JAIYAVARA

OTHER BOOKS BY THIS AUTHOR

 The Embrace and Stories

 Fear and Tenderness

JAIYAVARA

A Prophetic Novel

by Eleanor Glaze

a St. Lukes book
Peachtree Publishers, Ltd.
Atlanta   Memphis

St. Lukes Press
A Division of Peachtree Publishers, Ltd.
Editorial Office: 1407 Union Avenue
401 Mid-Memphis Tower
Memphis, Tennessee 38104
Business Office: 494 Armour Circle, N.E.
Atlanta, Georgia 30324

Library of Congress Cataloging-in-Publication Data
Glaze, Eleanor, 1930-
Jaiyavara.

I. Title.
P.S.3557.L384J35   1988   813'.54   88-1012
ISBN   0-918518-60-1
Cover Design by Larry Pardue
Typography by CST Typo-Graphics

Copyright © 1988 Eleanor Glaze.
All rights reserved. No part of this
book may be used or reproduced in
any manner whatsoever without
written permission except in the case
of brief quotations embodied in
critical articles and reviews.
For information address,
Peachtree Publishers, Ltd.,
494 Armour Circle, N.E.
Atlanta, Georgia 30324.

—For Valorie
 —my beautiful daughter

ACKNOWLEDGEMENT:

—For the story of Jaiyavara a journey was required, to a very remote and special place. Narrow, twisted roads—up one steep mountain and down another—a Zen transition just getting there.

—I wish to express my gratitude to the Tennessee Arts Commission for awarding me the 1982 Individual Artist Grant in Literature, which provided the means for that journey.

—Eleanor Glaze

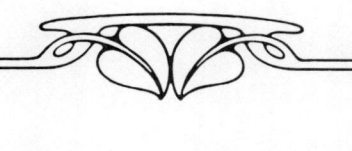

JAIYAVARA

Chapter One

High in the air above mountains and sea the birds congregate, lilt and circle, swoop and dive. Breaking away, one bird wings inland, flinging itself toward the vast, isolated mountains above the sea. Down drifting then, it slants at an angle, attracted by something below, almost hidden, a curious dark figure centered in the dense forest cathedral of valley.

The large and very fat monk sits on a crude wooden bench in the midst of the forest, doing nothing but dreaming.

Trees in this valley, as if effortlessly immortal, soar straight upward into the heavens.

Solitude. Stillness—accented only by slight flutter, scratch, chirp in the underbrush, in high interlaced branches, by finflip breaking surface in the stream, or by a sudden near and rushing whir of beating wings.

Near the feet of the large and very fat monk there is a diagonal path, silver-threaded at its edges by tracks of the lowly slug, a path worn through the centuries by animals on their trek to the stream which, as quietly as a serpent, slithers from the peaks down through the valley, downward to the sea.

Surrounding the valley, bold mountain sentinels sit ponderously as if weighing great issues, deciding eternal themes. Far beyond lie faint, translucent mountain vistas, sky islands floating in dawn's mist and haze.

Hands folded, eyelids lowered, on the lips of the large and very fat monk there is subtle enchantment. These are pleasurable dreams. Random images appear to him, evolve organically. He does not seek or invite them, he does not create them. They are simply there, given.

And the music is given. Slow, sonorous, an inexorable rhythm, plaintive, resigned, yet lyrical. Within that music all creatures captured in the net of forming light and time are linked, celebrated beyond their individual spans, each a part of that perpetual vibration, that sweet and sorrowful melody of being.

Both observer and participant . . . both teller and the tale . . . even as you and I . . . the large and very fat monk dreams himself into the world.

Now in his dreams a high wind rises. The sky darkens.

In pressure, complaint, the earth begins to shift and stir. Temperatures drastically fluctuate. The earth shudders, rumbles, begins to crack and split.

Heaving violence. The earthquakes begin. Volcanoes erupt. The barely buried and profane wastes of man are released. Thickened air is foul, poisonous; the waters become bitter. Lakes and rivers exude an evil smell. Fish float to the surface, belly upward. Wild and plunging, animals flee. Cornered, they attack. Masses of furious insects cast dreadful shadows.

A thick powdery ash settles down. Leaves droop in suffocation. It lies thick on swollen tongues.

For the large and very fat monk enchantment vanishes—yet he can not stop dreaming.

Crops are dying.

Tornadoes strike. Hurricanes sweep the coasts. Fragments of burning cities fall into the sea. Skylines are shrouded in red haze. The moon is blood red, the sun blackened and dirty at midday.

In cities the sick, feeble, drunk, and demented pile up in corners, are ignored, stepped over. Computers click out statistics, garbled solutions. Who to attack? In elaborate underground complexes those prepared to deliver total annihilation sit paralyzed, unable to retaliate.

Headlong flights of terror. Thronged, congested roads and highways, airlifts, mass exodus from the old cities. Looting, rape, mass slaying—there are new and diabolical forms of human brutality. Reported sightings of legendary monsters. Rituals on the rise. Desperate appeasements. Epidemics of conversion—of suicide. Sacrifice cults emerge.

JAIYAVARA

At night on crowded beaches pyres of dead bodies are put to torch by the sea. There are orgies of grief, followed by drunken orgies.

Amid these ravages the large and very fat monk hears a rising wail which merges with the music, the deep and mournful bells; the lament, the death march. Somber and resounding, the music, a dirge of dumb suffering. He sees all humanity as an endless procession marching slow, in step, in time, chained to the music.

The large and very fat monk wakes on his bench from these dreams. His eyes are dim. But here the sun is high, sustaining. Here, the air is pure, grass and leaves still blaze green.

He remembers himself.

He remembers you.

Time, he shrugs. A selection. A screening. An arbitrary convenience created by the human brain. But the present I speak from appears to lie somewhere in your future.

There have been in earth's history six major plagues. This, the Seventh Plague, born of ecological collapse throughout the world, has become a global malignancy. Henceforth that illusion called Time will be reckoned as Before or After . . . The Seventh Plague.

At the slanted drawing board she stood back, critical of the layout, a crane-peony motif for the entrance to the Educational Complex. Beneath the glass dome, afternoon light was still strong—Arizona light, still almost as penetrating as in Greece.

Down the hall in another studio someone turned on a radio. ". . . sharp increase of deaths reported in Germany, Hungary, and Indo-China . . . The scientific community still baffled . . . Plague has struck in seventeen major American cities . . . Heads of state are scheduled to meet in Washington the thirteenth . . . The Russians deny any use of germ warfare . . . The Vatican has issued a statement urging Christians everywhere to remain calm and keep the faith . . . Traffic is unmanagable in Rome as crowds throng the Vatican daily for the Pope's blessing . . . In India . . ." The sound snapped off.

In India, she thought, Shiva is dancing. Everywhere dancing . . . Creation . . . Destruction. She put down the pen, screwed the top on the ink pot, eased her head back, stretching. She hung up her work smock, replaced it with a black and white tunic over black pants. At the sink she washed her hands, knotted and pinned her hair off the back of her neck. Her hair needed washing, but the water supply was low.

Leaving the studio, in the wide vaulted corridor with long strides . . . still she walked like a dancer. Never could her body forget the years of labor, discipline, preparation. On the quarry tile the click of her heels tapped out emptiness. She imagined that she walked a pathless desert stirring up swirls of soundless dust—the last survivor.

From their inviolate places framed heroes and gods of art looked down upon her, through her, and let her pass. Yet she felt the grim burden of their now sightless eyes on the back of her neck, enough to wonder . . . is there yet time to justify my life?

At the stone railing of the open balcony she looked down to the uncompleted city of the future spread before her. A mere sketch, a futile skeleton. Far to the east precise mountains cast shadows as definitive as postcard pyramids. The desert stretched to a limitless horizon. Space. No mirages. And not much time. She had always equated space with time. She had been wrong.

Several levels below, Salvini's apprentices were still hammering, sawing, feverishly trying to bring the hope to life. Tirelessly they worked, as if man could ask for no higher fate than the subjugation of matter. Who would be the next to die?

Salvini undaunted. No trace of despair in his gaunt face. When critics had attacked her he said, "Easy to remain magnanimous with acclaim. How you conduct yourself in outrage is what matters." Long ago they had lampooned him also. He shrugged it off. Now, in his mid-sixties he was as incapable as ever of being influenced by anyone, anything. But the hospital was full. Within the gates of Citta Nova, in the astonishment of blatant youth, twenty-seven had died a lingering death.

Disease. Worse, she thought, than total war. And too damned much poetic justice. This global howl—who would live to commemorate it, as Picasso had commemorated the rain of fire upon his defenseless village?

Was she resigned? Her last telephone conversation with Kraft, trapped in New York, she repeated to herself in the middle of sleepless nights. She thought of her father, Malcolm Gottrell, whose manipulative greed had no doubt contributed to the present chaos, the plundered earth. For years after Varrick's death she had wanted to die . . . while still insatiable for every experience. Yes, even old age. How must it be, she wondered, to feel your good strong hands become fumbling, useless, unable to work? Yet not to experience every loss is in itself, she thought, a kind of loss.

Obsessively of late, faces appeared to her mind's eye. They were crowding in on her. She sketched them frantically. Tormented still by that hopeless lust, dreams of Varrick woke her, aching with loneliness. He seemed trying to warn her of something worse than death by plague.

She had buried her mother in a Mississippi downpour, a drapery of rain so thick nothing could be seen beyond dark figures at the grave site, and William and Lou Iris came, not as servants but as friends bereaved. A few other black people came to offer flowers, sing the staunch yet weary hymns. The rain ceased. The sun slashed out like a sword of wrath. Exhausted by shock and heat, in the empty mansion she had slept for days.

In this barren desert she was a creature without dimension, a mere point dot on a straight line. All a horizontal abstraction, as New York had been a vertical abstraction. With the sickness and death at hand she had been unable to form a solid concept. Or was it that gnawing depression which so often preceeded a burst of creativity? In youth she had declared that she could dance on an island with no hope of either audience or applause. But was it still true, in this the last outpost?

Intuition had told her in New York—Get out of here quick. It had saved her life. For awhile. Her face—which had appeared in *Focus, Time, Dissent,* was often presented by photographers as a "mood piece." Salvini called her face a November sky. Her eyes, large and very dark, regarded the world with a level, uncompromising, deadly serious gaze. She was forty-three, at the height of creative power, consumed by fervent aspirations, tireless drive.

But as she looked out over the unfinished city surrounded by sands so soft and final the earth seemed to have no bones, she let her eyes unfocus, blind to all but the monotone . . . and everything seemed to be quietly slipping away, all life disappearing as if lured by some distant, invisible, death vortex.

And now . . . her intuition told her nothing.

On the California coast a high wind, a gathering storm, and a whale had floundered in to die.

Gigantic waves came roaring in, smashed against mammoth boulders, tore at the base of the immense dark mountain which stood like an Olympian sentry protecting the interior. The sea kept raging in, struck with shattering force both mountain and brooding sky.

Beneath seething currents a whale was rotting, bleeding to death. Murky scarlet rose to the surface, was lost in foam.

Wind lashed, under the bombardment of lightning and thunder, a solitary figure struggled up the sentry mountain. His black robe swirled like a hostile flag. He reached the twisted peak. Holding to the rock, Giroux faced a world engulfed in darkness. And the sea howled like a wounded monster.

Dawn. Gradually it forms, the high, all encompassing and fearless light. Wispy clouds cast drifting shadows on the washed green mountains. On the ribbon of winding highway—once one of the most traveled and scenic in the world—nothing moves. Here the devastating boldness of nature is only slightly marred by destruction. Small pieces of mountain still crumble, fall to the devouring sea . . . yet beauty prevails.

In the mountainous interior a clear stream meanders downward to again gather some force at a small waterfall, a natural slide over smooth, glossy-slick, flat rocks, to form a small brilliant blue-green pool.

Young monks have thrown their clothing in a pile beneath the trees. They played in water, swam and dived. On warm granite rocks they sunbathed. Several girls sat together, feet dangling in water, shook out their long hair to dry.

Young female bodies. At the shallow end of the pool, water came high on their thighs to accent tantalizing curves and indentations of buttocks. Human flesh in all its hues. Arms, shoulders, bellies, and breasts, glistening in droplets of water. For Anthony

JAIYAVARA

it was visually lyrical, a paradise. Moving water—light dazzled his eyes.

With a glance at him, Karen disappeared into endless avenues of forest shade. He had been waiting for that signal. Always a risk. Karen was blonde, deliciously beautiful, but she played coy, cruel games. She sometimes led him on only to stop at the crucial moment. Yet that added to Anthony's intoxication. He took up his blanket to follow.

Shamelessly scratching her back against a tree when he found her, like an animal in rut. Anthony held the blanket to cover his erection. Hand over hand Karen circled the tree then, knees bent, legs around the tree as if it were a gigantic phallus. Her green eyes gave the invitation.

Toboggan style, their legs wrapped around each other, four monks, two male, two female, slid down the natural incline of slippery, water-covered flat rocks to plunge into the pool, screaming with laughter.

Dreaming still ... and the imperceptible smile on the lips of the large and very fat monk has not been entirely erased. For even as the earth shuddered in a plethora of suffering, writhed, wrenched free of betrayal, there were individual moments of heroism. In cities that glowed red before vanishing, vows were made, promises were given. Trapped in a sulphurous pall, there were those who armored themselves with a startling discovery, to become self-realized at the very last moment.

The sound of gongs.
Silence.
The sound of soft drums.
Silence.
The sound of clacking sticks.
Silence.

That part of the forest where the large and very fat monk sits dreaming is now enclosed within high stone walls—the ecumenical monastery founded by Giroux. All is within the natural barrier of impassable mountains, all roads destroyed.

The center is a labyrinth of stone, one-storey buildings. On a terraced hill the Zendo faces down toward the patio between dining room and kitchen. The patio, railed with benches, overlooks the mountain stream. Between the patio and the Zendo, the bench of the large and very fat monk and that changeless patch of forest remain intact.

Directly behind the Zendo—a narrow four-storey building, a tower by contrast. Giroux's study is on the top floor. Above his study, an open rampart, the bell tower. The three storeys below are made up of Giroux's living quarters, a few small vacant cells, large meeting rooms. Underground there is a library, a wine cellar, various storerooms.

Beyond the buildings are outlying fields of crops, pastures, a barn. Fenced off from each other there are geese, goats, cows, a small herd of horses. There are work buildings for pottery, metal working, weaving, carpentry. The monastery is self-sufficient, self-sustaining. Giroux's fortress, originally intended to house hundreds, now shelters about seventy people. It is still a community. Pastures, barn, greenhouse, pool, gardens, baths—all is enclosed by the high thick walls of stone. Gates of iron grillwork are guarded by two Oriental monks at a small post.

The large and very fat monk now wakes to what lies before him.

All that is lost. . . . But long before the Plague, life for many had become joyless and tiresome. Trees planted in good faith died when their roots reached the refuse. Numerous vague anxieties. An all-pervasive pressure. Psychosis so rampant as to seem the norm. Masses of people greed manipulated. For most there was little freedom, little choice. The constant threat of holocaust. Long before nature revolted, there was world-wide malaise.

At some distance, with a preoccupied scowl, Giroux walked past.

That lean and hungry look, said the large and very fat monk. *Just another ranting prophet they called Giroux twenty years ago. Then he grew a beard and people began to take him more seriously. And Giroux was fortunate. When the situation grew desperate, many who for years had cried warnings, were, by more devious methods than the cross, crucified.*

Karen waited near the patio until she saw Giroux. Flowing toward him in her long black robe, tawny curls danced about her shoulders. Impulsively she offered him a small bouquet of wild flowers.

Little fox, he thought, but accepted it, mildly amused by her maneuvers.

The end of the world, many pronounced it. But life, said the large and very fat monk, *here and in many primitive areas, still flourishes. In all its caprice.*

At the sound of gongs all work and study ceased. From every direction monks made their way toward the center, the Zendo. Soft drums. A rapid pulsation. Monks sedately climbed the wooden stairs to the porch of spaced slats, removed their sandals, placed them neatly against the outer Zendo wall. The sharp sound of clacking sticks. They formed two lines on either side of the wide double entrance, hands folded, eyes downcast. Each before entering bowed to the person in the opposite line. Anthony bowed to Karen, Karen to Anthony. Anthony saw the teasing of her mouth. Aroused, he looked away. He took the rituals seriously.

Entering the austere, candlelit interior they found their places. Subdued human voices rose upward in soft chanting. Of minor harmonics, serene, lulling—yet the higher it drifted out toward the impervious mountains, the more it resembled the subtle menace of insect drone. In ever expanding circles at last it dissolved entirely in the ubiquitous air.

Afterwards in the kitchen, working deftly, several monks prepared the midday meal. With much artful chopping, stirring, playful flair, they created an appealing variety of vegetables, fruits, nuts, seeds, and breads.

Anthony brought bowls of food to the wooden picnic tables beneath the trees. Fat audacious bluejays swooped down to the tables with raucous voices, fearlessly hopped and fluttered all over the tables. Squabbling among themselves, feet first, they plopped into bowls of food. Anthony ran back to chase them away. But the moment he returned to the kitchen, the bluejays dived back down to their thieving banquet. Infuriated, Anthony ran back, black robe flying, waving his arms to shoo them away.

A slim book in her rough, splotched hands, her place marked with a silver ribbon, Alexis descended the stone pathway. Russian Jew, rawboned, large, a little awkward, yet somehow stately, Alexis was fifty-seven. Her dark eyes were deep-set, her nose large. Her skull, utterly bald, shone with an ivory translucence. Second to Giroux, she alone had the privilege of wearing a robe of dusty rose. She came to sit beside the large and very fat monk. Fondly together they watched the flurry between Anthony and the bluejays. Alexis was partial to Anthony—the bold set of his shoulders, his thick unruly dark hair. "A handsome boy, don't you think? Just look at him. But oh, what a temper. He reminds me so much of. . . ."

In undeclared skirmish wars, one by one as they came of age, Alexis had lost four sons. Her robe—which Giroux indulged—was not a refusal to mourn so much as an aversion to black. The book of poetry was a gift from her youngest son, Nicholas, killed in Poland. It was Nicholas that Anthony resembled.

The large and very fat monk glanced at the book. Pushkin.

"So Italian," Alexis said. "He can't talk without using his hands."

"And he has," said the large and very fat monk, "a lot to say."

"So Italian," she repeated. "But what is it—this between him and the bluejays?"

"China . . . India . . . Japan. . . ." mused the large and very fat monk. "Such has it ever been. Such may it ever be. May there ever be bluejays and a young monk to scold them."

CHAPTER TWO

At the wide windows of his study Giroux stroked his chin with a black feather, scanned the cloudless sky as if awaiting a message.

In sharp contrast to the Spartan bareness of the monks' cells and his own living quarters, Giroux's study was luxuriously appointed. Scarlet velvet drapes outlined the windows. Paneled walls, covered with a dramatic black lacquer of subdued luster were accented with a molding of gold leaf at the ceiling. On either side of the white marble fireplace, floor to ceiling bookshelves housed his philosophy collection bound in scarlet. The shelves displayed an ivory goddess, a jeweled box, a priceless Greek vase, a Chinese inkwell.

A streamlined desk was before the windows, the leather swivel chair faced the interior. The black lacquered floor, visible only at the edges, was covered with a large Persian rug of scarlet, deep blue, black and gold. Before the fireplace a velvet sofa of navy and scarlet. The coffee table was Italian Renaissance, inlaid with onyx, garnet, mother of pearl. On the coffee table, facing the sofa, recumbent but alert, a large stag of opaque crystal by Lalique. On the table a golden bowl adorned with dolphins and water nymphs.

Giroux had never been wealthy. Assiduously scrupulous with monastery funds, each art object, slowly acquired, represented a painful sacrifice.

Against the wall behind the sofa stood an ancient Italian chest with numerous drawers and cubbyholes, a masterpiece.

Chapter Two

In the opposite corner a Rodin nude on a marble pedestal. Giroux had a special fondness for cloisonné, various ornaments carefully placed. His inability to resist small, perfect watercolors was almost feminine. Atop the Italian chest a watercolor by Su-Zan-Zee, flanked by cloisonné lions. On the wall above the chest an exquisite collection of small oil paintings by French impressionists—then centered, his prize, an original Goya, *The Asylum Faces*.

Two opposing sides of Giroux's ancestry, the French, the Spanish, often precipitated internal conflict, but in this eclectic atmosphere he was almost at peace. It had taken years, but at last all was in readiness. Nothing to do now but wait.

He sat down at the desk, unlocked a drawer and opened a worn scrapbook. The faded photographs, yellowed clippings, were as familiar to him as a personal diary or journal, as secret as his constant preoccupied vigil.

Degas would have loved it, he thought. Jaiyavara: age twenty-one. Nothing yet definitive, yet even then, in the evasive defiance of her downcast eyes, the side tilt of her stubborn jaw, a kind of trademark or forecast. Caption: "Young Hopeful Seizes Lead in London Competition." When she was twenty-one, he reflected, I was a late seminary student . . . hopelessly in bondage to that French prostitute. Adele. Dead by now. Or a worn-out hag.

He studied slick, but tattered, photographs of Jaiyavara in various minor roles.

Age four. She was sullen, unpromising; enormous dark eyes.

His favorite—twelve or thirteen, fragile, unsteady, attempting some torturous pose when caught off guard by the camera, glaring like a lynx.

Hawaii. The crashed hang-glider, one wing forced backward like an arm wrenched out of place. Caption: "Noted Dancer's Career Ended By Fall."

Next, Jaiyavara dwarfed by her own prodigious canvas. In a rigid stance. Years after the accident she still wore the back brace. Caption: "Washington Exhibit to Feature Work of Indian Artist." Printed interviews of the same period reveal that she is blunt, hostile, totally lacking in public persona.

Jaiyavara and Thandon arriving at the opera in Milan, Italy. Thandon's Cheshire cat grin on automatic. Jaiyavara aloof but glamorous in silver sequins. Caption: "The Romance of Negotiation?"

Next, courthouse backdrop. Jaiyavara conferring with Kraft, her lawyer. Caption: "Thandon Accuses." Libel, Giroux thought. Or slander. Thandon's paranoia was no secret. In a TV interview, when questioned about Thandon, Jaiyavara's response was so vehement she was cut off the air.

New York City Jail. Looking down her long nose from behind bars. Kraft obtaining her release. Caption: "Assault and Battery With Spiked Heel." Sub-title: "Secretary of State Has No Comment."

Salvini and Jaiyavara at the entrance to Citta Nova. Caption: "Revival Of Greek Drama In Dream City." Sub-title: "Jaiyavara Commissioned For Theatre Murals."

One last shot. It never failed to intensify his anxiety. Taken at the guest house converted to a studio at her father's Mississippi plantation—caught in that split-second before slamming the door on a reporter—her face blurred yet unmistakably haggard, her mouth twisted, her eyes savage.

The black feather, which had never lost its gleam, Giroux tucked between the pages and closed the scrapbook. Had she returned to Mississippi? What had caused her to retreat, hide out there three years before? Rumors of an attempted suicide. . . . Or was she still in New York?—surely the worst place on earth during a disaster.

For over three months he had heard nothing from Simeon in his search for her. How could he be sure that Simeon was still alive? Lost in worry, self-flagellation, he repeated a line from one of his own lectures. "This is the hair-shirt, my friends."

He had met her only once, had challenged her. She bristled with hostility. But she had been so much more than beautiful and extremely arrogant, when she bestowed upon him the black feather.

Directly beneath the bench of the large and very fat monk, Karen, Ruben, Doyle, Jethro, Sebastian, and Brother Bethune sat at a large table.

Ruben, the deaf mute, ate with his hands. He was huge, young, strong as an ox, the beauty of his face vacant and Nordic. Karen wiped his hands and mouth with a small damp towel. Already he was making an unsightly mess on himself and the table.

Jethro, the black monk, said to Brother Bethune, "How can we sit here and eat? How can we ignore all the shit? We should be doing something."

Behind rimless glasses Brother Bethune's eyes were misty-bright blue. Capped by a wreath of fine fuzzy light hair, the bald spot on top of his head glowed pinkly. "Perhaps pairing off and having children." But the fork in his delicate hand toyed with the food.

Doyle sat back and lit his pipe. "That," he said, "is what many of us came here to avoid, good brother."

Brother Bethune smiled. To pursue the matter with Doyle, homosexual, would be tactless.

Sebastian's red hair glowed even in the shade. He wiped moisture from his low forehead. Working his full mouth, he made a pronouncement. ". . . and their flesh shall rot while they are still on their feet, their eyes shall rot in their sockets, their tongues shall rot in their mouths."

Jethro slammed down his fork. "For Christ's sake! We're trying to eat! Who the fuck are you quoting now!"

Sebastian's freckles deepened in anger. He chewed, swallowed, answered phlegmatically. "The Old Testament. For Christ's sake."

Jethro swung his legs over the bench, turned his back on Sebastian and muttered, "Stupid, gross, son of a bitch."

Smoking a cigarette, entirely at ease, the large and very fat monk looked down to them. "For many death was preferable . . . the only escape."

"How did he hear?" Jethro whispered to Brother Bethune.

"He hears everything."

Karen looked up to the bench. "Innocent children . . . how can you say that?"

With a by-your-leave glance to the large and very fat monk, Brother Bethune explained. "We Buddhists don't think in terms of good and evil. You don't judge the bright colors in a painting, good . . . the dark colors evil. It takes darkness to see light. Everything is God."

"Call the plague," said the large and very fat monk, "a collective death wish."

Jethro swung both legs back over the bench, asked Doyle in a whisper, "I never see him eat. How does he stay so fat?"

"He grows fat," Doyle smiled, "as I do. On theories and smoke."

"You're right, my son," said the large and very fat monk. "Theories too are *Maya*."

Meanwhile, Ruben amused himself by swirling the food on his plate into patterns.

"Stop that!" Karen smacked his hand.

Looking up and down the table into inscrutable faces, Ruben's mouth puckered.

"Never mind, never mind." Brother Bethune got up, put his hands on Ruben's shoulders. "That's a good boy. Come along, it's time for your bath."

After the midday siesta Giroux brought a bundle of clothing down to the stream. Female monks had gathered to wash clothing. Karen watched from a boulder near the opposite bank. Would Giroux give anyone the honor of doing his laundry? No. As usual he walked further downstream. He wished to be left alone.

Giroux responded to her countless overtures with nothing more than reserved fatherly affection. He avoided, in fact, the slightest hint of favoritism. She did not understand his dry, laconic humor, but his lectures held her spellbound. It was not the content or his eloquence but the sound of his voice, his quirks and twists of accent, which thrilled her. My God, she thought ... what do I have to do to get through to him? Could he actually be celibate?

Anthony came down to the stream with clothing. He waved to Karen. Pensive, drooping, no longer in a pose as when Giroux was near, she ignored him.

In the quiet valley, long before they saw it, they heard the pulsating whir and beat. As it drew near, grew louder, those in gardens and fields, those at the stream, looked to each other, looked to the skies.

At the approach of the helicopter monks came rushing out from individual cells, the physician leaned out at the clinic window. He yelled to aids. They came running through the narrow corridors; one carried a stretcher. They ran out through the pastures to meet the helicopter which landed in a small field within the walls.

In a circle of waves the high grass bent low. Before the churning blades slowed to a stop, an unconscious figure was lowered to the stretcher. In a running walk two monks carried the body back to the clinic.

A cloth army bag and a large, gaudy, jeweled knapsack were thrown to the ground. Brother Bethune rushed forward to meet the pilot who jumped down; a large, burly, muscular man with a tough stubble of beard, a scarred face.

Legs apart, Simeon took a stance. "How the hell am I supposed to get out of here? That's the last of the fuel."

CHAPTER THREE

On a narrow, elevated bed, covered by a sheet she lay naked, bloodless lips parted. John Bain began an examination. Tensely Giroux watched. She appeared lifeless, desperately ill.

Sebastian, who helped carry the stretcher, stood just inside the door. Blocked by Giroux, all he could see of the woman was the spread thickness of her dark hair. He was full of suspicions, but having played a small role in an unusual occurrence gave him a rare sense of importance. He cleared his throat, about to speak. With an angry motion of his hand Giroux silenced him.

Bain, an almost delicate man with thinning dark hair, listened to the patient's heartbeat, made notations on a chart. Taking her pulse and blood pressure he might have been an anthropologist tenderly probing an unearthed treasure.

"What do you think," Giroux said finally. "You don't think it's the. . . ."

"Don't say it," Bain said.

Sebastian went pale. "Oh, my Christ! And infect us all!"

Whirling, Giroux's voice was a rasp. "Get out of here. Tell Alexis we need her."

Hurriedly, fumbling at the door, Sebastian backed out.

Giroux turned back to Bain. "I'm sorry, John. That clod gets on my nerves." Giroux trusted Bain implicitly, considered him highly intuitive, an expert at diagnosis. He had on Giroux a calming effect.

Focused on the patient, Bain spoke in a mild, reflective tone. "From what I've heard, it's the very young, the very old, who are most susceptible. I'll have to take a blood sample, but my guess is exhaustion. Possibly shock."

"Isn't shock dangerous?"

"Everything's dangerous. Depends on the inner state. Germs don't invade healthy cells."

"Can people die of shock?"

"Frequently yes. Particularly this type."

"Type? What type?"

"We're all mixtures," Bain said. "You rarely see a clear cut, classic type. But there are three basic physical types—Adrenal—Thyroid—Pituitary."

"Which is she?"

"Well . . . good muscular tone like an Adrenal, but that seems due to exercise, discipline, rather than innate capacity. Strong nose and jaw like an Adrenal, but you see," he said, his hands framing her face, ". . . the bone structure is finely molded. And her eyes large, predominate . . . conscious, no doubt, the sort of eyes termed soulful. So despite the thickness of her hair and strong jaw, she's definitely not an Adrenal type."

"Is that good or bad?"

"Depends. For sheer survival you can't beat an Adrenal type. They seldom die of illness. They're so aggressive, combative . . . usually get themselves killed, or die in an accident." He inserted his finger into the patient's mouth. "High palate. That's a Thyroid type. Their hearts are smaller. Can't take as much stress." Lightly he touched her throat. "See how long and graceful? A Thyroid throat. Small breasts, nipples exquisitely sensitive. Genitals also. Not exactly earth mothers, these women. Often great difficulty bearing children."

Bain pulled down the sheet. "Look," he said, as if lecturing a medical student, "at the hands. Even in repose, how expressive. Wrists and ankles delicate. Definitely Thyroid. But the high forehead and superior orbital ridges, the large upper lip . . . that's Pituitary."

"But what does it mean, John. Get to the point."

"Oh, meanings," he smiled. "You have strong Pituitary qualities. Pituitary types are always interested in meanings. It means that she is basically a Thyroid type with a lot of Pituitary. And yes, she could die of shock. They are extremely nervous, restless people. Vivid, even morbid imaginations. Perfectionists. Dreamers. Strong sex drive. And that drive often brutally sublimated."

"Amazing. I never realized. . . . What else?"

"A Thyroid-Pituitary dominance indicates an artistic temperament. Highly-gifted Pituitary types have to lash up the adrenals with stimulants, narcotics, a creative binge . . . a sustained, heroic effort. But when they do, the pituitary and thyroid become over-stimulated. What follows is depression, even a suicidal state."

Giroux frowned. "I never realized mere bodies could reveal so much."

"Mere bodies," Bain repeated. "They're our fates. But if depression did not occur . . . for these types it's a safety valve, a life-saver. Otherwise they would wear out the adrenals entirely. Genius types often die young. Now you know why."

Bain moved to Giroux's side of the bed. "Stand back, please. You're not helping any by hovering over her." He lifted the patient's right eyelid. Peering into her ears, her nose, with a narrow light, he then stood staring, lost in concentration. He sat down, crossed his legs, made further notations. "I'd like to know the conditions in which he found her. And it would help to know her age."

"Forty-three."

Slowly Bain looked up from the chart.

Giroux admitted, "I asked Simeon to bring her here. I know her." Giroux's tone indicated he was not amenable to further questioning.

Alexis came in with a small tray, wine and broth.

"Help me turn her on her stomach," Bain said to Alexis.

"Let me," Giroux offered, but Bain shook his head. Giroux stood back while they turned Jaiyavara, but he could not resist stepping forward to brush the hair from her face, her mouth.

Bain put his hands to her neck, head to one side he looked at the wall and said softly, "Oh, good Lord. . . ."

"A bad fall," Giroux supplied. "She wore a back and neck brace several years."

Bain nodded. "I don't need x-rays to tell me that. A lot of scar tissue. Was she paralyzed?"

"I'm not sure. Partially, maybe . . . for awhile. She was hospitalized a long while. All that happened before we met. I didn't know her then."

"But it was a complete recovery?"

"As far as I know. I know she did an enormous amount of work."

As if listening John Bain's sensitive fingers slowly traveled the entire length of the patient's spine. There were slight worried movements of his head. He pulled her arms upward over her head, as if for a dive she was stretched, her rib cage clearly visible. Looking at her thin body she seemed younger to Giroux than years before in all her finery and black feathers. The arch of her back, the sharp protruding hip bones, made him think of her as starved. His throat ached. He turned away.

When Bain and Alexis turned Jaiyavara once more on her back, her eyelids fluttered. "Try the wine," Bain suggested.

Alexis lifted her head, held the glass to her lips, but the red wine spilled from the corners of her mouth, making a pink stain on the white sheet.

"Well," Bain said, "we'd better have an I.V."

Charged with dedication Alexis left to get it.

The I.V. was injected—the bars of the bed pulled up, locked in place. As darkness came, the bed was centered in the dim illumination of two candelabra, one at the head, one at the foot of the bed. Giroux leaned forward in his chair, hands clasped between his knees. Finally he got up, moved about, arms folded, leaned against the wall.

Softly brilliant, a wide-haloed moon sailed suspended in the window. That she was here at last . . . all that it meant. Here and now, he thought. Wake to that moon. Yet never once did he touch her.

Muted by distance, the evening chant drifted down. Giroux went back to the chair, settled down for the long watch through the night. So still she lay, shrouded in sheets. Flickering shadows brought changing blue-dark designs to her covered body, her face; moving, they animated her stillness, made her in mute pantomine almost seem to speak.

Let her speak, he thought. And if she does not . . . I will speak for her.

In the darkened cell Giroux seemed to be keeping devout watch with a corpse.

At four A.M. Alexis and Anthony took watch.

"I want someone with her every moment," Giroux instructed. "Call me the minute she wakes."

Alexis began fussing about. Anthony sat down. The sight of someone that ill was repugnant to him. ". . . if I should die before I wake . . ." he thought morosely. Resolving to think of the confinement as a religious discipline, he yawned. Alexis' four A.M. business annoyed him. "What makes him so sure she's going to wake?"

"I think she will."

"Why? What makes you so sure?"

Pulling a protective rubber mat under the hips of the patient, Alexis ignored the question.

"Why is she so important to Father Giroux?"

"I have no idea."

"I mean . . . what's all the commotion? What is she, some sort of mystic?"

"That," she said, twisting her lips, "I very much doubt."

Anthony sighed.

"If you're that bored," Alexis said, "why didn't you bring a book?"

"It must be more terrible out there than we can imagine. The worst catastrophe in human history. And here we are . . . missing it all."

"Are you complaining?" Taking the patient's pulse, Alexis looked at her watch.

"I guess," Anthony yawned, feeling entirely useless, "that you will never cease being a good Jewish mother, Alexis."

"That's a cliche," she snapped. "I'm a trained nurse."

"You met Giroux at the children's hospital?"

She nodded.

Anthony sniffed, rubbed his nose. "Well, I was an orphan too you know, and no one ever adopted me. But then, those were very hard times."

"I would have." Alexis pulled the sheet to Jaiyavara's chin, covering her snugly. "I'm sure you were a beautiful child."

"Certainly, I was. I'm beautiful now, or haven't you noticed?"

"Oh, yes," she said with lifted brows. "We've all noticed."

"Why did Giroux adopt Ruben? Was it your idea?"

"In a way, yes. No one else could cope with him. He was terrible."

"And still is," Anthony said.

"Oh no, much better now. You didn't know him as a child."

Anthony stifled a heavier sigh. "Why did you want me here, Alexis?"

"In case of an emergency, you can get John much faster than I can."

"What's John doing?"

"Running tests. Besides," she added, "I just wanted your company."

Impatiently he tapped one foot. Nothing to do, nothing to do. "So . . ." he said finally, "Why did you leave the children's hospital?"

"Giroux needed me more."

A peculiar answer. He got up, sauntered to the window. The mists were clearing, the light growing vibrant. His shoulders slouched. "Well, who is she?" he asked.

"That I do know," Alexis said, and tightened the sheet at the foot of the bed. "She is Jaiyavara."

The pronouncement in Alexis' voice made him turn to face her.

"And Heaven," Alexis said wistfully, "gave her every blessing."

Head to one side, Anthony paused. "Yeah? Such as?"

"Health. Beauty. Money. Fame."

Dubious, Anthony moved closer. "I don't think she's beautiful. What sort of fame?"

"As a dancer . . . when she was young."

"She's too old to dance now."

"Oh! The arrogance of youth! She's young enough to be my daughter. It was an accident that ruined her career. Such a daredevil. Hang-gliding."

"Really?"

"Hang-gliding. Can you imagine? So foolish to take such a risk."

"Did you ever see her dance?"

"Do I look like I had that kind of money? Not in person. Once I saw her, a TV documentary of several dancers. She was by far the best, Anthony. All sorts of original dances she choreographed herself, adapted folk dances of India and Greece. One I'll never forget, an old Russian folk dance, she flew across the stage. Flew, I'm telling you! She seemed to defy gravity. Oh, it was thrilling."

To come to this, Anthony thought, peering at the woman as if she were a relic of her own past.

"But then . . ." Alexis said, "she recovered. She became a painter." Anthony detected the resignation, as if to say . . . She made the best of a blotched life. As if to say . . . No painting could compare to the way she danced.

"And what of love?" Anthony said dryly. "Did Heaven give her that?"

"Who knows?" Alexis shrugged. "She was Thandon's mistress for a time."

"Are you kidding?" Anthony was incredulous.

Alexis made a droll mouth. "No. I'm not kidding."

"The Secretary of State? Are you kidding?"

"For a time. Until she saw through him."

"So. . . ." Anthony's head moved up and down. "This is getting interesting."

Alexis gave him a side glance. Maleness, she thought. More interested in who she slept with than what she was.

"Giroux despises Thandon," Anthony said.

"Oh, don't I know it. I've heard him rant about Thandon often enough."

"So . . . it must be something political . . . that Giroux had her brought here."

"Don't ask me," Alexis sighed. "Your guess is as good as mine."

   pale green   the light
    under water   effortless   flowing upward toward the light soft radiance   all pale   all green
    breaking surface   too harsh   it hurts   get back down into water   separate hurts   let me flow again   let me be water   all pale   all green

Chapter Three

    in the boat with Varrick   drifting   it was not a dream soft warm day again   after his death and yet the very same time doubled back   duplicated   green waters rippling under willows close to that soft grassy shore   that rich warm sweet eternal day   again   to see him once more   re-live it   matter falls   spirit flows

    willow and water   arc of willows over still green waters   he was there alive again   and it was heaven   together in the small boat   my hand trailing in water   circles of water overlapping   his back to me   couldn't see his face   oh God the curve of his back   the beauty   the power   to be with him again in such a world   more beauty than was bearable sun-warm stillness peace   again   exactly the same

dying of love   and I could not speak   could not tell him that it was repeated   knowing he would die   powerless to change anything

    with my body I adore you   forever I adore you with my body and all my soul

    Her eyes opened. She saw square stones. Flickering lights. Where is the water? I need it. I need it. I need it again. Bars? What time? What prison?

    Her eyes focused. Someone in a chair. Eyes closed. Draped in something. Skin bone. Bald. Is death a bald old woman? Where is Varrick? No. No. Not this kind of death. I refuse it.

    Faces emerging from the stones. Memories. The stones will weep. Ye who enter here. All hope abandon. Faces in the stones. Demons. Labyrinths of torture. Tibetans warned us. Demons of my own mind. What happens at death. Try. Try to wake. Can't keep eyes open. The poor children. Blessed are those in the womb unborn. Children's faces. Bluish disease. It will eat out their eyes. Bronze, marble oozing down. All work melting in that furnace, that fiery hate. People eating animals. Animals eating children. Hell eating everything.

    Her head turned. Once more she saw the old woman. Another dream? Someone on the floor, head down. A black bundle. Is it human? Throat dry. Crave water. Crave water. Make a sound. Make a sound.

    "Help me," she whispered.

    No one heard. They were sleeping. Or dead.

Chapter Four

Each morning and evening John Bain checked the patient. Trusted monks sat to watch. It became a routine. Giroux paced the corridor, wandered in and out, or stood at the foot of the bed as if attempting telepathic communication with the woman who refused to wake.

The third day Bain confided to Giroux, "I don't know why she's still unconscious. Her vital signs are good. I could give her a stimulant."

"No! She'll come out of it on her own." He put an apologetic hand to Bain's arm. "Believe me, she would prefer it that way."

Later, as Anthony and Alexis again took watch Anthony could not repress his indignation. "If she's so important to him, why doesn't Giroux sit day and night?"

"Everything to attend to, you know that." Alexis was knitting a heavy black sweater for Anthony to wear beneath his robe in the coming winter.

"I think she's just going to lie there and waste away."

"No, she's strong. A lot of fight in her. You'll see."

"I saved a dog once. But then it got cancer, and I had to have it put to sleep."

"Any nurse could have told you that. Any living thing, it's only for awhile."

"I wish she'd either wake up or. . . ."

"Patience," Alexis warned. "I've heard of people in semi-coma for years."

Chapter Four

"Years," he groaned. "Thank God we don't have respirators. If it comes to that I believe in pulling the plug. Why prolong a vegetable existence?"

Her needles halted. Alexis looked from the sweater to the opposite wall. Her eyes were fixed, motionless. She swallowed.

Shamed, he watched her large, clumsy hands resume, work the yarn into a useable object. "You saw her dance. Did you ever see her paintings?"

"Once, yes. A place called Corcoran Gallery."

Anthony sat up straighter. "That was a prestigious gallery."

"Well, don't repeat it, but I didn't care much for anything I saw."

"Repeat it? To whom?"

"To her," Alexis said. "When she wakes."

Deferring to her unquenchable optimism, Anthony let it drop. The hours would drag, a slow labor of endurance. "Her work . . . can you describe it?"

Needles clicking, her hands in rapid motion Alexis said, "No, I can't."

"Come on, an impression . . . anything." He needed conversation to stay awake.

"Such huge, raw, shocking images. If you must know, it gave me the shivers."

"Art," Anthony pronounced, "does not have to be pretty, Alexis."

"I know that. What do you take me for, a peasant? Some of it was terrifying." In agitation her needles clicked. "She could dance like an angel, but she paints like a demon."

Anthony looked to the woman enclosed in bars. The comatose, he'd heard, curled in a fetal position. Why did she lie head back, stretched, as if about to levitate? "Maybe," he said finally, "she saw what was coming."

"Precognition?" Alexis shuddered. "That would be ten thousand deaths."

And maybe, Anthony thought, that's why she refuses to wake.

In the cell then, only the sound of the knitting needles. Each sat thinking of those they knew, suffering or lost, forever beyond reach. Alexis stood, put the knitting in her chair. "Enough of art. You can talk with her later. There are some herbs I want to try. I can add the liquid to the I.V."

"You'd better check with Giroux first."

"Giroux doesn't know everything. Stay with her. I'll be back."

Anthony sat. On the opposite wall near the ceiling, above the window, a moth fluttered helplessly. His resentment increased, not only for the confinement, but the begrudged fascination he was beginning to acknowledge for this prisoner of silence, who, as they spoke of her, did not rally to her own explanations.

Strong, Alexis said. She did not look strong to Anthony. Yet why was it, each day she looked younger to him? Some contradiction here. She looked forsaken, yet in that impenetrable stillness . . . invincible somehow. Alone with her, his imagination could conjure all sorts of forbidden possibilities.

He eased from the chair, moved close. Reaching through the bars he took a strand of her hair in his hand, rubbing it between two fingers. No one looks sleeping as they look awake. How would she look . . . speak . . . move? Her high slanted cheekbones, he studied. Ah, such a nose. Her nose looked Italian. Damn it, he thought. Wake up. I want out of here.

Cautiously, he lowered the bars. He reached to touch her bare shoulder. But then, he could not. He backed off, circled the bed, and went to the window.

And what was Karen up to while he was detained? When Karen locked her legs around him, grabbing in spasms his deep thrust, writhing in her own responding up-thrust, sending fire up his spine—good god what cunt. But trust Karen? Never. No telling who, at this very moment, she was fucking.

Patting the window ledge in frustration, he looked up to the ceiling. Stupid moth. Trapped. Still dangling up and down.

Until he found himself again standing over her, he did not realize he had moved back to the bed. His finger traced the curve of her neck, paused at the measured pulse, in touch with the beat pressed in. His finger in a slow lateral distraction traced her collar bone, then, more slowly still, dipped into the secret cleft between her small breasts. The ache began, an erotic swelling. Bending, ever so lightly he kissed her, flicking his tongue between her dry lips, parting them, seeking the sensation; his tongue with a will of its own tasted her hot dryness . . . and wanted more.

Both hands at her breasts, he felt a slight shudder pass through her body. Fearful of becoming entrapped in something he did not understand, he drew back. He would not have been surprised if waking she were to pull him down to the narrow bed. Pull him to her. Into her.

His heart was beating hard. He put the bars of the bed up, locked them, retreated to the chair.

"Goddamn you!" Springing up, he jerked the chair to the opposite wall, leaped upon it, captured the moth in his fist, took it to the open window, flung it out.

As long as possible he watched the fragile dot of life released . . . watched it flutter away, until it merged with air and wind and the world it danced.

Booted legs stretched before him, Simeon leaned back into the plush sofa, took a scarlet pillow to his lap, punched it softly, tossed it aside. "The bath helped more than sleep and food. I smelled like a pack rat."

"You still look very tired," Giroux said. He looked, Giroux thought, like a combat veteran in need of leave, his weather-beaten face etched with more wrinkles than Giroux remembered. Yet the strength, the integrity he had always admired in Simeon were still intact.

"That'll pass." Simeon paused. "Well, no . . . maybe it won't. Quite a set-up you have here."

"I'm glad you approve."

With a wave of his cigar Simeon indicated the entire monastery. "Enormous changes since I was here."

"I couldn't have done it alone," Giroux said. "Everyone has worked very hard."

"And not a single case of plague? Have you any idea how fortunate you are?"

"Probably not," Giroux conceded.

"As if you anticipated the whole thing twenty years in advance. But," he added, squinting, "I never said I approved."

"That's quite all right." With the Scotch bottle Giroux refilled Simeon's glass. "I've always preferred a good argument with you to agreement with anyone else."

"True test of friendship. Cheers again."

Giroux responded with his elegant wine glass.

"I've never been very original," Simeon admitted, "with toasts or signing autographed copies, but here's to two of the best damned debaters Columbia ever produced."

"Always," Giroux reminded him, "on opposite sides of any given issue."

"And then we'd swap up. Supposedly great practice for objectivity."

"I've never been objective," Giroux said.

"Oh well, who the hell is?"

"I don't think you ever realized how much I envied you."

"Me?" An abrupt laugh. "You were the one who raked in all the honors."

"But you were the man of action, in the thick of it, dashing all over the world to get the story, while I sat around mulling things over. And when you were anchor man for CBS . . ."

"That didn't last very long."

"But I envied the millions you reached. Remember my letters, all my advice, admonitions?" Giroux smiled, shaking his head.

"I wasn't cut out for it. Too confining."

"Your successor didn't pay much attention to my letters either."

Simeon puffed on the cigar. "Ratings . . . you know . . . all that shit. Ideas, you have to be damned sneaky slipping them in. Wonderful Scotch, Giroux."

"I've been saving it for you."

"You were that sure of me?"

"I knew if anyone could find her, persuade her to come here, you could."

"It wasn't just finding her, it was getting her back here. But, as it turned out, no persuasion was needed. She was unconscious." Squinting, puffing, his gaze turned to the wide windows. "I only know her by reputation. A trouble maker. That messy business with Thandon. As much as I detest Thandon . . . still, artists should not dabble in politics. They're too idealistic, too intolerant of the complexities."

"Listen," Giroux said, "to who's talking."

Simeon grinned. "Well, yeah. But when it gets down to it. . . ." He leaned forward, said soberly, "Citta Nova . . . city of idealists. And a man tried to kill me for the helicopter."

"Not Salvini?"

"Oh no, not Salvini. Salvini's dead."

Head lowered, Giroux did not speak for several moments. "That," he said at last, "is a terrible loss."

"I agree. A rare man. A world citizen. You know, I interviewed him once and I could hardly understand a word he said. But you couldn't help but be drawn to him. That quiet charisma, that mystic purposefulness."

Quietly they sat. Giroux sipped wine. Simeon gulped Scotch.

"Well," Simeon asked. "How is she now?"

"Still unconscious. We're doing everything possible."

"And it's not the Plague?"

"No, Bain assures me it's not. She'll come out of it soon, I think. I hope. But tell me, how was it at Citta Nova?"

"I didn't take time to look around, just found her and got the hell out of there. Those last few . . . holed up, avoiding each other, avoiding infection." He finished the drink. "I need one roaring drunk before I get back out there in it."

Giroux pushed the bottle toward him. "If that won't do it, I've got one more."

"Thanks." Simeon refilled his glass. "Are you sure this is an ashtray?" he asked of the golden bowl Giroux offered for his cigar ashes.

"Use it as that."

"Well, hell, what's the use?" He sat up straighter, crossed his legs. "We thought computers could do everything. We forgot just how much depends on manpower. We may be on the verge of becoming extinct, do you realize that? If we are . . . perhaps it's no great loss."

"But you found her," Giroux said, observing that Simeon was already pretty high, not wanting him to get side-tracked on who or what might eventually replace man. Simeon railed incoherently when drunk. "So . . . you are a great detective, as well as a great journalist."

Simeon squashed the cigar butt into the golden bowl, took another cigar from his jacket pocket; puffing, lit it. "Oh, yeah." He threw the match into the bowl. "Great time to be a great journalist. Decline and fall of civilization. Everything front page and not enough people to run the presses, very soon not enough paper. Great time to be a great anything."

"Oh, surely. . . ."

"I think I've got lice," Simeon interrupted, scratching his head. "And I'm smoking these cigars like I could run out to the corner drugstore for more." He laughed. "But listen, tomorrow, or the day after, I've got to get out of here."

Giroux was about to argue, but with a forceful gesture Simeon stopped him. "You know why I covered so many uprisings, revolts, minor wars? To see with my own eyes the unbelievable stupidity. And now, it's as if nature is saying, 'Okay, you bastards, you want destruction, stupidity, insanity? I'll give it to you . . . in spades.' "

Nature, Giroux thought ruefully, doesn't *say* anything. It takes man to interpret, man to deify, man to *say*. The room seemed suddenly dim, gloomy, damp. Clouds passing over. He moved his chair closer. "I'm still stunned by some of the things you told me last night. How quickly people revert to savagery."

"Worse than animals. Here lately, it seems to me that animals are very noble compared to man."

"Regression no longer such a preposterous theory," Giroux said, with a hint of I-told-you-so, thinking back to their youthful debates, refilling his own glass with blood red wine. "Stay with us . . . until things are better."

"No, I'm sorry. I can't."

"Perhaps," Giroux said, "there's a purpose to all this we can't yet comprehend. Perhaps it saved us from something worse. The bombs, the missiles. If we survive this . . . perhaps we will be wiser."

Simeon sank back into the sofa, his eyes dulled. "I don't know . . . I don't know. I've got to try to get back to Washington. We've got to form some opposition to Thandon. Nothing could have suited his purposes better than this chaos."

"Blame that," Giroux erupted, "on the idiot who appointed him."

Cigar and glass in hand Simeon got up, walked to the wide windows, looked down to the circular, winding, but clearly delineated pathways, all below was orderly, serene. "That idiot," he said, "got exactly what he deserved. I've often imagined the French Revolution. . ." He turned to face Giroux. "But try to imagine a thousand stadiums . . . the American people . . . the average person . . . an ocean of them, wave after wave of howling savages. The guards couldn't shoot, they were swept into it. The most awesome thing I've ever seen. My hair stood on end."

Giroux could think of nothing to say.

Simeon turned back to the window, his shoulders hunched. For a moment Giroux thought he was going to break down, weep. Instead he gulped more Scotch.

"It came to that. . . ." Giroux said.

"It came to that." The growl of Simeon's voice was wrenching. "He died with cake in his mouth, him and his silly wife. But to see the people . . . become. . . ." He shook his head, came back to the sofa. "Greatest story of the century, it would have been, had nothing else been going on. But now, lack of communication, that's the worst problem. People all over the globe in isolated patches, holding on, surviving, waiting it out, who know nothing of what's going on elsewhere. Maybe that's best. Maybe thinking they're the last makes them hold on all the harder."

"But who's in charge?"

"In charge of what?"

"This country . . . what's left of it."

"Oh, what's left of it, Thandon. Moved in immediately with his troops. Don't you understand! There's nothing left of Washington but a huge pile of rubble. People tore it down with their bare hands. That night . . . fires burning, ambulances wailing, and a man in a tuxedo, bleeding from head to toe, at a piano in a pile of debris . . . playing the *Marseillaise.*" He swallowed. "Thandon moved headquarters to what was left of the Commerce Building, surrounded by machine guns. A dictatorship. He'd been ready for a long time."

"Always an opportunist. I've always known that." Looking at Simeon's face he thought . . . if granite could weep. Still, he had one last question. "You covered so many fights, so many wars . . . but you never killed. If the opportunity presented itself . . . ?"

"Without hesitation," Simeon said grimly. "Without a second thought, if I got half a chance. I'd blow his brains out. I'd splatter him all to hell."

Alone with her—a numbed langor invaded his senses. Jethro and Doyle had relieved him briefly. As if avoiding contamination by osmosis, Anthony moved his chair as far as possible from the bed to a corner. Alexis' herbal mixture had had no effect. She was off in the kitchen concocting a different brew.

Still uncomfortable, he sat on the floor, knees propped, his back to the wall.

"You look," he said, "like a sea bird to me."

Double awareness. Awake, he began to dream.

He watched images form, flower in euphoric detachment. Two things occurred to him: first, that he was providing his only escape from boredom. Second, that she was speaking to him in the only way she could—projected images.

She was a mere speck in expanding, vague immensity. He drew her forth, enlarged her. Now that a certain aspect of his will was dormant, something more mysterious compelled him, made him creator, spectator, at one and the same moment.

Hang-gliding over a calm sunlit sea. Jaiyavara. But that disappeared quickly. He was too enthralled. He had to stay loose, relaxed, direct it, but let it flow. His desire called to her. She returned—with the body of a woman, the outstretched raven wings of a bird. All in slow motion. Gliding, dipping, turning, lilting on currents of air.

And he heard the music that her movements made. A slow dance in air over a green sunlit sea, prisms of radiance thrown upward from water to touch her in all her turning. He could see the blue-green-black iridescence of her flowing hair, her metallic wing feathers. At every angle as she glided, turned, she was in breath-taking juxtaposition to heavens and sea. Effortlessly curving, swooping, sensuously undulating, a slow death-defying dance in high air. And the endless sky, the endless sea, in rapt compliance, held for her their vast spaces wide.

His deepest desire satiated, Anthony slept.

Giroux was upon him, jerked him to his feet, hit him—a blow which knocked him to the floor. Giroux picked him up, shoved him brutally against the wall. "I told you to watch!"

Anthony fought down instinctive retaliation. "I did watch. I've been here since yesterday."

Slowly Giroux released him. "Oh. Why didn't you say so?"

Chapter Four

As furious as he was, Anthony was fascinated by what was happening in Giroux's face—naked rage smothered as the persona, the benevolent mask, regained possession. Giroux took a white handkerchief from the pocket of his robe, wiped the blood from Anthony's mouth. "I've been under a strain. I apologize."

"I know. You abhor violence. I've heard you say so many times."

"Your tone is insolent. If I catch you sleeping again when I've told you to watch, I'll put you out. Out! Do you understand? You know what that means?"

Anthony's eyes narrowed. Cheap threats? "Everyone knows."

"Where's Alexis?"

"Mixing herbs."

"What next!" Giroux snapped. "Stimulants? Herbs? I can do without all these gratuitous offerings! I don't want her given anything I don't know about! You understand!" Throwing his arms he paced up and down. Then, making a visible effort at control, he stopped, looked at Jaiyavara. "No change yet?"

Oh, quite a change . . . Anthony was tempted to say. Whatever it was that Giroux wanted of her, he, Anthony, had grasped a facet of her which Giroux in his severity could never approach. "No," he said, and touched his mouth; looked from the blood on his finger to Giroux with as much accusation as he dared.

"Go rest," Giroux said, dismissing the entire incident.

As though newly decorated Anthony left, wearing Giroux's attack like a badge of merit.

Patience, Alexis advised. What he'd seen in Giroux's face confirmed long, half-conscious suspicions that Giroux was not quite the messiah he pretended. But this incident had precipitated a discovery far more meaningful than Giroux's flaw—an indirect gift, which even unconscious the enigmatic Jaiyavara had the power to evoke.

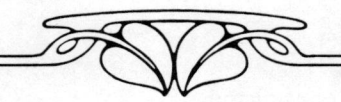

Chapter Five

"You see," he accused, "the trouble you cause me?"

Frowning, preoccupied, for quite some time Giroux considered Jaiyavara's exposed ankle before covering it with the sheet. "No end of trouble." He walked to the window, looked to veiled distant mountains. "No, I didn't mean that. Again, I apologize." He smiled. "Two apologies within the last ten minutes? I don't think I've apologized to anyone in the last twenty years."

Returning to the foot of the bed, he stood with his hands wide apart on the lifted bars.

"We now deserve . . ." he said, "some gift of Heaven."

The sound of gongs.

Silence.

"As if there were a Heaven. . . ."

The sound of drums.

Silence.

"Which I very much doubt."

The sound of clacking sticks.

Silence.

"But that is beside the point. One of those rare, fortuitous occurrences," he said somberly, "of time . . . place . . . person . . . which occur . . . what? . . . once in a lifetime?"

It occurred to him that he was making a speech.

But such seizures of language were a life-long habit. Testing the nuance of phrases, often he spoke aloud to himself. Rehearsing what he would say to her later? Wait, he'd lost the thrust of it . . . this message for her ears alone.

"Lifetime, did I say? Once in an age. Once Upon An Age . . . yes. To *seize* the moment. *Make it happen.* Paul on the road to Damascus," he emphasized in a better pitch, "saw only what had already been made manifest. But I see . . . I see . . . so much more. Convergence of necessity. Compliance with the avenging fates. Perhaps an advantage. Humanity has so suffered that the very nemeses of nature are now in our debt. There will be a reckoning," he warned, with lifted finger. "You will see that I have prepared a place for you . . . a place for all lovers of the Absolute in whatever form they choose to adore it. As if there were a God. Which I very much doubt. But that too is beside the point."

Simeon knocked, stuck his head just inside the door.

"It's all right, Simeon. Come in, come in."

Fearful of disturbing the patient, Simeon stood quietly, hands to hips, looking down at Jaiyavara. "Still out of it, is she?"

"Yes, but I think she looks better."

"I appreciate your hospitality, Giroux, but I have to leave now."

"So soon?"

"Today, yes. The weather looks good."

"You're certain I can't persuade you to stay?"

"No. I have things to do."

"Well then, take two horses. One to carry supplies. Tell Juan I said to give you the best. Switch back and forth, take your time so you won't tire them."

"I'll go like a pioneer," Simeon grinned, "watching for wild Indians all the way."

"How indebted I am to you. I know what a crusader you are, and yet without question you took time to do this for me."

"I now have a question."

"What?"

Simeon took a stance. "Are you in love with this woman?"

Instantly Giroux realized he should have anticipated that. "Oh," he said, his expression resigned, tinged with bemused sorrow, "if only it were that simple."

"What, then?"

"But what's the point, Simeon . . . until I know she's out of danger?"

"I went to a great deal of trouble. I'd like to know why."

"Yet it may all come to nothing. All I can say to you now is that . . . the future is sending me messages."

Simeon stepped back, folded his arms. "Messages? Through her? What messages?"

"Of what is needed."

"A cure is needed, Giroux. A vaccine. A solution."

"Oh," Giroux sadly smiled. "More than that. That's very simplistic. Much more. I know what you're thinking, that I've always suffered from enlarged expectations."

"Something," Simeon persisted, "you expect from her?"

"Well . . . yes. As you've often reminded me, I'm sometimes blinded by too much light. This place, you called it a pipe dream, remember? But now . . ." vaguely he gestured, "for the first time . . . perhaps life will meet me half way."

"Through her?" Simeon looked worried.

Giroux searched for a way to confide in him without sounding like an idealistic imbecile, like one indeed blinded by love.

Jaiyavara moaned. She flung out an arm. The I.V. stand toppled, the glass container hit the floor, shattered glass splayed across the floor in a thousand glittering pieces. Liquid seeped into cracks between the stones. In intense anxiety, Giroux tried to keep his voice normal. "Please, ask Alexis to bring another I.V."

"Sure. Then I have to leave. I'd like to hang around for more of an explanation, but then, I'm out to get the soulless bastard."

"Good. Do it." Giroux clasped Simeon's hand, his shoulder, with fierce affection. "And then come back to us."

"I will. By the way, I'm taking that last bottle of Scotch with me."

"Take it, with my blessings. I hope when you return things are much different."

"One way or another, I'm sure they will be." Simeon was about to say something more, but Jaiyavara began thrashing about. Deaf and blind to everything else Giroux bent to her. Simeon left.

Within the confining bed she emitted hoarse gasps. Fearing she would injure herself Giroux pulled the I.V. needle from her arm, tried to restrain her. Unconscious, she fought him. He had no idea what to do, nor did he dare leave to get Bain for fear she might fling herself over the bars, fall to the floor. Holding her, he managed to lower the bars and tried to force her mouth open with his fingers. Her teeth were clenched. He could not cope with her. Twisting, she struck out savagely. He was trying to lift her, get her to the window for air, when with astonishing strength she threw herself against him, sat up, and opened her eyes.

Her eyes were wild. Hoarse whisper. "Don't touch me, don't touch me."

His hands came away, he kept them protectively a few inches from her body.

"Water," she whispered.

Backing away, watching her, he brought the water. Her eyes calmed. Like a small child she took the glass in both hands, gulped as if sightless. He wondered if she had suffered brain damage.

"More." She pointed to the water pitcher.

The relief he felt was like a blood-letting. He brought the pitcher. She drank in measured greed, a kind of rapture.

She would think she was still at Citta Nova. "It's all right, it's all right," he said. "Lie back, now. Rest. You're safe here."

Without looking at him she whispered. "Now I understand . . . now I understand."

"Understand what?" Whatever she had accomplished, he thought, was as nothing compared to her eyes. Dark, dark eyes. He had forgotten their power. "Understand what, Jaiyavara?"

". . . the dream. The dream. Now I understand."

"Tell me," he urged, not daring to touch her in any way.

Her eyes came upon him, but without acknowledgement of him as a person, she seemed still within the dream. "In a forest," she whispered. "I'm a creature. A simple creature. Not yet human. No thinking. Yet somehow . . . I know."

Urging her to speak, trying to entice her from that suspended state, he paid little attention at first to what she was saying.

"Part of a clan," she whispered, staring past him again as if in a trance. "So real. More than a dream. Ten thousand lifetimes I lived it. Dominant male. Stronger. He takes food away from me. When I'm injured he leaves me to die."

"Yes, yes," he kept coaxing her. "Tell me all of the dream."

"Predators . . . and the baby clinging to me. Can't run fast. So many times injured I crawl away to die. So many females die. We don't think about it. We just die."

She did not look at him, but he saw that now she was aware of communication with a sentient being. "I take the baby . . . go alone through the forest. Find my way. A long time. Hard to find. Find my way at last . . . to the sea." Lightly she clasped her own breasts, in her eyes an expression Giroux could not decipher. "The others followed. Females led the way. All came finally to the sea. When the panther comes I run into the water . . . the baby clings to my back, my breasts, my hair. We're safe in the water." Slumping, she took a deep breath—as if naked on a beach in the pleasurable heat of the sun. "The sea saved me. I sit watching. Every moment the sea changes. Never get enough of watching, smelling, listening. It sings to me."

Entering, taken by surprise, Alexis halted just inside the door.

"For thousands of years," Jaiyavara said, "I am sitting by the sea." She fell silent. Moments passed. Neither Giroux nor Alexis spoke.

"Safe there. Good there. For thousands of years. We thrive. But the sand irritates. My body changes . . . genitals move downward, inward. So slowly I never notice. He can't get to me so easily. Angry that I'm no longer so submissive. He begins to . . . he's thinking. Thinking how to get to me. Frightens me. Both of us becoming more conscious, more human. Mating is from the rear, mortal combat face to face. Rage . . . lust . . . urgency . . . or call it inspiration, he throws me on my back. I'm terrified, fighting for my life. Think he's trying to kill me. He ignores my screams. Terror excites him. He overpowers me. The first rape."

Remembering, she fell silent. Then, a movement of her head, ". . . that ruthless aggression. Passed from generation to generation by the dominant male. Inbred, through all the generations. All the atrocities . . . now I understand."

Her eyes fixed directly on Giroux. His presence registered. Male presence. Her dark gaze bore into him. "There were," she said, "other solutions. You could have evolved a longer penis."

"Mon Dieu!"

Biting her lips, hiding her smile, Alexis came forward. "Penises, penises," she scolded. "Enough of penises. You need water. You were very nearly dehydrated." Glancing at Giroux, she flushed. "My herbs . . . that did it."

Jaiyavara looked from one to the other, asked the same question she asked from within many dreams. "Who are you? Where am I? Where am I this time?"

"Don't you remember?" Giroux said. "Years ago we met on the Riviera at St. Claire's hospital."

". . . Citta Nova."

"No, no, you're in California now. A mountain valley a little north of Carmel."

"Carmel," she repeated, struggling for orientation. "I've never been here before, have I?"

"No, but you were once invited. Don't you remember? The reception at St. Claire's?"

"Where's Salvini?"

Giroux hesitated. "He's still at Citta Nova."

"From Arizona . . . to California. How . . . how did I get here?"

"Simeon brought you in the helicopter. You were unconscious."

"Simeon?"

"A friend of mine. Please, no more questions now. You're safe here. You'll have friends here. This is a new beginning for you. We'll talk later. I'll explain everything." He took her unresponsive hand, kissed it.

Watching him leave, she lay back confused. Alexis gave her a brisk sponge bath, then left to get wine and a bit of solid food. Jaiyavara heard soft bells proclaiming gladness. Turning on her side, she tucked her head under her arm. What in this world was there to celebrate?

Had I not fought him . . . she thought of the dream . . . how different . . . how different . . . it all might have been.

Waking the next morning in a larger cell, a more comfortable bed, she was no more astonished by her continued existence than with every waking. Evidently they had moved her during the night. She felt drugged. Odd to be carted about without awareness. Like so much goods. Watching blotted darkness retreat, watching the world again create itself, did it matter? Substance. Duration. Cool morning air dense with moisture.

Absorbing the new, the unfamiliar, she lay wide-eyed, very still, testing sounds, smells, testing the light.

. . . man in black robe looming over her as she woke before. The one who kept saying . . . Don't you remember?

. . . woman with bald head who bathed her.

. . . Helicopter. California. Someone called Simeon. And then the soft bells.

. . . the way he kissed her hand. The way he said it. Evasively. Salvini still at Citta Nova.

Salvini was dead.

In the forming world another loss. Teacher. Friend. Substitute father. No one else could have taught her the things he taught her. She tried to consider that he was old, that under the best of circumstances he could not have lived much longer with his heart condition. But old only in years. In ideas, ideals . . . eternally youthful. She could imagine how he would smile, shrug it off . . . news of his own death.

Yet so many of his concepts, ideas, were within her, entrusted to her, safe within her as long as she lived. The light kept growing, expanding, transforming sorrow to resignation . . . to wonder.

Where am I now?

A white wicker chest. Above the chest a small mirror framed in white. Without a mirror you might never be convinced, you might think yourself a homeless phantom, or still a stubborn child. In a white spiral vase on the chest, delicate orchids, purple throated, splashed pink-violet. Her gaudy bulging knapsack on the floor beside the chest—someone had thought to bring that? Clothing, jewelry, keepsakes, gathered at Citta Nova as if preparing for flight, when she knew flight was no longer feasible. Yet someone provided flight. Someone called Simeon.

Bird song. Floating toward her in the meshed sieve of lateral spaces, between receding darkness and growing light. The world coming at you from every direction at every moment. That sensation she had first experienced with Varrick in the woods—that the world was soft, continuous explosions with the two of them at the center. Implosions? Was there such a word? In the forest beside him she would wake very early, after awhile the first birds would wake, sound a few trills, then go back to sleep. She would lie in his arms listening to him breathe.

Chapter Five

The old warrior. Varrick. The primal male. Dead.
Her mother dead.
And now . . . Salvini.
And I am still here? Why? Hearing the heart tick out the endless span. None that I love beside me now as I thrash through time.
She heard gongs. Silence. She heard clacking sticks. Very wierd. She heard ritualistic drums, which sounded like the panting of a mytical beast, white-winged; and felt a quiver of interest in the pit of her stomach.
Sound seemed to dissolve more slowly here than in the Arizona desert.
Her fingers traced the stitches of the patchwork quilt. Many women had worked on it—she was informed by the braille of stitches. Such a quilt could last for generations. Her fingers caressed it. A wedge of turquoise, an emerald square, a ruby star, a sapphire edging. It had a downy smell. From the grandmothers, the aunts, the sisters . . . the mothers. No one should take such gifts for granted.
Echoes of sounds lingered. They would be repeated, no doubt, circling around and around throughout the day. No doubt she had heard them in her sleep. Indoctrinated already? All sound, every spoken word, every thought perhaps, went into some vast reservoir circling the world to condense as mists or fog or falling rain when needed by the thirsting earth. Or those dry of soul. Nothing lost, the sounds said.
Alexis brought a breakfast tray, fluffed her pillows, then primly seated herself beside the bed. "Are you comfortable here?"
"Yes, thank you. Why are you so concerned, so kind to me?"
What a question! Alexis thought. "Eat," she said bluntly. "The muffins are special. You look much better already, but you need to eat."
Jaiyavara took up the fork, began, but found it unnerving for someone to watch every bite that went into her mouth. Half way through the meal she pushed the plate aside. "I seldom eat breakfast. I usually have just coffee and cigarettes."
Sympathetically, Alexis nodded, but did not budge.
"How brave you are," Jaiyavara observed, "to shave your head. Was it a religious act?
"No, it fell out years ago . . . it never grew back."

"Some sort of disease?"

"Oh, no. . . ."

"What then?"

"Shock, you might say. Too many shocks."

Quietly, looking into her eyes Jaiyavara did not press for details. "Your head is beautiful. I would love to paint you."

Politely, Alexis smiled. She nodded to Jaiyavara's knapsack on the floor. "Don't worry about clothing or any necessities. I can bring whatever you need."

"I have enough," Jaiyavara said of the knapsack, which now contained all her worldly goods. "When I danced, I traveled lightly. It got to be a habit."

Ill at ease, Alexis seemed waiting for someone in authority to take a position or attitude toward Jaiyavara. "Did you enjoy dancing more than painting?"

Jaiyavara blew lightly into the mug to cool her tea. "I love both, but dancing is innocent. Painting is ruthless . . . a kind of violence."

Violence, indeed! Hadn't there been enough of that? Was Jaiyavara, Alexis wondered, always so blunt, yet somehow rather tilted, off-key? "Well," she offered pleasantly, "no need to travel now."

Jaiyavara fixed her penetrating, hollow-eyed gaze on the older woman. "No way to travel, no where to travel . . . you mean."

"We have everything we need here. . . ."

"I doubt that."

"You'll have many friends here."

"I've never wanted many friends. Friends interfere."

At a loss, Alexis rose and took the tray. Placing the tea pot within easy reach she said, "Giroux will look in on you later. And I'll bring your lunch."

"Thank you. Tell me your name."

"Alexis."

"Thank you, Alexis."

Alexis left to seek what she habitually sought when disturbed —she sought the young. Jaiyavara seemed to her not only skeleton thin, but depleted by some sort of implacable weariness, cynicism. Anthony was right. It was worse than they could ever imagine.

Sitting up straighter in bed, Jaiyavara tried to recall the name. Giroux. Giroux. She looked to the window. Trees, layered terraces, circular and winding paths, all a luxurious profusion after the flat arid desert. Distant mountains, wispy as chiffon floated in mists—an ethereal dance. Unsteady, she got up, went to the window, kneeling, put her hands to the ledge. A beautiful place. A good place to work.

At a distance she saw several monks led by Giroux, walking by. A few paces behind a young woman came into view, very attractive, tawny blonde curls which sparkled, full of electricity. Giroux entered a latticed arbor; the monks, all male, formed a circle around him, their backs a barricade to the young woman who kept discreetly maneuvering for a position, a break in the backs, trying to edge her way in toward Giroux—who was evidently delivering a spontaneous lecture.

Every culture had spawned them, Jaiyavara thought. Giroux. Of course. The Riviera. The reception after his speech. He did not have a beard then—which was why she had not recognized him. Nor did he wear a black robe. But oh yes, Shaman he modestly proclaimed himself . . . even then, years ago.

Ravenous for coffee and cigarettes she got back in bed, poured another cup of tea, propped with pillows, sipped. Remembered.

Yes . . . that reception she had attended with Thandon. And Ethyl. Thandon liked to brag that he stayed on top of things, was alert to every subversive movement, every possible insurrection.

Yes . . . smarter than a Christian, that Giroux. Making a point of . . . "Those who are last shall come first in the Kingdom of Heaven." He seated two rows of the worst children up front. Children were also seated randomly throughout the audience of political and artistic dignitaries, like grotesque little puppets, the hopelessly ill and mentally retarded children. Children who drooled, wet their pants, rocked back and forth in their chairs, or mumbled incessantly. Or, even as normal children, laughed or cried aloud. One, she remembered, fell out of his chair.

Various people she had known at the time were easily remembered by their ill-concealed irritation, pity, or aversion to the children. And on the front row, that beautiful, stricken blonde boy of about twelve, who gaped at Giroux in canine adoration, without a glimmer of understanding.

Giroux on stage. Holding forth. Doom-saying.

The angry reach of his oration.

Never, even in a professional actor, had she heard such a voice. Quite an advantage. An instrument perfected.

Sipping tea in the quiet cell she recalled . . . his gestures . . . his words . . . his performance. . . .

". . . a warning prophet," he was saying, "has always been a joke. A cartoon with an amusing caption."

He was anything but amusing.

"While science is feverishly poking and prying into the secrets of reality—big bang or cyclic assumptions," he shrugged, "what does it matter? That the universe expands and contracts the Hindus signified as 'The Breath of Atman' countless ages before modern science was ever conceived. Has science offered us any real answers to anything? The deeper they probe the more incomprehensible the All becomes. Immanuel Kant once said, 'The finite mind can not grasp much of anything!' Ha! Primal mysteries can never be explained. (Certainly she could agree with that.) We can only celebrate them with ritual."

Compelling. Magnetic. Disenchanted with any hope of influencing Thandon, she had wanted to be charmed. And was, somewhat. Despite no doubt of Giroux's sincerity . . . what was it that made her wary? The set-up? His theatrical exploitation of the unfortunate children?

"Now," he said, stalking up and down, "there are those *imbeciles* who will assure you that whatever technology can create it can also control. Who will assure you that nature is so vast and forgiving that there is nothing that mere man, in his rapacious greed and stupendous arrogance, can do to harm Her." Dramatically, he paused. "But could it be—aside from our extinction— that if Earth dies . . . something in the mind of God is forever lost?" His hand indicated the children. "I place these innocents among you as a preview of what is about to befall the entire human race. The inferno," he said quietly, "is at hand."

A cough in the audience, a restless stirring, and as if on cue from one of the children, an angry howl.

Giroux waited it out. "Mohammed," he continued, "Moses, Confucius, came trying to teach you a few ethical basics. And failed. Christ came trying to teach you love. And failed! And here I stand with the temerity to ask for your help for the generations to come . . ."

He leaped down from the stage. Half suspecting he might walk among them, touch them, pretend to heal them, she would not have been surprised to hear the strong arousing chords of a fundamentalist hymn, as she had heard in passing outside the white churches as a child in Mississippi. "Onward Christian Soldiers." Something like that. But no, he did not over-play it.

In tones signifying the beginning of the end, he warned, "Early Catholicism stamped out the Gnostic movement offering salvation to the masses. The Gnostics were elitists. They saw Christ as a mystic, morbidly sensitive to suffering, appreciated by only a chosen few. They saw a man who, the night before he was to die, could stand beneath the stars in the Garden of Gethsemane, hold out his arms to his disciples, and say . . . 'Come, dance with me.' "

With deep finality, with the tender sorrow of a condemned poet, Giroux concluded, "I too am an elitist." He held forth both arms. "For the world as we know it . . . may I have the last dance?"

Charisma, yes. No applause. That jaded audience moved to silence. She was moved, despite her better judgement. And yes, she would have danced with him, had it been physically possible, if still she could dance.

But not the last dance.

It was, she remembered, at the hotel that evening that Thandon said of the dress she changed to, black lace, long sleeved, "Stunning simplicity."

"Perhaps I'm as morbid as our dynamic preacher." At the mirror she lifted, adjusted the head-dress of black feathers, tightened the beaded bronze band.

Thandon stood behind her, stroking from beneath her lifted arms down to her hips, pressing against her, breathing down her neck. Petty bastard. He liked to think he could arouse her when there was no time, no opportunity for consummation. For the reception she took a taxi back to the hospital. Thandon escorted Ethyl.

Walking the pale blue corridor which reeked of ammonia, just outside the doors to the dining room she saw the child she had noticed earlier in the front row. He was kicking and bawling, throwing a tantrum. Determined, she realized, to get in to Giroux. Two nuns were trying to drag him off to his room. "Can I help?" she offered.

"Oh, he's impossible," said one nun, exasperated.

"We'll handle it," said the other.

It?—she thought, and entered the reception. Dining room tables pushed back against four walls, loaded with food, drink, confections. All very lavish, festive, sparkling. Throngs of people, in every conceivable mode of dress, the current "anything goes" finery, much of it outlandish, garish. Giroux formal in black suit and tie. No longer needed as props, the children mercifully put to bed.

Unaware of his conquest, the little monster howling for the sight of him, Giroux basked in the limelight. All his show. Still disturbed by the child, Jaiyavara got a drink, wandered to the edges, uninvolved, avoiding contact. All dressed up, were they? For what? Eat, drink, mingle, and be merry, for we perish very soon? In those days—severe pain from the neck injury—she drank to excess. So . . . much of what Giroux later accused her was blurred, yet no doubt true.

Even now, years later, in the quiet cell, she could visualize exhilarated Ethyl, who had persuaded and commissioned her to do Thandon's portrait. Her own motive—a lust for revenge on Varrick's murderers, the hope of talking Thandon into ordering an investigation.

As if she had launched a successful advertising campaign, the night of the reception Ethyl eyed her with acquisitive approval. A streak of lesbianism? Or only that Ethyl was such a collector? The cold-blooded arrangement between Ethyl and Thandon filled her with revulsion. Thandon's reputation as a lover enhanced Ethyl's sense of power, his reported seductions included the Greek actress Theodora, the Italian soprano, Morenna. Nothing lit the strange fires in Ethyl's cold eyes more than believing that some individualistic female envied her prized possession. And, if interest were lagging, she pitched in, stirred things up a bit, in adroit (or so she imagined) procurements. Jaiyavara suspected that Thandon was forced to keep himself romantically linked for Ethyl's surfeited entertainment. Ethyl's standards were precise, if quirkish. Money bored her, as did political influence; her appetite dulled by lifelong association with both. And . . . a half-breed dancer would never do, yet a successful painter she deemed worth snaring.

Giroux making the rounds, eye to eye and hand to hand contact with every presumable contributor. By the time he got around to her she was in a foul mood and drunk. He grasped her hand possessively. "Ever since your London performance, I've been an ardent admirer."

Haunted still by the howling child, she made only a civilized murmur.

"They fairly devoured you."

"One should leave off being eaten when one tastes best." Not very original, but what the hell....

"Yes, I heard. The accident. What a terrible thing. But," he added, in grandiose tones, "like the Phoenix you arise from the ashes . . . from dancing to painting, what an astounding transition. How did you so easily manage that feat?"

Her eyes throbbed. Sullen with antagonism, she looked beyond him. "Nothing has been easy."

That mocking, aggressive smile. He loomed over her. Was this a flirtation? If so, it was only a ploy. The orator she would have danced with that afternoon seemed now nothing more than a professional solicitor.

"And what," he asked pedantically, "did that horrible experience teach you?"

To look up at him directly would have hurt her neck, and so she refused to look up at him. "Pain cleansed me, I hope, of some vanity."

Giroux threw back his head and laughed. "Forgive me, Jaiyavara, but if you are now cleansed I would hate to have encountered you previously."

"Some, I said. Don't fret, I still have plenty to spare."

He moved in, leaned down, as an amused conspirator took her arm. "I don't fail to notice that you are somewhat a social outcast."

"How observant."

With savor, he recounted her sins. "Yes, you insulted the Envoy to China . . . you called the famous Russian novelist . . . yes, I heard you . . . a pamphleteer. You referred to our new Minister Of The Arts . . . as a bee-keeper."

"Well, now," she drawled, her mouth twisted to accents of deepest Mississippi, "ain't that the truth."

"Which is why I have enjoyed it all enormously. What next, Jaiyavara? I can hardly wait."

Dislodging her arm she gave him a look reserved for politicians and turned away.

Blocking her, he asked, "Are you making a contribution?"

"But of course," she smiled. Plucking a long black feather from her head-dress she placed it firmly in his hand.

His glittering eyes narrowed. "Fitting, I suppose, for one who can no longer fly."

She looked directly up at him. "What next, Giroux? Next, is you. In this entire gathering of pompous supercilious egomaniacs, you are the ultimate. What is all your mouthing compared to. . . ."

"Dancing? Painting? If I am ultimate ego, and I readily admit to it . . . you are Queen of Eccentrics."

Why waste energy trading insults? She turned to leave.

Again, he blocked her. "Compared to what, Jaiyavara? I defy you to answer."

"Putting your life on the line. Putting your body, for instance, between whaler and whale."

"Ah yes . . . Varrick. Your unforgettable hero." As if measuring her against some preconceived faultless illusion, he refused to back off. "You've made one major transition. Make another. Join us."

Her eyes rolled heavenward.

"I mean it. Join us. As a symbol of. . . ."

"Who the hell wants to be a symbol! I have no idea of what you're up to. I don't *join* anything. And the essential argument, Giroux, is not between science and religion. You can't stop them, and building a place to hide is no answer."

"You have a better one?"

"Only for myself."

"Ah yes . . . for yourself." Looking down upon her, hands in pockets he took an Olympian stance. "How selfish. For yourself you danced your grief for Varrick through the cities of Europe . . . to standing ovations, true. But you could be so much more. Because beneath your hard pose, your hostility, there is an intoxicating spirituality."

"My perfume," she sneered, when they were joined by Thandon. In the hope of some grim morsel of humor she stayed to watch.

Stiffly, Giroux bowed.

Thandon extended his hand.

Giroux did not accept it.

Thandon's reaction, a confident smirk. Pugnacious Thandon, a foot shorter than Giroux, legs wide apart, undaunted by the affront, stuck out his chin. "Ah, Giroux . . . your old world charm. Interesting speech. Overwrought, but interesting. And of course you realize that proper legislation will . . ."

"Legislation has never solved anything."

"My contribution," Thandon continued, "will be anonymous."

"The only way I would accept it."

". . . the administration can hardly condone your dire predictions."

"In other words," Jaiyavara smoothly supplied, "he does not want you for an enemy, or publicly for a friend."

"My dear, as usual, you understand me perfectly." Chauvinistically, he put his hand to her waist.

She smiled. "Oh, do I?"

"My wife looks stranded," Thandon said. "Excuse me." Lightly he kissed Jaiyavara on the mouth.

She turned to Giroux. "Observant one, I hope you observed that he did not pinch me on the ass."

Giroux's jaw clenched. "Blatant, ostentatious, unscrupulous son of a bitch. What do you see in him?"

"Power."

"To change things?"

Unwilling to admit anything, she shrugged.

"In bed? Don't be a fool."

The tea pot was almost empty. What little tea was left, cold. She was still in bed when Giroux came in, pulled up a chair, sat down.

"Now I remember you." She waited for him to get settled. "Do you have a cigarette?"

"I'm sorry, no."

Quietly they regarded each other. "Salvini's dead, isn't he?"

"Yes."

"Why didn't you say so?"

"You seemed in no condition just then to hear such news."

She could not argue with that. "I was disoriented. But telling the dream . . . was I lucid?"

"Yes."

"Well," she said, looking down to the quilt, tracing a hexagon pattern with one finger, "that's all that matters."

"Absolutely, yes . . . all that matters."

"Except for the robe and beard," she offered, looking up, "you really haven't changed much."

"Neither have you."

"I'm anxious to get up and look around."

"Perhaps you should stay in bed and rest another day or so."

"No, I'm fine now."

"Do you feel like telling me what happened at Citta Nova?"

Looking toward the window she did not speak for several moments. "You feel so helpless. You can't believe it will come to the people close to you, the people you plan with, work with. But then, one by one . . . It's a nightmare. The strong nurse the dying until they too fall ill. I don't mean just physical strength. What surprised me . . . so many were so young. When I collapsed Salvini was still on his feet, still going strong. We all looked to him, depended on him. It's so difficult to imagine him . . . not being. . . ."

What greater tribute, Giroux thought. Would someone some day say the same thing of him?

Jaiyavara put one hand to her center, pressing inward. "This Simeon who brought me here. I don't understand. Why?"

"I asked him to."

"But why?"

Elbows on the arms of the chair, Giroux brought his fingertips together precisely, which made him appear, she thought, quite scholarly. "Let's just say that I could never forget you."

"That's very hard to believe, Giroux."

"Long before we met . . . you made a life-long conquest."

Head to one side, her expression was grave. "But I remember," she said evenly, "the night of your reception. We did not hit it off very well."

Chapter Six

She dreamed of a wind that neither moaned nor howled, but like a melancholy ghost searched relentlessly for a place to cease. She dreamed of windmills, tall, erect in a dead world, which sent telepathic messages over vast spaces to other windmills: each solitary, separate, against a streaked, downswooping sky.

Jaiyavara dressed—sandals, purple pants, purple robe—let her hair fall loose and went out to explore. The air was crisp, invigorating, the sky cloudless, as pure as an untouched canvas. In every direction the view was stupendous. She could smell the trees, yet there was the backdrop, the detachment of great vaulted spaces.

Brother Bethune rushed forward. "Wonderful, wonderful to see you! I'm Brother Bethune. How are you feeling?"

"Much better, thank you."

He grasped her hands. "May I show you about?"

His touch made her think of the Jade plant, cool and curling, slightly moist, his finger bones unbelievably fragile. To get her bearings she would have preferred wandering alone, but agreed —she liked his fine, excited air.

Level by level they descended terraces to the patio between dining room and kitchen. All the buildings, so nestled, dwarfed by mountains, seemed to her both old and new—old because they were of the same stone as the mountains, new because she had never seen them before, and because it was morning.

On the patio, against the kitchen wall, an outside wooden table, an urn of hot water; earthen jars of honey, cream, tea, instant coffee.

"Coffee. I'm dying for coffee. Do you have enough?"

"Certainly, help yourself. Most of us drink tea."

Adding honey and cream, she stirred and tasted. "The first coffee I've had in months."

"Just the immediate environs," he said, as they walked to a bench. "We don't want to tire you. We gather here for tea before the four A.M. meditation. But you probably don't wake that early."

"Earlier than that," she said, gluttonously savoring the coffee.

"Oh, then, please join us. Do you meditate?"

"No. I'll be like a fish out of water here."

"Oh, no . . . you'll see. Everyone will make you welcome. Everyone here is very anxious to meet you." Holding the tea cup close to his heart, he beamed.

Happiness? Was it possible? Some effervescence filled him which his slight frame seemed barely able to accommodate. Behind rimless glasses his weak eyes of startling blue would have been, in another face, icy—she was drawn into their watery light. Pulling back she had an urge to shake herself like a seal shedding water. "Now . . . if I only had a cigarette."

"You smoke? Why didn't you say so? Wait, one of our monks smokes. I'll get you a cigarette." He scurried off. She watched him ascend a terrace, disappear into a clump of white birch. Presently, bubbling and sparkling, he came back, handed her four cigarettes and matches. "Be careful. They're very strong. Hand rolled."

"The best kind. Thank you, so much." She put three in her pocket, lit one, inhaled. "I can't believe . . . I can't believe. . . ." Her eyelids drooped.

With keen interest Brother Bethune watched.

Tears came to her eyes.

"It must be. . . ." he said, "almost a religious experience."

"It's so. . . ."

"Yes," he whispered, vicariously partaking.

". . . indescribable."

"Yes."

Cell by expanding cell the tingling sensation in her toes inched upward into every part of her body, into her brain. Bliss. For a few moments. Then she re-adjusted more quickly than Bethune watching. Looking up, she admired the Oriental swing of roof on the central structure.

"Would you care to see inside? It's lovely."

"No, not now."

"I call it the Zendo," he explained, "but to the Christians it's a Chapel, to the Jews, a Temple, to the Moslems, a Mosque."

"Good Lord, all that?"

"Oh, we are all varieties here. Sufism. Pntanjali's Yoga. Khakti, a Hindu mysticism. Kundalini Yoga," he recited. "Zen. We study Grudjieff and Krishnamurti. I was an Angelican priest before I converted to Buddhism."

Jaiyavara looked over the railing at her back, down the rough sloping bank to the mountain stream shadowed by mature slender trees. On the sandstone ledge she saw two frogs slathered in iridescent slime. All to itself the stream sang with its silvery tongues, slithering along. One frog jumped in. Plop. "What is Giroux?"

"Oh," Brother Bethune smiled, "that would be difficult to pinpoint."

"I'll bet," she said dryly, inhaling.

"He studied longest under Trungpa, a Tibetan Llama. A paradox, a living legend, Trungpa. But Giroux can hardly be confined to a single view. He says that's extremely limiting."

"Yes, but what does he teach . . . the essence of it?"

"The essence," Brother Bethune repeated. He pressed bloodless lips firmly in concentration. "Well . . . the essence . . . the very essence would be, I believe . . . a fearless compassion. The man is fearless. Without reservation, I can assure you of that. Just look around you, who else would have had the foresight to so provide for us?" Pleased with himself, he asserted his small shoulders. "But you know, I never before tried to pinpoint it. I just absorb it, intuitively."

Nodding, she murmured, "I know . . . I know. . . ."

Bethune struggled to wring from intuition a concept which could be verbalized. "A fearless compassion . . . to destroy what needs to be destroyed . . . foster what needs to be fostered."

Had this frail person of such subdued radiance actually used the word *destroy*? "One would have to be very wise," she ventured, "to make those distinctions."

"Oh, but he is, Jaiyavara. He is wise."

Head lowered, sipping, she let it pass. No sense in antagonizing the followers. No telling how long she might be detained here. Conscientiously, she squashed out the cigarette. One had to be very careful of fire in California. "Where are the baths?"

"Come, I'll show you." They took their empty cups back to the table and began the tour.

Fully awake, her eyes began to sweep and probe. Endless nooks, vales, crags to investigate, a startling contrast between the immense and the exquisite. Flowers she had never seen before. Vivid minute flowers clinging to ravines, peeping through wedges of stone. Clusters of tiny flowers like jaunty hats on thorny cactus. All this expanding, limitless grandeur of nature put human endeavor into an extremely minor perspective. Within this earthy nest, this high protected valley, it was almost difficult to remember or mourn Citta Nova. The world disappeared, dropped away. Boston, New York, Rome, London, Paris, even Greenleaf, Mississippi, seemed no more now than illusions induced by morphine.

And he, the gentle monk, took it all for granted, perfectly acclimated to only this: the here and now.

"Tell me," she said, as they slowly walked, "your life."

"Good gracious, there's nothing to tell!"

"I'm sure there is. You're much too modest."

The question rendered him speechless, almost sightless, he nearly stumbled, groping his way along he peered straight down to the path before him. "I . . . oh, my goodness . . . well, I tried . . . I tried to minister to people. But they didn't seem to want what I had to offer." Speaking in a rush, a headlong dash, the moment it was articulated his vision cleared. "So," he summed it up, "I came here."

Trying to imagine that, what it meant, giving up, she asked, "Were you ever bitter about that?"

"Oh, no. It's not in me to be bitter."

Head down, step by step, she pondered that also. "I was," she said finally. "I was bitter."

"About what?"

The classic monk. She sighed. "You really can't imagine? You really have no idea?"

"No. Truly."

Removed from the stresses, conflicts, confusions of civilization —so long had he lived in this rarified air—such a barrier his innate innocence, his chosen isolation. "What was happening in art."

"Oh. But what was happening?"

"Everyone so goddamned mesmerized by moving images. Behold, the hologram!" She spat it out. "Petty cleverness, cheapness, tawdriness. People who would do anything for money. Years ago I was in such a rage I tried meditating, but then I quit."

He looked at her as if she had said, I quit breathing.

"It made me too passive, too placid. I need the tension, the fizzle, the highs and lows. Maybe I need the rage. But to feel the work grow out of all of that, beneath your hands . . . oh, there's no power on earth to compare with it."

Brother Bethune wagged his head. "There must be a great deal missing in me. I have no comprehension of any sort of power. . . ."

That stopped her. In the middle of the path she turned to him, put both hands to his face, kissed his pallid cheek.

His translucent flesh heightened to a glow, a flush. "Thank you. But truly, Jaiyavara, I don't worry much either."

"Good." Playfully, she touched his shoulder. "Don't let me contaminate. . . ."

Through the trees they continued on the path, passed buildings which Bethune said had once housed temporary students, summer guests and tourists. The monks looked forward to those visits. Now all the student barracks were empty. Through winding turns of the path the stream was now lost, now visible. Walking upstream, at the foot of a small graceful bridge they came to two wooden benches facing each other. On the opposite bank another stone pathway led to the baths. Following his example Jaiyavara sat down to remove her sandals, placing them, as he did, neatly under the bench. Barefoot they mounted the Oriental bridge and walked to the middle, the high point of its mild spanning arc. "And are we now," she smiled, "shaking the dust from our feet?"

He was quick to appreciate it. "A Biblical quotation."

"Oh, verily. I grew up in the Bible Belt, missionaries and evangelists tromping up and down all over the place. And I avoided them like the plague."

Stupidly, he blinked. There it was. Spoken. But he had handled it better, she noted, than the question of his life.

Here the stream was less deep but wider than beneath the patio, its perpetual song softer, more intimate. At the edges of the banks it threaded, fingering into individual silver snaking ribbons. From the bridge she looked straight down into water, watched it separate around jutting rocks in luscious frothing. Ever moving, yet ever in place. Water, she worshipped. Yet Varrick had died at sea. But, she thought, it was not the water that killed him.

And through the tall interlaced branches above, the dark overhead shadows, pulled as moths to flame, small minnows of light came swimming down to the water. So the water pulled by attraction small fishes of light down from the trees. In droves they came gliding down, to enter that which could never wait, and were joyously carried to the sea.

"So beautiful . . . so beautiful. . . ." she said. "Do we have a right to all this?"

"I think we do."

"I wish I could believe that." She turned to him. Something he was trying to decide. Whatever it was, she wanted to know. Lulled by moving water it was easy to wait.

"If we are living," he said, "there must be a reason."

"Oh, I do wish . . ." she drew in a deep breath, ". . . I could believe that."

"Once," he confided, "just before something very dreaded, I said lightly, as a bad joke . . . I said, 'maybe I'll get hit by a truck first.' I didn't mean it. I didn't. I should not have said it. I knew the moment I said it I shouldn't have said it. Two days later I was in my old car, stopped at the light, and in the rear view mirror I saw this black truck coming straight at me, some lunatic barrelling down on me at ninety miles an hour. No time to think . . . move . . . I was sure I was going to die. In that split second I regretted saying that."

Listening, leaning forward, elbows on the bridge railing, Jaiyavara could not take her eyes from the water. "What was it you so dreaded . . . once upon a time?"

"Heart surgery. I was afraid of dying on the table. The truck, well, don't you see, I was being chastized for that bad joke. And Jaiyavara, it comforted me to be so chastized."

She stood straight, turned, leaned with her back at the railing. "How is your heart now?" she softly asked.

"Oh, fine. Like brand new."

The pensive ghost of a smile came to her lips. "How sweet to know," she said at last, "someone with a brand new heart."

He was rather embarrased, yet pleased.

"But," she added, "isn't it a wonder that nearly being hit by a truck didn't give you a heart attack?"

"That's it, that's it," he beamed. "That's what I'm saying exactly."

"I see." Turning again, hands to the railing, she bent once more toward the water. For quite some time they merely stood, listening, watching, breathing.

"There's so much I want to ask," he began, ". . . if it's not too painful for you."

Sooner or later each will ask, she thought. Horrors enough to pass around. Placing one on each tongue like a sacramental wafer? His example of feeling chastized made her wonder . . . did he want her to punish him for having, if unintentionally, avoided it all?

It rose from the depths. The repulsive form rose before her as if from nightmares of evil waters. All there, intact. As if yesterday. "One of those bright sweet gorgeous days," she said, "when you feel so alive, so glad to be alive. One of those quiet pretty streets that goes through Central Park . . . I was riding my bicycle. Went through," she corrected herself, and as she did her mouth went dry, making her wish she were close to the water to splash it cold to her thirsting mouth, her burning eyes. "A man dashed out . . . running from cover to cover like a wild animal. He ran right in front of me. Froze there. I nearly ran into him. Everything stopped. I was too terrified to scream. His face was like . . . his eyes like . . ." She swallowed. ". . . like an animal caught in floodlights on the freeway at night. It was day. In pain. Panic. His eyes shining like an animal's. I can't describe. I've never seen such eyes. His face bluish. Swollen. A sore on his throat. Congealed pus crawling out like a fat worm."

"Oh, my God."

Not looking at Bethune, she said, "I left that night. I left work in galleries, work in the studio finished . . . unfinished. I just fled. Went home."

Brother Bethune turned completely around, facing the opposite direction, as if straining to see a more rational universe further upstream.

Chapter Six

Too late she realized he had expected some mild generalization, nothing so graphic. "I'm sorry. I thought. . . ."

His hands made furtive gestures.

Ashamed—she should have been more aware of his sensitivity—she said no more. As of one accord, yet now quite separate, they crossed the bridge to the other bank. Yet in the next moment had he looked at her, he would have seen something suppressed, smoldering. Sooner or later in every eye, the evasion. Spare me the details. I don't want to hear, I don't want to see, I don't want to know.

"Home . . . to India?" His voice was a thin rasp. He cleared his throat.

"No, my father's place in Mississippi. When I got there," she said matter of factly, "my mother was dying."

His face in distress, too soft, as malleable as the play dough Lou Iris used to make for her as a child. "Of the Plague?"

"No," she assured him. (No more of that.) "Of a broken spirit. Worn out, worn down. She nursed my father for years before he died. She loved the bastard. Actually," she shrugged, "I am the bastard. He never claimed me."

Leading up the bank he took her hand. His small hand trembled.

To distract him from the tale of Central Park she went on with it. "Well, he already had a wife, and a legal son and a legal daughter. My mother was born and reared in India, she followed him to this country after I was born."

"India," he breathed. "I envy that."

"Yes, always the faraway place . . . for my mother it was America."

Shoulders almost touching they reached the level path. "How did they meet?"

Weakened, she stopped a moment to catch her breath, leaned against a boulder.

"Oh," he apologized, "I ask too many questions, but then I've led such a sheltered life I love hearing other people's romances."

"It's all right, I don't mind." Automatically examining, her hands pressed into the boulder. "He was in India converting grain to alcohol. Such an entrepreneur. Always converting something to something, always converting something to cash, assets, profit."

"So . . . he was wealthy?"

"Oh, very. Wealthy and southern. Atrocious combination." She left the boulder and moved on.

In the small enclosed courtyard surrounding the baths Jaiyavara stooped to examine the tile. "This is from Italy."

"How did you know?"

"I studied there." Fingers to the tile, she looked up. "I loved Italy, especially Florence."

"You've been all over the world, haven't you?"

"No," she said, standing. "Most of Europe, but not the Orient. I would love to go to China and Japan. I've never been back to my birthplace, India. I wish. . . ." In bewilderment she turned, looked upward. "From whence comes our help? From the mountains?"

He smiled. "From the Lord."

"Oh. I'm still disoriented. I've never been good at directions. Geography confounds me. Fleeing New York in panic. . . ."

"What?" he urged.

"I deserted a good friend."

"Regrets are useless," said Brother Bethune. He had no regrets, and watching her eyes fix on the mountains, that seemed to him suddenly, equally useless. "Forgive me for saying so, I know you are a strong person, Jaiyavara, but you seem . . . well, how shall I say? . . . rather shattered . . . and certainly no wonder, but. . . ."

"And you're thinking it was the plague," she answered. Her eyes came down on him with that deep, penetrating, hollow-eyed gaze. "The Plague was only the aftermath. . . ."

"Of what?"

Reaching into her pocket, she lit another cigarette.

So soon? he thought.

"Years . . ." she inhaled, "of trying to grasp the ungraspable . . . express the inexpressible . . . and constantly haunted by the stupendous stupidity of trying. . . ."

It was all beyond him.

For the space of a breath she anticipated some answer.

"So," she said, turning, "these are the baths. On to the baths."

He took her arm, leading forward. "Mineral baths are very restorative," he said too cheerfully. They entered a large steaming room of blue tile with an enormous blue tub full of hot mineral water. Moist vapor clung to the walls, stung at her face. The sharp salty-iron odor was not pleasant. A kind of blue gloom.

She backed out. They returned to the courtyard, mellow in sunlight.

"That way," he indicated further upstream, "those are the male baths."

"You don't bathe together?"

"Not here. But far downstream, beyond the patio, there's a pool where the youngsters swim and bathe together. There, to your left, those are the female baths."

"I want to look." Behind the woven screen she took a turn which led to the first compartment and paused before entering. Habits of apprehension. Here, she reminded herself, she would see no one dying.

A sunken tub, pristine white, spotless. Beside it on the black and white tile floor a Zen flower arrangement in an oblong black vase. Three wide flat leaves, horizontal, small green hands cupped optimistically for alms of rain; two vertical leaves, palms facing, as in prayer. On slender stems amid scarlet petals the yellow fangs of lilies curved downward as if to bite.

Fully dressed she got into the empty tub, lay down, folded her hands, closed her eyes. Rehearsals, rehearsals.

Her eyes opened. A strong breeze fluttered the flimsy cotton curtain up and aside. Behind an entire mountain she could see Heaven.

Sheer magnificence. Mine to paint. Yet she shuddered, a needle-pricking at the back of her neck. The tub was too large, a pretend coffin which did not fit. Quickly she got out of the tub and returned to Brother Bethune, patiently waiting.

"It would take an hour to fill that tub!"

And yet again, his discreet angelic beaming. His resilience, his blessedness. "We have nothing but time here."

"Time is what I need. I'm tired," she conceded. "Let's go back. But could we ride tomorrow? Do you like horses?"

"To look at, yes. Not to ride. I'm a fearful, timid person, Jaiyavara."

She took his arm. "Not too fearful to admit it. Honesty takes courage."

He led the way.

And as all the world proclaimed, she thought, it's easy enough to die. But embarassing . . . somehow.

Having retraced their steps, from the center of the bridge facing downstream on the right bank in purple shadows, Jaiyavara saw something odd close to the damp clustered rocks. "Something I want to look at," she told Bethune and left him to investigate. As she drew close it became the color of jaundiced flesh; it was rounded, smooth, vaguely dappled, subtly ridged, indented. At first it resembled some creature which had struggled out of the water past sharp jutting rock edges . . . then no, it seemed something entirely alien which had evolved in the wrong place.

She stooped beside it. Rendered helpless by its own weight, it lay on its side, too large for the thick neck stem; exposed, indecent, an over-large toadstool or mushroom, or exotic mutant. Inert . . . yet it made her imagine pulsation. Its formidable hooded frontal lobes bulged into right and left hemisphere. It looked like a human brain.

Parasite. Tenaciously clinging beneath the trees, between clawing roots and stubborn rocks, obsequious. Why the urge to kick it, destroy it? Something which sucks its life from something else. There it is, and it's disgusting. So vulnerable, kickable, squashable, yet in clinging, persisting . . . somehow a menace. Each night in starlit secrecy it will grow while we innocently dream. Quietly it will grow and out-wit us all. Gobble up the world. Something which mindlessly persists . . . until it becomes mind?

Yet she could not kick it.

When she returned to Brother Bethune he was standing with his hands on the bridge railing, his face lifted, looking into the sky. Beside her on the bridge someone honest and intact, with the delicacy to give her time to grapple with her revulsions: above the moving waters a space for brooding.

"He was that honest . . . and so easy to be with."

"Who?"

"Kraft. My friend in New York."

"Was he an artist?"

"No, a lawyer. When Thandon . . . do you know who Thandon is?"

"The name is vaguely familiar. Someone in politics?"

"The Secretary of State. When Thandon had me jailed, it was petty revenge, a trumped-up charge . . . my portrait of him was unflattering . . . but Kraft said . . . oh, I called him Kraft rather than Harry, but sometimes, you know, I called him the whole name just for the humor of it. . . ."

Brother Bethune smiled, but did not grasp the humor of it.

"He came to see me in jail, Harry Kraft, that is, and he said to me, 'Let's see if you can talk your way out of this one.' "

"You're good at talking," Bethune offered, willing to wait for the details to fall into place.

She turned to him. "You think so?"

"Yes, really, I do."

"Well . . ." she shrugged, smoothed back her hair. "Which was so funny because he didn't think I could talk at all. Oh, but he could. And not just to a jury. He could talk all night. He could talk, as they say in Mississippi, the birds out of the trees. A kind of talk . . . evocative, rather than logical. I think he got tired of logic, being a lawyer and all. Oh, if he were alive now he could skip with words over every rock in this stream."

"You think he's not alive?"

She wet her lips, turned her head aside. Her hand went to the cigarettes in her pocket, to make sure they were still there. "Everyone I cared for . . . and there weren't really that many . . . I have to presume dead until I know. . . ." She swallowed. "Even that, I suppose, is no protection ."

"You're right. There is no protection."

"Is that a Buddhist concept?"

"Yes. Buddhism," he said, "began in India."

"I know. I know that. But I've made my choices. But it was wonderful having Kraft for a friend. Walking down Fifth Avenue we'd just go out of our heads together . . . fantasies shared . . . laughing our heads off. People would stare. That craziness I so loved in him. A kind of craziness I've never found in anyone else. He had the clan pressure to make a lot of money, but money was not important to him, it was expected of him, and he suffered from that. So," she shrugged, "he made the money, lots of it, just to get them off his back . . . but he should have been a poet. Well, when he talked, he was, he was a poet. A poet at heart. The last time I called him from Mississippi . . . by then New York was all panic . . . and he made a joke even then. 'It's so bad,' he said, 'no one is even bothering to blame the Jews.' And he said," she went on, unable to stop, "that a man swathed in bandages dropped dead on the sidewalk right outside Bellevue

Hospital and people were pulling on the bandages, rolling him all over the sidewalk. Plastered to his body under all those bandages were thousand dollar bills. Which means he swathed himself, a sort of camouflage."

She became aware of Bethune's stillness, turned to look at him. His face was white. "Oh, I'm sorry. I didn't mean to. . . ." Why was she punishing this harmless monk? "My God, I just now realize. Maybe Kraft told me that . . . maybe he saw that camouflage as a parody of his own life." Clenching her teeth, she stood straighter. Trees. Sky. Mountains. It was all fake. Painted stage props. They could roll it up, all this scenery, and push it aside. But what was behind? "Where's the music?" she wondered aloud.

Poor child, Bethune thought. Poor child.

"Where are we? What's this place called?" And she remembered asking that same question long ago in a dream. Of this very place. Standing on this very bridge. It gave her goosebumps.

"Simply . . . the monastery. We're north of Carmel."

Was that the right answer, the answer she dreamed? "I would have expected Giroux to give it some dipsy name."

Fingertips before her, sliding on the sanded wood of the railing, she followed her fingers, walked to the end of the bridge. Bethune came along. They retrieved their sandals. Kneeling, Brother Bethune buckled her sandals, revealing, she thought, by this act of humility how deeply her lack of reverence for Giroux had disturbed him. Determined not to further offend him she got up and followed the path, looking only to the path, concentrating on each step, the next, the next, heel hitting first. So different from dancing, from reaching with the toes, the arch, the entire body before the foot-fall.

Sucking in clean stringent air, as she looked intently to the path, someone fell in step beside her, matching his stride evenly with hers. Bethune, she noticed, was not really much of a walker. So enjoyable was that sensation of matching rhythm, movement, she did not look up, she did not need to identify that person. Gradually the length of the strides increased so that Bethune, out of step, had to hurry to keep up.

And so they came to the terrace directly beneath the Zendo. "But to worship with others," she said, squinting up at it, still ignoring the one who had fallen into step, "seems to me rather obsolete."

"Do you believe in a diety?" asked Brother Bethune.

Diety . . . such an obscure, amusing word. "God is music to dance to . . . canvas to paint."

Brother Bethune laughed aloud. "A true Buddhist!"

Smiling, in denial, she shook her head.

"Jaiyavara," said the young monk, "will you paint here?"

"Of course I'll paint." She gave him her full attention. "Ah . . . such a nose." She took his jaw in her hand, turned his head a little to one side for a better scrutiny. Her finger traced the large hook of it. He suffered this handling with sullen dignity. "Like Savonarola," she said. "You're Italian."

"Who is Savonarola?"

"Oh, don't you know? You look like a direct descendant. A great reformer who prophesied the 'Scourge of God.' A terrible man, a wonderful man. He was tortured, hanged, and burned. You must read about him."

"I will," said Anthony. "I have a request."

"What?"

"When you paint may I watch?"

"Why?"

"I want to learn. I want to paint," he said, holding his ground. "Once in a while would you have time to let me watch?"

"Brother Bethune," she teased, "says we have nothing but time here."

No response to her slight teasing. Intense, she thought, and waited—for what, some deft obeisance? But he made none. She liked that. "If you're serious about it."

His chin lifted. His eyes, level with hers, were steadfast. "I assure you, I am serious."

"Very well, then. What do you have here? Can you gather materials?"

"Yes, I'll see to it. Thank you very much, Jaiyavara." There was a swagger as he walked away, which the fullness of his robe could not conceal.

"Who was that?" she asked Brother Bethune.

"Anthony Giordano. I never realized he wanted to paint. You've made him very happy."

"Italian vitality," she mused. "Who knows . . . maybe even passion."

Eyes averted, Brother Bethune blushed.

It charmed her.

"Where," she asked, "do we go from here?"

On a ledge beside the stone steps they sat down in the shade.

... I once, she thought, danced all night with a handsome Italian. Walked with him at dawn beside the Arno River. But was that me?

... and once made love with a matador who would not take off his socks. Did he have webbed toes? I'll never know.

... and once ... that posh Iranian restaurant in New York with Thandon ... lounging on the floor on scarlet pillows. Entertained by belly dancers. A dazzling inlaid mosaic on the ceiling ... scarlet, purple, gold. From the same bowl we ate with our fingers. At another table three sleek models trying to impress an agent. At another table, on and on in the obnoxious voice of a commercial, a young man full of himself expounded on his spiritual development. Careful to wipe his fingers, Thandon took from his briefcase a proposal for aid to a small country at war, made a few notations. At another table that famous pudgy Southern story-teller, all alone, was getting very drunk. From every direction bits of counterpoint. Well, said Thandon, that settles that—and put the proposal back in his briefcase. Smiled that smile. As if to say—I decide the fates of men. Pulled another morsel from the bowl, chewed, swallowed, licked his fingers. Cock of the walk. Oh, he was crude. He wanted me to ask which country. So I would not. Guns. Tanks. Missiles. Between the third and fourth course, hundreds of thousands of deaths projected. Before dessert. The agent was explaining the contract to the models. In endless reiteration of himself the spiritual enthusiast droned on. The pudgy story-teller wiped his glasses with a napkin, put them back on and began to cry. "Would you care for a liqueur?" Thandon asked. Bombs went off in my head. I understood assassinations. But was that me?

"Hello. I am Jethro."

There stood a young monk, tall, slender, black, extremely good looking.

"I am Jaiyavara."

"I know." He sat down beside her, quite thoroughly looked her over. "I've been waiting to meet you."

"Oh?"

"I hear you were raised in the South."

"Not entirely. I was sent away to school in Boston, but yes, every summer I went home to Mississippi."

"Mississippi, that's the deep South, isn't it?"

"Pretty deep," she admitted.

"My grandmother was from Macon, Georgia."

"Pretty deep too. Not much difference."

Head back, he looked down his long aristocratic nose at her. A bit of French mixed in, she thought.

"I've heard handed-down tales," he said, "of terrible atrocities."

"I heard," she said, "the same stories."

"How was it for black people when you were there?"

"A lot of poverty and hardship. A lot of bitterness. No real equality . . . but some wonderful black politicians and preachers. Nothing I could tell you about black people would be true, Jethro . . . since I am not black."

Courteously, he appraised her. "Well said, Jaiyavara."

"When I was a child . . . an old black man I loved told such stories . . . such stories. Gatemouth of Memphis. He also made predictions."

"Did they come true?"

"Well, see for yourself. He once said, 'The rats will prevail.' No one understood at the time. They thought he meant music, they thought he meant a rock group."

Softly Jethro laughed.

Simply to listen, Bethune was content.

Jaiyavara picked up a stick. Chin in hand on her drawn up knees, she absent-mindedly drew spirals in the dirt at her feet.

After awhile Jethro took the stick from her hand, drawing large circles beside her spirals. "You're not black . . . but you're not white either."

Watching, she nodded. "A mixture. A mongrel. There are messages in my blood my mind knows nothing of."

Passing the stick back and forth they made compatible squiggles and doodles in the dry soil. Without looking up, Jethro announced, "I'm a poet."

"Fine," she said.

"And . . . when all this uproar is over and the dust settles down, I'll probably become famous."

"Fine," she said. "Only please don't ask me to read just yet. I'm weary."

"I understand weariness."

That made her feel comfortable. At home.

"Maybe," he offered, "weariness is in your blood."

"Maybe." She looked into his eyes. "Maybe in yours too."

"Maybe. If so, I will strive to overcome it."

"Fine," she said, and was suddenly faint with weariness.

Monks began making their way toward the dining room. The lunch gong sounded. Brother Bethune, Jethro, and Jaiyavara got up, leisurely walked down the path. From the opposite direction Giroux came to meet them. "You two go ahead. Jaiyavara is to have lunch in her room."

"See you later," Jethro said. He and Bethune went on without her.

"I'd rather eat with them. I'm just getting to know them."

It had never occurred to him that Jaiyavara would want to mingle with the monks. He took her arm, turning her. "Alexis will bring you a tray."

She dislodged her arm. "I don't want a tray. I don't want special privileges."

"It's no trouble. She prepared it herself. Come along now, please don't argue. You don't want to disappoint her. And tonight I'd like you to dine with me in my study." He was anxious to show off to her his varied art collection.

"Wait just a minute." She came to a halt. "I'm not accustomed to being ordered about. I don't even understand why I'm here."

"We'll discuss that later."

Karen, in passing, slowed, stared at Jaiyavara. Giroux threw her a stern glance. She had the good sense not to intrude.

"You keep saying that," Jaiyavara reminded him. "A simple answer. . . ."

"You're not fully recuperated." His tone solicitous, he again took her arm, brusquely guiding her along. "Please trust me. For the time being, please do as I ask."

Propelled by the sheer physical largeness, the force of him—were there certain rituals, she wondered, even to eating in this place? Did he fear that in her weakened condition she might catch something in the crowded dining room? Too exhausted to make an issue of it, she went along, but by the time they reached her room she reasserted her position. "I will not be treated as one of your docile monks, Giroux."

"Docile?" Surprised, somewhat offended, he looked down at her with genuine concern. "No. They are wise."

"Because they call you father?"

He made one of those hurt, apologetic, evasive French gestures.

"I call no man father," she said and flung open the door, turned, slammed it in his face.

Reverberations. As though hearing a crash of cymbals, he stood facing the door. There was no lock on the door—but her whirling made a blur of motion in his astounded eyes; he was left standing, caught in a harsh music he could not yet follow.

Chapter Seven

Temper, temper, thought Giroux, climbing the long narrow stairs to his study. She is not compliant. But then, I never anticipated immediate compliance. A challenge. Must give her time to become acclimated, indoctrinated into the routine. It's all new and strange to her. Inside, at his desk, his back to the strong sunlight from the window, he stretched out his legs, put a folded hand to his mouth. Don't rush. Don't push. In quiet talks . . . slowly lead, step by step persuasion. Or . . . if I could somehow maneuver her into thinking it at least in part . . . her own idea . . . her own discovery. Splendid. Splendid.

He looked about the room. Would the crystal stag look better on the hearth? Should he move the golden bowl to . . . to where? Perhaps it was too soon to invite her to dine here. Perhaps he should rearrange things a bit. He so wanted the study to make a perfect impression.

Suddenly he wished for something carved of cypress to place on the hearth . . . a figure tall, mythical, vaguely maternal. Her spirit was like cypress. Properly guided, molded, polished, preserved . . . ah, how it could last.

She once said the essential argument was not between science and religion. What then, he wondered, does she consider the essential argument?

Chapter Seven

In the dining room repeatedly Karen looked to the entrance alcove. Giroux's center chair at the head table was still empty. He and that woman seemed to be having some sort of argument. How it leaped out at you, the outrageous purple of her robe. All the speculation since her arrival, and no one knew anything. Where was he? Alexis was right, Karen thought, in demanding her own color. Black was no color. Flowers in her hair, she decided, dresses and robes of many colors, earrings and beads and bracelets, she should have them. She deserved them.

Where was he? Still talking to that woman? Here they were in the middle of a world crisis—and what was he up to? Why a painter? The sight of her close—someone seen on television years before—somehow a shock. She did not look much older now. Well preserved, Karen thought maliciously. Yet that one quick look in passing had caused this breathless nervousness, this queasy hollowness in the pit of her stomach. What the hell, Karen thought. I am only twenty-six. She is at least forty. Time is on my side.

No answer to her knock, carrying the tray Alexis pushed through the door with her shoulder. Face down, Jaiyavara lay on the bed, tangled strands of hair fell across her cheek, shadowed her gaunt face. What a waste to let the food get cold, yet Alexis was hesitant to wake her. All that tromping around outside all morning, she needed the rest.

Shifting in sleep, Jaiyavara raised one knee, her hand clutched aimlessly. "Mama? Is that you, Mama?"

Only a murmur. Yet how it pierced. Quickly Alexis put the tray on the table and left.

Hands curled to her mouth, closed in sleep. How many times had she seen their hands just so? Peter. Berman. Karl. Nicholas. Did the pain never leave? What did all the world's righteous mumbo-jumbo have to do with it? Disciplines and rituals and philosophies . . . what help? Her body felt heavy, something she dragged along against her will. Earth's gravity seemed to pull down harder each year.

But then on the stony path before her Alexis noticed how her shadow looked still eager, how it leaned ahead of her pointing the way like the prow of an old battleship, lunging through undulations of light as if they were waves. Day and night, she thought, I am growing old. And no wonder. Look at the old skull bone shadow still plowing through. Idiot. Anyone old should have the good sense not to bare their skull to the cold indifferent world. Old skull bone, where are you going? Days and nights come and go.

Yet the longer she walked, the more she tried to throw off the sensation of becoming even more of a fool than her bald head proclaimed. Within the dull anguish of that one word murmured in sleep, now at last subsiding a little, something more; diffuse, new forming, forgotten, such a wisp. Could it be . . . some sort of happiness? New flutters in old veins? Peter. Berman. Karl. Nicholas. When a life was ended on earth where did the essense of it, the secret of it, go? I am an insignificant speck, she reminded herself, waiting to be crushed by death. And no curled and aimlessly clutching hand could ever change the shapeless lost dust of their hands . . . their eyes. . . .

Twisting on the bed Jaiyavara sat up. Someone had been in the room. She saw the tray. No appeal. It was sleep she craved. She loosened the robe from her neck and shoulders, lay down with the good hot sun on the back of her neck.

Night. The ship. Torrents of rain. Why were we on deck rather than in a cabin? Did she think if the ship sank she could get to a life boat faster? Crouched in a corner, Mama held me. Towering waves crashing down. Fiendish hiss and roar and howl. The wracked old freighter floundering, throwing us this way and that. Thunderbolts. Hurled by homeland gods angry at our leaving? Old ship, groaning, creaking, the lash and crack . . . rising up up up then dropping out from under us that terrible swoosh a bodiless fall. Mama terrified. Singing.

Mama sings right through.

Out in back at the clothes line still I see her . . . an apron of big pockets for the clothes pins over a thin house-dress the wind blew against her legs. In the flat distance scrubby fields, a muddy pond, and beyond the pond thick splotches of dark green. Wind carried the smell of trees. First lesson in perspective brought by the wind.

—"Your Mama," scolded Lou Iris, "is jest a little chile herself."

Through the front screen door I could see more scraggly fields of weeds, scorched grass—that isolated little shack, our home, intended for sharecroppers. But Mama bounced me. Could have gone naked in the front yard, no other houses anywhere. That orange and yellow dress she wore . . . and another dress of lavender roses, green petals, my favorite. Flies and mosquitoes. Constantly swatting flies. And that fat old Basset hound came waddling down the front dirt road every morning as if he owned the place. Stole the cat's food off the front porch. Even sometimes stole the tinfoil pan. I've seen Mama chase him down the dirt road waving her skinny arms like matchsticks and she would come back fussing at how that dog had plenty of food and was too fat already. That dog from the big house. . . .

Where was the big house?

Mama sings like a crazy sea.

"...be-ware of lof-ty...clipp-er...ships...
they'll be the death of you...ooo...oooh...
It was there...he made...me...walk the plank
...and pushed...me un-der...too...ooo...oooh...

Sitting in the front yard for our own private picnic, dry as parchment from the sycamore it floated down, a snake's shed skin. Mama yelled, scrambled out of the way.

I never saw her in a sari. Cast off her homeland as easily as a snake shedding its skin. Everything American enthralled her. Especially the gadgets. Year after year, holes in the front screen, cracks in the windows, the leaking roof. My cat was black. Dipsy. Fat hound that waddled down from the big house out of sight belonged to Gottrell. No other children to play with. No one to tease me that I had no father. She never told me, but I came to understand from the way she danced to the phonograph, the radio, that I had no father . . . and never felt the need.

"She had a dark and a rov-ing...eye...ay...ay....
...and her hair...hung down in...ring-a-lets....
She was a...nice girl....
a...prop-er...girl....
but oh!...one of the...rov-ing...kind...."

Mama's hair did not hang down. Frizzed in the silly current fashion. *Vogue, Mademoiselle,* and the Sears catalogue came to the mail box by the dirt road. Postman waved and tooted his horn. Once in a while Lou Iris would come to stay with me. Mama walked the dirt road a mile to the bus stop, brought home books from the library by the armload. Maybe she thought one day she would teach again. Pouring over slick magazines she would say—"The look is arrogant and bored."

Traded her birthright for an electric can opener, a black and white TV, a sewing machine.

Saturday mornings William came for the grocery list, Saturday afternoons he brought the groceries. She would ask him when Lou Iris was coming for another visit, would beg him to stay for a cup of tea. Politely he excused himself. It took her a long while, I suppose, to catch on, the unspoken law that it would never do for a black man to mix with the boss's mistress.

What an actress. Sitting on the front porch, a Bible in her lap. —"Isn't it lovely, my darling! This Christianity!" And she would leap to the yard, striking a pose to perform it before me. —"Entreat me not to leave thee: Or to return from following after thee. Yes. See, it's in his own black book that he says is holy."

Or she would say to William,—"Oh, I forgot to tell you I need matches. I forgot to tell you I need curry."

And William would say,—"You got to tell Mr. Gottrell that you got to have a telephone. There's such things as emergencies. Things can't go on this way."

She would look at a fat slab of bacon or side meat or ham hocks in bewilderment.—"Lou Iris says this goes in the greens?"

Fluttery Mama primping in the mirror, two high spots of feverish color in her cheeks. I must have been three or four, fooling with her gaudy array of trinkets and junk on the dresser. Agitated, she smacked my hand, but immediately grabbed and hugged me. —"Listen, listen. Your father is coming to see you. Be a good girl. Be an angel." She kept scrubbing my face, changed my dress twice. Her perfume was like incense.

At the screen door, blocking the light. He was huge. A heavy jacket. A cowboy hat. Boots caked with mud. Flinging open the door she hurled her small self upon him. No real embrace from him. He was looking down at me. I saw something in the sack wiggle. She was pushing me forward and I had my heels dug in. —"Your daughter, Malcolm. Isn't she beautiful?"

—"Christ," he said. "What strange eyes."

And I thought he might put me in that big sack and drop me through a hole in the bottom of a ship into unimaginable depths of blackness, drown me like a stray cat. She got my crayons and coloring book, got me settled on the front porch. I was quiet for a long time. I was being a good child, I was being an angel. Pretty soon it began to rain. When I went inside the house was dark with his invasion. The bedroom door was locked. He might put her in that sack to steal her away from me. Pressing to the door I heard her voice. —"Am I only your rainy night woman?"

That was a summer . . . like so many . . . miserable with heat . . . almost every day a sudden storm, a lot of noise and bluster but little rain. You could hear the first drops spit and sizzle like water in a hot frying pan, steam smoke curling off the porch, limp dust-coated weeds on the side of the road would stand erect, renewed for awhile, sprightly, almost courageous; then go limp again with fatigue when the rain went elsewhere. Those quick inland thunderstorms unsatisfying, nothing to compare to a storm at sea. When he left her arm was stretched out on the back of the sofa, her head resting on her arm, and I put my face against her silky black robe, the one with red edging, red on the inside of the wide black sleeves. She was distant. All her effusiveness drained. —"Thy people shall be my people," she said like a waif. "Thy God, my God. And so forth," she said. It started raining a little again. I felt despair. He had stolen something from her. Her very heart. Leaving me nothing but the remote shell.

I wandered into the kitchen.

The floor mud-smeared from his boots. On the rubber-maid draining board two squirrels and a large grey rabbit, limp, lifeless, their eyes glazed. One of the squirrels twitched. A puddle of blood beneath them slowly trickled into the brown stained sink.

The kitchen floor mud-smeared; blood down the drain.

I call no man father.

When he walked through that house in heavy boots the splintery grey floor boards rattled, the thin walls trembled.

What did he do . . . sneak into her bedroom at night while I slept in my crib? Only his rainy night woman? Yet, when I was a child she never failed to bounce back, like spring water at its source she threw off the dirt he smothered over her, bubbling back to life. How graceful when she danced, not to the common radio blare . . . but to music remembered. More graceful when she danced than any of those flat commercial poses in magazines. —Greta Garbo! Would you look! Look at her eyebrows! I must have tweezers! —With small brown hands, fingers so quick, so nimble, she wove for me an elaborate head-dress of clover chains. A little sparrow she was, gathering bits of this and that to make a love nest. With small brown hands she would part the grass, pushing down with her fingers, eyes closed, to feel the rhythm, catch the throb of the foreign land, the strange place.

Or she would grab me up in the front yard swinging me around, around, gleefully reciting:
    —Listen my children and you shall hear!
    of the midnight ride of a bottle of beer!
    Down the alley and through the fence!
    Ho! Ho! Ho! Old St. Nick!
    And you can buy him for fifteen cents!

One friend for Mama. Plump, rounded, and perfect, Lou Iris sat at the kitchen table; neat slacks and a knit blouse, gold rings on her fingers, loops of gold in her ears. William worked for Mr. Gottrell but Lou Iris cleaned houses free-lance. Gallons of coffee she drank at our table. Her pursed lips, lifted brows, her little finger held out from the cup handle. The perpetual poise of one who has conquered the world with a vacuum cleaner, Pine-Sol, a hymn, and a mop. —"Miz Hendrix, she fixed me a waffle breakfas' for my birfday. With sausage an' eggs and all, 'cept grits. An' Miz Wilson, she gave me an extra ten dollars to put my coat in th' lay-'way. Then I got to git me them red shoes an' a purse to match 'cause we got somethin' goin' on ever' night at church nex' week. Miz Langford, she axed me would I work for her sister, Miz Shooey, but she's th' one that sticks them dirty pots an' pans back in the oven th' whole week till I gets there. It's unsanitary. So I says no, I got my hands full, I got all I can handle with William's son, that terrible Houstin, comin' in on us, an' 'sides, this ain't one a my better days. I ain't takin' on anyone else 'less they got 'specially good references."

Two highly esteemed gold teeth displayed when Lou Iris laughed at anyone's jokes, including her own. Draw near, draw near, to the comfort of Lou Iris at the kitchen table. Such a bosom I have seen nowhere since. Starved for female companionship Mama listened to trivia by the hour, with unobtrusive little coupons of wisdom, advice slipped in. Which Mama never used.

Only once, Mama asked . . . only that, nothing more. —"Have you ever worked for Lucile Gottrell?"

—"That hellcat! Not for a million dollars!"

And Mama learned the names of American presidents, the capital of every state, recited to him like an adopted school child. He was not amused. When they went to the bedroom and locked the door I was afraid he was hurting her.

Special hat, special black suit William wore when he came for us that morning in the long black car. Children, mothers, going in when we got there. Unappealing red brick building. William opened the car door for us with flourish. He whispered to Mama, —"Now you walk proud."

Crowded inside. Mama sat down in an armless chair beside the desk. —"This is my daughter. This is Jaiyavara. We are here for the registration."

Twigs of short mousy hair, the teacher. Pale. Not friendly. She wore a starched grey blouse with a high collar. It irritated the skin of her neck. —"Jai . . . a . . . what?"

—"Jaiyavara," Mama said. She spelled my name.

—"We'll call her Jai," said the teacher.

—"No, please. She's accustomed to the whole name. It's not that difficult."

—"Last name?"

—"Gottrell," Mama said. "It's on her birth certificate. G . . . O . . . T . . ."

—"Everyone in this town knows Malcolm Gottrell." She glared at me as if I had scabs and sores.

Lucile. Lucile. And who was to blame? Certainly Mama knew he was married when she met him. Certainly Mama was not entirely innocent. High in the sycamore, beyond flat striped fields of cotton I saw it at a distance, speeding through. The faint roar. Like a bullet, metallic green. Trailing clouds of dust, dust churning against the deep-hued afternoon sky. It kept coming. I knew it would. The roar dimmed as it disappeared behind a clump of trees to swing out taking a wild curve, lost momentarily in its own spewed dust on the turns. As the roar grew louder, nearer, I climbed down from the sycamore and hid behind the fig tree on the side of the porch. All of a sudden it shot past the house, swerved, the back end pivoting. She gunned the motor, foot to floorboard no doubt; came back, jerked to a halt. The car shuddered like a horse about to drop. She got out, slammed the door, and came staggering toward the house; tall she was, thick hair the color of burnished copper. Silky dress, patterned like a snake skin, green and gold, wrinkled, spilled on, dark splotches down the front. Smeared mouth. Bleared eyes. She wore no shoes. Extremely drunk. —"Where is the little shit? This I've got to see."

I thought she meant Dipsy. I thought she hated black cats.

Lucile in the house, pulling at the bed covers, jerking dresser drawers out onto the floor, smashing lamps, while my mother stood in the doorframe between bedroom and kitchen, etched in shame and terror. I began to feel some sort of terrible guilt for my mother, some sort of pity for the wretched woman in that frenzy of rage. Lucile hollering, —"Where's the sacrifice! Where's the heathen altar! Where is the little bastard!" and she whirled to face my mother. —"All this time I thought it was niggers living here. I don't ordinarily tramp around investigating the shanties. Right on our own property! Any of the nigger girls he could have had, but no, ole Malcolm Gottrell has to have for himself an imported whore!"

Crazy. On the attack. Going for my mother. I ran. I grabbed her leg. I bit through nylon. She screamed. Rattled my head trying to shake me off. I held on with my teeth. I tasted blood.

IMPORT: *To bring in from the outside. To introduce.*

To bring (goods) in from one country to another.

—"We will leave this place," Mama said. "We will shake the dust from our feet and leave."

The same burlap bag he brought the rabbit and squirrels in, she threw some of our things into and we started walking down the dirt road. She held my hand, dragging me along. Before we got anywhere I was tired and thirsty. Endless road. Bits of rock got in my sandals, hurt my feet. We got to the asphalt road. Every time I heard a car, I cringed. I could imagine that green bullet running us down.

Then it was dark. We were on a bus.

Then she was propping me in a scoop of slick plastic in a greasy bus station. She went to a pay telephone. The lights hurt my eyes. Some men were playing a pinball machine. One of them kept leering at me. I wanted Dipsy. I wanted to go home.

Waking in a bed at the end of a long narrow room, an aisle down the center, beds against two walls. There was a night stand, a ratty curtain for some pretense of privacy. Mama stood at the window. Tears that did not slide but stuck to her face like rain drops on a window pane. We had to stand in line in that place and then wait for someone to pray over the slimy food, over the entire motley gathering of the homeless. Very few women, very few children. Mostly men. Sullen. Mean looking. Dispossessed. Shifty eyes. At the table a lot of the men tried to sit by Mama, strike up a conversation. She was uneasy, cowed. The next night we slept together in the same hard little bed, so tightly she held me I could hardly breathe.

How long before he came for us there? I don't remember. I remember his boot heels resounding on the hard bare floor as he walked down between the long rows of bed. An old woman sat up in bed, working her toothless mouth, held out her arms to him, thinking he was some long lost relative. Another fat frowsy woman sat up, pointed at him and laughed. —"Well! Mr. Gottrell! Welcome to the Salvation Army!"

—"Where did you think you were going? he said to my mother."

—"I don't know. Home maybe . . . somehow."

—"Get your things."

Without knowing where he was taking us or for how long, she did as she was told. Greatly relieved, I think. I guess I was too. Goods . . . but he wanted us. At least he wanted her. Took us to that apartment over a liquor store on Naylor Street. Even . . . a telephone.

But just before we left he picked me up and set me on the bed and looked into my strange eyes. —"Open your mouth," he said. "Show me your teeth."

I did.

He was handsome when he smiled. I thought he wanted me.

—"By God," he said. "You are a Gottrell."

Chapter Eight

Doyle sat facing the open door of his cell, his heavy swollen legs propped on a footstool, a copy of *The Folklore Of Ireland* open on the floor beside his chair. Tuning, picking at his dulcimer, he waited for companionship, indisposed with gout. Once fear had made him chaste.

Now and then a monk would stop in his doorway to inquire about his health. The one he awaited did not appear, but Doyle was at ease. For the past several years his love life had flourished.

He had never known torment.

Picking and tuning, morning passed gently to midday. Just as he was dozing off in his chair, he heard Leon's dry crackling laugh. Wiry little Leon appeared, high on dope, his greasy unwashed hair in coils down his back, his chin sprouting spaced, long hairs that did not gather to a beard, his eyes like dry ice. Oblivious to the facts, Leon launched into his latest manic enthusiasm, ideas for putting the monastery on the map.

Patiently, Doyle listened. "What map?" he finally said.

Clipboard in hand Giroux moved among the storeroom bins and shelves taking inventory, ordinarily Doyle's assignment. The sea was within riding distance, he was not concerned about salt, it was the ebbing supply of antibiotics, insulin (two monks were diabetic) and anesthetics that worried him.

In the kitchen Karen had three batches of bread working. While one batch baked she timed the rising of the second and mixed up the third. Working the dough with rolled up sleeves, her taunt breasts pushed against the cotton snugness of her blouse, a cotton petticoat under her long flouncy skirt teased at her thighs. Giroux was near. Glancing through the door to the storeroom she tried to gauge his mood, his accessibility. Her face was flushed. Heady yeast heightened her impatience. Her pulse quickened. She rinsed her hands and went after him in the storeroom.

"Giroux. Excuse me. I've been thinking," she announced.

"Not too much, I hope."

"Maybe too much," she ventured. "I've been thinking that maybe I came here too young, too inexperienced. Maybe I know too little of the real world."

"Oh?" he relented. "So that's the trouble, is it?" His arms folded around the clipboard. "What do you mean, the real world?"

Having gone after him in heated impulse, unprepared to elaborate, Karen none the less bravely floundered in. "Things like . . . ambition. Competition," she said, grasping at straws.

"Why are you suddenly burdened with these thoughts?"

"How am I to judge my spiritual progress if I have so little to compare with?"

Thoughtfully, Giroux's tongue moved to his upper teeth. "What sort of progress are you striving for, Karen?"

Detecting his sarcasm, she helplessly shrugged. "Oh . . . you know. . . ."

"No, I do not know. Please be more explicit."

"I need," she persisted, "some idea of contrast. I need someone to tell me more of the real world."

"Please don't keep using that trite expression. What gives you the idea that this is not real?"

"Nothing, nothing, excuse me. I mean, I'm not saying it right. Things I never experienced. Those . . . how else can I say it? . . . those worldly things."

"Ambition? Competition? It all went to hell because of those very aspects. You were spared a great deal."

"Really?" Her eyes made appeal. He did not respond. Defeated, she then avoided his eyes, ready to drop the entire matter.

He decided not to scold. Dalliance. The young female who constantly pestered him with her frivolous attentions, a useless vessel. Almost any male on the premises could shoot his hot sperm into her, and it might just as well be spilled on concrete. Lecture her? He would do better to lecture stones, she was that dense. Yet leaning, he wiped a bit of flour dust from her cheek. "You've been working hard this morning, haven't you? You're a bit dishevelled."

Aroused by the compliment, Karen lost her head. "Do you think she's beautiful?"

His eyes narrowed. "Who?"

"Jaiyavara."

"Oh," he nodded, peering over her head, far past her.

There was no turning back. She waited for an answer.

"Physical beauty," Giroux said with restraint, "you consider it that important?"

"Well, yes, I suppose . . . doesn't everyone?"

In mock gravity he regarded her. "I don't know, Karen. You see, I don't know everyone."

Her armpits began to itch and sting. Surprised at her own audacity she doggedly repeated, "But do you think she's beautiful?"

"I presume you are somehow relating this to the idea of competition? Well, to answer your question . . . no, she is not beautiful." Tongue to upper teeth he watched Karen dangle before him, incapable of defense. "But she has," he elaborated, "a quality much more significant, much more essential."

Her voice was breathless. "What quality?"

"The ability," he slowly enunciated, "to project beauty."

Unable to withstand the rebuke, his finality, she wiped her hands on her apron.

"Hadn't you better get back to the kitchen, Karen? Your dough is rising."

"Yes. Excuse me."

"Gladly."

Repeating and replaying every spoken word, every gesture, and expression, as she punched and kneeded the yielding, resilient dough mass, Karen began to wonder . . . essential for what?

Giroux finished the inventory and returned to his study. The pain in his left temple, he realized finally, was due to a toothache.

Poppycock, he thought. Up with which I will not put.

A clutter. A nice mess. At odd hours, when it was convenient for them both, Anthony and Jaiyavara worked together in her room. For the array of earthen paint jars Anthony had constructed a narrow table, for canvas he coated burlap with white paint, tacked the burlap to frames. Preparations complete, he stood before the stretched whiteness, lying in wait. Suddenly, he had nothing to express.

"Well . . . it's tentative," she told him. "A kind of groping. Just fool around and see what happens. Something happens . . . while you're working."

In dumb resignation he faced the substitute canvas. "To begin. . . ."

Yes, she thought. To begin. Beginning again. Nothing ever but beginnings.

Here, at long last, perhaps possible . . . the pure thing? All the trappings, distractions put aside? Influences. Evaluations. No flash bulbs to defensively prepare for, no pressure to finish something in time for an exhibit, no thought of what to donate to the latest charity. What freedom. All that bother behind her now? All that led down so many wrong paths, twisted detours. That business with Thandon, playing the enemy within the gates, where did it get her? Trying to beguile him into doing something worth while. Who was I, she thought, to presume to try to change the world? Playing the rebel, she accused herself, you rather enjoyed it, you got caught up in it. Disgusting.

"These crude materials," Anthony apologized. "You're used to much better."

"So . . . we'll be ingenious. . . . I'm not accustomed to anything. Everything amazes me."

Murmurs passed between them. And those questions he asked that she was still possessed by, almost as if she were speaking with a former, younger male version of herself. What is beauty? What is desire? By what means does the revelation emerge?

A kind of barter, solitude exchanged for a framework. Anthony provided a border or bulwark which seemed to keep Giroux peripheral. Of late she sensed Giroux was biding his time. When she met him on any path she was civil, in perverse curiosity having decided for the present to humor him, comply with his peculiar restrictions, play the hand he dealt.

Giroux was in for a rude awakening. Sooner or later he would approach with some work in mind for her to execute, there could be no other plausible explanation for his interest. Working with Anthony was a way of preparing him for the fact that she had no such intention. At Citta Nova she had been much under Salvini's influence—not that she regretted it, he gave much in return. But once she got back in stride she would do no work but her own. She was too depleted, too haunted to consider some chapel depicting Giroux's odd mixture of mythologies.

Anthony at last dipped his brush, stroked the canvas. But not for long. "What you said the other day, about learning to put up with your own compulsions. . . ."

"Hmmm."

"I have a compulsion," he stated.

Silence.

"Meat."

Working something close, intricate, she made no answer. Several minutes later she stood back eyeing the work quizzically. "No wonder. Not enough protein. And then, anything taboo. . . ."

"Ordinarily, I prefer white meat, the whiter the better. But here lately I crave bacon, ribs, steak. Charcoal grilled. I can taste it. Thick and juicy. Smoky."

"Hmmm."

Anthony asked what she liked to eat. No answer. She was locked in, inaccessible.

But half an hour later she said, "Hmmm," and sighed. "Well, vegetarianism doesn't solve it. Vegetables don't scream as loud. Murder in the kitchen. If you kill something, animal or vegetable . . . you ought to honor it by preparing it as beautifully as possible."

Humble in his growing desire, almost abject, he patiently timed his next interruption. "You're not giving me any criticism."

She came to stand behind him, look over his shoulder. He was not well enough into it so that she could offer criticism. "You have a light touch."

"Which is better, definite or evocative?"

"Which is better," she shrugged, "the circle or the spiral? You must believe Anthony, that your vision is as valid as any other."

With the hard end of her brush she pointed, making circular motions. "Something interesting beginning here...."

"You think so?"

"Ummm. Go with that."

Pensively together, as they contemplated the given area, she did not realize that her hand was on his shoulder. He wanted to turn her, put his hands to the lean flow of her, stroke the flesh covering her long bones.

"Besides," she said, turning back to her own work, "the world is full of half-ass critics. Or was. Critics who never attempted anything themselves. Ant hills of frenzied activity."

A gong sounded.

"What's that for?"

"Meditation." He had no intention of leaving.

She wondered if his absence from rituals would cause problems.

"Karen," he offered, "thinks we're up to something."

"Your girl?"

"Sort of."

"The pretty blonde?"

"How did you know?"

Without looking up, she smiled. Karen, she thought, is up to a great deal herself.

Anthony waited for her to ask what it was that Karen thought they were up to. She had warned that she did not like to talk while working. Fearful of irritating her, he let it go. Was she unaware that she was being courted? Seize her boldly? Some instinct warned against that. He waited for one of her lapses, when she stared out of the window or at a blank wall in vacant remission. As for her unrealistic canvas, he watched it change, evolve, centered metallic ambers, pale greens pulsated with radiance, froth edged turquoise and white spewed out, at the edges dark blue deepened to black. The more he looked it seemed from the viewpoint of a sea creature breaking surface, bubbling up from watery depths. "What is it?" he finally asked.

She kept working. That his question hung unanswered made him more cautious.

"... if I could explain ... I wouldn't have to do it. Maybe," she said, again standing back, "it's pain ... or ... something attained despite ultimate defeat."

And so the hours passed. Anthony worked.

At the table, mixing a more definite shade, she smushed a hardening blob with her finger, wiped her hands with a cloth.

"What was it like being famous?"

"Oh . . . I don't know. It's for the young," she said, working her brush into the mixture, swiping it on the edge of the jar. "I thought," she looked directly at him, "you were going to ask about pain." Then rapidly, again and again she repeated the mixing, swiping process. "There was a time," she said, turning back to the canvas, ". . . after the accident . . . when I wanted it back. Not fame so much as the same body. Trapped in that body. Unending horror. Months of superhuman effort . . . and the damned thing still couldn't dance. Oh, how I hated it."

Suspiciously he stared, yet the earlier imprint of her hand still burned in his shoulder. Hate the body? And now he could not look at her without remembering the music, her movements, the secret space, extant, between her small breasts, her dry parted lips, the pleasure of that plundered kiss. Plunging his brush into red-violet, in forceful strokes, thick and wet, he laid it on. Damn! Ruining it! Incensed, he cleaned the brush, went to the window to sulk.

For some time she failed to notice that he had stopped working. "Tired?" she asked.

"No." His voice was despondent. "I'm considering a different approach."

Male ego, she thought. Added to that, the well-known Italian humors.

"Jaiyavara, why are you teaching me?"

A long pause. "Potential. Not that many artists left now. . . ."

Nightmares.

When she woke in the middle of the night she lit the lamp and sketched in bed to calm herself. On occasion she got up and dressed to restlessly prowl outside until the monks took pre-dawn tea on the patio. Waking briefly, or turning in sleep a monk might see her floating by his window, or her shadow gliding across his bare wall.

One morning just before dawn she met Jethro, stalking his own dissident muse. Together they sat down on a hillside to watch the sunrise.

Ruben came lumbering up the hill, golden-orange light splaying wide at his back. At one and the same moment she recognized him as the child in the corridor at the Riviera and saw the sun at his back as a raging lion . . . and a sudden vision exploded in her mind's eye. She saw a male giant, a sun god, crashing through a wall of stones. A huge fist shot through the wall and the wall began to crumble. A gigantic leg crashed through and the earth trembled. What did it mean? She shuddered.

Child mind. Body of power. As if begging to be petted, Ruben squatted beside her; he was stinking of urine, unwashed, his square long fingernails filthy. He grabbed for her hair and she suffered him to fondle it. Then he grabbed for her beads. The strand broke. Like tiny creatures trying to hide, beads went rolling in every direction. She caught a few in her lap, offered them to Ruben to play with.

"Don't," Jethro said. "He'll try to eat them."

She patted his shoulder. The sounds Ruben made were an eerie mixture of purr and growl.

Gazing through Jaiyavara's window Anthony saw nothing but the fantasies of his own indulgence. Superimposed on every tree and distant mountain peak, he saw imagined previews and teasers of penetration. Tonight he would think of her, torment himself with thoughts of her. Some word, some encouragement he needed for the long night. In shameless stealth he moved close as if watching her work. Twice she almost glanced up, but was not to be intruded upon. At last she sighed. "What is it, Anthony?"

"Jaiyavara. . . ."

"What, Anthony?"

"I have to say it. . . ."

She frowned. "Say what?"

"I love you."

No change of expression. She kept working. Close beside her, suffering the ache, he waited for his declaration to register.

"Good," she said, matter-of-factly. "I loved Salvini."

"I mean as a woman."

Stepping back, she scratched her neck, complained of the canvas, "Not enough mass," reached toward the table irritably, hand poised above the keyboard of colors, ready to pounce, searching for heaviness, density. He watched her seize upon it, dip and stroke until she stood back, temporarily satisfied. "I loved Salvini as a man. But I never made love with him."

"Why not?"

"It would have ruined something perfect just as it was. Lovers are plentiful, a good teacher very rare."

His jaw tightened. "I know that." Sullen with resentment he retreated to the wall, folded his arms. Never had he told any woman that he loved her. The barrier was not distance, nor was it years. His rival was the canvas. "Why are you angry?"

Her shoulders twitched. "When you soar," she said, "someone will always try to shoot you down." But she was speaking to herself, the canvas, certainly not to him. "My best work ridiculed. The mediocre praised. Enough to make you . . . all I wanted was the right evaluation. I just wanted them to see in a new way."

Sympathetically, he nodded. Not that she noticed.

"When it came . . . the Plague . . . I was ravaged with guilt. As if my fury had called it down."

Head back, leaning against the wall Anthony's pupils dilated. "Maybe," he whispered, "it did."

With an involuntary gasp, her eyes flew to him. For a split second he had her full attention.

Without warning Giroux was there, towering over them. In that suspended state of instantaneous contact both were startled, as if caught in some furtive alliance.

Slowly Jaiyavara turned to Giroux. "Good morning," she said dryly. "Don't you ever knock?"

"Morning?" Giroux growled. "It's nearly three o'clock."

"Oh, dear me. I must have left my watch at Citta Nova." Then the smirk slid from her mouth. "You're interrupting. What is it you want?"

"You missed two meditations, Anthony."

"So?" she shrugged. "What's the problem? He can catch up later."

"It is not something you can catch up on. It's a daily discipline."

Fanatics. Malcolm Gottrell and the Church of Christ. Fat matrons with useless hands, steely eyes. Straining a gnat, swallowing a camel. In a crowd of thousands, anywhere, Fifth Avenue or at the Mid-South Fair, she could spot them. "So is this," she said.

Giroux was grim. "It's a spiritual discipline."

"So is this."

"Leave, Anthony. And take all this stuff with you."

"Stuff! I'm teaching him to paint!"

As if under military command, with studied dignity Anthony began putting paint jars in a box.

"Stop that! Take your canvas if you have to. Don't touch the materials."

Unable to look at her, Anthony pulled his canvas from the easel. "You don't understand."

"You're damned right, I don't." She turned to Giroux. "And what the hell do you care if he paints?"

"He has other duties."

"Get someone else. You have plenty of cheap labor. He has a right to a better explanation than that. And why," she demanded of Anthony, "are you letting him bully you like this?"

"I took a vow."

She flung her arms. "Vows come and go." In measured emphasis she repeated, "Don't touch the materials! I'll be using them."

Trapped between them, Anthony looked from Jaiyavara to Giroux.

Giroux gave a relenting nod. "Just leave," he said. "I'll talk with you later."

Jaiyavara lit a cigarette. As Anthony left she folded one arm to her body, fixed on Giroux her implacable gaze. "Whatever it is you want from me, I warn you, this is the wrong way to go about it."

"You must be, while under my protection, utterly chaste."

Her eyelids flared. Her lower lip dropped, then closed as if on a spicy tidbit. Her head dipped, her dark eyes slanted toward the floor. Giroux withstood her derisive laugh. "Are you serious? You can't be serious. What in God's name," she laughed, "would I want with that young stud?"

"After Thandon? Thandon was such a lover?"

"Thandon! Ha! Thandon could not even get up. . . ."

"Please. Don't be vulgar."

"My, my," she taunted. "Aren't we prim? An erection," she concluded, blowing smoke in his face.

"Who then? Varrick?"

All humor left her. "Discuss Varrick with you? Never." Shaking her head, she began to move back and forth. "This is the most . . . this is . . . Chaste!" she erupted. "I've never been chaste!"

Giroux favored her with a slow sardonic smile. "Then perhaps now would be a good time to start."

Advancing, she grabbed a long brush, pointed the hard end at his chest, used it to punctuate every word. "Listen, you. You listen good. You go to hell. You go straight to hell. I never asked for your presumptuous protection."

"Jaiyavara, may I remind you, you would have died at Citta Nova."

"So?" Her scorn was pitiless. "What of it? Millions died."

Late afternoon. No gongs. No drums. No clacking sticks. A daylong accumulation of that stillness which had shocked her awake. Waking, she should have guessed. Between the bold foreheads of two mountains, the pre-dawn moon had squatted in a hollow like a sullen squaw.

Wrapped in a rust-colored shawl, Jaiyavara walked, hands thrust deeply into the low pockets of her vest. A cow had broken her leg and had to be shot. She wore the cowhide boots Anthony had made for her. All day the monks were enclosed in the Zendo —a wierd celebration of sensory deprivation. Deep meditation, they called it.

And the damned weather complied. Prison gray clamped down on the landscape. Most of the day she had huddled in her room, unable to work, in a kind of daze, gray-blind. A mood induced by the weather. Collective morbidness of the monks influenced the weather, and the damned weather was infringing on her. A hollow aimlessness induced by the lack of direct light, the absence of shadow, the absence of contrast. No glow to illuminate the intricate veins of leaves. No depth. No exposed, startling detail. A day unredeemed by the slightest sparkle, sliding down the drain hole of time.

Chapter Eight

The cold opaque sky, darker at the top, in gradations filtered sluggishly to earth. Billions of grey pinpoints, as if imposed by a psychotic Seurat. Distant mountains, which in normal weather seemed to drift around and around the valley throughout the day, were blocked by fog. What little light there was crouched close to earth, a mere watery halo for nearby mountains streaked with ragged snow.

She shivered. But it was not actually cold. All day nothing would gather, converge. No forms would sort themselves out. Finally, she gave up. Finally, she walked. Leaves were deepening, dying, beginning to fall. Letting go.

Old earth entering another cycle, a layering down of dead bodies. Squishy fat padding this year, another year of the Plague. But she was becoming almost as indifferent as the pallid moon glob, no longer even very curious or anxious about the outcome. In a million years what would it matter?

In the slow unfurling of earth's tattered scroll, what did it matter if some composer groped for new melodies with numbed fingers? Or if some poet grappled with phrases, unable to test them with a swollen tongue? New ideas, new images, flowering no doubt in a thousand dying brains. Like leaves, she thought, we should know our time of falling, wither in this void, take the downward plunge.

The gamble Giroux took in bringing me here. What made him so sure I would not bring in the disease? Why did he risk it?

To see how it fared in the heavy hours she went to look for the mushroom that masqueraded as a brain.

In that unlikely place, among sharp slabs of rock and slate, still growing. She squatted beside it. It looked gorged. A darker motley brown softly flooding upward through the thickening stem. Son of a bitch. Ugly, she thought—too squeamish to touch it, yet inspired to a kind of perverted admiration. Still clinging? Still thinking? Gorged on what?

A moan pulled her to her feet, back to the path, but whether a wandering gust or the echo of a chant, she could not decide. No, no chanting today. On the winding leaf-strewn path she walked head down; a few leaves dryly scraped and scuttled across the path, or followed along with her for a few steps . . . until glancing ahead she saw that the path led to a wooden bench within a clump of white birch . . . and there he sat, the only other person not enclosed—very large and very fat. The monk. Here, a rare light. Trunks of the birch white-soft, yet vivid, stood out from surrounding grayness like a photographic negative.

Hands still jammed in the pockets of her vest, without invitation she sat down beside him, stretched out her legs. No gongs. No drums. No clacking sticks. Nothing to count. Nothing to measure. Jaiyavara sighed.

The large and very fat monk merely nodded.

She got settled on the bench.

Shifting his ponderous weight, he reached into the folds of his robe, brought forth a packet of hand rolled cigarettes, offering her one. Holding it with two fingers, in un-centered distraction she considered the tight little cylinder. And yet another wonder, he produced a box of matches, struck up a tiny fire, offering that also. Bending to him she saw the flame reflected in his depthless eyes.

Smoke looped, fanned, lilted upward. Caught in an updraft, it dissolved. But more kept coming. Fantastic compositions, metaphysical essays in smoke. No sounds from the kitchen, no one working, no one moving about. Suspended, she sat. This vague, suppressed, strange world she and the monk had all to themselves.

And it occurred to her that the entire day, perhaps her entire life . . . had led to this bench.

Then something plaintive, distant, some animal or bird lost in the wilderness. No. Wilderness was a human assumption. Lost was a human assumption. Curling a tag of fringe around one finger, she looked at her boots, wiggled her toes snugly inside them.

"Something very strange," she said at last, "is going on here."

A compatible murmur. The large and very fat monk lit his own cigarette, lay one arm across the back of the bench. A dry leaf twirled to earth. "Something very strange," he said, "has always been going on here."

Sunk down on the bench she moved her head to study him. A pleasant face. Full. Substantial. A face from which all pettiness had been vanquished. "What do you do?" she asked.

"Nothing," he said.

In slow silence she almost smiled. "How original."

He nodded.

A long lapse. She smoked. "Absolutely nothing?"

"Nothing," he agreed. "Absolutely."

The wind whispered. She listened. "And . . . are you content to do nothing?"

He was silent so long, she herself, forgot the question. Finally he said, "Obviously."

Stretched out, she frowned, she sighed, she looked at her feet. "I've never known how to do nothing. I only know how to work."

The moments passed. She was aware of her heartbeat, her pulse.

"Are you complaining?"

"Maybe. I suppose." Heavily she sighed. "No, not really."

He tapped ashes over the back of the bench. She wondered if the ashes baptised some insect. "A saint may simply be," he said. "An artist is one compelled to work."

Impenetrable gray pinpoints. Her right hand held the cigarette, her right elbow rested on her left arm, clasped to her waist. Holding herself. Holding in emptiness. "Are you," she asked, "a saint?"

He shrugged.

Another leaf floated down.

"By your own definition you are."

And by the time she realized he had made a murmuring sound, it was gone.

The fringe of her shawl rippled, air currents made visible. But nothing was certain. Far away she seemed to hear a faint, high pitched humming. It prickled the back of her neck. Trees whispering secrets among themselves? How to get rid of us? No, other than silence nothing was certain. Only so many human assumptions accumulated, compounded. Perhaps a trill of air in mountain crevices. Her bones felt odd, disjointed. Finishing the cigarette she dropped it to the damp ground, squashed it with the toe of her boot. Arms folded, she sat back. Time. Different here. Somehow both expanded yet slowed down, a kind of warp. "Well . . ." she said, "How did you come to be here?"

That she had asked, he was pleased, he was amused. "It seems . . . I've always been here. And by and by, all this . . ." he indicated with a lazy motion of his hand, "came to be around me."

Head down, she became very still. Brief light, she thought. Brief lie that I live.

A rending. An opening. From the very heart of vagueness a stupendous intuitive grasping. Beyond rationality. An awakening.

Transfixed, she slid from the bench, knelt before him.

"No, no, please . . . none of that. You'll embarass me." He reached for her hand, touched it lightly, beckoning her back to the bench.

Slumped, overcome, she put a hand to her mouth, blinked to clear her eyes of unshed tears.

He offered her another cigarette, which she mindlessly took, forgot to light, simply held in her hand. "There's nothing . . . nothing . . . for me to tell you then. . . ."

"And," he added, "nothing to ask."

In slow apprehension her hand lifted. "Ask?"

A long pause. "For what is to come."

"More?" It was anguished. "No. No!"

"Surely you realize," said the large and very fat monk, "that suffering never ends. It's the price of consciousness. A cruel price, you're thinking. But would you have it otherwise?"

Clouded anger dimmed her eyes. Flinging the un-lit cigarette in a high arc, "Who," she asked bitterly, "was given any choice?"

CHAPTER NINE

Following the stream late that afternoon, Jaiyavara came to the place where the stream made an exit beneath the stone wall. Gratified that nothing could contain it, she sat down close to the water, her back to the wall, fatigued with the day's labor. Each day with first light she began. Work without distraction, without the bulwark Anthony.

Sunset was bleeding light like an open wound, glorious streamers of color spilling down the edged ravines to the far meadows. In a sky not yet dark the moon emerged, pale yellow. Bits of reflected moon began dancing on water. Moon Over Water. In the Book of Changes what did that signify?

What is to come. The monk's warning.

Impossible to doubt him, yet she was not a fatalist. Having thus far survived so much, she felt armored with certain immunities. Whatever it was it would find her on her feet—working she could withstand it.

Just beyond the wall on a mountain ledge an enormous ragged wolf appeared. An electric thrill shot through her body. As if unconsciously she had called to him. Moon Over Magnificent Wolf. What did that signify? He glared down at her. Hungry? Would you like to devour me? Burning eyes that reminded her of Varrick. Or was it that she was ever ready to seize on any occurrence, make of it a sign, a reference to him?

Details long forgotten resurfaced, just as in that void beyond the moon stars were not faintly visible. Details obliterated by and time—or as Giroux expressed it, danced through the cities of Europe—yet all still there.

At the inn with Varrick. The irony of viewing on *Sixty Minutes* his own premature obituary. And it gave her the full scope. A photograph of Varrick's birthplace, the barren stone house where he was born. A treeless field. Eldest son of a wheat farmer. Goodland, Kansas. The heartland. Wrestling a living from that stony ground. He got a football scholarship to Kansas State . . . easy to imagine him as star player for the Wildcats. He married young. Without warning that night, her face filled the screen. Larraine. She died in childbirth. . . . The infant stillborn.

But I, thought Jaiyavara, refused to be blinded by those haunting green eyes.

That rebellious summer. Varrick was thirty-seven. I was seventeen. I wanted to paint. I wanted to dance. I could not decide. . . .

Letters from Mama, dispirited, written in short childish notes. "I don't do much work now. But I am not very happy." Gottrell luring her back to that miserable little house with a renovated kitchen, a microwave oven. Lucile too sick to object. Had Mama stayed in town . . . well, what's the use in thinking of that? Her suffocating dependence on me, her passivity, that I couldn't return to Greenleaf that summer.

Saving and scheming, writing to Gottrell in New York with invented, padded expenses. So accustomed to *their* outrageous demands he sent the money. That was the year he had Lucile twice in sanitariums for alcoholism. Both her and my mother mere chattels. And there was Helen approaching thirty, still unwed, a frantic debutante. After the ball. All those extravagant parties and no one asked for her insipid hand. Troy dubbed town playboy. Nicer word than wastrel.

By contrast to his legal children I suppose he considered me sensible. Impressed with my grades. Misinformed by Mama, Gottrell thought I was going to become an architect. All those early dancing lessons he paid for considered gilding to the lily, proper finishing for southern young ladies. "See that you amount to something," he admonished . . . whenever I saw him. Which wasn't often. Sensing some resolve in me he liked to imagine that he bequeathed. But no affection. Ever.

Heading North . . . that rebellious summer. Cold air. Adventure. Mountains. To help form my resistance to him. Oh, I knew, sooner or later, we would fight it out. New Hampshire. Michigan. Maine. Tromping around. Fortified by savings I could work cheap, even in those hard times easily found little jobs. Waitress. Clerk. Usher. Ithaca, New York. Niagara Falls. Wandering, searching, trying to come to a decision. That was the summer I was obsessed with green.

The last lap into Vermont by helicopter, as far as the eye could see, in lush undulations over all the mountains, nothing but trees, nothing but green. More than for people, the earth, I thought, was made for trees.

A cool, clean place. People hearty, energetic, and sane . . . none of the craziness of humidity, none of that avid southern propensity for meddling. Homey little country inns tucked in pockets along high curving mountain roads. What air! What vistas!

Odd, I can't remember the name . . . that small community college gone broke, up for sale. Deserted campus, deserted student barracks. No one about but caretaker and wife. Inexpensive. Settled in back, the left room on the ground floor. Best view. Loved the fireplace. Bought a hot plate and bed covers. All on my own. A glorious independence, freedom. Pushed that overlarge chest into the hallway. Got the best working table from a room upstairs. Tied it to the bannister, let it down step by step. Heavy table. Had I known . . . I would have waited for him.

Clyde Watkins. The stable. Best summer job I've ever had. Grooming, feeding the horses, cleaning muck from the stalls. Leading riders through those winding mountain trails. Constant stream of tourists. A stop-over for people on the way to Canada. The best summer of my life, except for the nagging guilt. Mama begged me to come home that summer. But I was young and selfish. Had I not been I might never have known him. With me still. And more than memory.

Still he sustains me.

Must have been three or four weeks . . . a cough in the middle of the night. I woke instantly. Upstairs. Male. A heavy tread. I imagined someone young who would turn on a blaring radio, give noisy beer parties. Furious at the invasion of my private hide-out.

Jaiyavara looked up. The wolf had vanished. On the mountain ledge an emptiness, a vacancy in reality's fascade. Loneliness more acute. Loneliness she had lived with, learned to accommodate for many years.

Ten thousand times she had remembered it, dreamed it. Those first moments.

Back to the wall, she dreamed it still.

Up at dawn . . . on the side porch sketching . . . watching for him . . . waiting . . . the strangest sense of stillness . . . anticipation . . . certainty . . . as if I had lived it all before.

Soft fog mists . . . from that long distance across the open campus I saw him walking toward me, returning . . . and the light seemed to increase as he emerged from those mists. How he looked even at that distance. How he walked. And he brought the light. He wore boots, heavy brown jacket. A damp white towel slung around his neck. Swimming at night in that icy stream. His hair still wet, not long but a thick dark mane of it . . . his hair and the way he walked . . . I thought of a lion. He was not young. Large. Rugged. That slow measured walk. My god, male magnificence . . . nothing less. Before he saw me he adjusted the shoulder holster inside his jacket, but never for one moment was I afraid. Did he actually see me, or was it that instinct, that animal wariness that he changed directions, made a wide detour circling around toward the front entrance. Avoiding me. Why? Even at that distance I knew somehow . . . recognized . . . outlaw.

Had I never seen him but once. Had I never known him, of this I'm certain, still I would have remembered him the rest of my life.

But he kept to himself. Day after day . . . torrents of rain. Mountain trails were mud slides. Didn't have to work. Stayed in and painted green unicorns, green lions, green rain. In pouring rain went out for groceries on my bicycle. Occurred to me to ask if he needed anything, to make the first move, but I didn't dare. Coming back wet sack collapsed on the porch. White milk spilling into a brown puddle by the steps. Suddenly he was there. Helped me get the groceries to my room. Too stunned by his presence to say much of anything . . . offered him a cup of tea. No, he said. Said he'd bring me some dry wood for the fireplace.

The rain ceased. I waited. Freezing nights. Sometimes he was so quiet I thought he had left. And then . . . oh, and then . . . the night I came in from work and the firewood was neatly stacked by the fireplace, a fire was burning in the fireplace. Happiness struck like a knife wound.

Ill with flu, in bed, consumed with self-pity. Burning and freezing, aching, wretched. No right to be hurt that still he avoided me, no right to expect anything. When I recovered passed him once in the hallway and stuck my nose in the air.

One night I heard him coming down the stairs . . . shivering with fear, leapt out of bed, threw on my robe, met him in the hallway. Thanked him for the firewood, insisted he have a cup of tea. That long, serious look before he accepted. Like walking on eggshells, like walking through land mines, my head light and dizzy . . . felt so small and airish, yet powerful . . . leading that man to my room. Sitting before the fire. The sight of him close rendered me inarticulate. Perhaps no one else ever saw him as I saw him. Helpless before him. No choice. None. It was absolute. He was the most beautiful living thing in all creation.

But burdened. Worried. Holed up. Hiding. He asked if I minded if he had a drink, took the bottle from his pocket. I was very careful not to spook him, as with certain wild, unmanageable horses, I let him do exactly as he pleased. He finished the bottle, said he enjoyed it. Left. I couldn't sleep. Sat before the fire all night in a wondrous daze.

He was not to be bothered. Timidly, persistently, I pursued him. Brought newspapers, books from the library, left them at his closed door. Liquor, iced cupcakes, cigarettes, left at his door as at an altar. It took weeks to gain his trust. Posted a few letters for him, picked up his mail. Letters to him from all over the world and so I began to guess . . . some sort of underground movement. He was hunted. I never asked why. Only why he liked to swim at night. We were in my room before the fire, I was drinking tea, he was drinking liquor.

"You have to stay used to it. The shock can kill you."

Icy water? The sea? I let it go. But later I said something about his tolerance, his patience. He had learned that, he said, in prison.

"To tell me that . . . does that mean you trust me?"

"Yes."

"Why do you trust me?"

Raised bottle almost to his mouth, he paused, put the bottle on the table. "You work with horses. You're young. And you're so out of it."

"Out of it?"

"Uninvolved with politics. Issues. You're a strange girl to accept me implicitly on my own terms."

Suddenly bold, I said it. "I'm not a girl. I'm a woman."

"You're young enough to be my daughter."

"That doesn't stop most men."

"It stops me. Don't get foolish on me."

We kept it abstract, platonic; we talked of events, places, ideas, books. Ideas most of all. I was famished for that kind of talk. Things he said left an indelible imprint. "Anyone who has more than enough is stealing from those who are deprived." For the first time I seriously contemplated my father. Gottrell exploited the system, Varrick fought it . . . yet some indefinable quality in common. We talked of everything but the awesome male-female magnetism. Out of my depth and new it. He had memories of a different time, a different world. I could never be his first love, as he was mine. He never talked about her. Razor-edge values. He feared subjecting me to danger. Even those talks before the fire cost him a great deal. I could sense the strain, the inner conflict. . . .

She heard the wolf howl.

Conditioning of photography, cheap art, that flash of imagery. A shaggy wolf head thrown back against a mile-wide moon.

At eclipse savages fear a dragon is swallowing the moon. Maybe wolves fear also.

He had to fight the devil to do it . . . take me to that inn for supper. A turning point. Bitterly cold. Treacherous roads. We walked. It made me quake to think of following him into that icy hell, Canada. Figured he would cross where the borders were unpatrolled. Presumed dead, we went to watch the recap of his life. He took the risk to find out exactly what had happened.

"Holding down the fort," said the waitress. She was old and spry. Eager to entertain on a lonely night. A constant stream of chatter between her and the unseen cook in the kitchen. "They love the soup!" she hollered. "See, I told you that soup would bring them out, even on a night like this!"

Television over the bar on the right station when we got there. We sat toward the back, finished eating before it started. Varrick's exploits reported by the well known liberal, Wallace Armand. Whaling was banned. But Russia, Norway, Canada, Japan still dealt in black market. Can replay it like a tape, Armand's voice, his earnest, soulful eyes. ". . . The one man who has fought this battle for many years alone in his own unorthodox way. . . ." No surprise to me that Varrick was literally a hero.

Off the coast of Nova Scotia an unidentified man shot by whalers for interfering. His body not recovered. Varrick's ship, *The Zodiac*, confiscated by Canadian authorities. The murder incited world-wide demonstrations. "But . . . was it in fact, the notorious Varrick?" The Sea Warriors were established by him. Once he got it going, struck out on his own. In the Philippines he rescued dogs slated for human consumption. Gruesome photographs of miserable, tortured animals, front legs wrenched, tied behind their backs. I could hardly look. In Chili, Peru, he filmed pirate whaling operations. Blew up helicopters in Montana used for hunting wolves from the air with rifles. Jailed in Wyoming for the sabotage of a freight train full of mustangs on the way to becoming dog food. Film clips of *The Zodiac* in action. Thrilling. Headlines: *Zodiac Crew Halts Plans to Slaughter Baby Seals in Orkney Islands*. All that. Old Viking. Archetypal.

Years after his death . . . to see his documentary, *The Birth of a Fawn* . . . such sensitivity, beauty, captured by a man who was primarily a fighter. Poetic. How he loved life! I wept.

And that night yet another escapade humorously, indulgently reported at the inn. Armand enjoyed relating it. Drunk in Oakland, California . . . he broke open cages in a pet store, handing out kittens and puppies to people who fled with them before the owner could get the police. Beside me that night, oh how I loved him . . . he calmly put his bottle on the table, leaned back, drank his whiskey. Growing older. Still larger than life. Until then all my heroes had been great artists, dancers. He was incensed at the murder. And he wanted his ship back.

"Fearing death every day," he once said, "what good is a long life? I never figured I'd live this long." And once when I said, "hero," he smiled and added, "Of the absurd."

He must have anticipated the childhood photographs, high school, football . . . but not her photograph, her face. My breath stopped. Blonde. Delicate. Ethereal. He saw only her. And she still caused him pain. Looking at the screen . . . I will not be your shadow, I thought. You're dead. I'm alive. He's mine now. Mine.

That was when the patrolman came in. Startled, I jumped up, then to cover my blunder rushed to the ladies room. Got control.

By the time I got back to the table the program was over. Patrolman sitting at the counter. Small talk between him and the waitress. Later, elbows out—he looked like a weight lifter—he ambled over to our table. "Bad night. Didn't see your car out front. You folks need a lift?"

Watching Varrick, old pro, bluff it out. "No thanks. My wife's running a few errands but she's picking us up later."

"This your girl?"

He nodded. Fatherly teasing. "Such as she is."

"Fine looking young lady, I'd say."

"We think so. A little stubborn sometimes."

"Oh, don't tell me about stubborn. I got three boys. I know all about stubborn. Always wanted a girl. She don't favor you much though."

"She favors her mother."

Patrolman regarded me with a benevolent leer. "Well, you folks take care," he said and left.

I was shivering.

"Don't worry," he said. "You did fine. You made a conquest."

Held to his arm when we left, we ascended the hill against a freezing wind.

"The man who was killed . . . do you know who it was?"

"Some young hot-head who didn't handle it right. He should have left it to me."

He was going, I knew . . . back to the fight, back to the sea. Useless to argue. Walking beside him. Just the two of us, alone. He guided me through that pithy darkness. That was when we watched the eclipse and he told me that a dragon was swallowing the moon.

Back in my room before the fire. "Why do you drink so much?"

"I don't like myself sober."

"Don't like yourself? All you've accomplished?"

"That TV bullshit. Hype to pay their sponsors. Year after year when the crops fail, a man who keeps farming, goes in debt, gambles on the elements. My father, now there was a hero. But for that kind of endurance you need. . . ."

"A woman?"

"The right woman. He had that." He took a long drink, wiped his mouth with his hand. "Well," he said finally, "it was God I wanted to fight, but the son of a bitch has always avoided me."

How to follow when he left. Sleepless nights. Plotting. Getting it all together. Getting ready. Black mare. Fast. A lot of spirit. Venus, I named her. That vast wilderness. I might lose him. Might lose myself. Suicidal recklessness. He would keep to the back roads. At the junction I cut through, she took a fence, we went straight over the mountain. Three more fences she took like flying. We got to the crest, could see below where he kept his horses. He was already there. Just a few more minutes he might have left me behind forever. Watched him get started, an easy pace. Morning sun on my shoulders I was fearless, ready for anything. If I followed him far enough he would have to relent, take me with him. He kept stopping, looking back. Suspicious. By midday I lost him. Throat tight, so scared my vision blurred.

He circled around, came up behind me. Furious. "What the fuck do you think you're doing, Jaiyavara?"

"You didn't even say good-bye."

"You knew I was leaving."

"I'm going with you."

"The hell you are."

As we argued it flashed before me, the storm at sea, the floundering ship. What my mother had dared in following my father. "You can't stop me," I said. I never should have said that.

God, he looked brutal. Brought his horse up very close, took the gun from his shoulder holster, held it to her head. Said through his teeth, "Oh, I can stop you. I can shoot your horse."

"You wouldn't do that. I can't find my way back alone."

"You stay on this road all the way. If I shoot your horse you walk. Serve you right for being such an idiot."

Begged. Cursed him. He wouldn't budge.

Turned back, walking Venus. What could I do, take a plane to Montreal, try to find him there? He might head for Sherbrook, the crazy bastard. Or he might stay clear of even the smallest towns, head straight through the wilderness for the St. Lawrence, which led to the sea. What then . . . swim out to his ship? If I lost him my entire life would be desolate. I would read of his death in the paper some day. It was now, or forever too late. Far ahead I heard one of his horses neigh. Venus heard, wheeled, fighting the bit, she wanted to follow. As if the heavens opened and trumpets blared. The conviction that what I felt was the strongest force in existence, the gods themselves astonished before it. Gave Venus her head. We raced after him.

Twice caught sight of him far ahead, riding faster. By dusk was sure I had lost him for good. Back and forth, back and forth between a deathless desire and stupefied indifference. Why should I want to live if he could abandon me? No sense of direction. I began to feel as if I were floating above the horse and my own body. Darkness. Despair. The sheer terror of losing him, of dying alone, without meaning. Then from a hill saw the light of his fire and straggled in.

Still unrelenting. Said he would take me back in the morning. We fed and watered the horses. Ate dried apricots, salmon, fried potatoes, raw broccoli. Pitched camp in front of the cave. Numb with fatigue I sat before the fire wrapped in a blanket. He would not talk to me until he had a few drinks. "Guess you think you're one smart-ass little Indian, don't you?"

I asked for a drink.

"Mix it with water. All I need is a drunk Indian."

"I'm not going to get drunk. I'm cold. I'm freezing. I'm half Indian and half southern and I had no idea you were such a goddamned bigot."

He grunted.

The drink gave me courage. "I deserve a drink. I was so scared I was out of my head. Half the time I felt like I was out of my body."

"How very interesting," he said dryly.

"I had no idea you could be such a bastard."

"Shut up. Drink your drink and go to sleep."

"You shut up!"

He lit a cigarette. "You've cost me too much time already. I should have left weeks ago. You read too many romantic novels."

"No, I don't." Had another drink.

"That's enough. Give me the bottle."

Handed it back to him.

"Well," he said at last, "at least you're no cry baby."

Threw back my head. Stars so close, right in my face. Could not bear to look at him. Love would consume me. My heart was breaking. Knew even then that I would never be free of him. His death would not free me. Words I didn't think or intend. . . . "I read about you in the paper after that program. It said you boast that no prison could hold you."

"True."

"That you boast, or that no prison can hold you?"

"Both."

"That last part I missed, when I ran to the ladies room, will you tell me?"

"I'm not telling you anything. You know too damned much already."

"Won't you even talk to me? Do you hate me?" I moved from the rock, a few inches closer to him.

"Don't crowd me," he warned. "I'm tired. I'm getting old. I don't know what you want."

"Oh . . . but you do. You know I love you."

"I should have shot your horse."

"You couldn't shoot her, her name is Venus."

"All the more reason."

". . . but that's not all of it, that I love you. I want to learn from you. I want to be a warrior."

He stared. "You want to fight the whalers?"

"No."

"What, then?"

"I want to paint. I want to dance. I'm going to war for art."

He was holding the bottle. A long silence. "That's a tough one, Jaiyavara."

"I know."

>   a tough one, Jaiyavara,   I said, I know.
>   I didn't know anything then.

We gazed into the fire. He kept drinking.

"Dance first," he said. "Dance while you're young."

So, I thought . . . that settles that.

He went to the saddle bags, brought back another bottle, leaned back, stretched out, shook his head, had another drink. "I throw rocks at you like a stray dog and you just keep on following."

Didn't dare move closer. Felt like a stray dog.

"You've got to finish school. Use your head. Take the advantages. Have some fun while you can, grow up a little before you fall in love."

"Is that what you did?"

"No," he admitted.

"Do you regret it?"

"No." He admitted that.

"I'm not going back to school. I'm going to dance."

"I don't give a damn. I didn't take you to raise. Just get off my back. I've got work to do."

Inching closer then. "Wolves . . . seals . . . mustangs . . . every fish in the sea and bird in the sky . . . and nothing for me?"

"Four months with you. More time than I've spent with anyone in the last ten years. You're a good kid, but it's time for you to go home now."

"I read somewhere. . . ."

"You read too much."

"I read . . . that to live alone a man must be either a demon or a god."

"Nietzsche." He grunted. "Are you drunk?"

"A little." I hiccupped. "Why do they hunt you? I have to know."

It was the hiccup that eased him down. "I kept breaking out. This guard at Lexington trailed me for two years, some sort of private vendetta. A real psycho. It got on my nerves. I shot him."

"Killed him?"

"I didn't intend to. Only intended to make a point. But he died a month later of complications."

Trying to get a little closer I held out my cup. "One more drink. Please."

He handed me the bottle. I mixed the drink with water. Still, it burned. Then I said, "You never had time for love?"

"I loved . . . Larraine."

"She was beautiful."

"That's not why I loved her."

"Why, then?"

"So gentle. Her spirit."

"And no one else?"

"No, not really."

"In all that time?"

"I've had other women. But no, not really. No one else."

"I love you so."

He shook his head. "You're so pitifully young, Jaiyavara."

"Don't say that. I could say that you are pitifully old."

His grim smile. "And you'd be right on the money. I'm beginning to feel it, and it's not just the years."

"Young . . . old . . . what does it matter?"

His face softened. "In a way you're right. It's all sorrow, Jaiyavara."

    I know   I know
    but not yet   not yet

"I could dance for you. I know how to dance. I'm going to dance for you the rest of my life."

"Fine. Good. Just go home." Harsh voice. "You're slowing me down. You're interfering. The last thing I need is an idealistic virgin tagging after me."

I tried to bluff it. "What makes you think I'm a virgin?"

"Obvious. If not, you'd have better sense."

"Don't you care for me at all?"

"You've been a good little friend, but it's only a matter of time. . . ."

"Before they kill you. I know that, Varrick. That's why I'm so desperate. We have so little time." I had not acknowledged it, even to myself, how deeply it registered, his aura of doom. That got through to him, yet still he tried to fend me off, maintain the barrier.

"You have a father complex. Where's your father?"

"How should I know? He only gives me money. So what if I do, what does that matter?" Moved a little closer. "I love you so."

"For God's sake, don't keep saying that. I'm trying to protect you. It'll be worse for you later . . . when. . . . No. I can't."

"You're wrong! You're wrong! Don't leave me with no memories. Nothing. I know you will die and I know how."

He looked straight into my eyes. "How do you know?"

"I just know, that's all. You'll die fighting. I know that. A doomed warrior knows how to die."

Our eyes held. Without warning, he laughed. Then, again, he was angry. "And where the hell did you read that? You're so damned young, so damned poetic. It's not going to be poetic, Jaiyavara. It's going to be ugly. You don't know how obscene death is. It can wound you for life. I'm not putting you through that. Now get away from me. Leave me alone. I mean it."

      her   green eyes   gentle dreamer   because of her
      he courted danger   courted her still   courted death

"Maybe it's death that attracts you, you little whore."

"Call me virgin—call me whore—it doesn't matter. No, not death. Life. The force of it in you as in no one else I've ever known." I touched his arm, put my head close to his shoulder. "Only please . . . please don't lie to me, Varrick. Don't say you don't want me."

He wouldn't answer . . . wouldn't look at me. But he did not move away.

"Open the blanket. I'm so cold. Please, please just hold me for a little while. My God, Varrick, take what life offers you while there's still time. Don't leave me with nothing. Don't make me an outcast the rest of my life. Don't lie to me, don't say you don't want me.

      could feel the resolve   the fight   ebbing away

"Please, Varrick. My God, please."

He opened the blanket, pulled me close. Holding. "I do," he said. "I do want you. I want you like a hungry wolf." Kissed me . . . so slowly . . . so thoroughly . . . taking his time.

      before time began you were my love when the earth dies
      the stars when all the fires of all creation die to
      frozen nothingness still you will be my love

On the cold hard earth he took me. My eyes open. Filled with the depthless black sky. Millions of burning stars. Soul is not simply given. You have to reach for it, cry for it, beg for it, follow after it through a wilderness. Fight for it. So much more accomplished than a seduction. A valid existence.

Before the fire, holding me, he slept. I could not quit looking at him, committing to memory every line and angle of his face, the texture of his flesh, his hair, the smell of him, touch of him. I was looking at him when he opened his eyes.

"I was afraid of hurting you," he said.

"No, no . . . you're not afraid of anything."

"Of you I was."

"You hid it well."

Even in darkness, I told him, I can see it . . . the light of your eyes. In darkness I can feel it, the light of your body.

And with you, he said . . . I might just as well say . . . it's only air . . . it's only water.

Held close all through the night. Pressed to his body. There was never a night we spent together that he did not hold me all through the night. Father complex? When he held me I was as protected, secure, as cradled as at a mother's breast. Waking beside him that first dawn, a sky full of spun spirals of pink and white . . . all life new, radiant. Heaven. And it was green.

Four days traveling with him through the wilderness. I did not feel the cold. It could not touch me. In Montreal he put me on the plane, as he persuaded I went back to Boston, finished school. We got messages to each other, passionate outpourings. Totally honest he was, always. It did not detract from his love for her. He would never have believed, he wrote, that it could happen twice, love that deep. My Boston debut . . . Swan Lake . . . I danced for him. Soared beyond an immature body, because he was there.

Two more summers together . . . before he was killed.

Injured in battle. The sea took him. A man who loved the wheat fields of Kansas. A man who thought he was not brave enough to become a farmer. A man who gave all that he had, and yet did not like himself sober. But was it failure to spend his blood on endless waters? At twenty-one I knew, I knew . . . that no matter what I achieved, my personal life would be empty, a mere postscript, a pointless epilogue. . . .

Giroux stood before her. He pulled her to her feet.

As he guided her back to her room she moved like a sullen hostage.

She did not light the lamp. "I wish," she said, "that you had left me at Citta Nova."

"You don't mean that."

"You'll never know what I mean." In darkness she found the bed, stretched out.

Giroux pulled up a chair.

"Is there no privacy in this place? Leave me alone. I'm in no mood for anything."

"Conversation?" said Giroux. "Seduction? You've seduced many."

"No. No one but Varrick. . . ."

"As a dancer you cast a spell . . . you can do it still."

"My spell is spent," she said. Turning her back to him she closed her eyes. "I'm as old now as Varrick when he was killed. Leave me alone. I have to sleep. I'll work in the morning."

"There is for you now, Jaiyavara, a higher destiny."

Half asleep, she made no sign . . . that over-large idiot and his small mumblings.

"You will become the perfect symbol."

. . . words . . . drifting down . . . falling on her face . . . her hair . . . the pillow . . . like withered petals   words . . . without meaning . . . only the tone registered . . . the growl of intimacy. . . .

For more than an hour as she slept Giroux brooded over her: his hope, his torment. Resigned, he rose from the chair, went to the easel and methodically slashed the canvas. Jagged fragments slid to the floor.

Where they lay, he left them.

Moon-glow. The knife Giroux held gleamed at a phallic angle.

Chapter Ten

Avoiding the light Jaiyavara pushed her head down between the pillows to postpone waking, bring back certain past faded fragments.

She was nine. Her mother walked back from the wobbly mailbox at the edge of the scorched yard, a white envelope in her hands. Beneath her thin grey kimona Jaiyavara could see the outline of her body, the veiled shadow of pubic hair.

Oh! From your father! A check for your birthday. So generous. I can buy you a new dress."

"I don't want a new dress. I want a swing in this tree. I want to swing high."

"No, look my angel. Look at this nice check. I can buy you a new dress, I can buy your ballet shoes."

Snatching the check from her mother's hands, she whirled and ran, tearing it to bits.

"No! No! What am I going to tell your father! Oh, you terrible child!"

Bits of paper confetti, in a rare wind draft danced up a circling swirl.

Gottrell's office on Wall Street.

At the wall of amber-tinted glass it was as if she could see the confetti of her childish refusal merrily twinkling at the high steel and concrete edges of those monstrous vaults and tombs. All the way from Greenleaf, that indestructible little vortex—bits and pieces of check—still it danced. Below, beyond, as far as the eye could see, the vast storehouse, the Jupiter Department Store, Manhattan, goods piled up, goods bought and sold, goods hoarded, pushed this way and that, catalogued; tiny humans scurrying and squirming like ants beneath an avalanche of goods. Mere stuff. And no exit but UP.

Gottrell's preoccupation not even that basic, that real. Shoes, chairs, coats, rugs at least gave creature comfort.

"Money wasted," he ranted. "Do you have any idea what those snotty schools in Boston cost me?"

Money he seldom saw or touched. Figures on paper, mathematical abstractions. Ego. Identity. Power over the lives of people he had never seen or known. There was not enough money in the world to absolve his insecurity.

"Pay attention when I'm talking to you!"

"Working my way through that maze of cubby holes out there, I expected to at least see a cluttered desk. Decisions, you call it? All you do is finger punch buttons. You call that work?"

"There's no future in dancing. You've got no sense. You're danced thin. You look emaciated. Are you anorexic?"

"Not yet."

"If you're not going to pursue architecture then take a business course. Teach. Or learn to type. Do something useful, practical."

Before her eyes, to her satisfaction he was shrinking. As a child she had tried to cling to some shred of respect, had absorbed against her will some of her mother's enthusiasm for the American Soap Opera, this son of a dirt poor itinerant picker who had become a crop-dusting pilot, had studied the stock market to become . . . da da da dum! . . . this. Every year he became smaller, meaner, uglier, more paranoid.

Such stuff as dreams are made of. She was. She had auditioned at the Joffery that morning and had been accepted for an apprenticeship. Like a pearl on a beach the world was waiting at her feet to be picked up, put in her pocket. She was nineteen. She could dance. And the bravest man in the world loved her.

". . . if you want to get ahead in this world, for Christ's sake take an American name. Even your name is ridiculous."

"My name? What kind of idiot names one child Helen, the other Troy? Everyone in Greenleaf laughs at you behind your back. It never ends, your redneck stupidity." She walked to the door. Above it, the plaque, "If You're So Smart Why Ain't You Rich?" made her burst out laughing.

"We haven't finished this conversation. Where are you going?"

Opening the door, she flung it back to him. "To rehearsals! To the theatre! To my future!"

"Tell your mother. . . ."

"Oh, you tell her. Send her a telegram. I'm not your flunkie. Tell Helen and Troy to take business courses. I'm a dancer."

Against the starched white collar his flabby underchin bulged. "They won't need it. I take care of my own. They're inheriting my money."

She smiled. She smiled big. Flashed back at him those by God strong white teeth. "The sooner the better, Gottrell."

Mid-air. Hawaii.

Muscle spasm. Caught in a paralyzing vise she could not control the glider. Earth spinning up and up and up. Earth and sky a crazy rotation. The black volcano, a wide ravenous mouth, leaping up to swallow.

When she regained consciousness she felt nothing, no physical sensation whatever. Then there was pain so immense it could not possibly originate in one body. A sheet wrapped bundle she was carted along, passed from hands to hands, stretcher to stretcher —to where? —some dumping off place? —the crematorium? Lights in ceilings. Injections. Operations. Faces, forms appeared above her, glided beside her, came and went. God no . . . putting her back together . . . how many times? Periods of oblivion. Countless rooms, corridors. She howled like an animal, howled in rage as well as pain, howled until she vomited bile and blood and there was no sound left. Nurses wept.

Jaw wired. Nose mended. Ribs. Pelvis. Collar bone. Spine. Teeth miraculously intact. Total of broken bones she never asked.

Face down, she was suspended in a machine that resembled a space casket. Whoever came near she begged for death, spat at them when ignored. Suspended on her back, arms, legs stretched and strapped—*a Dali diagram*—she wafted gently in air like a cross anchored in calm waters, floated in and out of consciousness. Above the discreet perpetual click and whir of her mechanical prison apparatus she heard voices, orgies of horror hallucinated. One part of her mind, even so, snapped like a shutter. Grotesque demons of the netherworld forever imprinted. In lucid moments she plotted revenge. Massacre. Carnage. She would kill them all, all who had wired her back together with dope, cat-gut, glue and spit—she would machine gun splatter their scientific, self-righteous little brains all over the ceilings and walls.

That this long ordeal shortened her mother's life, she had not the slightest doubt. Delicate, beautiful Denise . . . spooned water to her, waited through every operation, wiped perspiration from her face, massaged her legs and arms by the hour and became a frail husk.

No coherence. No cohesion. Reality's shattered jigsaw pieced itself back together in a thousand discordant ways. She came to know how blocked, insignificant, the normal waking brain, fit only for gross survival. Consciousness separated from body— where to this time?—her essence sucked into and out of what she could only refer to as other dimensions. Or was it simple insanity? Yet no matter how disoriented, some flimsy thread linked her to sea and earth, some part of her mind questioned every apparition she met, tried to verify her own identity, what time or world had promiscuously sucked her in.

One night she woke and saw red neon. It blinked off and on from somewhere outside. In a chair beside the window her mother curled, even in sleep her hands were knotted. On. Off. Red. No red. Dazzling little triangles, the print black and white of her mother's dress, every triangle retained the red aura. She could only whisper. Mama. Denise woke instantly and was at her side. It occurred to her that there was a transforming dimension of real earth, real life that she would never experience. Motherhood.

"A few moments, Mama . . . no pain."

But the tour through hell was not over. Morphine withdrawal. Every atom a fizzling insanity of craving. She bit her tongue. They jammed a rubber guard into her mouth. She wanted the pain back. Anything was preferable to that lethal craving. She was addicted to morphine, addicted to pain.

Held by strong indifferent hands, dipped and lowered into rushing waters, the sight of her own naked body, limp, pallid, withered, made her ill with nausea. Water songs, water therapy. An electric tingling, tiny riverlets, inroads of feeling. The water reclaimed a finger, an elbow, a knee, a shoulder, a quiver in the pit of her stomach. Ferocious atoms gradually were soothed and silenced in water. The water giveth, and the water taketh away. In all its forms and names, blessed is the water.

In rain. The monsoons of Mississippi. Was that the preordained linkage, that her mother migrated to and made a home in a place of tidal waves of rain?

Past the No Tresspassing sign the taxi eased through the long winding driveway under a lush canopy of dark dripping leaves. Gentle now, the rain, yet she saw evidence of its devastation.

In the back seat she sat rigidly composed. The neck brace made her look static, emotionless. She had been told that the rest of her life she would be subject to peculiar sensations, spasms, the unpredictable illusion of weightlessness. Eight years she had danced. Now it was ended. The taxi entered the clearing. Going home. But not that ostentatious white mausoleum visible through three acres of rain, no matter how long her mother lived there. When the weather cleared she and her mother would return to the shotgun shack, sit on the front porch, or what was left of it, talk, scratch at mosquito bites, remember. . . .

"Leave the suitcases in the driveway," she told the driver, not only because he was old but because she saw Gottrell out on the portico. By then the rain was fine billowing mists. Carefully she got out, walked up the curved steps. The taxi turned, pulled away.

Feet propped on a wrought iron foot stool, he sat beside the glass and wrought iron table, drinking. Bleary eyed. Hostile. He did not rise to greet her.

"Good afternoon, Gottrell."

No answer.

She walked to a straight chair and sat.

"You can't leave those damned suitcases in the driveway."

"I can't carry them."

With his hand, rather than the silver tongs, he grabbed ice cubes from a bowl on the table, dumped them into a large iced tea glass, poured Scotch to cover. "Well, I sure as hell ain't carryin' 'em. I have heart trouble, in case you haven't heard."

"You still, I presume, have servants."

Chapter Ten

"Goddamned rain," he snarled. "Been raining a month. Cotton's rotting." He hollered for William. Willie, he called him.

Always within earshot, an actor hovering in the wings, William came out through the screen door.

"Get the goddamned suitcases out of the driveway, Willie. The notorious exhibitionest is honoring us with a visit."

"How are you, William?" He had not aged, not changed one whit.

Under Gottrell's wrathful eye he quickly took her hands, squeezed them. "Doin' very well, thank you. An' it's so awfully good to see you now. We been prayin' for you, me an' Lou Iris, we been prayin' right along."

"Thank you, William. How is Lou Iris? I can't wait to see her."

"Oh, she got a few aches now and then, but she stay on her feet and her mouth never stop, you know. She be glad. . . ."

"Cut th' shit," Gottrell interrupted, "and get the goddamned suitcases out of the driveway, Willie."

The well worn and rightful anger, how good it felt. Fishing cigarettes out of her purse, she lit and inhaled, savoring hatred. "You never let him finish a sentence."

"Worthless son of a bitch never finishes anything. Since when did you start smoking?"

"Since wanting to die."

A sarcastic laugh. That, he liked.

He settled back, regarded her. Was he trying to gauge how much he could fight with her, ease his boredom, without letting it get out of hand. "You want a drink?"

"Why not? Don't holler for William. I'll get the bourbon."

Down the gloomed hallway, past the banquet dining room with all that hideous furniture, Lucile's treasures, hideous wallpaper, hideous heavy drapery, hideous silver and crystal. A young black maid in the kitchen in uniform, looking bewildered and useless. Her name was Nancy. Jaiyavara introduced herself, found the bourbon, coke, a glass, carried it all back out, sat and poured her drink. "Where's Mama?"

"At the country club. Some kind of women's something."

"I told her I was coming."

"You should have been more explicit. Everyone's supposed to sit around holding their breath for your stupendous entrance?"

She drank.

He drank.

"My, my, my . . . the country club, no less. So the local Bible thumping puritans accept your whore of thirty years."

"Watch your mouth. You're here on my charity."

"If your generosity is strained I can always sleep in the shack."

He kicked the footstool aside, sat up straighter.

"Oh, excuse me Mr. Gottrell, your part-time whore of thirty years."

He put another garish chintz pillow at his back, held his glass close to his chin. "What did you do, Jaiyavara, fall on your head?"

"An entire year that you never once came to see me, never sent so much as a post card."

"I warned you about dancing."

"It wasn't dancing that put me in the hospital."

"Flying, dancing, what's the difference? I warned you. Why the hell didn't you get a pilot's license? Well, what the hell do I care? I have a few problems of my own, in case you haven't noticed." He fondled his chest.

"Oh, I've been aware of your problems all my life. Troy. That effeminate weakling. Helen, a blood-sucking parasite. When Lucile crashed her pink Cadillac I thought you might finally have the decency to marry my mother."

A tight smile, the drawl loose and exaggerated. "Well now . . . that's just none of your goddamned business, now is it? God knows how many men you've shacked up with. I've heard a few barroom stories of how you twitched your ass all over this town. Still a know-it-all. And still wasting your life on one damned harebrained. . . ."

"It's my mother's life that's been wasted."

He kicked a chair over, slammed his glass down on the table. "I pay the bills! Your hospital bill alone, over half a million dollars! Your own goddamned mule-headed stupidity! Hang-gliding, for Christ's sake! Very arty and avant-garde and all that shit! Flaunting your body all over the world, you got exactly what you deserved."

In mock salute she raised her glass. "So did you, Gottrell. You got me. That I was a success as a dancer, you're mad as hell about that. You envy that. You wanted me to fail. Even in a drunken stupor you know as well as I do that I'm the only decent thing you've ever produced."

His blood-shot eyes focused hard. "That strength you have, Jaiyavara, where do you think it comes from? Your silly mother?"

Without the neck brace she might have gasped.

"And this painting thing. Art," he sneered. "You go against my wishes again and I will not leave you one thin dime. You're a liability. You've cost me too much already." Unconsciously, once more his fingers spread over his heart.

That he was weakened, she gloated. She would miss his final attack, be cheated of the pleasure of watching him turn purple in suffocation. "People are dying slowly in factories and coal mines because of your greed. I never wanted your filthy money. Your feeble threats, after what I've been through? You were never anything but a monstrous bore." She got up, went in. In the damp hallway she heard him call after her.

"My filthy money put you back together, you loathsome bitch!"

"Not his money," her mother said later. Careful not to disturb Gottrell's prodigious rest they sat together in the window seat alcove off the blue bedroom. "They're not as impressed with money as your father thinks. That skinny little Jaiyavara, they say to me, aren't you proud of her? They read about you in the paper, they see you on television. I'm the mother of a celebrity."

"Not any more, Mama. I'll never dance again."

"Success and defeat, it takes both to have a whole life. But it's not just the dancing, it's the way you fought to live. It's courage that counts around here. There's more to a lot of these people than you think."

So . . . it flowed. Like water found its way, sought its own level. "You paint like a maniac," someone said. From hands, heart, endurance, and dreams it flowed to form the flowering, explosive rhythms of passion, delirium.

Berkeley. A summer night. On the lecture platform Salvini; tall and gaunt, with thinning hair, slender hands, a soft snake-hiss voice. The screen as he spoke flashed a series of enlargements, complex futuristic city designs. The contrast—between those intricate, detailed labyrinths and his quiet vague eyes.

Still wearing the neck brace, she sat in the audience making notes, questions she wanted to ask later. Everything provided... but would you want to live there? Yet moment by moment she became more intense, the opening of a new direction before her.

"We must put a stop," he lectured, "to an accumulate waste which makes constant war on the environment. The automobile must be put to death, not just to pasture. Rather than the abject squalor we now tolerate, the new cities will be concentrations at vital points, leaving the land uncontaminated for farms, forest, wildlife, parks. The city of the future must become the image of man."

A burst of applause. But he was not yet finished. "A work of generations, but we must begin now. It is never easy... the transmutation of gross matter into spirit."

More applause. In the tiered auditorium in two's and three's they rose to their feet; then it swept through, they rose in waves, the applause was thunderous.

The visionary leap. The fervor of a movement.

Returning to Florence after a ten year absence. Coming in she could see as before the green terraced hills, red tiled roofs of the stucco houses. Ageless Florence much changed. Swarms of tourists. The center off limits to cars. This heart of the Renaissance seemed more like a neglected museum than a vibrant city.

It was summer. Vendors everywhere. She drove through Piazza Della Liberta where masses of snapdragons were in bloom, to Via Tripoli, a dusty street near the Arno river to look for the woman who made the best cappuccino in Italy. Carlena had departed. On the counter there was a smug stainless steel automatic coffee machine. Political posters blatant and glaring. Computer games in some of the bars. Music still in the best cafes. "The artisan tradition?" a man said, throwing up his hands. "Not as it once was. They want security. They prefer to work in factories now."

Punk and Doop had surfaced but were quickly passe. With the typical love of display, young Florentines strutted the latest fashion to the fountains, the galleries, the operas. There were new clubs, new restaurants, but the shops seemed smaller. More signs. More advertising. Depressing, the shop that once sold live falcons, peddled computers.

She drove up and down the steep winding hills looking up old acquaintances, looking for those glamorous villas where she had been a house guest, was offered hospitality as a dancer. After ten years the villas were less impressive but those she had known briefly seemed like long lost friends. Rossi, ex-dancer, advised her, "Don't go to the theatre. It will break your heart. The troupe disbanded. Pornography at the theatre now, and it is in terrible disrepair."

Tuscan cuisine still a tradition. Roast quail on long spits. At Gilli celebrities still met for coffee in the late afternoon, at Rivoire you could still order warm white wine with sugar on cool evenings.

At the museum he designed she met Salvini. He showed her through. A three-storey mosaic wall of beautiful pale wood. Intertwined staircases, spun gold, pure magic. They walked a long outside corridor of pink brick archways. "How long," he asked, "are you going to be here?"

"As long as my money lasts. Florence is still my favorite place on earth."

"You've sold more work?"

"Some, yes. I could do commissioned portraits, but I don't want to yet."

Sympathetically, he nodded. "I'm glad you looked me up. At the end of the month I'm returning to Arizona, the first new city in progress. It's exciting. Come with me."

"Maybe too exciting, too much of a distraction. I really crave...."

"I know, a quiet corner, a private studio. Could you imagine the first city of the future does not provide for solitude?"

At the gentle rebuke, she smiled. Ascending curved steps which led to a rampart they could see much of Florence, a city, despite the changes, more memorable, more eternal to her than Rome. "Tell me," she said, "in the villages, does the bridegroom still put the wedding night sheet out on the balcony for all to see that his bride was a virgin?"

"I'm afraid so. Some things in Italy never change. Female liberation never got very far here. So? What are you thinking?"

JAIYAVARA

"That esthetically we're in perfect accord. And I'm very grateful. How often is one offered an apprenticeship to an Italian master? But...."

"Speak," he urged.

"Your ideas are overpowering. I want to do something as unique, as original as you have . . . but in my own way. I keep struggling toward that breakthrough. But...."

"Go on."

"They pay to learn from you. I have only a little left now."

"Oh, no," he smiled. "Only the neophytes pay. You don't have to pay. I'm selfish. I'm looking for those able to carry this work forward when I am no longer here."

Of one accord they restlessly turned from the rampart, walked again. From time to time as he spoke he put his hand to her shoulder, the lightest touch. All slow and thoughtful, he was ever the teacher. "Listen to me," he said. "All we can ever own in this life is what we create. Yes? Everything else, the so-called rational world, is only a scaffolding to it. Life itself is what we create. Race consciousness. Yes? What does it matter what sells? That's only craft. Don't waste your time on portraits. Don't waste your time earning money. Strive for the breakthrough. Craft requires time and place. Art transcends time. Art creates its own birth."

Listening, she thought of Varrick. *That's a tough one, Jaiyavara.*

"I need you," she said. "I'll come with you. I need to be constantly reminded of the things that matter. I'll absorb so much," she warned, "it will be like stealing from you."

"As an apprentice," he shrugged, "I did the same thing. It's always that way. The anointed artist takes what he needs."

"You've given me so much."

He took her hands, kissed them. "And you, Carina Mia . . . give much to me."

"What? What could I possibly give you?"

"I sense in you an anguish no work can touch. A priceless gift. Use it well. The world is transformed by unabatable anguish."

Morning. Time and place.

Not the end of the world, Salvini. Only an interval, an interim. When this horror is over I'll go back to Citta Nova. I owe you so much. I'll find others to help me. Meanwhile . . . I'll work toward the next breakthrough. New images to take with me when I return to Citta Nova.

Why am I nervous, Salvini? The human body is seventy percent water. Water is not nervous. Why do I shiver? Well, water is ageless. I am aging.

Sitting up, her bare feet touched the cold stones of the floor. She saw on the floor the slashed canvas, pieces scattered at her feet.

A sharp breath. And then she became motionless.

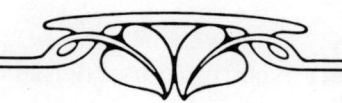

Chapter Eleven

Giroux woke to the throbbing tooth, woke regretting his deed. What was it about Jaiyavara that made him behave so compulsively, so rashly?

As she burst into his study Giroux quickly closed the scrapbook, slid it into a desk drawer and stood to face the music.

She braced against the door. "You gutless bastard. How dare you?"

"I understand your anger. Please sit down."

"You arrogant idiot. What possible explanation?"

"It's very complicated."

"Just be good enough to tell me how to get the hell out of here."

"Don't be absurd! No one can leave now."

"Simeon left."

Giroux sought to placate. "Be reasonable. Simeon is a strong man accustomed to every sort of hardship, a seasoned mountain climber. Please sit down. We need to talk."

"No. I'm leaving."

"Jaiyavara, please listen. It's almost November. Even in normal times the roads are impassable, we're totally isolated here in winter. Now the roads are destroyed. A woman alone, it's impossible."

"Anthony could go with me."

"Oh," he nodded accusingly. "So now you want to take Anthony from me."

"Whatever it takes. I'm getting out of here. I can't tolerate this kind of oppression."

"Even if you could make it, where would you go?"

"Back to Citta Nova."

"You couldn't survive there. Everyone is dead. It's a dead city. You're safe here. Everyone here cares for you. Why should you want to leave?"

She sprang toward him. "To get away from you! What is the matter with you, you crazy bastard! Why do you keep interfering with me? Why do you destroy my work?"

"Work?" He moved one arm in a vague gesture. "Who cares? Who do you think is interested? They're only interested in survival now. Work? For whom?"

"For me!"

He shook his head, regarded her with parental concern. "And ignore all that's happened? Your idealism makes grim demands. That kind of idealism should aspire to higher goals." He turned toward the window. "You were meant for much more."

"And who the hell are you," she demanded, "to say what I was meant for? Turn around. Look at me. Answer me."

Turning, he was blocked, mute with frustration.

"And what was that silliness you mumbled last night, something about symbols?"

"Everything. But you're too distraught to discuss it now."

"Oh, yes," she said with quiet force, "we will discuss it now. To deliberately destroy something you did not create, what stupidity, what arrogance."

"Yes, I realize now the way I went about it was stupid. Please forgive me."

"You had better explain. And it had better be good."

"I wanted to give you time to . . . all right, but please sit down. We can't talk like this." He pushed a chair before her. "Sit down, I say!"

Seething, never taking her eyes from him, she accepted the chair. He pulled up a chair to face her. How sallow his face, she thought. How morbid. How ugly. *And these women find him attractive, fawn upon him?*

"So many years," he said, leaning forward. "So much thought. So much preparation." No, that was not the way to begin. He got up, moved to the fireplace. "When you could no longer dance you found another mode of expression. Granted?"

No answer. She kept her eyes fixed upon him.

"I mean . . ." he faltered, "when that way was closed to you. . . ."

"Don't stalk up and down in front of me like that. I'm not here for one of your famous lectures."

Once more he sat down. A different tactic. "Our lives . . . our lives are not entirely our own."

"Mine is," she said.

"I mean there are circumstances, forces beyond our control. We are sometimes used to ends beyond our comprehension. Would you agree to that?"

Glaring, she folded her arms.

Her unwavering rage put him as on a witness stand. After saving her life he felt he deserved better treatment. He tried to take her hand.

"Don't touch me," she warned. "Get to the point."

"After your break with Thandon, I have to ask . . . what happened then?"

"What the hell has that got to do with anything! I'm not here to answer *your* questions. Stick to the point. Why you destroyed the canvas."

"Believe me, it pertains. Let me make you understand in my own way. What happened?"

"Nothing happened. What are you getting at?"

"After Kraft got you released, I understand that you did not paint for a time. There were rumors that you attempted suicide."

"As who in their right mind hasn't," she said furiously, "at one time or another. Contemplated, not attempted. And certainly not because of Thandon or his trumped-up charges." Full of disgust, she twisted in the chair.

"Then why?"

"That," she said, "is none of your business. What is this inquisition? But since you're so interested, the following year, the year of the Plague, I fought like a wildcat to live."

"So," Giroux insisted, "first premise. One has to stay alive to accomplish anything."

"Obviously. I see you want to labor through some long involved Socratic dialogue." She lit a cigarette. "You destroyed my work. I demand to know why."

"To make a point."

"What point? I wish to God you would make a point!"

"For the concept. The vision. The future."

Her mouth made an acrimonious twist. "This is where I came in. Even Thandon convinced himself that he had a vision."

"Compare me with Thandon?" He was deeply offended. "We are now speaking," he said with Olympian dignity, "of my vision."

Smoking furiously, Jaiyavara crossed her legs.

"During the exodus to the suburbs I thought, ah, that's a good sign. People are fed up with the destructiveness of this society. Which—and this is the point—goes back to the myth that God gave man dominion over all the earth. Which implies a right to conquer and exploit nature."

"Pedantic, Giroux. All old hat."

"Bear with me. But in ancient cosmologies the Source was considered androgynous, both male and female. And those societies," he emphasized, "flourished."

Her flicked ashes fell to his priceless rug. "Would you please get to the point."

Conviction powered his eyes. Yet he thought to push an ashtray toward her. "That is the point. Drastic diseases require drastic measures. Drastic innovations." His voice was urgent, hoarse with emotion. "The feminine principle, Jaiyavara. A new and unifying myth which goes beyond all previous myths of actualization. I as organizer. You as focal point. Can't you visualize it? When the Plague is over a new beginning. There are enough people here to spread the word to the far corners of the earth. I can teach it. You can personify it. A new path."

She could not make sense of it, could not make the connection. "My patience, Giroux, is wearing thin. I have no idea what your peculiar mind has wandered into. You're avoiding the issue. No idea what this has to do with my canvas."

"Listen. Suppose, for instance, that St. Paul had said to himself . . . I know what is needed. I have the message. I must find the Christ to fulfill it."

Queasiness. It occurred to her that she'd had no breakfast. Cigarettes and outrage on an empty stomach, and this conversation was getting her nowhere. She was a little dizzy, nauseated. "But it wasn't like that. Even I know that."

"What do you mean, even I?"

She blew smoke toward the ceiling. "No interest in religious theologies."

"But for the moment imagine." Giroux's eyes begged. "Imagine, that's all I'm asking."

She stared. That avid hunger. People who had lost their last dime at the race track. People who lost fortunes at the gambling tables of Monte Carlo. The ferocious ardor of the lioness for her prey.

"Imagine that Paul found him. Imagine that he said to him, 'I have the message which you are to signify.' Paul organized it all, you know. It could have been that way."

"Who cares! This long winded shit!" She stopped. Frowned in concentration. "You mean . . . you want . . . you have some great message you want me to help propogate?"

"A total synthesis, beautiful and complete. Which you will come to understand and love." His face glowed as with a feverish malady. "It's so obvious. So profound, yet so simple. It astounds me that no one else, no one before me has put it together, formulated. . . ." Watching her intently, he broke off.

Curling a hand to her face, she was fascinated. Almost hypnotized. There was once a preacher who confided to her his unshakable conviction that in the hereafter he would be personally in charge of an entire universe. Pitiful. Laughable.

Her vision blurred. Objects seemed to slide, fade in and out. Perhaps she was in the hospital dangling still in the machine, and everything since that she had thought real was only a demented escape from pain. Smiling, she shook her head. "This must be the best joke I've heard in a million years."

"It's no joke. A new beginning. A revelation."

"I can't believe . . . let me get this straight. You want me," she said slowly "as some sort of puppet for your. . . ."

"No, no, not puppet. An equal partnership."

"For some sort of message . . . myth . . . ideology? Some sort of fantasy of saving the world?"

"It's no fantasy, I tell you. It can happen. It will happen."

Quietly, hysterically, she laughed.

"When you've had time to consider . . . Jaiyavara! Ideas change the world!"

"Why me? What about my work?"

"Rather than a male trinity there will be. . . ."

"I *said*, Giroux, what about my work? Don't you hear anything I say?"

"Of course I hear you. Your work has impressed me with your capacity for dedication." His hands were expansive, his voice now coaxing, seductive. "But in view of the world situation, I know, I know that you are magnanimous enough to put that behind you now, to relinquish it for the good of those suffering horribly out there in that chaos."

"My god. . . ." she breathed. "You're serious. My god."

He took her hands. Limp with shock she allowed it. "When we met on the Riviera," he said, "how can I ever express to you what that meant to me. It was for me a moment of stupendous recognition."

Her mouth went dry. "How long," she managed, "has this . . . this scheme been on your mind?"

"For years. Years," he repeated. "It evolved so slowly, but it really began when we met. But there was so much to do here. And then I lost track of you. And then the Plague. Now I am utterly convinced that the time is right."

Cautiously, she withdrew her hands.

"Just as you once went beyond dancing to a more intelligent art, now is the time for an even greater transition, now you will transform all that talent and creative energy to a much more significant task. Just give what I've said time to . . ."

"Time!" She exploded. "Time! Look at me! I'm not young! I don't have time!" Pale, one hand to her throat she sat back. "Water. I need water."

He poured from a silver pitcher, water offered in a crystal goblet. She drank in slow concentration, then looked at the sparkling goblet, almost amused at the value he placed upon silver and crystal—as if they could help.

"Think about it," he said in a steadier tone. "I'm offering you nothing less than a kind of immortality which you could never achieve on your own."

Her eyes narrowed. "Go save the fucking world. I don't give a damn. It's full of lunatics. One more won't matter that much. Just leave me out of it. What time is left to me I will do my own work, no one else's. Least of all yours."

Head bowed, he pulled the drained goblet from her hand, his fingers pressed into the cut facets of crystal. "As much as anyone," he said sorrowfully, "I appreciate and love art. Look around you. But these, my treasures, so slowly accumulated, most of them for you to enjoy, are after all, only things. Can't you understand that? Things. It's ideas that matter, that move life forward. If I did not love you, Jaiyavara, I would not have recognized you, chosen you. All that you are has led to this. You have chosen it for yourself, only you don't yet realize it. Please, I insist, you must not paint now. You must become still and centered within and prepare yourself for a new beginning. If you persist, for your own higher destiny, I will have no choice but to stop you."

Trembling, she rose from the chair. "So. You've warned me. You're incomprehensible. You are everything I have fought all my life. The collective. You are everything I loathe. You are the enemy."

The sound of gongs.

Hands clasped to elbows, head down, Jaiyavara walked back to her room.

The sound of soft drums.

Her ankles wobbled. Her back and neck felt like rubber.

The sound of clacking sticks.

The others—how long had they been brainwashed? Did they have any grasp of his insane schemes? Monks of subdued demeanor—were they conspirators?

For what is to come. Nothing to ask.

The sound of chanting.

Once, long ago, Giroux had tried to lure her here. She had laughed. The chanting grew louder. She tried to block it out. Nothing to ask. She tried to walk faster. Nothing to ask. Nothing to ask. She was not Giroux's guest. She was his prisoner.

Pre-dawn tea with the monks on the patio. Jaiyavara wore a rough work shirt, pants, an old Army combat jacket Jethro had offered. The sun came up. She headed for the stables.

Chapter Eleven

No one in attendance. Most of the horses grazed in a pasture. Of fourteen stalls only six were occupied. Walking the dirt floor hard as concrete she appraised each beast. Two Morgan stallions, powerful, of great endurance, good traveling companions. An Arabian stallion, all spirit and speed no doubt, but probably unmanageable, used only for breeding. A grey gelding of questionable descent—his eyes were spooky. Two mixed-breed mares, one chestnut, one black. She found bridle and saddle in the tack room—saddled the black mare—rode out at an easy canter.

On the rampart above his study, surveying with binoculars, as was his early morning habit, Giroux sighted her. Close to the wall beneath tall trees she followed an entwined path. Only a little morning excursion? No. Giroux knew instantly what she was thinking.

She came to a clearing, halted at the edge of shade. Flushed from a nearby tree a hawk took wing, beating upward in clapping strokes; her eyes followed as it glided into wide indolent circles beyond the wall. It dipped back toward her, she stretched upward in the saddle. The sharp wing edge glinted like gun metal. The jeweled ferocity of its eye made that eye seem magnified. Giroux's eyes were fixed upon her, as hers were upon the hawk. A few minutes later he lost sight of her.

By noon she had searched the wall's entire irregular rectangle, found it impenetrable, came around at last to the iron gates. Outside their post two Oriental sentries sat at a card table playing chess with mythological figures of carved ivory. Dust raised by the mare's hooves disturbed their concentration. Wiping his eyes with both hands one of the monks came forward to greet her.

She made her smile pleasant. "Good morning."

Politely he bowed. "Good midday."

"Do you have keys to the gates?"

"Why do you ask, lady?" He too was smiling.

"I'd like to ride out for awhile, just look around. Please open the gates."

"Please, lady. It is not permitted."

"Really? Why not?"

Palms upward. Big smile. Big teeth. "Too dangerous. Gates never open without Giroux's permission. Plenty of places to ride inside gates. Acres to ride, lady."

Unwise to argue. She shrugged, then nodded toward the chess board. "Who's winning?"

"We play for years," he said, a reptilian twinkle in his black eyes. "No one wins."

Wheeling the mare she dug in her heels, spewing dust.

Early evening. On a gentle hillside a gathering of monks. They set up folding chairs as if for a theatre performance. Once everyone got comfortably seated on the ground and in the chairs, two bowls of buttered popcorn were shared, passed along. Some took fistfuls into their laps, some stuffed it directly into their mouths to chew and swallow fast, while others poured the morsels to a cupped hand to delicately savor one by one.

They had come to view the sunset. Between two jagged vertical peaks, shooting splayed fireworks of color the sun dramatically descended.

Brother Bethune's pale eyelashes were illuminated. "Glorious. Glorious."

"It goes down," Doyle said, "like a brave ship."

Leon cackled.

A nice phrase, Jethro thought, resenting Leon's obstreperous laugh.

"As if sending out signals," Anthony said. On the ground he sat close to Karen, intoxicated by the smell of her wheat-honey hair, imagining that he received from her more intimate signals.

Karen's cheeks were rouged, in the strong light a trifle garish. Flowers and strung beads adorned her. But beneath her robe her undergarments did not fit right, they pinched or slid or tucked in all the wrong places. Her flesh was sensitive, itched and stung, there were large areas of rawness on the inside of her thighs.

"Signals," Jethro repeated. "But not of distress." His critique of the sun's performance.

Returning from a long bath, her hair wrapped in a white towel, one terrace below Jaiyavara walked past.

"Come join us," Alexis called. "Come sit and watch the sunset."

Preoccupied, she stopped, frowned as if she did not recognize them. Finally she said, "Sunsets depress me," her voice edged in contempt.

Alexis watched her walk away. She looked like an alien dignitary. Karen watched also until Jaiyavara disappeared, then squinted up to the sun so sure of its falling. "One day it too will die."

"It knows that," Leon cackled. "It knows that."

Jethro said, "Everything knows. So what?" and sat back vindicated that he was not yet reduced to translating all that he felt, saw, and sensed to polished phrases.

Rain. Cleansing. Renewing. A rain so rare—that in good spirits despite the aching tooth, despite their last encounter, with a jaunty stride Giroux set out for Jaiyavara's room. Stopping by the kitchen he asked that breakfast for two be served in his study.

At the easel near the window she worked in a dim light. She did not acknowledge his presence.

"And still you persist?"

The tacked up paper was more porous, more fragile than canvas. He waited. Her silence a door locked in his face. By her stance he knew that she had anticipated his visit. "You were always a fanatic," she said without looking up. "But at least honorable. Now, under all this zeal there is a horrible bitterness."

"Bitterness! Bitterness! I came to invite you to breakfast!"

Dipping her brush into blue-violet, on the edge of the pot she stroked it lean. "What happened to you?"

His jaw tightened. She made the room her own. It seemed off limits, no longer a part of the monastery. Breakfast carried in the rain, up the long stairs would be cooling. "What happened?" His hands made extravagant gestures. "Years of warning, preaching, pleading . . . and no one would listen."

Her voice was flat, yet not harsh. " 'Cast not your pearls.' Remember?"

Sucking in a deep breath he tried to adjust to her atmosphere. "Well, I have a few more pearls to cast."

She nodded.

He moved behind her, looked over her shoulder as she worked. Perhaps it was the sound of pattering rain, the smell of rain, the damp dim intimacy of her room that for a few minutes he almost enjoyed watching her deftly apply and overlap thin, nearly transparent layers of color for a variety of prisms, an intricate jeweled web. "But I told you. I warned you."

"Yes, Giroux. You warned me."

Her hair hung loose about her shoulders, the lightweight purple robe shot through with golden threads hung loosely about her thin body. She squinted in concentration, and in her obstinate continuity, patience, there was something abject, subservient, something very ancient. For the first time he sensed in her an Asian pulse, a haunting chorus. "Did you not believe me?"

"Oh yes, Giroux. I believe you." She kept dipping the brush, tenderly applying delicate color. "Etched in stone in Florence . . . above the unfinished work, a quote from Michaelangelo. . . . 'Time destroys both warriors and thinkers.' And, sooner or later, art also." She turned to the table mixing pale yellow, white and green, moved back to the watercolor. "So . . . like one of those funny old Chaplin movies, I have decided to think of you as speeded up time."

That rendered him speechless.

Head tilted, she stood back then, considering the work with such quiet, musing intensity she seemed entirely alone.

"I will never understand," he complained, "your fascination with matter. And I don't even particularly like your work."

"Most of the time I don't like it either." But she went back to it, dipping and stroking, dipping. "What you see," she said as if talking to herself, "depends on where you are. And, as Einstein said, every viewpoint is valid. Theoretically, I agree. But not really."

"If you know it will be destroyed what's the use, what's the point? Tell me that."

"Ah. A good existential question, Giroux." All gentle acquiessence she turned to him. "Being French, you surely know the answer." She smiled. War was declared.

Like a swinging camera her vision tried to follow, it was all a blur, his furious eruption; her vision froze on his hands tearing the work from the easel, crushing it. Sightless she turned, got out of the room, walked into the rain.

Water dripped from her ears, eyelids, hair, fingertips, trickled down the back of her neck. Her eyes burned. Blood pounded in her ears. Stoically she walked, straight and slow, then . . . in undulations of motion she began surging toward the stream.

She sat on wet stones grasping her knees, holding herself tightly. No thunder. No lightning. Only tree trunks glistening darkly, writhing in silver riverlets of water. Only the leaves enlarged, saturated in wetness. Only remorseless rain, its slanted ping against the flow, millions of tiny silver arrows. Unbelievable. She kept seeing it. His crushing hands. If I'd had an ice pick, she thought, I would have stuck it in his guts. What is the matter with these tight-assed people that they put up with him? Their compliance creates him. Presidents. Priests. Secretaries of State. What have all these fathers ever done for us?

Hunched on the bank the wet robe clinging to her body like an extra wrinkled skin. Fingers clasped close to her mouth, she thought of certain martyrs. Socrates. Jesus. When she refused to concede to Giroux's psychotic fabrication, perhaps he too would crucify himself.

As long as the rain lasted she crouched near the stream. As the sky slowly cleared there were no solutions inscribed in bland light.

Cold stones, washed and radiant, fingered in stillness.

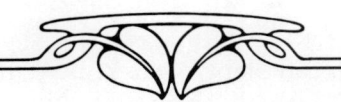

Chapter Twelve

Denying her work, said the large and very fat monk, *a diabolical coercion. Functioning normally, Giroux realized she could forever withstand him. In her favor her Asian blood; the stubborn endurance of ultimate dust. But then, Jaiyavara was not entirely Asian.*

Both Giroux and Jaiyavara . . . such monumental egos. Consider the capacity of each to sustain an unequivocal tenacity during the most drastic fluctuations of fate. Chaos reigned, yet as moths drawn to separate flames, neither would deviate one iota from the light which beckoned, pulled like a magnet.

    sky   night   depthless black
    piercing needle point sparkle of numberless stars

Within the Zendo the old man lit candles, padded about on quick, white-stockinged feet. It was two A.M., the time he most loved—the Zendo all to himself. He dusted the meditation shelves, fluffed each pillow, placing it just so in each space, arranged fresh flowers, selected and lit the incense. As content as he was to be the only soul awake at that hour all preparations were made with deft, belligerent efficiency.

Aged and small, he was—yet his face smooth, unwrinkled. With his bald head, very large ears, dark eyes rimmed with delicate pink folds he looked not quite of this world, almost resembled a fairy tale gnome or space alien.

It was said he seldom slept, well known he seldom spoke. When not occupied with the meticulous keeping of the inner sanctum he tended a private garden of exotic herbs and plants, off-limits to everyone but Alexis. Whatever the religious preference, it was the old man who initiated all into the rituals of the Zendo—sanctioned procedures of entering, leaving, how to conduct oneself within; learned by imitation rather than spoken instruction.

The four A.M. meditation he considered most sancrosant, was most easily offended at that pre-dawn hour by breaches of conduct. If one overslept, failed to appear, at some unguarded moment the offender would be confronted with a glare of such ferocity as to effect the reform of the most negligent.

Once he was dying of cancer. His potent herbs of no avail. Forbidding orthodox remedies he took to his bed, like a soldier at his post took up watch for death by day and by night. Pestered with the sympathetic ministrations of those who cared for him, he spoke of the cancer in a protective growl. "It too wants to live."

At the threshold of extinction the old man's flesh took on an unnatural luminous sheen. It was rumored that by his very acceptance of the disease he was saved, but his miraculous recovery had not the slightest redeeming effect upon his notoriously bad temper.

By light of small kerosene torches spaced along the paths, one by one the monks came down to the patio in darkness for tea. Each took his cup to a bench, sat blowing on the tea, sipping, trying to wake—each separate and silent, yet linked in a psychic communion of preparation.

In slow uncertain stealth, terrace by terrace, Jaiyavara moved down toward the patio. The black toga floated about her wispy as chiffon. As if listening she moved and paused, hesitant, yet stalking. At the edge of the patio, hidden, she stopped.

She waited for music.

She entered the edge of the patio. It became an arena. The inner music began.

Within that dark cloud of toga she was barely visible, she seemed a detached movement brought to that arena of night, or some part of the night itself becoming silent music, movement . . . as one by one the monks' eyes came down from the cold bright stars, turned from somnolent contemplation in that hour before waking, to focus upon her, to realize that it was Jaiyavara, and that she danced.

Tentative and slow, graceful, fluid, rhythmic movements. Those she danced for had never seen her at her best. Those she danced for had never danced themselves. With no male to balance her, lift her high in flying leaps, poised; with no male partner, she was earth-bound, grounded. The body she danced with was a mere replica, a poor substitute for the one she had once possessed —a body worn down, reduced by pain and labor and age. A body shattered, put back together in a thousand odd configurations of compromise, compensation, defeat. Constraining bands of scar tissue which no amount of heroic will or zeal could loosen held her down like chains. Yet still in her dreams she could dance, still in her dreams she could do every amazing thing; could leap, soar, hang suspended, perform the spirit's gift, execute pure ecstasy.

Within that black-soft cloud of toga, turning, swaying, dipping, the music grew stronger, more demanding, beginning to pulsate throughout her body. What did it matter that the instrument was inadequate? As a swimmer entering the sea she gave herself up to it, the music took her, swept her into its currents, the slow unending dance. Her body began to grope, to gather power.

What does she want, Doyle wondered. What does it mean?

This too . . . thought Brother Bethune, watching with quiet appreciation. This too is a path.

For reasons he himself did not understand Sebastian was embarrassed. He tried to look away, but his eyes, against his will fastened upon Jaiyavara.

Loneliness and sorrow, thought Alexis. What else is there? Only its momentary transformation.

She's dancing the Plague, another monk thought. The travails of earth.

Hearing her music Jethro was incapable of translations.

Karen was startled, then angry, envious . . . until at last she surrendered some part of her fear.

From the Zendo balcony Giroux looked down to the patio circled by lamps, and it became for him a stage. Caught in that counterpoint between past and present he watched; his previous visions, memories of her, rendered more poignant by the scene below. Leaning, he put one hand to the post straining to see her face, obscured by darkness.

This is her task. She can do magic.

What he envisioned for her—for them all—was a leap of consciousness, the feminine principle predominant—yet a rational cosmology with him at the helm, the sustaining Logos centered, keeping all balanced, workable. There was no one he could trust as he trusted himself to keep the ultimate goal ever in sight.

But look at her, he thought. She's not thinking. She's not rational. She acts impetuously, on an intuitive level.

Let God handle the details? Perhaps, he thought, that was not so wise. Was she capable of subverting them, capable of leading them off like some pied-piper into paganistic rebellion. Why, for that matter, was she dancing? *I found my way to the sea alone*, she said on waking, telling the dream. *The others followed.* It gave him an eerie foreboding. What irony if her very defiance of him was beginning to form in her what he sought to evoke.

Enough. He sounded the gong, calling the monks to meditation.

No one moved. No one seemed to hear.

Meanwhile, the old man, disturbed by the delay came out to the balcony, shot Giroux a look of vexation.

Should he go down to them, Giroux wondered, stop the dance? That would appear heavy-handed.

The old man looked down to the patio. Jaiyavara danced a slow twirling undulating circle. As though printed by stars in the black sky the poetry leapt out at him:

> Except for the point, the still point,
> There would be no dance, and there is only the dance.

Again, louder, more forcefully Giroux sounded the gong.

Facing mountains beyond the stream, beyond the wall where the hungry wolf prowled, where the moon hid, Jaiyavara sank down to the earth, palms upward in supplication, head bowed she ended the dance.

As monks entered the Zendo the old man saw in their faces a childish freshness. He bowed to each. Last in line, with no partner to bow to came the strange woman, the outsider, the uninitiated.

She bowed to empty space.

JAIYAVARA

Her bare foot arched and reached, crossed the threshold. For the first time she entered the Zendo. The old man bowed to Jaiyavara, she to him. For an instant, in mutual fascination, their eyes locked.

Sedately the monks move in two lines in opposite directions, one clockwise, one counter-clockwise. There are more meditation spaces than monks, a reminder of how their number has diminished. Last in line, Jaiyavara selects a space far from the others in the extreme left corner near a wall. The gong sounds its somber vibration. She bows to her space. She climbs upon the shelf, gets settled on the large bright blue pillow. Black night presses at the small window high above her.

Prescribed position, structure remembered. Belly forward. Eyes open. Thumbs and fingers lightly touching, barely touching in front of the navel—center of the universe, according to the masters. On the white wall before her the faintest shadow of flickering candles. She stares at the wall. She sees white sand, she sees white snow. Try to keep those shadows from forming images. No. Not to force . . . or hold anything back by force. All paradoxes. Contradictions. What one must somehow strive to attain, without striving? Leave it to the images. Let them decide if they must form. Supposed to let sounds, thoughts, sensations flow through, without impediments. The mind like a monkey in a cage, very difficult to quiet. Silly thoughts. Now Is The Time For All Good Men To Come To The Aid Of Their Whachamacallits? O Lord let me go. Gatemouth. Gatemouth.

Bits of commercials. Soap opera titles. Newspaper headlines. Trite songs. We were all saturated with trivia. When Christian monks of old fasted, Huxley wrote, some part of the brain, low on blood sugar, opened to a different reality, a higher vista.

Opium of the masses. Old theories. Aphorisms. Under swathed stillness her sigh is audible. She feels conspicuous, the exact antithesis of what she is supposed to feel. Then . . . on the wall before her, moving from right to left, the distinct shadow of the old man as he stalks on white stockinged feet behind the seated monks. Against his shoulder, slanted like a rifle, his large whacking stick. His shadow alerts her. She sits straighter. Her eyes refocus. His ears make her think White Cat.

No thought. No naming. No judgment. Do not put life under a graph, a grid. Impossible, she decides, opening cages, letting thoughts leap out, chatter as they will. No thought? No naming? No goddamned cigarette either. An hour without a cigarette! What am I doing here?

. . . and the morning mists, the vapors. How he walked toward me. Varrick. My god my god forever lost. At the center, raw overpowering pain. By what insistent dedication to slavery, work, have I kept it at bay? Why work, Giroux said. It's like trying to climb Mt. Everest inch by inch. Gain three inches, fall back two. Like trying to chisel stone with a tooth pick.

That force that love Varrick which must have preceded in all existence the birth of either pleasure or pain

In the small high window beginning light Can I honestly say it is never taken for granted? Distant sound sweet faint first bird one high pure note sailing through soft repeated another oh, Varrick now the song

distant rattling of pots and pans from kitchen seeing, it is real association seeing food brought out fires lit seeing, it is more imperishable than the actual useless this whatever it is, I can't do it. whatever it is, it's beyond me

Loud! Oh! Like the crack of a whip! Oh. The old man whacked someone on the back for falling asleep.

Give us this day our daily bread? Our daily bread *is* this day.

She looks to the window. The light is seven times stronger. An interval then . . . of no mind? The gong sounds. An hour passed which seemed only a few seconds. If one cannot remember what was achieved with no mind, of what use is that? Too esoteric. I can't be bothered. One life only.

Quietly the monks stretch, flex their muscles. An escaped hour, but aren't we now a little too complacent, too self-satisfied? Paid our dues, have we? By sitting? Too easy.

Yet Jaiyavara performs the balming rituals, climbs down from the shelf, bows to her space, falls in step at the end of the line. Consider the accumulative coating of such acts in unison, repeated four times a day, year after year. Letting your soul know you mean business, Bethune had said. Ah yes, the rituals. Compensation for unquenchable cravings? Defense against the remorseless ravages of time?

Reality is old age sickness despair death decay. So be it. But not yet.

Emerging once more into the world of stones, water, animals, trees, creatures who did not have to try to manage their minds, she saw Giroux waiting on the balcony, arms folded. His benign approval turned her stomach.

Beneath tall trees Anthony caught up with her, grabbed her at the waist, kissed her on the back of the neck. Hot breath on the back of her neck. Merely annoyed, she disentangled, tossed her hair, walked on.

Assets. I did not die of my father's indifference. I did not die of grief for Varrick. I did not die of pain or morphine addiction. I did not die of the Plague.

While the flocks were gathered at supper, Jaiyavara slipped into the underground labyrinth beneath Giroux's tower study. Invader, she entered, feeling along damp stone walls until her eyesight adjusted, through the narrow murky corridors. Giroux's very foxholes and ditches.

The first door she came to was locked. Further down the corridor another door, also locked. What was he hiding down here? At the first cross-section, turning right, she would not have been surprised to come upon medieval instruments of torture or skeletons chained to the walls.

But a wider door opened to a small library, lit dimly by two lamps. There were a few straight chairs. Perhaps monks studied here at night. Crude unvarnished shelves were filled with old books, thin and voluminous, ancient classics. A small alcove to the right of the shelves was provided with light by day with three large overhead windows. Someone worked here. On an elevated writing stand someone was in the midst of laboriously copying *The Tibetan Book of The Dead* in calligraphy. Brother Bethune? Who else? And this, she thought, is how he spends the sameness of his days, ruins his weak eyes. Exquisite work. Her heart was wrenched.

She returned to the shelves and wandered, browsing. High in a corner, a large black book titled in gold. INDIA. She had to stretch to reach it, work it forward on the shelf with her fingertips. With the feel of a ripe heavy melon it toppled into her hands. How dry and brittle its pages, brown tinged. Tucking it under her shawl she left, hurried through the corridors, fearful of becoming lost or locked in for the night.

Venturing past the intersection she found yet another unlocked door which opened to a wine cellar, well-stocked. A supply to last well nigh unto the Second Coming. Ho! Ho! Ho! as her mother would say! Another asset! Humming a little tune under her breath she filched a bottle of white wine and happy as a thief made her way back to the entrance.

Remembering Giroux at the Zendo that morning, his impervious conceit, she smiled. We'll see. We'll see.

She would stop by the kitchen for a loaf of bread, dine in her room alone, unmolested.

Book and wine and bread. What greater weapons! What greater assets!

"Wine for breakfast?" Alexis exclaimed. The day before as she danced Jaiyavara had projected something timeless; now, lounging on the bed in loose pajamas with the wine and bread and book, she looked innocent and earnest; she looked like a young girl. Alexis had difficulty accommodating these abrupt changes.

"Delicious bread." She tore a chunk, stuffed it into her mouth, swallowed it down with wine straight from the bottle. "This book I found last night. Gandhi's strategies."

Pulling up a chair Alexis glanced at the title. "You remember nothing of India?"

"I remember the heat." Jaiyavara took another swig of wine, capped the bottle and set it on the floor. "Before we got to the boat I remember a long train ride. Very crowded. I could see out of the window . . . jungle, mountains, dirty little huts. On the train, a bad smell. People's feet sticking out in the aisles. Children crying, wetting on the floor. The train straining to get up steep hills. But this book . . . I must not fly into rages."

"Rages? At who?"

Jaiyavara sat up straighter, braced herself at the headboard, pushed her hair out of her face. "Giroux. Why are you loyal to that bastard?"

Shocked by the question, Alexis folded her hands close to her body. Jaiyavara's eyes demanded an answer. "He was very kind. He pulled me from the depths of depression."

"You? In depression? That's hard to imagine."

"I felt I had nothing to live for."

"Why?"

"I'd rather not speak of it."

"You must. I have to understand."

"I . . . I had four sons . . . each killed in a war. It was Nicholas, the youngest . . . when I lost Nicholas. . . ."

"Oh. How horrible. Oh, Alexis. But . . . that was a long time ago. Why do you stay here now, out of gratitude? Is that his hold on you?"

"In part, maybe. We are all, in a sense, displaced persons. It's home to me now. When we first got news of the Plague many of us wanted to leave, go back, try to help. But Giroux convinced us that it was important to stay, make this place secure, wait it out."

"Why? What was his reasoning?"

"He said . . . there seemed some sort of immunity here, he said that to return would be futile, we would die for nothing. And he said it was important to maintain an island of safety, so to speak, that those most needed for world recovery would be drawn here."

Jaiyavara turned her head in disgust. "And you believed *that?*"

"He has a prophetic gift. In a way he was right, don't you see, you were drawn here."

"Drawn," Jaiyavara sneered, "or abducted? It was not my decision. I'd have more respect for him if he tried to rape me every day. That kind of lust I could understand."

"Lust? What are you talking about?"

"So . . . you're not in on it?"

"In on what, for heaven's sake?"

"He's obsessed. He's destroying my work. He told me he would destroy any attempt. And he means it."

"Oh . . . I can hardly believe that. That's a terrible accusation."

"Believe it. I am only to him some sort of amanuensis."

Aghast, Alexis sat back in her chair. "I don't understand . . . what does that mean?"

"It means," Jaiyavara said, leaning forward, "that he wants to use me to puppet his outrageous fantasies. Help propogate some sort of wierd new religion when the Plague is over."

Chapter Twelve

"What?"

"You heard me."

As if she were hearing an incomprehensible foreign language, Alexis frowned in confusion.

Giving it time to sink in, finally Jaiyavara said, "Bring no more trays. I'm going to eat with the others, I'm going to talk with them, get to know them. And somehow, gradually, I'm going to let them in on what an egocentric fanatic he is." Jaiyavara got up, began throwing strewn clothing about, looking for something to wear. She pulled the pajama top over her head, put on a loose black blouse. Searching for a skirt, she pulled off the pajama bottom.

Stark naked from the waist down—in front of the window! Alexis thought—fearful she would be seen by passing monks. Why couldn't she pull the curtain?

Putting on a long loose skirt, Jaiyavara buttoned it quickly, grabbed a brush from the chest, lashed at her hair.

"I'll do everything I can to help you," Alexis said, "but I won't betray him. He's been very good to me."

"Oh, who wouldn't be good to you? Mother to us all. He's using you."

Doesn't she wear undergarments? Alexis wondered. "He's devoted his life to helping others," she argued, her eyes wounded.

"Devoted his life to his own grandiose image." Jaiyavara slung the brush to the chest, sat down on the bed. "Lord and master of his enclosed setup. Emperor Giroux. Everyone else works. What does he do but sit on his ass and dictate! Have you seen his ivory tower up there?" she gestured with a wave of her hand. "He wallows in luxury!"

"We all share in it. We are all invited there from time to time."

"Bullshit! My father used to have his yearly barbecue for the workers, the niggers white and black. A lot of white niggers to impress. Let them wipe their feet and humbly come in to the *big* house, so he could glut himself on their envy. And when his alcoholic wife killed herself, why then he could trot out my mother in her gaudy dime store jewelry, and her little bastard to try to prove he was not a bigot."

"You're judging Giroux from your own unfortunate childhood," Alexis replied, but there was little conviction in her voice.

"Try crossing him," Jaiyavara challenged. "Try it. Just once."

"He sincerely cares. . . ."

"Just try it and see how much he cares."

Jaiyavara got up, paced the room. "My god," she said furiously, "did I survive that entire holocaust of devastation only to wind up in this god-forsaken ditch!"

Alexis rose from the chair, pulled herself to full height. "This," she said sternly, "is not a ditch. This is one of the few places on earth that God has not forsaken."

"Makes little difference to me, blocked by that bastard."

"Learn to wait, endure. When you leave here. . . ."

"I don't have time. Believe me, I don't. All my life I've been harrassed by time. But—he's not going to stop me." Distracted then, her anger spent, she looked about the room. "Where are my shoes?"

"I don't know, where did you put them?"

Jaiyavara flung her arms. "If I knew that! Oh," she sighed, "I get so . . . so . . . sometimes at night when I can't sleep . . . I think I hear the sea."

"Maybe you do." Alexis' eyes were suddenly full of fatigue. She beckoned as if to a distraught child. "Come to the window. You see that mountain? Before Giroux put up the wall we used to climb that mountain to look at the sea."

"I knew it." Jaiyavara pressed to the window, one hand to her breast. "I knew I could hear it. I knew I could smell it."

"And sometimes we wrote wishes on bits of paper and let the sea wind take them."

"If I could get beyond the wall, beyond the mountain. And if there were a boat, even a small boat. . . ." Together at the window they stood close. Jaiyavara turned to Alexis, searched her face. "What did you wish for?"

Alexis lowered her eyes.

"Please . . . I tell you everything."

"Oh, you know, it's odd about wishes. First you think only of yourself. No more wars. Peace. All the children safe. Everyone safe. Good health. Love. Prosperity. You imagine all that for yourself. And then you think, why not include everyone? What I want for myself, I want for everyone. But then finally I was selfish. Something I wanted just for myself. Something I realized I had always wanted."

Lips parted, Jaiyavara memorized her face. "Was it a daughter?"

She nodded.

Gently Jaiyavara put an arm around her. At the window together, as allies, they looked toward the mountain.

Then Jaiyavara saw Anthony walk past. Remembering his hot breath on the back of her neck, she shrewdly wondered . . . another asset?

Chapter Thirteen

Stepping carefully from stone to stone, Jaiyavara crossed the stream. From the central terrace beneath the Zendo, Giroux watched her. He moved to follow but Alexis came quietly up behind him, put a detaining hand on his arm. Irritably, he frowned. "Where is she going?"

"Only for a walk."

"She walks a lot," he said, squinting at the exact distant spot where Jaiyavara vanished into the forest. "And she hasn't continued with the meditation."

"Leave her alone. Please. Don't push her on that."

It was so out of character for Alexis to advise, he took offense. "What do you mean, push?"

"She defied Thandon," Alexis reminded him. "There is violence in her."

Later, when Jaiyavara returned to the patio for a cup of tea, cautiously Giroux approached the bench where she sat looking down to the stream. "You've been walking in the woods again. I have to warn you, they're full of snakes."

"No worse than here."

"Isn't trite sarcasm beneath you?"

Holding the tea cup, her eyes settled upon him. "Confronted with a tyrant, nothing is beneath me. I'm capable of anything."

Sitting beside her, he pleaded, "I'm not a tyrant. Thandon's the tyrant."

"You and Thandon," she shrugged. "So much alike."

"How can you say that? No one here considers me a tyrant."

"No one here is trying to live a life of their own."

"Can't we be friends?"

She threw the contents of her cup over the railing, refused to answer.

Head bowed, in thought, at last he came to some idea of how to proceed. "I've heard from Simeon on the radio."

"So?"

"Don't you want to hear?"

"So . . ." she shrugged, making it obvious she would prefer to sit alone, "all right, what's going on now in the battered world?"

"No recent earthquakes, for one thing. And the death rate has lowered."

Arm on the railing, she put a hand to her chin.

"Hopeful, don't you think?"

Still she refused to answer or look at him.

Compelled to speak, he began carefully. "Nature threw off her chains in preparation for a new way. The feminine archetypes have been lost for centuries, but with the teaching I have formulated . . ."

"Oh?" she erupted. "World-wide catastrophies, all for you! All creation moved to open a way for you! You're inhuman. If I were not involved personally I could almost sit back and observe your megalomania as spectator. Theatre of the absurd."

"What if I am God's way of speaking to you? What if I see in you what you yourself are not yet able to see?"

"Oh, good Lord. You don't even believe in God."

"Don't you understand," he implored. "I'm trying to help."

Moving back, she glared. "Help who? You would use me as if I were wood or metal or clay. Give it up, Giroux. You have chosen a resistant material."

"Because you're a woman? History, I tell you, has come full circle. It's because you're a woman that you're so perfectly suited. . . ."

"I'm the most unlikely candidate in the world for what you have in mind. Find some female as fanatical as you are. What a fake you are! You've perverted everything to your own ends. These so-called great teachings, what the hell have they done for you?"

"And what," he said, "is so marvelous about shaping crude materials to your own ends?"

"I follow my own path. I don't bother anyone else. It's art," she said, folding her arms, "that speaks to the generations."

"Philosophy speaks. So does religion."

"Salvini said it, and it's true. And so far beyond you. Art is man's highest compassion."

"What nonsense!" He heaved forward, then clamped down; put tightly clasped hands between his knees, frowning severely.

To Doyle, seated on a low distant wall, who could hear nothing, with their violent movements and gestures, it looked like a quarrel between passionate lovers.

Backed against the railing she was as impenetrable as a fortress. "And suppose," she insisted, "that someone locked you in a room with canvas and paint and said to you, now look here, Giroux, all you have to do to save the world is create a masterpiece. Could you do it? No more than I can. . . ."

"Why are we in conflict? We both want essentially the same thing, a better world."

"No, we don't want the same thing. You want a better world. I want a better self."

"There's no redemption in a painting," he said. "Turn the lights off and where does it go?"

"There is light, you idiot!"

"Here, yes. Not everywhere, obviously. This is the second age of darkness, more tragic than the first, because so much, so slowly and painfully attained is now lost. Perhaps forever lost. But the word," he said, "proceeds and makes a path through the most terrible darkness. The word endures. The myth prevails." He stood then, looming over her like a monolith. A stalemate. Wordless, drained, she watched him walk away.

No, he did not believe. (He did not deny it.) And yet . . . such God-haunted eyes.

A hand cupped to her mouth she watched dead leaves fall to the stream, twisting as they fell and floated, carried to sea. Leaves, she thought, escape.

"The leaves are dying," Anthony said.

She looked up.

"You were meant for life."

More pontificating. She resented his youth, she resented his ignorance, she resented his maleness. "Oh, Anthony . . . if you don't want to paint go amuse yourself. Go fuck one of the pretty girls."

He sat beside her. "I do want to."

"Not enough to fight for it." She turned back to him.

"Jaiyavara, what's the matter?"

"Cold weather is coming. I can feel it. My bones ache."

"All your bones?"

A half smile. "No, not all. Not quite. Only those broken."

Her mood made him bold, he put his hands to the back of her neck. She stiffened. "Relax," he whispered, "I love you," and he began massaging the tense muscles of her neck and back and shoulders. The strength of his hands was good. Her head drooped down. Close to her ear, he whispered, "Let me come to your room tonight."

Through the kitchen window Karen saw them. Anthony hot for that older woman? Rinsing her hands, she whipped a towel from the rack. A cold day in hell, she thought, before he gets to me again.

Furiously she scrubbed her work space. When she glanced again through the window Anthony had gone. Jaiyavara sat alone, in profile. Projected beauty? What the hell did that mean? Other than reputation—and that past tense—what was her allure? Men were attracted to that? Giroux's fascination with her was still a mystery . . . and now, Anthony's defection.

Meanwhile, Jaiyavara sat wondering what to do with the long hours which stretched before her. Go for a swim? Too cold. Walk down to the stables, visit with the horses? What would that solve? Imposed leisure was becoming unbearable. Here and now, the canvas of the world stretched before her, freely given, and she was cut off from it. Aimlessly she got up and wandered to the kitchen.

Seated at the table, Karen peeled oranges for a luncheon salad.

"May I help?" Jaiyavara asked.

"If you like," Karen said, but her voice was hostile. "There's a knife in that drawer."

Jaiyavara found the knife, sat down at the table, picked up an orange. "Well," she said, "we are both well-armed."

Shocked, Karen said nothing.

"Why are you saving the peelings?"

"For marmalade."

"It's very late for oranges, isn't it?"

"They come from the greenhouse."

"I see." Utterly predictable, Jaiyavara thought, bored before it ever began. She disliked Karen's maneuvers, yet understood why she was forced to make them. Quietly they sat, peeling and slicing. "I once overheard," Jaiyavara said, "a remark Doyle made about you."

"Oh? And what was that?"

"He said, 'It must be nice to get everything you want, just by smiling'."

"I don't get everything I want."

Jaiyavara picked up another orange, started another ring of peeling. "I know that, Karen." If Karen could learn to temper her "me first" attitude, she would be, Jaiyavara thought, much more personable. She could detect in Karen no creative potential, she might just as well live her part, enjoy the advantages bestowed by nature. But she needed some focus other than beauty. Otherwise, as she grew older, she would become the victim of her own devices. She reminded Jaiyavara of those discarded models and starlets on the streets of Hollywood, often chic, but starved, pallid, garish creatures, feigning self-assurance, living in haunted desperation on outlandish ambitions. Life is shipwreck, she wanted to say. Before your beauty fades find another source of strength, otherwise you are going to be stranded. But Karen was not ready to hear that. Not yet.

"How long have you been here, Karen?"

"Nearly four years."

Bit by bit, Jaiyavara pulled from her, her story. Karen was not nearly so innocent of the world as she had tried, in her unsuccessful ploy, to make Giroux believe. Unexpectedly, she answered Jaiyavara's questions without evasion or embellishment. (Perhaps because interest in her life, rather than her looks was rare.) The Chicago slums. A broken home. Desertion by the father, a mother who became alcoholic. Two older brothers constantly in trouble. Little education. Poverty, hardship. Karen had worked in the garment district, had been seduced by her employer, a married man, was forced into an abortion. Jaiyavara could appreciate the appeal of the sanctuary, Giroux, to a young girl in that situation.

"And what," Jaiyavara asked, "do you think of Giroux now?"

"I still think he's the most wonderful man I've ever known."

"I see. What do you know about his life?"

"Nothing," Karen admitted. "He doesn't talk about himself. He talks about ideas."

"So I've noticed."

"Why are you asking me about Giroux? Aren't you two old friends?"

"Hardly. We're not friends at all."

Karen put two melons on the table to cut and scoop, add to the salad. "But then . . . why are you here?"

"Giroux had the mistaken idea that I might be of some help to him in the future."

"How? I don't understand."

"Sort of as . . . well, organizer. Like Alexis," she said evasively. "That's all I want to say about it now. Except that it was an unfounded assumption which I deeply resent."

"But he saved your life."

"With an ulterior motive. Nothing very noble or selfless about that, now is there?"

Karen made no attempt to hide her surprise, her relief. "Well," she said, with an air of pronouncement, and began peeling and slicing the melon. Jaiyavara sat and smoked. After awhile Karen coyly glanced up. "How old are you?"

"Forty-three."

Karen sweetly smiled. "You are certainly very well preserved."

Jaiyavara laughed. "Why, thank you, Karen." She stretched, eased back in the chair. "Let's have some coffee."

"Yes, I'll get it," Karen offered, moving quickly, lightly, smiling, as if they shared a private joke. Bringing coffee to the table, she said, "I'm glad we talked. The others will be here soon to help prepare the rest of the meal."

"Then I think it's time," Jaiyavara said, "to lay our cards on the table."

"What do you mean by that?"

"I mean, that I have no designs on Giroux. I try to avoid him. You and Anthony are lovers, but. . . ."

"Well . . . we were. . . ."

"Whatever," Jaiyavara shrugged. "But it's Giroux you care for, isn't it? It's Giroux you want."

Karen's poise vanished. She looked trapped, guilty.

"It's nothing to be ashamed of. Why don't you seduce him?"

Her mouth opened. She sucked in and then heaved out a deep breath. "Don't think I haven't tried."

"Try harder," Jaiyavara said, matter-of-factly.

"Do you mean that?"

Jaiyavara got up from the table. "I certainly do. You have my blessing." She walked to the door, turned. "It might be exactly what he needs. It might do him a world of good."

Migratory flights of geese swarmed the skies, their cries pulled her eyes upward to follow as they disappeared into the tattered scarves and shreds of clouds. In wet twirling fat flakes the first snow came, in dancing flurries which did not stick, melted on contact. Obliterated by snow, distant peaks merged with the sky, were lost from sight. As if fighting off freezing the stream coursed, louder, stronger, lavish with trills of foam.

Wrapped in a blanket, wearing boots, early that morning Jaiyavara crossed the stream. Like a friendly dog, thrashing and sloshing into icy water above his knees, Ruben followed after her.

Turning, she shouted, "No, you can't follow. Go back, Ruben. Go back."

His ears were very red. Confused, still grinning, he halted. Waving her arms Jaiyavara tried to shoo him away. He would not budge. Not intending to hit him, only to make him go back, she hurled a small rock. It dropped into the water. Thinking it a game, Ruben stooped to search for the stone. He saw only reflected sky. "Go back!" she shouted, and hurled another small rock. While he searched she gained the sandstone ledges, crossed and hurried into the trees. Looking up to find her gone, Ruben's lower lip puckered with a betrayed and childish grudge.

Lost in the deep shade of evergreens she entered the forest, where everything was remembered.

Periodically Giroux called meetings in the dining room for the discussion of practical matters. Theoretically, everyone was given a say. That afternoon Jaiyavara was neither informed of the meeting nor invited. In the fireplace a fire crackled. Monks warmed their hands on large mugs of tea or coffee on the tables before them. Outside, snow fell steadily, now sticking, piling up.

Giroux was in pain. Pus oozed from his upper back infected gum. John Bain had lanced, cleaned, and cauterized it, which had helped briefly. Several monks complained of leaking roofs. A volunteer committee was formed for the inspection and patching of roofs. Pasture fences needed mending. A few rusting water pipes had to be replaced. As mundane necessities were acknowledged Giroux's offending tooth incessantly throbbed. Standing at the head table he put his hand to Ruben's head from time to time to keep him quiet. When all business was concluded he spoke directly to Juan, in charge of the stables. "One last thing. You must not allow Jaiyavara to ride in this sort of weather. The paths are treacherous now."

"She comes very early. She saddles up before I get there."

"Then," Giroux smiled, "you'll have to rise a bit earlier, won't you?"

"Yes, Father."

"I'll speak to her also. Any further injury could leave her paralyzed."

"Yes, Father."

"We must all," he continued, to the entire assembly, "be very protective of Jaiyavara. This is a brave, but extremely headstrong woman who has suffered the loss of family and friends . . . the unspeakable horrors of the Plague. Safe and secure here, it's impossible for any of us to realize the full consequences, the aftermath of such experiences. For her own good I've asked her not to work until she's stronger. But," he smiled, "she is ambitious. She strives beyond her physical capacity. I'm not certain she will accept my advice."

About to enter, in the alcove entrance Jaiyavara stopped and overheard.

"But, Father, excuse me," said Brother Bethune. "Perhaps she knows best her own needs. Isn't work therapeutic?"

"Good Brother," Giroux said gently, "trust me in this. Work is not therapeutic when one is exhausted. Believe me, I know the danger signs. I've worked many years with the emotionally ill. Jaiyavara, I fear . . . could be on the verge of a breakdown."

"Liar!" she shouted, striding forward. "Son of a bitch!"

Shocked faces turned to her.

"You idiots!" she shouted, and flinging her shawl over her shoulder stalked out.

All were stunned by her outburst. Blushing in embarrassment, a few could not lift their eyes from the table.

As if to say . . . "You see?" Giroux indulgently spread his hands.

Most of the monks were indignant on Giroux's behalf. Some few, however, were not quite convinced, hid their doubts, their first hints of anxiety.

Crashing through the woods Jaiyavara walked fast. Clouds of panting breath erupted before her face. With a huge stick she wacked savagely at obstacles. Diabolical bastard! No honor whatever! Nothing was beyond him! Worse still, her shouting only gave weight to his vile accusations. Ambitious! she thought. My ambitions are as *nothing* compared to his! How am I to defend myself? Still seething, she finally came to rest against a boulder, got her breath, and watched a large grey rabbit scurry for cover.

High above her head a raucous bird was squalking at her invasion of his territory. Nothing new, she thought. I've dealt with ruthless males all my life. Egocentric dancers out to upstage me. Yet even Gottrell, even Thandon did not prepare me for this. What would Varrick do? Varrick would fight him. How am I to fight him?

At a slant, steadily, snow kept falling, it made an almost inaudible hiss. Trees were etched and outlined, all white on one side. Evergreen leaves cupped in their small hands pristine whiteness. If she thought of the world far away, she was fortunate. She kept reminding herself of that. But surrounded by the dead and dying, the arid stench, would she have been any less desperate? In such a world did anything matter? Stalker and prey, hunted and hunter, everywhere. Cold penetrated to the marrow of her bones. If I could get out, she thought, I would strike out alone. I'd rather freeze to death on a mountain path than stay here. Overpowered, oppressed, she sightlessly stared.

Without realizing it her cold fingers were tracing lines and indentations in the raw stone, its scars, its markings. Her hand on its own came to a backward inner curving; as her hand explored gradually in a sideways leaning her body followed.

She turned to look. A cave.

Did the loss of a tooth symbolize, Giroux wondered, loss of power? Would its absence affect his speech? No longer could he tolerate the constant pain. He thought of asking the physician to pull it but he was allergic to anesthetics and was afraid of behaving before John Bain in an undignified manner.

Before the bathroom mirror he braced himself. Close at hand the ice pack was ready. With a pair of pliers he took hold of the tooth, inside his head he could hear a loud crunching and tearing as he pulled and twisted and wrenched it out of his head. Blind with pain he dropped the pliers, staggered from wall to wall, both hands to his face. Scalding tears streamed down his face; he made no sound. When he got control he spit blood into the sink, rinsed his mouth, stuffed a wad of cotton over the bleeding hole. He took the ice pack to the bed, lay with it pressed to his face. In less than an hour the pain lessened. He removed the cotton, with his tongue tentatively explored the empty space.

The cave entrance in warm weather was hidden by underbrush, which was why she had never seen it before. With some fear—not of snakes, snakes were dormant in winter—she pushed aside smaller rocks and stooped to enter. It was dark. She crept forward a few feet until able to stand in a wide area filled with light. There was a natural wide opening high above her head. Snow swirled down into her face, caught on her eyelashes. There was a wide slab ledge to her right. Plenty of room and on a clear day the light would be good. Directly below the natural opening she saw the remains of a fire. Perhaps shepherds of long ago took shelter here. Or perhaps escaped convicts. Tasting cold air she sucked it deep. A good feel to this hidden place.

Jaiyavara crawled out of the cave and walked down rough sloping banks to the stream. Squatting near the water, brushing away snow, she fondled small rocks. With both hands she dug down deep into the cold moist clay. She took it in both hands, stood with it, moved it up and down; weighing it. Her eyes narrowed. A sly, secretive pleasure played across her mouth.

Scalloped in black at the hem and at the edge of the long sleeves, the dress she wore was long and simple and straight. The dress she wore was scarlet. Cords of scarlet were woven into the elaborate braids at the crown of her head. Jaiyavara swept into the dining room, took a seat at an empty table, her back to Giroux. It was the evening meal.

Giroux tapped a spoon to his glass for that moment of head-bowed silence. Her head remained high. Lifting a water glass to her lips her eyes met Jethro's. There was nothing overt, no invitation was extended, but presently Jethro got up, brought his plate and wine glass and came to join her. A few minutes later Brother Bethune came to her table. "Did not Christ," she quipped, "dine with thieves and harlots?" As conversation resumed no mention was made at her table of the earlier dining room fracas, that subject was assiduously avoided. Mid-meal Doyle got up to refill his plate, ever so casually he moved to Jaiyavara's table. Now she was flanked by three.

Alexis yearned to go to her but stayed in her chair, beside Giroux, her appointed place.

Once again paying court to Karen—Jaiyavara he felt beyond his grasp—Anthony did not dare go to her, or so much as glance in her direction.

All very civilized. The meal proceeded. Yet Jaiyavara sensed that out of boredom, and perhaps to their own shame, some of the monks were enjoying the undercurrents. And there were those who met her eyes with more empathy than anger or curiosity.

As the dining room began to clear, waiting for Giroux's next move, she dallied. Before the room was entirely empty he got up, walked to her table, stood behind Doyle, inclined his head in a stiff bow. His smile was tight. He said nothing.

On his upper lip the red she saw was a tiny dot of congealed blood.

Chapter Thirteen

The snow piled high. The weather was dreary. It was difficult to move about, almost impossible to keep warm. The simplest task became a chore. Almost everyone was feeling resentful and trapped.

In defiance of the weather Jaiyavara flung them out on the bed, draped them about the room, large swaths of material Alexis let her select from a storeroom. As she patterned, cut, and stitched, as her needle dipped and pulled, dipped and pulled, she could not help but wonder . . . why am I doing this?

For one thing, the history of India was not much help. All human history, she suspected, of not much help to anyone right now.

With what we wear we play a role. While working she had always been careless of her appearance. But wasn't it more than an urge for flaunting her flairs before the black robed monks, more than the urge to prove Giroux a liar? Here, she was powerless. Here, she was the intruder. Here, she had no future, only a past. Well then, she would parade not only her sanity, but her vitality, her ingenuity as well. She and the monks, at opposite ends of the spectrum. Perhaps she reminded them of a world they had turned their backs on long before all hell broke loose. In their endless dedication to repetition they had renounced individuality.

But working alone in her room, pensively from time to time Jaiyavara would gaze through the window . . . as if expecting Maya for a moment to lift her veils.

But think of it—once so ordinary, so taken for granted—a shortage of wire coat hangers! In her small closet she hammered up nails. Each finished garment promptly hung up. Stocking the arsenal. Colorful corsets to wear over long skirts, bright vests and scarves and shawls. Years in the theatre gave her endless ideas. And for the pain in her neck an occasional bottle of wine.

To walk about in this walled place, yes! a role, a camouflage! Giroux would destroy every canvas? Very well, she would become the canvas. Should worse come to worse she would make her face a mask of exaggerated evil, she would paint her naked body to walk about in this constricted prison. Could he attack her physically? Could he tear her up? Her needle dipped and pulled, dipped and pulled. When the thread snarled and knotted, when a piece did not exactly fit, she threw it down, calmed herself with a walk in snow.

Still scheming, some of these fineries she shared with Karen. "I can never believe," said Jaiyavara, admiring her handiwork on Karen, "that men get the pleasure from life that we do. And Giroux," she prodded, "seems to me very badly in need of pleasure." Preening before a mirror, Karen was grateful for the encouragement as well as the gifts.

When the wind moaned and wailed and the grey sky clamped down hard, she took her sewing to the dining room and worked before the fire.

In her room, while chanting monks praised the Lord of Creation, as the sound seeped through her walls, she tried on a new garment, tightened the belt at her long narrow waist, put hands to her hips, tilted her head toward the mirror. Here am I, Lord. Still beautiful. Still usable.

As her needle dipped and pulled, dipped and pulled, beneath all artifacts she held to the image, stark and steadfast, of her true self. As her hands formed these contrivances, she kept to the center of stillness; the place she had found alone, lying in wait, the cave; the entrance to that secret place most holy, most hidden.

Leaving the wine cellar on a cold night with a stolen bottle Jaiyavara bumped into Anthony. He grabbed her in his arms. "Wait," she whispered. "We have to talk," and pulled him back inside, out of sight.

"I don't want to talk. You know what I want."

"Wait . . . so damned cold down here. I'm freezing." She pulled the cork, took a long drink, then offered the bottle to Anthony.

He put his hand on the wall close to her head, and as he drank he never took his eyes from her face.

What was it?—what was it?—something about him very different.

Together, inside the wine cellar they sat down on the floor, leaned against the wall passing the bottle back and forth. "Drink," he urged. "Drink. It will warm your blood. I want it hot like mine."

"Do you believe," she finally asked, "that I'm on the verge of a breakdown?"

Anthony shrugged. "Understandable . . . if you were."

"Look at me. Do I look like someone on the verge of a breakdown?"

"I see only a desirable woman. I want you, Jaiyavara."

"And I want you . . . to help me."

"Help you what?"

"Leave this place."

"Are you serious?"

"Utterly."

"You would go back to all that?"

"Yes. Yes."

"Why leave? I can make you happy."

"Not here, you can't. I've got to get out of here."

"No, listen. We could be entirely content. Why leave?"

"Giroux. He'll destroy me. His crazy obsession."

"Which obsession are you speaking of . . . he has so many?"

As he took the bottle from her she flexed her empty hands. "That goddamned wall."

"The wall is nothing," Anthony bragged, moment by moment his masculinity more pronounced. "A rope with a hook, I could easily climb the wall."

"Well, I couldn't."

"Actually leave? To actually leave," he speculated, "we would have to steal more than wine. We'd have to take horses, supplies. Nothing less than mutiny, is that what you're asking?"

"He doesn't own your life, Anthony. Or mine."

Thoughtfully, he looked into her eyes. "A big price for a piece of ass. Are you worth it?"

Tilting her head against the wall she almost smiled. "Frankly, no. I'm not a great lay."

"Don't worry, I have every confidence in you. I'll inspire you. I'll make you great."

A quirk of her mouth, she looked at him sideways. Yet the wine cellar was becoming mellow. Drinking, passing the bottle back and forth, it reminded her of Kraft, almost as if in this hidden underground dungeon they were having a little party.

They finished that bottle. "I like red," said Anthony, and he got another bottle, brought it back to their place on the floor. Jaiyavara fished around in her pockets, found a cigarette, lit it. Tension in her neck and back, painful in release, easing away. Getting a glow going. Make love with Anthony on the cold stone floor? No. She had to keep her head, get what she really wanted.

"Who knows what's out there," Anthony was saying. "The old man of the Zendo says this is to be a particularly severe winter. He knows the signs. But the old man says it will help kill the germs of the earth, help stamp out the Plague."

Jaiyavara groaned.

"No, no, that's good. Think of us together, warm under the covers." He took another long swig.

Jaiyavara let the heavy wool shawl fall back from her shoulders, loosened the collar of her blouse. Anthony pulled her close, put a hand to her breast. Only her feet were cold then. She tucked them under his strong thighs.

"What obsession?" he asked.

"So radical . . . you'll never believe. . . ."

"Try me."

"If it doesn't all just slide down the drain . . . when and if it's over, he wants us to sojourn out there amongst the suffering masses with some sort of message shit edict." She belched. "Something about the feminine principle. Whatever the shit that means."

Anthony grunted.

"And what the fuck does he know about feminine? He has no woman. Has he ever had a woman? Do you think he's queer?"

"No, I don't think so."

"Well, anyhow, that's what he's had in mind all along. All along! For years, Anthony! My life means nothing to him. Nothing! I'm only a pawn in some grandiose scheme he's been hatching in that sick, isolated brain of his for years and years."

Anthony nodded. "Like a tiger . . . twitching his tail. I've always felt he was waiting . . . for something. So," he said, highly amused, "it's you."

"It's not funny. You don't know how relentless he is."

"We all used to constantly speculate, discuss the things he taught us. I was once very impressed with him. But now . . . we speak of Jaiyavara. A lady messiah!" He snorted with laughter. "Not to me, not to me, thank God."

". . . stupendous gathering of the simple-minded." She tilted the bottle.

They kept drinking.

"I wonder," Anthony mused, pulling her closer, tighter, "if Jesus was a good lay." Hurriedly, with his left hand he crossed himself. "Excuse me, Lord. You see what you do to me? I'll get another bottle."

"No. That's enough."

"One more."

"No, I said, that's enough. I want you to plan it, a way for us to leave in the spring."

"I want you now."

"No. In the spring. And only if you help me." Disentangling, she got to her feet, dropped her cigarette butt to the floor, stepped on it. Anthony stood. Both tipsy, they leaned at the wall. "Can I depend on you?" she persisted.

"I didn't realize it, but I was waiting for you too."

He tried to kiss her. She held him at arms length. "Will you help me?"

Lowering his head, extremely serious he studied the floor. "Yes, I think I will. I've had enough of this place. Yes, by God, I think we'll do it."

"Savanarola," she murmured, moving close, and put one finger to his nose. "I could make love with a Savanarola." Holding him, she lifted her face. He kissed her passionately.

As good as a vow, she thought, when he looked into her eyes.

He took her by the hand, led her down a corridor.

"Where are you taking me?"

"You'll see." From the pocket of his robe he produced a key ring, heavy with keys, unlocked the door. He pulled a lamp from the wall, held it aloft. They entered a storeroom stacked and crammed with objects.

"Old relics," said Anthony. "Pick a keepsake. There's a music box somewhere."

"Good Lord, so much stuff! Where did it come from?"

"Hoarded over the years. Everyone brought things. What do you want? A fan? A ring? A feather boa? What about a moth eaten mink cape?"

"It's like a grandmother's attic."

"Look at this, Jaiyavara. This great bull. Guess who. Brother Bethune."

Poking among the piled up objects, all were old, interesting, many were priceless antiques, many grotesquely ornate. An old victrola. A child's small rocking chair. A Tiffany lamp. Treasured heirlooms of families, people long dead. Things, she thought. And yet they outlast us.

Anthony kept insisting she select a keepsake, but other than an old diary, a life of the past revealed, she could think of nothing she wanted.

Then, far off in a corner something glass caught her eye, as she made her way closer, it looked like an enormous case or box. Anthony helped her remove a lion inkwell, suitcases, picture frames, and books from the top. "What is it, what is it?" she said. "Let me see. It looks like . . . oh my God . . . it is."

"A coffin."

"In here? What for? My God, it is a coffin!"

"Giroux's," Anthony said.

She ran both hands over the dust coated surface. "But look . . . look . . . it's beautiful. Edged in gold. Where on earth did it come from? And look at the work on the lock. The tree. The figures. It's Adam and Eve. Oh, look at the golden serpent!"

"I think he's saving it to be buried in."

"He really intends?"

"Probably," Anthony said sardonically. "Forever enshrined and admired. Gruesome, isn't it?"

She could not keep from imagining Giroux within, smooth, stiff and cold, lifeless as a wax dummy. Yet something more than death, some epiphany of dread made the hair at the back of her neck stretch in its roots. She backed away. "Let's get out of here. I've seen enough."

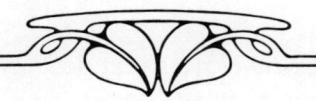

Chapter Fourteen

Wrestling with the large rock at the entrance to the cave Jaiyavara heaves, pulls, pushes, laboring furiously. It is bitterly cold, she is wet with perspiration. High above her head on icy branches sparrows make an incessant fussy chatter as if supervising. For leverage she uses a branch thick as a club. Inch by grudging inch the rock moves. Panting, she leans down to the vanquished rock, rests anchored, wipes her face on the flounce of her heavy long skirt. Having labored like a peasant she stoops to enter. The entrance is now wider. Now the light is stronger. Beneath the high overhead opening she looks up to soft white fluffs of sky stuffed into the opening like angel wing feathers.

Out of small frozen rocks and stones, out of bits of wood and clay warmed by her bruised, forceful hands, she has a work in progress.

Stung by the sharp wind Brother Bethune's eyes glistened bright blue, watered copiously. He and Jaiyavara had taken a brisk morning walk. He had to scurry to keep up with her. He tried to understand her anger. Pacing if off, with each hard, heel-dug stride she seemed intent on marking off the magnificent arc of the planet. They stopped on a hill to sit and rest.

"The cold gets to me," Bethune said. "My blood is thin. But I try to walk every day, otherwise I get very short of breath."

Jaiyavara got her long skirts wrapped around her legs, put both arms around her propped knees.

"Wouldn't you be warmer in pants?"

"I do have on pants under my skirt."

"Oh. Good. It never used to get so cold here," said Brother Bethune. "Everything has changed. But then, in this life, change is the only thing you can really rely on."

He was still short of breath. She regretted her pace. Her eyes fastened on a distant black tree, beautifully contorted, leafless and bleak; alone in that pasture—the cows were in the barn—it stood like the last survivor in a dead battle zone. "Do you ever think of leaving here?"

"Oh, no," he said cheerfully, patting his shoulders, trying to stop shivering. "Even before the Plague I could not have survived out there."

He knew his limitations. She would not pursue it.

Bethune took off his gloves to rub his hands. As if rouged for a clownish act, two high spots of red throbbed on his pale cheeks.

The squawk of a blackbird cracked through the sky. Was the blackbird calling to its mate?

"I wish," he said, "that God was as lucky as we are. I'm so happy."

He did not look happy. He looked cold. "How do you mean?"

"All this." In the spread of his fragile naked hand the blue veins looked scorched by cold. "Just look, all this."

As he spoke scudding clouds rushed eastward to the edge of the world, sunlight raced across the snow-covered pasture below. She thought it might leave the unblemished snow trampled as if by gigantic footprints.

"All creation," he was saying. "Such a masterpiece."

"And the least we can do," she added, "is be here to see it."

"Show up! Yes!" With one delicate finger he scratched his forehead. "Such a masterpiece, that is, until you come to man. We have not turned out quite right, do you think? Sometimes I wonder, maybe God can't decide whether to destroy us and start over, or hope we evolve into something better. I sometimes wonder if that is what the Plague is all about."

"The dinosaur was destroyed, and other species . . . constantly becoming extinct."

A noisy swarm of blackbirds flew to the black tree, settled in its branches. Now the solitary tree was fully adorned and bedecked with blackbirds.

"Well," she said, "if my vote counted I'd be for letting us fumble through. Even Ruben, for instance, has his own peculiar beauty. And he heightens sensitivity, he evokes protectiveness."

Brother Bethune's head wobbled slightly. "A place in the scheme of things."

So benignly he smiled, her spirits were lifted. Instantly, of one accord the blackbirds flared into the sky and soared away.

"Tell me," she ventured, "how does Giroux elicit such trust, such obedience?"

"Foresight."

Quick answer, she thought. As if forearmed, braced for the question. She would not argue. Not yet.

"The compelling power of his psyche."

She was quiet so long he turned a little to look directly into her face. Dark heavy hair close to her face gave it depth and shadow, the wind lifted the tag ends of her hair up from her shoulders and for a moment held them there, coiled upward as if held aloft by invisible wires. Mystified by the image, Brother Bethune's lips parted—an image he knew he would never be able to erase or forget. It was quite extraordinary. Eyes downcast in her expressionless face, hair lifted, she looked like an Indian goddess, the incarnation of some timeless force.

"Power," she repeated, lost in thought.

From the dining room alcove Alexis made a furtive signal. Jaiyavara rose from the patio bench and went in to her. They withdrew to the recess of the alcove, concealed from the others. Alexis took several knives from her robe, a hammer, a chisel, passed them to Jaiyavara who tucked them up her sleeves beneath her shawl.

"Be careful. Go while he's teaching."

Jaiyavara aimlessly edged away from the monks on the patio. Beyond the bend, out of sight, she crossed the stream.

Chapter Fourteen

Intermittantly it throbbed, yet another tooth near the right front of his mouth. Certain that anger inflamed it, he avoided Jaiyavara, biding his time. It was more than fear of pain or disfigurement, all his power was in speaking. A lisping philosopher? Was nature intent, tooth by tooth, on rendering him ridiculous, impotent? Sooner or later, no doubt, he would lose every tooth in his head, but not—good God!—before be had convinced Jaiyavara of the urgency of their mission.

Let the offending tooth get soothed and settled, let him hold to it yet awhile; he would try with her again.

He saw her walking to the baths with Karen. They carried heavy white towels. In the steaming hot tub, water lapping at their naked shoulders, hair piled high . . . what did they talk about? What could they possibly have in common?

Or he saw her in the dining room before the night fire with Doyle, observed the pains she went to to make him comfortable; such little niceties, pushing a footstool under his gout-swollen leg, bringing a glass of wine to his chair.

And he could not help but notice how often Jethro and Jaiyavara lingered at the dining room table, long after the others had left, pouring over notebooks, papers, deeply engrossed. What could it mean? She had always seemed to him unapproachable, so consumed with her own efforts she had no time for anyone else. That close intimate contact with Anthony day by day, he had forbidden, yet often he saw them together. Not quite daring to interrupt or impose further restrictions, he could not prevent her from mingling to some extent.

Almost every time he saw her she wore a different costume. Why all this sudden frivolity?

One morning in passing he overheard her attempting to engage the old man of the Zendo in conversation as he shovelled a path through his private garden. What was she up to?

Was it deception? ". . . though I speak with the tongues of angels, and have not love. . . ." Look around you, she told herself. You have, most of your life, cut yourself off from people. Make the attempt. See who there is to love here.

Jaiyavara was not agitating, not trying to incite anyone against Giroux, not openly (except with Anthony) trying to instigate rebellion. She was testing, probing, seeking other possible allies in case Anthony did not come through for her. She was trying to remain composed, prove that she was sensible and sane. She was trying to defend herself.

Her motives, even in this, were not entirely ulterior. Unable to work normally she was depressed, lonely, aware of isolation, thus more gregarious than usual. She was attempting to bridge the gap between herself and the others. But for all her soft adroit socializing she was left with the impression that nothing much was accomplished. Alexis was sympathetic, but she would never confront, much less challenge Giroux.

Anthony was still her only real hope.

The first star of evening quivered above the bench of the large and very fat monk, the only star visible; the only celestial offering.

Jaiyavara approached.

"So. . . ." he greeted her. "It goes well, the work?"

"How did you know?"

"It's in your shoulders . . . your face . . . your walk."

She sat beside him, looked down to her hands but did not offer them to him as any sort of gift or confirmation. "Well, then," she said, "I'll have to be more careful. I'll have to make of my face a mask, as you have."

He chuckled.

But suddenly, her sense of well-being, accomplishment dissolved. The world loomed solid, crowded in from every direction. Everything seemed futile. "Why does he hate me?"

"He doesn't hate you," said the large and very fat monk. "He sees you as the solution, all that he's waited for. He sees you as the feminine archetype, the image of his own soul."

"Damn his soul. What can I do?"

She waited. It took quite a while for him to answer. "You could lie to him," said the large and very fat monk. "Pretend to go along with it . . . until he himself leads you out of here. . . ."

"Never."

He nodded. "Well there is another possibility."

"What? Tell me."

"You could simply accept the situation."

"Accept this concentration camp?"

"Well, then . . . perhaps there is yet another possibility."

"Tell me."

"You are yoked to him by conflict. Perhaps . . . if you loved him as he loves you."

"Love him!"

"Love him or ignore him," advised the large and very fat monk with a shrug. "It's your choice."

Twisting toward him she demanded, "How can I ignore him? He won't leave me alone! He's always watching, waiting, thinking up a different tactic. How can I ignore the goddamned wall!"

The large and very fat monk crossed his legs, put one arm to the back of the bench. "You've seen walls before. What do you think is beyond that wall, but other walls. In that sense it's an illusion."

Head lowered, she said evenly, "I will concede nothing. I will at least die with my spirit intact."

"You ask for my help," said the large and very fat monk, "but you set your own terms."

"Honorable terms."

"Honor matters most to you?"

"Yes."

"Are you sure? More than the work?"

"Oh . . ." she sighed, weary, exasperated. "I can't make such abstract distinctions. I can't really separate them. They're really one and the same thing."

"Well, then . . . you see why I can't help you."

On the bench, within herself, she sank down. "Yes," she said finally, without looking at him. "And you see why I both love you and hate you, for one and the same reason."

He nodded.

So they sat for quite some time.

"Wait a minute . . . wait a minute. . . ." Head lowered concentration. "I don't have to fight him. Why should I fight him? Reason. That's it. I'll reason with him." Abruptly she got up and left the bench.

Full of renewed purpose. The large and very fat monk watched her walk away. *Males*, he thought, shaking his head, *seem to harbor illogical emotions. Females, illogical ideas.*

Centered with hothouse gardenia buds in an onyx bowl, the small table before the fire in Giroux's study was set with hand-painted china, edged in dragons of black, red, gold; white candles, utensils of gold.

For the conciliatory occasion Jaiyavara had gone to a great deal of effort to gild the lily. Her dress was deep turquoise, a necklace of turquoise entwined in her hair, the largest stone at her forehead. She was making a heroic effort to be charming, yet beneath all the gilding the strain was apparent. The effort, the wine, the heady gardenia incense had given her a dull headache. Her waist was cinched too tightly. The fire was too hot.

Giroux also, she realized, was making a special effort, he was behaving gallantly.

"Did you notice the date?" he asked, flourishing the bottle. "I've been saving this for just such an occasion. No wine like French wine. It's the subtlety of blending." He refilled their goblets.

"I have always appreciated," she said, "French subtlety."

"Blending. Yes. Well." Puzzled, a little suspicious, he settled back in his chair, watching her. "I must say," he rallied, "that's a beautiful dress. Did you make it?"

"Yes."

"How very clever you are, Jaiyavara. You know, I think you're even more exotic now than when I saw you on stage years ago."

"Back then," she said, toying with her fork, "I dreaded the years. I feared growing older. Now it doesn't matter."

"No, no," he assured her. "You're ageless. Eternal."

"I said . . . that it doesn't matter."

"It's the planes and angles of your face, the high cheek bones, the bone structure. Has anyone ever painted you?"

Inch by inch, her eyes lifted.

"Someone," he fumbled, "certainly should have. . . ." Dangerous ground, he realized, too late, and cast about for a better topic. "I have something to show you." Giroux went to his desk, unlocked the drawer and brought the scrapbook to the table. Pulling his chair close, he placed it in her lap.

"You saved all this?"

"Over the years, yes. Some of them very difficult to come by. Look at this one at the ballet school. One of my favorites. And this one. Do you remember? Marvelous, isn't it?"

"Even my mother," she said, slowly turning pages, "never kept a scrapbook." But she seemed, he noted, more bewildered than pleased. She kept shaking her head, making small comments. "I'd forgotten." Or, "Not very good." "I wish they hadn't." "But none of these," she said finally, "except when I was very young, are really me. It's all a sort of fascade that's forced upon you. Just the system," she shrugged. "But I was guilty for complying."

"You complied less than anyone I've ever known."

"No, not really."

Tolerantly, she waited it out, as Giroux poured over every clipping and photograph. She closed the book, picked up her wine glass. "I'm flattered," she said.

He stiffened. It was what people said to nonentities they wanted to be rid of. He had said it himself, many times. He took the scrapbook back to his desk, returned, moved his chair back in place, sat down facing her.

Hands folded in her lap, she was very quiet, very measured. "Giroux. I'm prepared to be reasonable. I'm prepared to listen . . . to your . . . your plan."

"Excellent! You see, when civilized adults make a sincere effort. I'm so relieved. Hear me. Let me speak. That's all I ask."

"I will. But in return, there's one thing I want."

"I knew there was a catch to it. What?" he asked tightly.

"These walls. I can't breathe. I'm getting claustrophobic. Take me up to that mountain that faces the sea. I can't tell you how I yearn to go there. I'll listen there."

"But I can tell you here," he said, spreading his hands. "The perfect ending to a pleasant evening."

"No, not here. I'm groggy with food and wine. I need to breathe. Close to the sea I can think more clearly. Compromise, Giroux."

Shifting in his chair, he said pedantically, "You're being inflexible."

Anger flared, her eyelids widened. She subdued it. "So are you. The French," she reminded him, "are famous for compromise."

"I don't know. It's a long ride and the weather is bad." He cupped one hand to his chin, fidgeted with the knife. "Too difficult now. And then, there's your back . . . the risk."

"I've ridden horses all my life. Going slow is no risk. I'm not accustomed to being so confined. We have to decide on some terms that are acceptable to us both. We could start early, take a lunch. It would be an adventure."

"I should think," he said caustically, "that you would have had enough adventures to last several lifetimes."

Head tilted, she became a little flirtatious. "I'm insatiable."

"Yes . . . well, I don't know. I'll have to think about it."

"Do, then." She put both hands on the table, pushed back. "Do think about it." Rising, she said, "The supper was lovely. Thank you."

"So soon? You're leaving now?"

"I walked a lot today. I'm tired."

"I'll escort you to your room," he said, rising also.

"That's not necessary. I think I can find my way."

"Please. I insist."

Walking the lamp lit path he did not touch her, he did not take her arm. For so long he had rehearsed his ideas, close to his heart there was a sinking sensation, much as an actor whose one great scene has suddenly been cancelled. He carried a terrible grudge of disappointment. Low and long and wavering, they heard a wolf howl. Apropos, Giroux thought. Barking whoops and calls answered. "They're not all wolves," he explained. "I've seen them with the binoculars. The first was a wolf. The others are domesticated dogs who have reverted to the wild."

"Then it hasn't all been for nothing," she said, feeling Varrick's spirit near.

Giroux turned his head sharply. "What a strange thing to say."

Arms tucked inside her sleeves, she kept walking.

Veering from the path, hoping to be invited in, he took a shortcut to her room. Unable to see in the dark she took his arm. "You never did tell me," he dared, "why you contemplated suicide."

"No, and I never will."

Passing close to the arbor shelter they overheard the unmistakable struggles, panting sounds of arduous love-making. Without comment they continued. Finally Giroux said, "Out in this weather. What fools."

"Back to nature," she smiled. "Do you realize that Karen is in love with you?"

"What do I care? It's of no consequence."

Chapter Fourteen

"She's very attractive."

"Oh yes, the little slut. That might well have been Karen back there. I have more important things on my mind."

A lamp hung beside her door. Turning, she could see his face clearly. "When I said that Thandon was impotent . . . is that your problem, Giroux?"

Momentarily caught off guard, shocked, he quickly recovered. Tenderly he took her hand in his, lifted it to his lips, kissed it. "I don't want to possess you, Jaiyavara. I want to give you."

Leaning against her door, watching him disappear into the cold night, she was forced to admit . . . that in that one moment . . . he was superb.

Ceaseless snow. At the window Jaiyavara watched it accumulate to an engulfing overlay. Four books, open at her place, lay face down on the bed. "Boring, boring, boring. How long can this last?"

"All winter," Alexis replied. She sat sewing, a mug of tea on the floor beside her chair.

"There's no music in this place."

"Doyle has a dulcimer. But . . . come to think of it he never plays it. He's always tuning it." Alexis sipped tea. "How did the supper go?"

Jaiyavara sighed. "Very strange. We were both extremely polite. I tried to negotiate. I asked him to take me to the mountain." She put a hand to her center. "But I can't be near him without feeling something go out of me. Physically drained. He somehow . . . just sucks the life out of me."

"That is odd. Everyone else seems invigorated by him."

A long silence.

"You would think," Jaiyavara said, "with all the stuff carted here, someone would have wanted a piano, someone would have brought a violin."

"Someone did, years ago. Neville, I think his name was. Very lively music, he played. Fiddle music, he called it. But he didn't stay long."

"And no wonder." Restlessly, she moved from the window. "My hands nearly froze in the cave yesterday. So I quit and came in. I offered to help in the kitchen. They didn't need me. Work! How vital! I could scrub some floors, paint some walls. He won't let me do anything!"

Before Alexis' eyes she switched from moodiness to strident anger, began pacing, enjoying her rage a bit; there was in her a great deal of Denise, the urge in venting it, to dramatize. "Why? Why?"

With some inkling of what she was up to Alexis decided not to be taken in. "He thinks you're special," she said dryly, and never dropped a stitch.

"Special enough to die of boredom."

"Well, I get bored. It's the human condition. I miss newspapers. I used to read the newspapers when I was bored to death. Giroux asked me, what does she do all day? I said, she reads, she walks, she bathes, she thinks. It's good for you to stay in for awhile. He's becoming suspicious."

"You lied for me?"

"Well," Alexis said, her eyes on the sewing, "I think you're special."

Once more at the window, Jaiyavara folded her arms, took up her watchful stance.

"I have some wonderful green velvet I've been saving. Would you like to make another dress?"

"To wear to the opera, I suppose."

Alexis sighed.

"I have never before in my life felt so superfluous. So utterly useless. Maybe that's how he wants me to feel. Maybe that's his strategy for wearing me down."

"You're not useless. Bethune adores you. And Anthony . . . and. . . ."

"Just out of morbid curiosity," Jaiyavara interrupted, "just what the hell would he have me do?"

"Participate. Become interested in the future of this place. Attend lectures, meditate, chant. . . ."

Hissing vehemence. "Ssshit!"

Casting about for some advice or solace, Alexis put down the sewing, went to Jaiyavara at the window. "Listen, when the weather clears . . . just by chance, if he does take you up to the mountain . . . promise me that you won't do anything foolish."

A hurting twist came to the corners of her mouth. "But," she said, gazing out of the window, "I am an entirely foolish person, Alexis."

Through nights of silence, monotonous days, sporadic in its gusts and swirls, still the snow falls. Wrapped in a blanket Jaiyavara sits on a patio bench overlooking the frozen stream. The gong sounds. Monks move toward the Zendo. Dully, she watches. *Day after day. Year after year. Ever the same.*

On his way to the Zendo Anthony stops before her. Her dark eyes glitter too brightly in her numb face. "Jaiyavara?"

"Waiting, waiting. Everything on hold. Waiting for what? I could almost wish for an earthquake."

Only then does he realize how serious her talk of escape. He walks on toward the Zendo. The swagger drops from his shoulders. *We were high on wine, for God's sake. Easier said than done,* he thinks.

The chanting begins. Jaiyavara gets up and walks to the underground entrance. She thinks of digging tunnels under the wall. Who would help? Standing in the doorframe of the library, still she can hear them from above, chanting, chanting. Her glazed eyes stare at the burdened shelves. *Sick to death of verbal visions. Sick to death of second hand visions. Hearsay.*

She walks back to the wine cellar, walks up and down, up and down among the racks. She grabs a random bottle by the neck, tests the weight of it. Through the creaking roof of the wine cellar another chant seeps down. She hurls the wine bottle against the stone wall. *Satisfying. That little crash. Something happened.* She grabs another bottle, turns, hurls it against the opposite wall.

Could stay down here all afternoon, fill the cellar with spilled wine, broken glass. Another bottle in hand, raised to hurl to hell. But her arm in a wide weakening arc comes down limp. *Why cut off my nose to spite my face,* as Lou Iris used to say. *What would that prove? What's the use?*

Jaiyavara takes the bottle to a dim corner, sits on the floor, one knee raised, pulls the cork.

At the head table, centered by the most loyal, Giroux's throbbing tooth has abated. His children are drawn close. The snow falls. The fire crackles. It is the time of the evening meal. Yet outside, beyond the subdued clatter of dishes, the buzz of voices, the domestic warmth, a razor wind trills and slashes in its headlong rush toward the sea.

Alexis keeps watching for Jaiyavara.

Still disturbed by the way she looked earlier, Anthony sits apart from Karen, apart from everyone, alone.

In his pocket Jethro has a new poem to share with Jaiyavara, written to her, for her.

Would she think me ridiculous, Doyle wonders. If I asked her? If Jaiyavara laid her hands on my swollen leg . . . could it help? It couldn't hurt.

Karen's hand curves gracefully to the stem of her water glass, her wrist droops. Sure that she is within Giroux's view, in some unexplainable anticipation her heart thuds hard.

Bottle in hand, Jaiyavara staggers in. She has been drinking all afternoon. Wine cellar cobwebs are in her hair, gray-green. Strands of snow wet hair hang in her face as if tangled with seaweed. All conversation stops. In childlike alarm, monks look from Jaiyavara to Giroux. She stumbles, catches herself against an empty table.

Giroux's eyes darken, but he makes no move to restrain her. She has made an entrance. So be it, he resolves. Let the curtain rise.

Spilled wine splotches the front of her green blouse. Wine-smeared, her mouth is lewd. She tilts the bottle, drinks in lecherous gulps, wipes her mouth on her long sleeve. Mouth hidden by her sleeve, she stops, she stares at them with burning eyes.

Cowered, Ruben does not move, but like a beaten dog who would like to sneak away, his eyes roll slowly sideways. The two Oriental monks are as fascinated as if a medieval witch had appeared. Jethro senses a soaring wrath. Bethune trembles.

"So." Sagely, she nods. "Holed up for the winter, cozy little family supper, are you?" Voice slurred. "Why aren't you out slaying dragons? This time of year." She mimics Giroux. "Hmmm?

Hmmm?" She waves the bottle at them. "You smear shits." Then, head back she rises up within herself, nodding, stalks up and down between the tables looking into each stunned face with haggard contempt. "We just sat there too. Waiting to die. What do you know? Nothing. You know nothing. So. What else was there to look forward to? Well, guess what, this end of the world retreat. You holy holy ass tasters."

As if the disease itself walked among them, rapt with revulsion they follow her every move. Staggering against another table she knocks dishes to the floor, each separately reverberates, shattering. Alexis rises, her face shadowed, old and pale. Never taking his eyes from Jaiyavara, Giroux puts his hand to her shoulder, with silent force pushes her back down to her chair. Alexis sits rigid, as if strangled with a gag.

"So many . . . so many . . . despised the earth while sucking it dry. Vultures. Picking its bones. Missed it all, didn't you? Sitting up here in your up-down valley on your soft asses. Sitting on your shelves like dolls in a closet." Hand to forehead, she looks down, disoriented. "Where am I? Where was I?" Her head lifts. "Minding my own business, for one thing. Great woe at last to middle men. The first to go when the center shifted. Stockbrokers. Speculators. Analyzers. Theorizers. Advertisers. Woe at last to arrogant head waiters," she laughs, raising the bottle high. "But not to teachers. Twenty million of you," she says with a sweep of her arm, "could dance on Salvini's eyelashes and never be noticed. Teachers and warriors. A few last warriors. People feared, more than all your fake gods, each other. Back to the mine shaft. Back to the cave. What did eternity ever have in mind, but burying everything. But," she laughs, "thanks to your great leader here, I am that fiend taken into your gates who will suck your insipid blood while you sleep. There's a mushroom out there that intends the same thing. Do you believe me? Well, where do you think you came from? Hmmm? Think you drizzled down from heaven like snowflakes? Blood and slime you came . . . from between a woman's legs. You diddlers. You turded clods."

Near Jethro she blindly staggers. He leaps to help her. She whirls in fury. "Sit down, mother-fucker! Hide in your half ass notebooks. Traitor! Where the hell is your blood!" She points to Giroux. "You're not on to him *yet*, are you?" With violence she turns to the others. "Still in chains, all of you, all of you. Those who died first, like pitiful dogs, bred to such rarity, a few simple basics out of them. Generations of inbred greed. Couldn't smell, couldn't touch, couldn't hear, couldn't see. Couldn't love. Couldn't even fuck." She drinks, wipes her mouth. "You screwdrips. You voidholes."

Very carefully she sets the empty bottle on the table, makes a "stay there" motion to it with her hands. Brother Bethune puts a trembling hand to his downcast eyes. Jaiyavara sniffs, looks for an instant as if she might cry aloud in pain. Instead, she smiles, wipes her mouth again. "Don't worry, I'm about to pass out. Threw up twice already. It didn't help. No, it didn't help. Oh," she snarls, "don't let any of those mere artists of the past disturb you. Ignore them. Kill them. Let big daddy here take care of you. Do as you're told. Like them. Big executive on the fortieth floor. Big decisions. Will he join the exodus? Not him. A responsible person, he is. Responsible for all the shit. Entombed, no doubt on the fortieth floor . . . to this . . . this very day. . . ." Her head rolls back. As she falls, unconscious, Anthony grabs her.

Giroux moves swiftly. Anthony hesitates. Their eyes lock. Anthony forfeits Jaiyavara. Giroux carries her from the dining room.

Throughout the night Giroux sits beside her bed. At dawn she mumbles and turns, reaching as if for a lover, grasping at emptiness. Then she moans, holds her head.

Elbows on his knees, Giroux leans forward as she wakes. "Not bad, Jaiyavara. Not bad at all . . . for a first sermon."

Chapter Fifteen

Fine and white powdered, soft puffy little piles of snow accumulated on the broad shoulders of the large and very fat monk, lay undisturbed in the spread black robe of his lap.

If anyone, said the large and very fat monk, *expected remorse from Jaiyavara for that vituperative outburst, they were very much mistaken. She acted as catalyst. When the winter wind howled there were those who drew close to the fire, and saw in licking flames those lit pyres for the dead. More than a few, thankful for their spared lives, went to their appointed tasks with energy renewed, purpose reactivated. Brother Bethune painstakingly copying ancient manuscripts bent with renewed dedication to his thankless task. And . . . it occurred to many to give thanks to their separate deities that they had not been born . . . as Jaiyavara.*

The cock crowed. The snow began to thaw. Dripping, trickling, it came down from the rooftops, seeped from the crevices of rocks, in merry riverlets raced down hills and banks to converge at the stream. Netted lines in the ice of the stream reached and cracked, in whisper splits spread as if animated. Solid chunks of ice separated, turned in the flow, in growing momentum began to move, breaking away.

Facing the stream, sunk down between claw roots Jaiyavara sat against the enormous oak which dominated the hill, spread majestically against a sullen sky. The roots were beaded with pale green moss—was the sea once here? Beyond the upper branches, still bare, a stagnant amassing of clouds. Cloud haloed, barely visible, the sun glowed like an iridescent pearl. Her drunken ravings, what had they accomplished? Nothing. Now the others avoided her. Even in those few who did not move away she felt an inner recoil, withdrawal; they spoke to her, peered at her from behind a polite veil. As perhaps nowhere else on earth, peace reigned here—but at what price? Limbo. Ironically, the only person with the slightest glimmer of what she was trying to say was Giroux. Only the enemy applauded.

How did they exist entirely in the present? Even the youngest of them seemed to believe that they were changeless, as fixed and finished as manufactured products. She knew herself as a progression. Layer on layer she was saturated with memories, deepening, mellowing in time. Memory expanded the present, gave it depth and detail and contour. She could not, like a serpent, shed her skin every spring. Even the future, she sometimes suspected, like plaintive music reverberated, echoed back to the here and now.

Working it out. In every line and angle, every balance, counterpoint of color and composition. How could she make Giroux understand that these multitudinous complexities, choices, were as necessary to her as water and air, granted her life day by day? Nor was it only a personal past which she could not deny. In the dim recesses of human history, the pre-birth of consciousness . . . those who had scrawled on the walls of caves, those with the compulsion to convey something of what they saw and felt . . . in their lives . . . in their time. They had bequeathed a heritage. She could not forsake them. They had stalked the elusive, ever fleeing prey—beauty—from all ages and races they had driven it forward.

It was there still. Hidden, lurking, lying in wait. Her turn now, to hunt, to stalk, pray humbly in darkness, flush it forward toward the open future. Where did it come from?—the unfounded, yet undying conviction that every work of art, known or unknown, seen or unseen, hidden, buried, or lost; still, somehow . . . helped keep the universe in motion.

She had been sitting for hours. The clouds dispersed. The sky became gaunt and stretched and hollow, inverted like a useless drum.

An eerie tingling at the back of her neck, a ringing in her ears, she felt as if she were sinking, fainting away. Colors were fading, lights were going out. She was cold. She felt an icy perspiration. A knot of force gathered at her center, became motion, heaving, roiling.

In a soft eruption it broke from her center. Physically she felt it leave.

It became separated, the scene before her, with its own inner luminosity. She saw Anthony climb a tree close to the wall with a thick rope in his hands. The scene then skipped, jumped, it was not time linked. She saw herself as a young girl in a frothy white dress replete with pink ribbons. I never wore such a dress, she thought critically. She watched the young girl climb into the swing Anthony made for her. Existence doubled, both observer and observed, she was one consciousness in two separate bodies. She was both beneath the oak and in the swing.

In the swing, the hard board beneath her, she could feel the scratchy rope in her hands. Pushing upward she felt the swishing flow of her hair, heard air rushing in her ears. Below, Anthony stood watching as with each pull she worked higher, higher. Soaring to the full reach of the swing she was on a level with the top of the stone wall. Reaching the peak of the arc she will leap from the swing, fly over the wall. Anthony disappears. He is on the other side of the wall, waiting to catch her in his arms, bring her safely to earth.

Now! Now! Launching into the air, a leap for escape, an effortless slow motion flight.

Gottrell appears with a shotgun, takes aim.

Soundless explosion.

Gottrell becomes Giroux. A bow, a gold tipped arrow in his hands, Giroux takes aim.

Arms outstretched as she flies, the arrow catches her in midair. Gasping at the impact, it pierces between her breasts. In heartbeat spurts blood gushes out; hot, red-vivid, soaking her white dress. Backward, head first, in a slow motion dive she falls.

Gottrell stoops to pick up a dead bird at his feet. Swaying from his hand its neck and head hang down limp. He puts the bird in the large burlap bag, stands, scans the sky for something more to kill.

Giroux picks up the dead bird pierced through with the arrow, turns to a large wooden symbol of Venus, grasps the arrow in his fist, stabs the dangling bird into the soft apple-wood.

The scene vanished.

Giroux, at a distance, saw her in profile, sunk down between the roots, leaning head back against the oak, fallow hands open in her lap, apathetic, lifeless, dazed.

This will not do, he decided.

The gates are opened . . . said the large and very fat monk. *I watch them leave. Giroux and Jaiyavara. As they begin that arduous ascent on horseback of the mountain which faces the sea . . . I hear it again . . . the somber bells, the sad, deep, inexorable music. Jaiyavara sits forward in the saddle, taunt with expectation. Tugging at the bit, the black mare dances beneath her, working herself into a premature, excited lather. Giroux urges her to hold back on the mare. Giroux's dark red stallion, a sober beast with a powerful arch of thick neck, plods earnestly forward. Clinging to the narrow twisting path which circles the mountain, Giroux in the lead, they labor upward. Jaiyavara is frustrated that she must meekly follow, there is no room on the path for her to pass him. They reach the summit. The music ends. Walking their horses they cross the wide grassy plateau to the edge of the cliff.*

Beneath vaulted heavens, limitless waters spread westward before them. After a long silence Giroux dismounted, walked his horse back toward the trees and rocks, tied him to a scrubby bush and left her alone there.

Slumped down in the saddle Jaiyavara inhaled, a gutfull ease spreading through her, the relief of one who has finally reached home. Taking the now-settled mare to the very edge of the cliff, she looked down, a sheer drop of three hundred feet. Then she backed off. A strong sea wind whipped and tangled her hair about her face, beat her clothing against her body. Up and down the empty beach she watched white scrolls of foam on each wave crest and curl in, curl under, disappear into the sand. Her eyes swept the horizon, searched the indistinct transfiguration where sea and sky merged. Mama, she thought. How brave to make that long dreaded journey on that ratty little boat, a child in your arms. Looking down the beach to the left, a pile of boulders jutted out into the water, basking in sun and spray.

What were the gardens at the palace of Versailles compared to this? Nothing man-made—all the palaces and cathedrals of London, Paris, Rome; all the temples of Greece—could not compare with it. Here no evidence of anything man-made, like looking backward in time. How beautiful the entire planet must have been, she thought, when the world had itself all to itself.

Head high, she whispered fiercely, "Vishnu . . . Vishnu . . . to work . . . to accomplish. I serve Vishnu. Krishna, warrior. Vishnu . . . Krishna . . . Varrick.

Wheeling the mare, she kicked her into a reckless gallop, raced the full length of the plateau. Still the daredevil, Giroux thought, watching anxiously. Back and forth four times she raced in sheer exuberance, exhilaration; in sheer celebration of the wide expanse of freedom. At last she dismounted, tied her mare close to the stallion. Giroux took their lunch from the saddle bag, close to the mountain boulders spread a cloth beneath a tree. "So," he said, "Are you satisfied?"

"Yes." She was still breathless. "I thought I would never see it again."

"Come then, let's eat."

She helped him spread the lunch. Gourmet vegetarian. He unwrapped crystal wine goblets, wiped them clean, held them to the light. *Mais oui, mais oui.* How precise, how French. He poured red wine. "To the future," he said, lifting his glass.

"I'll drink to that." Against the boulder she got comfortable. Eating, she kept her eyes on the sea. Here they were sheltered from too much wind. Jaiyavara was ravenous, but Giroux, despite the long climb, had not much appetite. He appeared as they sat and ate, increasingly morose.

Finished, she took a cigarette from her pocket, turning away from the wind ducked down, got it lit. "Come, pour more wine," she invited, and he did. Her cheeks flamed with color, her eyes sparkled. She lifted her glass to the sea. "Mother of life. Mother of all."

Never had Giroux seen her more glowing, more vivid—he drank the wine, but merely grunted to the toast.

"And what a place to dance! Just such cliffs I used to leap from when I was flying."

"Don't you want to forget that?"

"The fall, yes. But not the flying. Never the flying." Flushed and excited as she was, still she remembered her promise. "Well," she said. "Here we are."

He avoided looking at her.

"That's your cue, Giroux."

No answer.

"What's the matter now?"

"It's difficult to speak here."

So much more masculine, she thought, without the robe, in heavy corduroy pants and jacket, a dark shirt open at the throat, dark chest hairs visible. "Why is it difficult?"

Sprawled back, leaning on his elbow, he looked down into the wine glass. Wine red light played on his hands. "I don't know. Words seem ephemeral here." He squinted up at her. "And you knew that, didn't you? You wanted to make it difficult for me."

". . . just give you a different perspective."

"I have concepts. You have instincts." He sat up, held the glass between his knees. "Jaiyavara, think of it. What we could accomplish together."

Having recovered zest, spirit, she could afford to be generous. "If all this intimidates," she suggested, "turn around then, turn your back to it. You face the mountains, I'll face the sea. We'll each look to our own strength."

Dourly, he humored her. They sat facing each other, facing in opposite directions. Gravely he said, "Where to begin. . . ."

"Anywhere but the beginning." Her head was tilted, her mouth flirtatious.

"What a strange woman you are." Sadly he scrutinized her. "How in the world did I ever get mixed up with you?"

"Fixated, you mean. And when you figure that out. . . ."

"Yes, I admit that. But I don't want to figure it out. Psychology does not amuse me. It's all so. . . ."

"Beside the point," she supplied, mimicking him.

"Oh . . . Jaiyavara." Weary, he drank wine, poured more for them both.

"Try the ending." She meant by that, try telling what all this is supposed to lead to. But as usual, he misunderstood, he was much too stolid, literal, sequestered.

"The ending," he said, "began, I think, with modern physics."

His pedantic pause—Now, let's let *that* sink in—irritated her, and so she let herself become distracted by swooping sea gulls far beyond him, so tiny in the distance, diving between his earlobe and shoulder.

"A chaotic universe," he was saying, as she squashed out her cigarette. "All the boundaries of time, space, energy, matter, as distorted and interchangable as *Alice in Wonderland.* Full of sound and fury, signifying . . . God knows what. . . ."

Reluctantly she gave down, submitted to the slant and cast of his disputations, although in this boundless place it all seemed not only trite, but profane. But for the moment she went along, playing modest initiate to his guru. "But didn't they expect that to lead to new discoveries?"

"No, that's when they began to realize that they would never come within light years of figuring out anything. But they wouldn't let go. They were not prepared to turn science into raving mysticism. They clamped down, harder and harder, airtight dogmas. Their frustrations were let loose on us. A backlash. A reversal. Anti-Einstein. All that. It took me years to realize that the real solution was to replace male Logos with female Eros. As a world view. Eros can accept the unknowable." He swallowed more wine, tried to ascertain if she was still with him.

"Go on," she said, like a good housewife.

"The ancients knew the force of the Mother Mysteries . . . Diana at Ephseus . . . the Oracles at Delphi. Four Mothers. The Plague can't last forever. It's a cleansing, a catharsis, to start over, wipe the slate clean. The Greeks and Jews were right to pull out of Mother Consciousness, but now it's time for a return to it."

"Four Mothers," she repeated, more interested in him as a person, at the moment, than in his ideas. Yet the preoccupied scowl she detested was gone. High on the plateau, beyond walls, beyond his crushing dominance, she found herself almost attracted to him. He seemed almost capable of real humor, gentleness, human kindness.

"The Good Mother," he was saying. "The life force. She is the teaching, nurturing Mother. Then also, the Teeth Mother, who stripped man as he passed through, from adolescence to manhood. In primitive cultures she is depicted with teeth in the vagina. Then there is the Stone Mother, or Death Mother. And finally, the ecstatic . . . or the Dancing Mother."

She leaned forward. "The Dancing Mother? Tell me about her."

"When a man feels the force of her," he said slowly, thoughtfully, ". . . he is content to be alone."

"I see . . . I see . . ." Her voice was soft. "Content to be a priest or monk?"

"Yes."

She had an urge to touch him, reach for his hand.

Their eyes met . . . held.

On some level, he knew, he had reached her.

But she looked down, broke the spell. But I am not a mother, she wanted to say. I was too young, too stupid. I should have had Varrick's child. I will always regret that I didn't. An urge to confide, yet some intuition stopped her. Giroux avoided the personal, and he was not yet finished with theorizing.

They could be, he thought, on the threshold. Wanting it so desperately made him cautious.

"In Indian mythology," she offered, "Shiva dances both birth and death. . . ."

He nodded.

". . . both suffering and ecstasy."

Careful, controlled, again he nodded.

She was thinking about it. He gave her time to think. Looking up, looking again straight in his eyes, she asked, "What's in it for women themselves?"

"They will become . . . like pioneers in a new wilderness. Leading the way. They will become," he said, "the high priests . . . to instruct, to celebrate all rites of passage. Not just birth, puberty, adulthood, death, but the phases of the moon, the harvest and the laying by. They will sing and dance and paint and write poetry, once it is all established. They will teach the essences, the omens, and the signs. They will exorcise evil. . . ."

"Exorcise evil? How?"

"By believing," he answered calmly, "that it *can* be exorcised."

Simplistic, she thought. But wanting him to get through it, once and for all, she did not argue.

"I can't do it alone," he added.

"Why not?"

"There must be . . . it's essential at the inception, a charismatic central figure. People no longer trust male leaders, the male principle."

"How right you are about that," she said levelly, without anger. "And I can never trust you . . . the way you destroy. . . ."

"I wanted you to become focused. I'm not infallible. I misjudged . . . your obstinacy. When we join forces, become attuned and trusting, you can keep me from making that kind of blunder."

"I have better things to do, Giroux. And I don't know how to collaborate."

"Better? No, listen. Will you listen? When you found yourself in a strange situation, you dreamed, you danced. Help me teach others to do that. That's all I'm asking."

"What makes you think that sort of thing can be taught? By anyone?" Leaning away from him she dug her fingers down into the gritty soil, taking a hold on tough yellow grass. "You presume too much," she frowned. "You want to remake the world according to ideas. But the world is not ideas. The world is the world. Accept it. You will anger the gods with that kind of inflation."

Agitated, his voice rose. "I'm not trying to compete with the gods! I'm trying to help!"

"Oh, really? That's exactly what science said, remember? Don't you ever learn? Besides, they don't need your help."

"How can you say that? After all that's befallen us?"

"Which did not teach you a damned thing!" She sat straight up. "Male principle, that's the problem. Don't you ever quit meddling? With all these lofty intentions, you begin by trying to force me into something I don't need and don't want. As if the end justifies the means. As usual. As always. You want to control, dominate; only instead of mere physical matter, oh no, you want to manipulate their very souls. Tear down your walls, Giroux. Then maybe, just maybe, I'll begin to listen."

"The wall protects!"

"You lie."

"And what the hell do you want?" he demanded. "Sheer anarchy?"

"You would call it anarchy. I wouldn't. Every man his own builder, his own dreamer. Every man his own artist, his own priest, his own nation. His own everything."

"Impossible! Now more than ever, people need a unifying myth."

"Congratulations, Giroux." Her mouth twisted sarcastically. "You know how to think. Great accomplishment, thinking. But totally insignificant. And why unifying? Your whole scheme is the wolf dressed up like Little Red Riding Hood's grandmother. Logos," she sneered, "in a long skirt. Millions of new myths! To each his own!"

"They can't do that," he pleaded. "They're not strong enough! They don't know how!"

Head back, her face was cold, implacable. "Then," she said, "let them die."

His jaw dropped. It so stunned him, for moments he could not speak at all. "Cruel mother," he accused. "Teeth mother. Death." Deeply pained, he turned away, shook his head. "No. I can't believe it. I refuse to believe you said that."

"Your perverted humanitarianism," she shrugged. "Believe what you like."

Impasse.

For a long while he sat, head lowered, clenching his jaw. Then, his head swung back toward her. "Insignificant!"

Rising to her knees, arms outstretched to the open sea, her voice lifted. "Compared to this!"

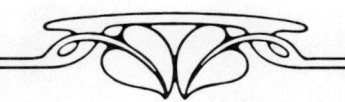

Chapter Sixteen

Near the stream at twilight they strolled beneath tall trees. Anthony and Jaiyavara. Her long skirt made a soft rustling. It was almost spring. As they conspired she took his arm, from time to time put her head to his shoulder. They heard a mockingbird's call, repeated three times. They heard the plaintive whip-o-will.

"Jethro and Brother Bethune are going with us," Anthony said.

"When?"

"Soon."

"Anthony, don't tease. Tell me when."

"Two or three weeks. A month at most. We're making ready."

"And Giroux doesn't suspect?"

"No, he's busy. He's planning more buildings. That's why I think the Plague is under control. He tells us nothing, but I'm optimistic. We'll head east."

"I thought San Francisco . . . or Los Angeles."

"Too dangerous. Los Angeles is under water by now, or floating toward San Francisco. I have friends there, I hope it floats." They came to an embankment. He lifted her hand, studied her jade ring. "We'll go inland. Some small community. We'll paint," he said, brushing her brow with his lips. "We'll make love and grow our own vegetables."

"And then," she smiled, "you will outgrow me."

"Never."

"Of course you will. But that's as it should be." Anthony lifted her, set her on top of the low wall of stones, stood close, his arms around her waist. Jaiyavara plucked a leaf. It lay curled in the palm of her hand. "Some day," she told him, "I'll get to the sea. I have such plans for work, floods of images."

In twilight, he thought, how girlish she looked, her hair loose, her eyes dreamy. He kept his hands at her waist, narrow and warm. "I know . . . I know . . . water dammed up gathers force."

"If I don't get them out I'm going to drown in them."

"You will. Nothing is lost." And like a lost child he buried his head in her lap. She stroked his hair. The moon was full.

"I'm glad," she said, "that Jethro and Bethune are going with us. Did you talk Bethune into it?"

"No." Anthony's eyes were nearly closed. "It got to him, what you said, the night you were drunk . . . sitting on shelves like dolls in a closet."

As they lingered his hands moved from her waist to her thighs. Then he lifted her down from the wall. Arm in arm they walked back toward her room. His throat ached. He was prolonging each moment, unable to believe that she would be with him through the night. And she could feel the pounding of his heart, the hot gathering force of his anticipation. She felt for him a bemused sadness, yet she envied his passion.

In her room Jaiyavara started to light the lamp but Anthony stopped her, stood behind her holding her tightly. Brushing aside her hair, he kissed the back of her neck.

"The male," she said, "approaches from the rear."

He murmured.

"Nothing . . . never mind . . . only a dream."

Lifting her, Anthony carried her to the bed. Descend to this, she wondered? Mere barter? He thought he loved her. Call it compassion, if nothing else, yet such a trite gift, the body. She lay back unbuttoning her blouse, and thought of the large and very fat monk. If he knew of their tryst—and somehow she imagined that he did—he would now be indulgently smiling. Moonglow. She watched Anthony take off his robe. He came to the bed, on his knees beside her, stroked from her bare shoulders to the tips of her fingers.

"It would please me no end, if I got pregnant. For simple biology to defeat him."

"Defeat who? Giroux?" He drew back. "You're using me."

"No more than you're using me." She put one finger to his large Savanarola nose. "Let's be honest."

"Honesty, between lovers?"

"The highest tribute." Her head turned on the pillow, she looked beyond him. "I'm almost tempted to stay and fight him . . . as if we had rehearsed this conflict for a thousand years. . . ."

Anthony unbuttoned her skirt, she lifted her hips as he pulled it down, tossed it to the floor. One hand beneath her neck he lay down beside her. "Now I need to look at you," he said. "When I first saw you under that sheet, you looked half dead. I thought you were going to die. I kissed you, Jaiyavara . . . while you were unconscious."

Promise, she thought, of rescue. She was touched by that school boy confession in contrast to his urgency of lust. She turned to him, feeling his maleness against the full length of her naked body. So long it had been . . . and with every lover since Varrick there was a sense of emptiness, futility. She had been almost celibate, her sexuality sublimated, submerged in work. Passive, willing but remote, she lay against him. When he mounted her she felt invaded. She thought it would be over quickly. But Anthony wanted more from her than mere compliance, ardently worked her into a response.

Not bad, she thought. And then they slept.

In the middle of the night he woke, pulled her to him, full of power, intensity. "Oh," she whispered, "you're insatiable. That's a good sign."

". . . sign of what?"

". . . what you are to accomplish."

He was biting her neck and shoulders, kissing her hotly, ramming his tongue into her mouth, rolling her on the bed, sucking her breasts, goading her with husky whispers; it was words which vanquished her last reserves, writhing in abandonment she was overcome.

They parted, lay back, panting, satiated, spent. Mindless langour. Finally she reached for a cigarette, lit it, smoking, lay on his shoulder, her thick hair spread over his chest.

"Got to you, didn't I?"

Chapter Sixteen

"Yes . . . you did."

"It'll get better and better, believe me."

"Well, you said you would inspire me."

Under all that swagger, she should have guessed, he badly needed that triumph. Karen, evidently, withheld something. One part of her was wide awake, wanted to get up, walk, paint— another part of her was cleansed, easy, reflective. She finished the cigarette, squashed it in a bronze saucer, put both arms around him and snuggled down to go back to sleep.

Giroux burst in, Ruben with him. They were blinded by the glare of Giroux's flashlight. Ruben lunged for Anthony, dragging him from the bed. Anthony fought back. The light swung wildly across the walls, the ceiling, as Giroux got into it. They were beating him. It was all very quiet. Jaiyavara leaped up naked, grabbed a chair, rushed at Ruben. Giroux caught her, with slamming force hurled her back to the bed. Yelling, she grabbed her neck with both hands, crouched where she landed against the wall, immobilzed with pain. They pounded Anthony brutally. She could do nothing. She could not even manage to pull the sheet over her body. She could barely see. They had him pinned to the floor. Giroux held a knife at Anthony's throat. He said to her, "It's up to you."

"You gutless bastard. Blackmail? You won't put that shit on me. Do with him what you will."

Backing down, Giroux growled to Ruben, "Let's get him out of here." They lifted Anthony, barely conscious, dragged him to the door.

He managed to turn, shout back at her. "Bitch!"

They were gone. No barking dogs, no offer of help. If anyone nearby heard anything, they ignored it. Non-involvement. They were famous for that.

Against the wall, hands at her neck, eyes closed, teeth clenched, she eased down slowly on the bed, refusing to weep.

Something woke her, she was not sure what. Moving her head cautiously, testing for pain, she sat up, listening. She went to the window. Narrow iron bars. Outside she saw the two Oriental monks slipping away. They had quietly screwed the iron bars into the window frame as she slept. She walked to the door, tried it. Bolted from the outside. "He wouldn't dare!" she whispered.

She put on a robe, facing the door sat down to wait.

It was mid-morning before Giroux unlocked the door and came in with a breakfast tray, which he put on the table. "You're not dressed?"

"What's the point?"

"Don't be alarmed," he said, nodding toward the window.

"I'm not alarmed. I'm disgusted. You must be desperate. How long," she taunted, "do you think the others are going to allow you to keep me locked up in here?"

"A temporary measure, for your own safety. I don't want you tempted."

"Tempted by what?"

"Aren't you going to inquire about Anthony? Well, Anthony is not seriously hurt, but he is to be put outside the gates."

"And you consider *that* a punishment?" she laughed. "He wants to leave."

"But not alone. He wanted you to go with him." Folding his arms, he leaned against the wall. "For what you have done to him, Jaiyavara, I hope you are contrite. Anthony came to us as a young orphan and found a good home. And no matter what your opinion of me, no one here is dying of hunger or disease or exposure to the elements. It might interest you, however . . . Jethro and Brother Bethune are going with him."

"Your little kingdom begins to crumble."

"No great loss. They'll be back, mark you, banging on the gates, begging to be taken back in."

"Bethune . . . maybe. Not Jethro. Not Anthony."

"Well,'" he shrugged, "we'll see." He gazed toward the window. "How's your back?"

"Stronger than ever," she assured him.

"Good. I didn't mean to. . . ."

"Shut up! No apology can ever undo what you have done."

Unperturbed, still gazing toward the window, he seemed to consider some splintery philosophical detail. "By the way, just out of curiosity . . . who seduced whom?"

She walked to the chest, lit a cigarette, sat down on the bed, crossed her legs, inhaling. "Well now . . . let me see. Oh, well . . .

Giroux ... I seduced Anthony, of course. Think of it, Giroux ... how long can you keep wet towels on my feet of clay?"

"I think you're lying."

"Oh, really? And I think you are."

"About what?"

"Simeon. The radio. Everything. Anthony thought so too."

Again, he shrugged, walked to the door. "Anthony leaves with bitterness toward you. He expected you to care whether he lived or died."

"I do care. I called your bluff. He'll figure that out. And now," she said with cool loathing, "you can begin to wonder who I'll seduce ... next."

Some satisfaction, she thought, as he left. That glassy-eyed glare.

Late afternoon. Feeling too aimless and depleted to attempt even a sketch, she sat on the bed, sure that by now two friends and a lover were gone.

"Jaiyavara."

"Jaiyavara."

Startled, she went to the window. Jethro and Brother Bethune stood close outside. Jethro was tall enough to see directly into her room. Brother Bethune's eyes were just above the window ledge. The better to see and speak with them, she knelt on the floor at the window.

"We've come," Jethro said, "to say goodbye."

"I thought you had already left. Where's Anthony?"

"He's waiting at the gates."

"Is he all right?"

"Badly bruised and sore and enraged," said Jethro. "He'll survive."

"Thank God, you're going with him."

Their faces were solemn, strained.

"Tell him," she said, "that I do care for him deeply, but I could not betray what I am, what I believe."

"I'm sure he knows that," said Brother Bethune. His voice quavered.

"No, I'm not sure he knows. Tell him."

Brother Bethune nodded.

"So . . ." she said, biting her lips. "You're leaving. You see," she said to Brother Bethune, "how strong you are? And you, Jethro . . . I think you will become very wise."

"It was your anger," said Jethro, "that set me free." He looked purposeful, resolute. For the first time she felt some hint of his full potential. "Give us a message," he said, "for others not free."

She smiled. "No message, Jethro. As you can see . . . I am most confined."

"Your prison," said Brother Bethune piously, "is not of your own making."

"I don't know . . . I wonder. . . ." she mused. "I wonder if my own vanity has not made it."

"You look exhausted," said Brother Bethune.

"No, I'm all right. Watch out for vanity, Jethro. It's very destructive." She took hold of the bars. "I wonder . . . if it's possible to cheat the devil by refusing to suffer."

Brother Bethune took heart, made a pronounced effort. "I believe it is, Jaiyavara. I believe it is possible. Christians would call it grace . . . Buddhists would call it acceptance. . . ."

A dark fire lit her eyes. "I would call it the best possible revenge."

"Please," said Brother Bethune, ". . . don't speak of revenge."

"Speak what you speak," Jethro said stoutly. "I will remember."

Tightly, with both hands she grasped the bars. "Tell Anthony to paint as if his life depended on it."

She tried to push one hand through, but could not squeeze it through the tight bars. She could not reach them. "If only I could touch you. . . ."

Brother Bethune's eyes brimmed with tears. "You have, Jaiyavara. You have touched us."

"Go quickly now, before Giroux changes his mind."

"We'll come back for you," Jethro promised. "Depend on it."

"No, don't think of coming back. I'll find a way out. I won't be here. Everything out there will be very different now, very difficult, but I envy the journey that awaits you. You'll help create something new. You'll create something more of yourselves. There's nothing more to say. Go now."

"We'll never forget you," Jethro said.

"God be with you," said Brother Bethune.

"Something . . ." she smiled, "is with me. Take care. Have a good journey."

When they had left she could not move from the window. Oh, but to imagine them walking boldly through the gates. In view, she hoped, of all the others. They would climb that steep path until they reached the ridge to the left of the mountain, disappear over the edge, all eyes upon them. A long road before them. Sunsets depress me, she thought, but light from the setting sun shot through spaces of mountain was focused into slanted glorious prisms. Visible through the trees, the edges of that nearby mountain blazed like new hammered gold.

Orange-gold light as she knelt at the window touched her brow, traced her cheek bones, left cold shadows beneath her eyes.

Two good friends . . . and a lover . . . now they were gone. . . . A long road before them through that arid wilderness.

And so as they departed the sun came down and slowly vanished. Gradually light was sucked out, leaving ephemeral outlines and recesses which filled with depthless pools of shadow and darkness. And as the sun came down, so that day had forever vanished. And still she could not move from the window.

A long road before them . . . A melody. . . .

Chapter Seventeen

Locked in. At the small mirror above the wicker chest, Jaiyavara made exaggerated faces, horrible and droll. She paced. Lying on the bed she relived first sight of far flung cities. She repeated ballet exercises she had labored through as a child. Each morsel of food explored, tongue pressed, was forced to reveal nuances of sensation. Sitting on the floor in yoga position she examined the woven textures of the straw mat, the fibers of the bedspread. Each stone in the wall peered back at her with a separate and invincible secret. Nothing to do but endure it, wait it out; absorbed in gradations of shadow and light, absorbed in contrasts, she was shoring up, storing.

Must make and hold to plans . . . definite strategies.

Fondling all that was left of her gaudy jewelry, reduced to basics, she yearned for the companionship of a cat.

Giroux had lied to the monks that she was on the verge of a breakdown. If, through deprivation, she began to hear voices, hallucinate, he would try to convince her that it was some sort of mystical experience, another argument to include her in his improbable fabrication. This was the worst he could do to her. Let him play his trump. With sheer self-reliance she would defeat him.

The third morning Alexis came to her window.

"What took you so long?"

"I've been attending the old man of the Zendo. He took to his bed again. He's ailing."

"Is it serious?"

"I don't know. He's so cranky and bad-tempered, it's hard to tell. I didn't know about this. Giroux has kept me very busy."

"I'll bet."

"Do you need anything?"

"Cigarettes."

"I'll get them for you."

"Thank you. What's Giroux telling the others?"

"That you're not feeling well. That you are indisposed."

"All this," Jaiyavara sneered, angrily back-flipping her fingers across the bars, "locked up like a criminal, a lunatic, because I am indisposed!"

"I know," Alexis said, guilty by association. "It's terrible, I know. Maybe he thinks they're camped out not far from here, waiting for you to join them."

"Oh, that's not true. They're well on their way by now."

"I know that, but does Giroux know it? Do you want me to talk to him?"

"No. Leave him alone. Let's just see how far he'll go. Given enough rope maybe he'll hang himself. Surely the others will begin to wake up."

At a loss, bravely Alexis cast about for some form of solace, some solution. "Ask God to help you," she advised.

But Jaiyavara's thoughts drifted away, she seemed evasively elsewhere.

> he lifted me and said . . . Show me your teeth
> and I did.   I showed him.
> He smiled   and he was handsome when he smiled.
> for one moment I loved him.
> By God, he said.   You are a Gottrell.

"Jaiyavara . . . did you hear me?"

"Yes, I heard," she said. "I don't want God's help. Just bring me the cigarettes."

Soft drums.
Silence.
Gongs.

Vibrations, spreading circles of sound outward and outward . . . where they reach and touch. Seurat dots and gradations of color, layer upon layer, bounced like sound waves back upon themselves. Some day, to paint those sounds; profligate, spreading. I'll paint blue-white water lilies in pristine iridescence, gently rising, falling on waves, un-anchored, floating out to sea.

Pushing the bed, chair, table, the mat back against a wall, in the middle of the room she began a new dance. To be young again. And remember it all. When I was alone and young I danced in the woods, my partner a slender young tree, turning around it, hand over hand. What music we heard. Memories. Images. Dreams. Enough to last? Oh, yes. Oh, yes. Images . . . slow them down. Don't let them slide through. But then . . . don't wallow in them either. They're all still there, in stillness intact. Don't think of death. To strike a balance between deliberate movement and concentration. But then . . . I'm beginning to feel weightless. In death . . . no time . . . no thought.

This then is eternity.

She went back to the mirror, frowned, stared into her own dark motionless eye with a neurotic, slightly transcendent glint. "Thus she talked to herself," she whispered, "because there was no one else to talk to. Tried to console herself."

And yet again . . . the bells. Ever the bells.

Far out to sea . . . I hear the bells. I am floating in water. Then, this is the past, which is now the present. The future? A precognition? Oh, what nonsense. She shook her head, turned, let her arms float upward, outward, swayed and turned and dipped, ignored the fear, danced it aside, to the corners with the furniture.

Fog. Vaporous, deep, all pervasive, obliterating delineations, boundaries. All is hazy, indistinct.

Approaching the bench of the large and very fat monk, Jaiyavara stops a few feet before him, stands with her hands clasped demurely before her.

As they speak their voices are merged, remote, yet unified . . . as if only parts and echoes of the fog were conversing with itself.

"So . . ." said the large and very fat monk. "You are out on parole."

"The bars are still on the window," she said. "But this morning the door was unlocked. Did you unlock it?"

Softly, he chuckled. "Surely by now you realize . . . I don't go about unlocking doors."

"I can't see very much. . . ." She paused. "I'm just groping through . . . but when the fog lifts I'm going to the cave."

"Going to your love," said the large and very fat monk.

"Yes. Always new."

"It continually amazes me," said the large and very fat monk. "The human capacity to substitute work for love. Or, as the poet once put it, 'The force which through the green fuse drives the flower.'"

"Drives me," she said. And it was final.

(Pause) "Won't you sit down?" he invited.

"No." (A long pause) "So," she said wearily, "it's all love."

"What else?" said the large and very fat monk.

"Then how do you explain Giroux?"

"But I don't explain him. . . . Him, or anyone."

(Pause) "Why does he imagine that the world can't do without him?"

"Some people," gently said the large and very fat monk, "do seem to imagine that, don't they?"

She could not clearly see him, but she knew by the tone of his voice that he smiled. "Why," she persisted, "is he the way he is?"

"Why?" repeated the large and very fat monk. "Why ask why?"

She sighed. (Pause) "I can't seem to keep from asking."

"But Giroux is not the question." (Pause) "Won't you sit down?"

"Just sit down," she said, "and just sit? No. I can't do that. You can just sit, but I have to work." (Pause) "If Giroux is not the question. . . ."

"Why don't you leave Giroux to his own devices."

"I *am* one of his devices. As you well know. Wait. If Giroux is not the question? Wait . . . what is the question? Oh, wait . . . the question is . . . you and the fog. . . ."

Once more he invited, "Won't you sit down?"

"No."

The large and very fat monk nodded and smiled.

Hands folded, shrouded in fog, Jaiyavara inclined her head and backed away, uncertain herself if her obeisance was a mockery or sincere.

"Are you on a hunger strike?" Alexis asked. "You weren't in the dining room this morning."

In a tattered cotton robe Jaiyavara lay on her stomach across the bed, palms down, her legs crossed at the ankles as neatly as if bound. "I got sidetracked . . . the sun in a drop of water on a blade of grass."

"You also missed lunch."

"I'm not hungry." Her long finger trembled as it traced a loop in the bedspread.

"Aren't you feeling well?" She seemed to Alexis, despite lying in bed, very intent on something.

"Would you ask Giroux to have supper here with me tonight?"

Alexis was dubious. "What are you plotting now?"

"Everything."

"Oh, can't you leave it alone for awhile? All this tension between you and Giroux puts everyone in a strain."

"Tough shit," Jaiyavara said, and sat up, pushing her hair back. "We need, once and for all, to get it resolved. A special supper, you know what he likes. I'll fix the flowers, set the table . . . and I need a white tablecloth."

"Giroux," Alexis said primly, "always expects a white tablecloth." He has all the power, she thought, and yet is increasingly humiliated and reduced by every victory over her.

"So . . . you'll do it?"

"I probably shouldn't, but . . . well, all right."

Jaiyavara got up, began pushing furniture, making room for the table in the center of the room.

Revitalized, Alexis thought. Unpredictable, as ever. "I hope you do resolve it. Is this," she asked, "your idea of some sort of celebration?"

Jaiyavara threw her a distracted glance. "You might call it that."

Evening light. The days were longer now. Waiting for Giroux she lounged on the bed, smoked, drank red wine. Black speckled tiger lilies in a black vase. Perfect. On the wicker stand beside the table, covered bowls of food. She stroked and smoothed the large pillow at her back. Everything ready.

Nearly an hour late, when Giroux arrived it was not yet dark.

Chapter Seventeen

"Come in," she said.

Awkwardly, he entered, uncertain of what to expect. Freshly washed, full of rich gleamings, her hair hung thick about her shoulders. Snake thin in a long snug dress of deep rust, she wore necklaces of glittering jet, earrings, many bracelets. Her excessive jewelry seemed to him rather ominous. Her musk perfume was strong. As if the small room was center stage, she lit candles, performing for him alone her unholy sacraments.

"Why are you late?"

"What's the occasion? What do you hope to accomplish?"

"A little privacy. In the dining room you hold court, you reign. Here. . . ." She glanced up at him. "What's the matter, Giroux? Afraid I'm going to poison you?" Facing him, one hand on the back of her chair, she smiled, then picked up her wine glass, as he watched, she drained it.

Cannibalistic, he thought, the red smudged corners of her mouth. "I hope," he said evenly, "that you're not intending to get drunk again."

"Oh, it did occur to me. But no, I'm not going to get drunk. And I'm not going to poison you. Relax. Sit down, please."

Play it out, he thought, as they got seated, as she passed food to him. See what she wants this time. He was not fool enough to believe that she had forgiven him. But perhaps with time to think things over she was now somewhat more amenable to arbitration. Instead of eating, she lit a cigarette. "No one," he frowned, "in the best French restaurants is served while smoking."

"No one is served while smoking in the worst French restaurants." She squashed out her cigarette, picked up a fork. "Have some wine. Maybe it will improve your disposition. Temporarily."

No topic seemed safe, uncharged. Should they, he wondered, talk of her visits to France, to Spain? No. That might lead to inquiries of his youth, his family, his life there. Giroux ate without enjoyment. Eyes averted, Jaiyavara put one elbow on the table, propped her chin in her hand, picked at her food. After several glasses of wine Giroux was still on guard, and his stomach was queasy. Against his better judgment he had taken a mild narcotic for tooth pain. She looked coiled, ready to spring, yet controlled, sure of her timing. Her eyes were very heavily made up, her face gaunt and pale. The thought struck suddenly, could this be a set-up, a sexual enticement? She was not above it with

Anthony. He watched her light another cigarette. Here it comes, he thought, watching her tensely, uncertain whether to expect a verbal attack or a seductive ploy.

Yet neither materialized. Finishing that cigarette, she lit another.

"Who gives you the cigarettes?" he ventured.

She rubbed her temple with one finger. "The fat monk . . . the one who sits on a bench."

Giroux leaned back, shook his head. "I wonder where he gets them."

"He rolls his own."

". . . I mean the tobacco."

Head down, studious, she touched one of the tiger lilies. "You know some of the kids grow their own stashes of marijuana. Why all the fuss over a little tobacco?"

As prologue to this edict, Giroux pressed a white napkin to his mouth and looked down at the table. Something was missing. "You'll have to quit, you know."

She became motionless. The whites of her eyes were very white. "Have to?"

"Surely you realize how destructive to your health, not to mention the bad influence. . . ."

"Oh, I see," she interrupted. "An inhaling symbol would never do. No," she exhaled, blowing smoke at his face, "I do not have to."

He saw her lifted head, her smoldering eyes; saw nothing but her cold relentless hatred. The defection of Bethune, Jethro, Anthony bothered him a great deal more than he let on, even to himself. Jaiyavara had incited it. She could be very dangerous. He had no real allies, no friends, only sycophants, and he carried the burden of the future alone. "It occurs to me," he said with weary deliberation, "that I could kill you."

"Oh, I knew it would. Sooner or later. You think the same thing hasn't occurred to me?"

He let out a deep breath. All his years of waiting, of preparation, had come to this? All his dreams sliding away. . . .

His lack of response cooled her a little. "Even if I loved you . . . I could not do what you ask."

"Love? By love you mean a sexual involvement."

"Oh," she said harshly, "I don't mean that at all. You don't know me at all." She drank more wine, wiped her mouth with her hand, and took note of his distaste. "Might as well accept it, Giroux, I'm a peasant."

"What nonsense. In every way you're an aristocrat."

"No, I'm a peasant. You never listen. Why can't you listen?"

He shrugged.

Not much fight in him tonight, she thought. "Ironic, isn't it? Love, that was your mission, remember? Odd, how many of the so called great lovers of humanity so often speak of killing."

"I only said it occurred to me. Forgive me. I am very tired and you are very stubborn." Giroux kept looking at the table. Something was missing. What was it? He made yet another conciliatory attempt. "It's a pleasant night. Would you like to walk?"

"No." Nervously, she smoked. Constantly, contemptuously.

A sudden buzzing cricket chorus sounded outside, untouched by all human assumptions, sing-song, jeering, a reminder that they shared the planet with life forms which seemed alien, unreachable, repulsive.

"What is it you want, Jaiyavara?"

"I've told you that. Countless times. I want to be left alone. But that's impossible for you."

"And I have told you," he said with measured force, "that I am striving for a future that becomes a poetic essence. Can't you reach beyond yourself? Can't you put aside your selfish ambitions?"

"The future," she said, throwing her napkin to the table. "What babble. Your perpetual alibi. Do you really expect me to believe that tomorrow's truths will somehow emerge from today's lies?"

"What is it you want, some sort of fame?"

"I've had that. That's not what I want." Tensely, she leaned forward. "If you say the time is at hand for this new truth, whatever ... who knows, you may be right. You were right about Thandon. Granted. You were right to see that a disaster was coming. Granted, granted! You may even be right about this symbolic *She*. But, even if by some miracle, *she* did exist ... I could not follow *her*. Where's your common sense? It should be obvious to you by now that it's not me!"

"You're wrong. It is you," he argued. "I've never been more certain of anything in my life. This is a sacred obligation. We must begin. If we fail, at least we fail magnificently. Only by such magnificent failures has human consciousness inched forward. But we won't fail. The myths are all there, in the ashes of the past, waiting to be reactivated, given new meanings. We can create them and we can live them."

"Is this the only idea of your life?" She sprang from the table, moved the candles to the chest. "Give it up! Find someone else. Or think of something else. My God, it's insane! Answer me! Will you give it up?"

"Never."

"You don't see me as I am," she accused, backing away. "You see only what you want to see, only your own projection, something made up from scrapbook fragments." All in one motion, she pulled from beneath the pillow the folded tablecloth, flung it out over the table, unfurled before him.

Blood-smeared, leering. The self-portrait. Hideous. Obscene.

"Mon Dieu! Comment? . . . Qu . . . est-ce que c'est?"

"Feminine principle!" she hissed. "Painted in blood. My own. Menstrual blood."

Clutching his napkin Giroux staggered back from the table, overturning his chair. His eyes bleared, color drained from his face. Holding to the wall, he gagged.

"Try again, bastard."

He heaved, vomit erupted, gushed to the floor. At the edge of the straw mat it lay in a small puddle, steamy and vile.

"Now," she said. "Maybe we're getting somewhere."

Mortified, Giroux wiped his mouth with his napkin, threw it to the floor. He looked to the table for ice water. There was none. Ice water missing. White tablecloth missing. He looked at her. His watery eyes were red, full of violence. "You . . . you're deranged."

As he blundered from the room the cricket chorus rose again, reached a higher, jagged, discordant pitch.

"Oh yes. Oh yes. Does it matter?" she whispered, and soundlessly laughed.

Chapter Eighteen

Deep woods beyond the stream.
The cave in full sunlight.
The cave at midday.

At the waterfall, the blue deep pool.
Young monks in the water, swimming, splashing, playing.
Naked they lie in the sun, stretch flat on the rocks. A lizard slithers close, hides in a dark cool crevice.
Monks climb to the high diving rock. Jaunty and clowning, Leon dances a jig to the edge, flops in for the dive.

At the stream Jaiyavara splashes into the shallows in her boots, leaping from rock to rock, gains the steep bank and enters the woods.
Standing in the shaded arbor Giroux watches. Giving her some time and distance he follows, crosses the stream, tracks her as she makes her way through the woods to the cave.
Stumbling and sliding, laboring to catch up, Ruben follows Giroux.

Chapter Eighteen

Within the cave, on a low stone slab to the right, an array of instruments and small earthen pots. Jaiyavara is crushing powders, mixing colors, with a wooden mallet. In procuring materials, finding substitutes in nature she has had to be extremely resourceful.

The primitive crudeness of the materials is appropriate for the work—a large male figure. The left leg is forward, the right arm is lifted, spear in hand. The figure half crouches, advancing in battle. In rage and resolve the face is tragic, already defeated, heroic. It is the primal male. The warrior. The protector. The pagan God. Varrick.

As she turns to begin she touches the figure on the face, the neck, runs her fingers lightly down the swoop of the shoulder, curves her hand to the hard rib cage. Taking clay in her hands she smooths and strokes it into the thigh.

. . . without failure, Varrick . . . close to death by my own hand, I could never have done this. I could never have dared.

I can touch you again. Out of this mere clay. Earth as you are. Sea as I am. If it takes ten million lifetimes I'll create you again. I know, I know . . . this is arrogance. Conniving with hands, blood, brains, endurance and dreams. You are all I need. It's truly spring. Nothing can stop me. Today I feel immortal. Shiva dances.

The shadow falls. The light is blocked.

Slowly, her wet hands let go, come away from his body. She is very still. Before turning, she knows.

Giroux looms in the entrance of the cave.

Cornered, desperate, she faces him.

Giroux advances. He takes it all in. In these crude tools and materials he sees, as never before, Jaiyavara's boundless endurance, determination. "You would try the patience of a saint." His voice is hoarse.

Behind her, backing her up, full of vengeance, the warrior dominates.

But then, it is only clay.

Giroux advances. "This barbaric image has possessed you long enough. Too long."

She is ready for him. A last defense. She grabs the wooden club. "Don't come near me. Don't. I'm warning you. Don't make me kill you. I will. I will."

Without hesitation, again Giroux advances.

With all her strength Jaiyavara swings back the club, hits him in the head, a dull whacking thud. Giroux falls to his knees. He groans. Blood gushes from his head.

Ruben stumbles in. He sees Giroux on his knees, wounded, bleeding; he sees Jaiyavara drawing back with the club to hit him again. Bellowing, he charges, throws Jaiyavara to the floor of the cave.

Ruben above her, a huge rock in his hands.

Waterfall.

Nude young monks plunging down the slide into the water *screaming* with laughter.

    The cave in full sunlight.

    The cave at midday.

    From within the cave, a loud long agony scream.

Giroux staggers out of the cave, Jaiyavara in his arms, unconscious. Wailing and howling, Ruben follows. Blinded by blood, not keeping to the paths, Giroux pushes through the dense underbrush. He tries to run. His shoulders crash through. The tower bell is sounding. In his head there is a bursting, thunderous roar.

Giroux reaches the stream, wades in up to his waist, flounders, falls. Jaiyavara floats from his arms. He regains his balance, grabs and lifts her again. From every direction monks come running down to the banks, plunge into the stream, reaching to help.

As they are pulled to the bank others watching begin to weep.

Jaiyavara's bloody hands and arms dangle from her body at an unnatural angle. Her wrists are broken. Her hands crushed.

Small and narrow the cell, mean in its austerity. One small window too high to see through provided little light. The stone walls were very high, the rafters and ceiling obscured in shadow.

Her back to the archway and heavy wooden door, Alexis sat by the bed. Jaiyavara lay with both hands and arms heavily bandaged, only the swollen blood gorged fingertips visible.

Chapter Eighteen

A good thing I never had a daughter, Alexis thought, and braced herself as she stirred, dreaded her awakening. Her own dry knotty hands ached and hurt, felt like brittle sticks. A daughter could ravage your heart in ways a son never could. All the years past of dull peace and routine were now a false shattered memory.

Somewhere water was seeping, dripping. Twice Alexis went into the closet bathroom to inspect the rusty plumbing but could not find the source of irritation. Where would it all end? The sight of her lying there, helpless, mutilated, filled Alexis with anguish. Yet so much of it she had brought upon herself. As fathomless as the sea, Jaiyavara's capacity for suffering.

Watching, as her eyes opened, Alexis silently prayed. Dear God, have mercy . . . Dear God, have mercy. . . .

"Where am I now?"

"Next to Giroux's study."

"I didn't kill him?"

"No."

Jaiyavara's clouded eyes moved slowly over the damp walls. "Looks like a dungeon." Her voice was thick, slurred. "What is that sound? Is there a clock ticking?"

"No, it's water dripping somewhere. I couldn't find it. I couldn't stop it."

". . . no, you can't stop it. You can never stop it . . . clock of water." She licked her lips. "Feel so strange. What is it, what is it?"

"John gave you morphine."

"He shuffles me around like an antique. Maybe I am. Refused to paint by computer . . . one critic called me an anachronism." She raised her head a little trying to focus and stared at her bandaged hands and arms. ". . . Oh, my God. . . ."

Tightly gripping the arms of her chair Alexis' back stiffened, for an instant her eyes closed, her lips soundlessly moved.

"Oh, my God. Ruben. It was Ruben. I can't . . . can't move my fingers. Oh, my God." She raised both hands before her. "Two dead mummies."

Alexis leaned to her, wiped her face with a damp cloth. "No, now . . . don't talk like that. They'll heal."

"Feel so strange . . . so strange. Suppose if I were a singer someone would cut out my tongue."

"No, hush now. You're being morbid. Can you sit up a little?"

"I think so."

"Try. There, that's it. Push with your elbows. Sit up a little now and let me feed you." Alexis fussed with the pillow, helped her. It had not fully sunk in, Alexis thought. Anything for a distraction, anything to postpone it.

Dazed, drugged, Jaiyavara at first did as she was told, opened her mouth, swallowed the food Alexis fed to her, but soon shook her head, turned away.

"A little more. Just a little more. Please, my darling, you must eat."

"Can't. Feel sick. Nauseated." The grotesque right hand moved to her mouth. "Useless. Hopeless." As she held the hand before her face, her mouth twitched spasmodically. "My God, I'm helpless!" Her burning eyes turned on Alexis. "Food. It's your cure for everything."

Alexis felt it coming, the attack.

"Work . . . in the cave?"

"Let's not think about that now."

"Tell me. He destroyed it, didn't he?"

"I don't know . . . I'm not sure."

"Don't lie to me, Alexis. He destroyed it, didn't he?"

"I think he went back . . . I'm not sure. He's badly hurt himself."

As if to control the twitch in her mouth her upper lip curled back.

"Stones . . . all those stones . . . clawed out with my bare hands. Hands cold and raw. One by one, all those stones." Her eyes closed, she put both bandaged hands to the side of her head, slid down in bed.

Alexis was afraid to touch her. She looked crushed at the center.

"His horrible jealousy. His horrible vengeance."

"Jaiyavara, please. . . ."

"Go away. Go away."

"I know this is a terrible shock, a terrible thing for you, but believe me everything will look better in the morning. Believe me, you'll leave here some day. Things will some day be normal again."

"Never for me."

"You're not helpless. I'm here. I can do everything for you."

"You don't understand. Leave me alone. Go away." From her closed eyes tears flowed, streaked her face into a mosaic of small separate pieces.

"Even if you can't work . . . you can adjust to it. You can teach. You can be an inspiration to others. . . ."

"Adjust! To this? I wasn't born to adjust! My God, I'd rather be dead! Give me something, Alexis. Let me die quickly."

Alexis recoiled. "What are you saying? Is it the pain? I can give you something more for pain."

She lifted her hands. "This pain, it's nothing. Without it the other would be unbearable. Give me something. Let me die quickly."

"I can't! I love you! What are you saying?"

In drunken fury Jaiyavara raised on her elbows. "Get away from me! Get out of my sight! I can't bear the sight of you! I can't bear the sight of anything!"

Backing toward the door Alexis pleaded, "Just stay still. You'll hurt yourself. I'll get John. . . ."

Viciously Jaiyavara lashed at her. "A good mother knows how to give death, as well as life. Did it ever occur to you your sons might have gotten themselves killed to escape from you? Spoon-feed someone else! Find another victim! Get out of my sight!"

Struck to the core, Alexis fled.

At midnight John Bain came to the cell to administer another morphine injection. By then the throbbing agony of her hands had spread throughout her body; she did not resist.

"I'm staying," Bain said, "long enough to attend you. Then I'm leaving. They saw Giroux bring you in like this, some of the others are leaving." He walked to the door.

"Wait."

He turned.

". . . fat monk who sits and sits on the bench . . . where is he now?"

"Still there. Why, do you want to see him?"

"No. I want to see Ruben. Karen and Ruben."

"Wait until morning. Take advantage of the injection. Get a good night's sleep."

". . . won't sleep until I see Ruben."

Useless, he realized to argue. "All right, I'll tell her to bring him."

She fought to stay awake. Slanting from the high window, a hazy moonshaft.

Ah . . . and lespedeza. Fields of it, that clover green hay, thick, whisper waving in a breeze. She could see it, could smell its sweet pungent aroma. Cut green, baled brown. Fed to livestock. The only faith Gottrell ever kept. To the land. Bequeathed by generations of farmers. Nitrogen extracted from the soil by cotton, replaced by lespedeza. And the tall tough serica . . . planted on hills, ravines, to prevent erosion. Sweeping acres of lespedeza and gullies of serica . . . as beautiful as their names. . . .

. . . or if shattered rock and clay should fall like seed . . . if works of art could spring up seeded, renewed, in remote and unlikely places . . . if someone should find them. . . .

Ethereal configurations forming in air. Accept the gifts of morphine at midnight. He had not changed. No, never would he change now. Leathery skin crinkled, etched in a network, tight wiry curls of hair bushy white. Humming and rocking . . . rocking and humming. Gatemouth.

". . . ole rock-in chair . . . got me. . . .
an I'm . . . sing-in . . . th . . . blues. . . .
. . . ole rock-in chair . . . got me now . . .
. . . an I ain't got nothin . . . to lose. . . ."

Soothing, lulling her violent wrath, easing it down. Struggling upward she sat with bandaged hands on her knees. From far beyond other black voices took the refrain, that low sweet melody. Eyes closed, Jaiyavara rocked and swayed. One soprano, pure and lilting, sang out, perfect in counterpoint.

Punch drunk fool at midnight. Never mind, never mind. Nothing to lose. Music fills the cell. Accept the music.

As the door opened Gatemouth faded, the music vanished. Ruben hung back, cringing, quietly sobbing, guilty. Until she saw him she did not know what she intended. Tricks her eyes were playing?—that in the shadows, how beautiful his raw angelic innocence. Everyone had given up on him, refusing to acknowledge in his perfect body the faintest spark of selfhood. What was his karma? Why was he used so? Karen, in a pale blue bathrobe, her scrubbed face formless and wan without make up; she too seemed fearful.

"Bring him here. Close."

Karen had to urge and lead, pull and coax him to the bed.

Chapter Eighteen

Sitting on a hill with Jethro that early morning . . . just before Ruben grabbed for her hair, grabbed for her beads, and the beads broke rolling in every direction . . . how she saw him coming up the hill and recognized as the child in the hospital corridor on the Riviera. How she saw him. The sun at his back, a roaring light . . . and a huge fist shot through a wall and then a leg, and the stones and the wall began to crumble. Was that what it meant, then? That only innocence could destroy those walls? Could destroy her? But Ruben was not responsible.

". . . and I don't understand anything," Karen was saying. "What can I do, Jaiyavara? Why did it happen?"

"Ask Giroux. He's the one to ask." Her eyes were on Ruben. "Bring him here. Bring him close."

Karen urged him close to the bed. Crying, he went to his knees, buried his face in a sheet.

"Ruben . . . no. It's not your fault. I'm not going to hurt you. Don't cry, don't cry. I don't blame you." Jaiyavara pushed to the edge of the bed, put her bandaged hands to his face. "You were protecting Giroux. I understand that. It's not your fault." She looked up to Karen. "Do you think he understands?"

"I don't know."

Ruben quieted a little, but suddenly it was too much effort, and Jaiyavara lay back on the bed. "He's only a child," she said, her eyelids heavy. "Watch. . . . Take care . . . of him."

"But what should I do? Karen pleaded. "I love Giroux. I can't help it. What should I do, Jaiyavara? I mean for me!"

No answer. Arms stretched at her sides, Jaiyavara slept.

At dawn Giroux faced in the mirror his livid reflection, streaked and blossoming purple, red, malevolent blue. He lay back on the sofa with a cold compress, dozed, dreamed of Adele. He was hurrying through the steamy lamplit streets of Paris, only to find her door locked while she entertained a more prosperous client. She came to the door in a black satin nightgown, invited him in, only to snap a chain around his neck. Then she was Karen. Then she was his mother! He woke groaning, sweating. But he switched it off, refused to dwell on it, immediately consumed with thoughts of Jaiyavara. He felt less hostility toward her for felling him with the club than for the repulsive tablecloth portrait. And she was paying a terrible price. They both needed the world. They could both die of infection from wounds inflicted. Could it all end in just such absurdity? But then, how many now suffered from total loss of faith in any pre-established correspondence between the logic of thought, language, and the logic of reality? The truth was, as Nietzsche proclaimed, that man must learn to live without truth.

Congested with pain, his head seemed to grow larger by the moment. His left eye was swollen shut. The tower bell sounded, out of sequence with anything, one dismal note, off-key. Odd. He should investigate. But he lay back, decided not to, an aversion to showing his swollen, discolored, and shameful face.

Several monks climbed the outside stairway to the bell tower. The thick pulling rope stretched over the narrow railing. The sun was hot. A few feet below, his head stretched to one side, Ruben dangled slowly in a circular motion. His eyes bulged. His face was blue. In contrast, as if painted by a cartoonist, his blonde hair gleamed brash, yellow-bright. A large fly zig-zagged up his chin, over his mouth, and on to his nose.

Karen rushed forward. Catching her in his arms, Doyle blocked her. "Don't look, don't look. You'll never forget."

"Oh . . . it's Ruben," said Sebastian. "The idiot is dead."

"Long live the idiot," Doyle said, as he stroked Karen's wild hair.

In the high, hot, airless cell. Burning with fever. No peace.
Too many visitors.
But from the small high window ledge Dipsy smiled down at her.
Then, some long convoluted story, hard to follow, Lou Iris was into, with righteous indignation her bosom heaved. "Sister McFadden . . . she walks me down th' red carpet in front of the cross an' she says, 'Do you want to give a testimony?' An' I says, 'I do, I do.' An' I says my heart is pierced but I'm givin' honor to God anyway. Somethin' happen in my home last Friday. . . ."

Working the water pitcher closer with her clumsy bandaged hands Jaiyavara sipped through a straw. No such thing as interrupting Lou Iris.

"It ain't William, it's Houston, his son by that first trashy wife. It's Houston that's terrible! All th' time goin' behind my back to William with untruths about me, so I just stood up in church an' told it. I says I ain't namin' no names, but I got to unburden my soul and I can't handle it no more, so I'm givin' it to th' Lord. An' I says that I'm so glad, *so glad* that God is God all by hisself, 'cause He don't need no help . . . but I sure do."

Jaiyavara pressed her burning face against the cool water pitcher.

". . . an' I says I ain't namin' no names, but to think that some people will plot behind your back within your very own home while smilin' in your face and sittin' at your table an' eatin' your food, it disturbs me mightily. An' I says I am feeling rejected! neglected! and betrayed! Amen. If ever you been there, you know what I mean."

"I know what you mean, Lou Iris. I know."

"Listen now, I ain't finished."

"I'm listening, Lou Iris. I'm listening." And Dipsy winked.

"So I just stood up and told it to th' whole congregation, tears rollin' down my face, and the Lord, he sure commenced to deliver me. An' so I could finally, yes, yes, rejoice in the Lord. A-men! I'm tellin' you, Miss Jaiyavara, had it not been for th' Lord, I coulda been in jail for murder today."

Cardinal sin of the South, interruption, rudeness. She sank down, turned on her side, covered her ears with the pillow.

Humidity. Density. Heat. Her ears were ringing.

The memory of all home so green in the far away flatlands. Sneaking through fenced pastures and paddock, up close to the sprawling barn. Hiding in the long grass. Weekend guests for the fox hunt, mounting up. All that was denied her, that showy elegance and finery and serious gaiety in which she could never participate. Helen and Troy also excluded—Troy was usually drunk. Helen feared horses. Baying hounds, a sound both joyous and mournful. Hunters streaked and thundered past on the lean, eager horses. Run little fox, run for your life. Barbarians, all.

The memory of Gottrell atop Delmar's Alexander, double reined. A dull glow of copper buttons on his rust velvet riding coat, the toes of his black boots shining like evil little spotlights. Held at a standstill the black horse gingerly lifting his hooves. *Soring.*

"Bastard, bastard!" She rose up in bed. "For torturing that horse! If there is not a Baptist hell for you to burn in, there should be!"

Echoing in some void behind her, Gottrell's hollow laugh. "My children are grown and gone to hell."

Very quietly that evening Giroux and Alexis entered the cell. "See for yourself," Alexis whispered.

Unaware of their presence Jaiyavara sat up in bed talking with someone invisible to them. "So becoming, Mama. You should have worn it all along."

At the foot of the bed Denise stood wrapped in a red sari, her left shoulder draped in a shimmering gauze of red and gold, a red dot centered between her high arched brows.

"Does this mean we can go home now?"

"America," Denise smiled. "This is our home."

"No, Mama. No."

"In our family, Jaiyavara . . . only one daughter each generation for seven generations. Didn't I tell you? I must have told you. It's true, it's true. Some thought that a curse. I called it a blessing. Before we left India a holy man told me that you would bear a special child . . . an eighth daughter."

"Too late for that, Mama. All my life I've dreamed of trying to find my way home."

"Your daughter will help you. She will lead the way. Earth is not your home. You too, my darling, have a dark and roving eye."

Looking through the wall to the left, Jaiyavara saw far beyond and understood. "The sea . . . the sea. . . ." And then softly together Denise and Jaiyavara sang the song.

"It's the fever," Alexis whispered. "She's delirious."

"And maybe not the fever." Shrewdly Giroux squinted with his good eye. "Racial memory . . . the collective unconscious . . . where myths may be born." He stepped forward. "So . . . Jaiyavara, we both survive."

With a long curious scrutiny she studied him. "Peculiar, isn't it?"

"What?"

"How the physical follows the psyche. Your eye looks very bad," she observed. "But then, you never saw but half of it anyway."

"And you will see no one but Alexis and me."

"Oh, I see many, Giroux. Perhaps too many." Closely watching his face she put the question to him. "How is Ruben?"

"Ruben is fine. Don't worry about Ruben."

"Ever a liar," she said flatly. "Ruben is dead."

Giroux and Alexis exchanged awed glances.

"Who told you?" Giroux asked.

"No one told me. No one had to tell me. You should have taken better care of him. He saved your worthless life."

"I don't deny that he saved my life. I do deny that it's worthless." Drawing up a chair, he sat down, his tone confidential. "There was something about Ruben from the first moment . . . a kind of precognition, if you will, that he would some day do me a great service. But, at any rate, it's time to dismiss all that and look to the future. Your hands . . . has John said. . .?"

Tucking in her lower lip, nodding sagely, her mouth droll, she mimicked, "If you will. At any rate. At any rate, if you will. If you will, at any rate."

Leaning sideways, Giroux folded his arms. "Any reason for levity at this point escapes me"

"Give me a cigarette. I can hold it, but I can't light it yet. There, on the table."

Giroux put the ash tray before her, handed her the cigarette, lit it, marveling at the way she got it to her mouth with swollen fingertips.

Inhaling, leaning comfortably at the headboard she became detached, estranged. "Most of our messiahs," she reflected, "have had no hands. Christ had good strong hands. I like that. I saw him this morning. He was a good boy, wasn't he, Alexis? But you were right not to adopt him. You know what he said? He said, 'I was only thirty-three. I never experienced old age or menopause problems. I never gave birth,' " She smiled. "Very bright, don't you think?"

"An excellent point," said Giroux. "I must make a note of that. But still . . . he was not, I take it, theologically embarrassed?"

"Oh," she shrugged, "who cares?"

"What else did he say?"

Greedily sucking the cigarette down to its nub, head tilted, she eyed him sideways. ". . . said he hadn't been around for two thousand years. Said he was out of touch and couldn't be much help with the terrible mess we're all in now. . . ."

Thoughtfully, slowly, Giroux nodded.

Meanwhile, Alexis stood gaping from one to the other in avid disbelief.

Surrender had its compensations. When John Bain changed the bandages and examined her hands Jaiyavara refused to look. Having escaped time's urgency and pressure she lay passive, drinking water, dreaming. The dripping water no longer mattered, each drip no longer reminded her of work not yet begun. It was difficult to distinguish morning from evening.

Waking in that watery gloom, she turned her head on the pillow and he was there, sitting by the bed, very tanned as if from working in the sun. Salvini.

"How does it go?" she asked.

"Not bad. Not bad. But not finished either. What are you doing in bed? Why are you not working?"

She indicated the bandaged hands and arms.

With his tongue he made that familiar scolding sound. "No excuse. You can find a way."

"Oh, really? Tell me about it. Tell me a way."

"Carina Mia, I can't believe this. All that I taught you, you're going to just lie there and let it go to waste? You were closer to a breakthrough than you realize."

"I doubt that," she said.

"That's the worst they can do to you, make you doubt. So what did you expect? Freedom? Happiness? A life of your own?"

"Not exactly. But I certainly never expected the world to turn out like this, either."

"Neither," he smiled, "did Sisyphus. Remember? Authenticity, integrity, that's all that matters. Sisyphus chained to his rock in the underworld, condemned and privileged to push it up the mountain day after day through all eternity, only to watch it fall, only to begin again. Again and ever. You know that. Through the rock you transcend a private self."

"But I am denied even the rock."

"Don't let them kill you. A living dog is better than a dead lion."

She made a wry face. "Oh, you're a fine one to talk."

"Well, don't do as I do, Carina Mia. Do as I say. I didn't let those who despise art kill me. It was those irreverent germs of the Plague. Be original, be audacious." He smiled gently, his eyes sparkled. "By the way . . . I'm glad you asked about the wedding night sheet in the villages. I like what you did with the tablecloth." Palms upward, he spread his hands. "Everything connects, you see?"

He faded.

"Don't go, don't go," she whispered. "I miss you so much."

Her back itched. Pushing against the bed post she rubbed and scraped her back against it. "He would say . . . paint with your toes, paint with your teeth."

In the right corner deeply shadowed another forming image. Lou Iris had depleted her, she was very tired and wanted privacy. But there seemed no stopping them, without her consent they appeared. "Who is it now?" she said crossly.

He looked leaner, tougher, taller; he wore tight black pants and no shirt. There were a few more hairs on his chest. He held a bouquet of scarlet flowers, in the center a tapered brush, thick and wet with scarlet.

"Salvini," she said, "is a tough act to follow. What is it you want, Anthony? Speak. Did you come back to forgive me?" She waited. "No? What then?"

One bold step forward and then he hesitated, his body poised, tense. He was sweating. She could smell it, the sheen of lust.

"Oh, good Lord, Anthony . . . I'm in no mood for that."

The scarlet flowers drooped down. The paint brush fell forward, as limp as soft rubber, red paint dripped to the floor. Anthony's haggard eyes still pleaded mutely.

"No," she said. "Never. Never. Never again."

Keeping her eyes upon him she sipped water. It immediately made her tipsy. Water became wine when Anthony appeared?

"Fare thee well, Anthony. Go marry. Go screw."

He was beginning to fade.

"Probe the night and swill the brew." (Jethro's influence, the rhyming?)

With weary tenderness she admonished. "Purge the fool in you. Do it, Adam . . . and get through. But," she added, sliding down, closing her eyes, "not to me. Enough. Enough. Lights out."

Chapter Nineteen

Wasting no time with preliminaries, early the next morning Giroux came in, seated himself beside Jaiyavara with note pad and pen. "These visions you're experiencing . . . accept them. They tap the source. You see, it's exactly as I've been telling you all along."

Stretched flat, emotionless, she paid no attention whatever.

"I want you to tell me precisely what you're seeing, what you're hearing. It's of the utmost importance to get the details. Please describe the details."

Never far behind, Alexis came in, overheard, and charged down upon him. "And still you hound her! Can't you leave her alone! Can't you see that she's ill. I forbid you to say another word!"

In astonishment, pen in hand, for a split second he froze. "You!" He leapt from the chair to face her. "You! Forbid me!" Up and down the cell, waving his arms, Giroux raged like a wounded martyr. But Alexis held her ground. As they argued Jaiyavara turned her face away from them, toward the left wall. Far beyond the wall the sea came roaring in, she let it overpower the awful sounds of their commotion. Giroux tromped off toward his study. Determined to have the last word, Alexis followed close behind. The battle continued elsewhere.

Something within rising and falling, a buoyant sensation.

Jaiyavara turned her eyes to the wall facing the bed.

Another scene seeped through, melting the wall.

Chapter Nineteen

She was standing on a swelling slope of hill, the grass a fiery green yet so very fine, so tender. A deep tableau of stillness. Nothing cast a shadow. All the surrounding hills were vivid, the sky a solid backdrop. There was that peculiar iridescence, as if light radiated from within each hill, each blade of grass. Below her, at the foot of the hill there were many people, many monks, faces averted; they were grouped and posed, motionless, as if for a stage setting. Jethro came swinging up the hill, all motion, full of confidence, swagger; as flamboyant as a gypsy in purple trousers, indigo shirt, a wide orange sash, gold loops in his ears, his chest adorned with golden chains. Delacroix, she thought, dressed him off stage.

Jethro handed her a bright green garden hose. Water, she thought, and it shot from the hose in a straight hard jet. To water the yellow flowers at her feet and the taller purple ones beyond, she adjusted the hose to a misty spray. Still the people were static, unable or unwilling to move or speak.

And so again she adjusted the hose, playfully turned it on them. They came to life!—moving, speaking, laughing—some ran, ducking the water, others lifted their hands and faces to it, cavorted in it like children at play. But where were the children, she wondered. Why were there no real children present?

Suddenly the hose was an enormous golden serpent, hissing, wildly writhing. She could not control it. "Jethro." she yelled, "Help me, help me!" He grabbed the serpent behind its head, together they struggled to hold it as it thrashed. Her hands were frozen on it, throbbing with pain. She was terrified but could not let go. The serpent spewed venom, it rained down on the people. Under that shower of poison they fell to their knees, heads bowed. What did it mean, what did it mean—a subdued ceaseless babble of prayers in many tongues? Even as she and Jethro desperately held to it, the serpent's neck swelled, fanned to a dreadful hood, and the shower of venom became soft warm rain. The people became flowers, larger than life, larger than themselves, now rooted, holding to their places, yet still they swayed and spoke and prayed and sang.

The serpent went limp. It was spent. It was dead. Jethro eased it from her hands, reverently placed it upon an altar which was an enormous turquoise ring. Then a lovely girl-child came from behind Giroux carrying the head of the work in the cave, Varrick's head; and she placed it also on the altar.

JAIYAVARA

As from high above Jaiyavara could see the altar of ring, she could see that it was a cove of turquoise water ringed and edged with pure white sand.

Night. The large and very fat monk sits on a crude wooden bench in the midst of the forest in a mild listing rain. Drifting down from the candlelit Zendo a chorus of human voices in singsong chant.
Well . . . what happens when we are expelled from the Garden? We can't go back. We must push forward.
Even as his eyes lift to the tower, to Jaiyavara's lighted window, the lamp is extinguished.
A gift perhaps . . . for Jaiyavara.

In the darkened cell she listened to the monotonous, hypnotic chant, but the wind rose higher, louder, the chant was swept away by rushing waves and gusts of rain. A storm on the way. The chanting ceased as monks were dispersed to their sturdier stone cells. Distant thunder, little more than a grumble, rushed in close, on the attack. The cell sporadically lit with soundless electric flares.
Like an old freighter in high waves the tower began to groan and heave. Closer now, lightning spit and crackled. Miserable, miserable night. When younger she exulted in such storms; ozone in the air or the release of pent-up tension, her best ideas often came in all that uproar. Younger still, as a child she would run out in back of the house, dancing, leaping naked in the rain.
And now in darkness she could see millions of pinpoints of frenzied energy, could feel in her body hard percussion thunder blows. If lightning struck, it would be the tower. Wind howled. A veined white-hot purity marked the walls. Like painting with thought. Some demonic energy painting the night world. Huddled down in bed, she shivered. It was an apprehension beyond her helplessness in the raging storm.
The sound made her pores stiffen, expand—something cracking, opening a supernatural splitting of primal elements. She

had heard tales of light which could mysteriously condense during a storm. It was happening now in the cell. Pinpoints of light gathered to a luminous sphere, an unearthly golden light.

Within the light, a human form.

"Oh, my god . . . oh, my god. . . ." Rapt, she went to her knees on the bed. "Is it you? Is it you? The light held him. The light was a cage. He had to separate from the light. She stretched to him her bandaged hands and arms, her entire body taunt and pleading. "Closer . . . closer . . . I can't reach you yet. Oh, my god, my god, how long I've waited. . . ."

Reaching through the light, he held forth his hand. Stretching, reaching, trembling, she made the contact, her swollen fingertips touched his. Through the tips of her fingers the electric current throbbed. He came to her then.

He was flesh and blood. He was real.

He was Varrick, and he lived.

Singing birds. Singing. Singing. Beyond these walls, she knew, outside, the natural world was washed and new, exquisitely created. Within the cell the light lingered, a hazy radiance outlining every object. Bandaged hands and arms stretched above her head, she lay naked, luxuriating in the afterglow. Nothing to fear now. Ever. True. All true. Other dimensions did exist. None of the previous visions had convinced her of this. Salvini, her mother, Anthony . . . the others only spoke to her, they did not touch her. Somewhere still . . . Varrick lived. Somewhere still . . . she was loved.

The moment Giroux came in everything changed. The cell was once again a mean drab prison. "I can see you're feeling much better." Mock cheerfulness. He immediately sensed in her a state of grace, was envious that she somehow enjoyed clandestine transcendences beyond his reach, behind his back. "So am I, Jaiyavara. And I have good news. I've been in contact with Simeon. He assures me that the Plague is subsiding. So we must prepare now for leaving, we must seriously prepare for the work before us. . . ."

She yawned, stretched and smiled.

"Why are you smiling?"

"I think not, Giroux. I won't be in any condition to travel."

"Oh, come now . . . good food, exercise, a real purpose, you'll recover your strength. Get those heavy bandages off. You can wear long sleeves to hide the scars. Of course you'll be able to travel, all the great cities of the world."

"I'm not going anywhere. I am, as they used to prosaically put it . . . with child."

His jaw sagged. His one good eye stupidly blinked. "You're not serious."

"Oh, but I am."

"You can't be serious."

"Decidedly, definitely, gloriously pregnant. Every cell in my body is singing."

"Anthony?"

"Oh, who knows?" she taunted. "I had to fill my leisure in some way. I slept with them all, even Ruben. It could be anyone."

His jaw set, sternly with one good eye he regarded her. "You're lying."

"Or so you hope," she said, and sat up. "But you're not really sure. How can you be sure, Giroux? It seems you have on your hands a very wanton and pregnant whore." The word, whore, she noted, had more of an effect than she had hoped for, seemed to strike at some peculiar vulnerability. "Too bad, too bad. Should word spread of me, it will not be as the bearer of great new tidings, but as a great lay."

"Why are you lying? I warn you, I will not be cheated."

She swung her legs over the side of the bed, got to her feet. He moved to help her. "Oh, get out of my way," she snapped. "You bother me. You're only a bother now. I have to bathe and dress. And if you don't believe me," she said, "then just sit back and watch me grow. I am blissfully pregnant, eternally pregnant."

Alexis rushed in. "Is it true? Is it true? Giroux just told me."

"Of course it's true," said Jaiyavara. "I want to go to the baths now. Then I want to walk. You'll have to help me dress, I'm so awkward."

"Oh, my angel," Alexis beamed. "Sweet miracle! And thank God for Anthony."

"Thank God for them all, Alexis. With all their territorial imperatives . . . still, they get through to us somehow."

"Wait, wait. I'll find you a robe. Something with large sleeves." As if twenty years had dropped from her, Alexis went into flurries of help. "Wait . . . where are your shoes? Oh, I'm so excited I can't think! Oh, to have a child here. What do you want, a boy or a girl?"

Jaiyavara sat down on the side of the bed. "It's a girl."

Finding her shoes, Alexis knelt to put them on her. "What makes you so sure? How can you know?"

"My mother told me . . . on her side of the family, one daughter only for seven generations. She will be, on my mother's side, the eighth daughter."

"How wonderful, how wonderful. The eighth daughter," Alexis repeated, impressed.

After taking Jaiyavara to the baths, helping her bathe and dress, they took a short walk. Alexis left her sitting on a bench in the shade, facing the stream and returned to Giroux's study.

"Please don't behave like this," she urged. "Please share in our happiness. Think what a joy it will be to have a child here. What greater message than a new life, a new beginning?"

"Any cow can give birth," he growled.

"Come, make peace with her. For everyone's sake, let there be an end to all this conflict. It's become unbearable."

At his desk Giroux stared at her with an inconsolable glare. "Peace? With her? There is no peace! The bitch. How she gloats."

In disgust, Alexis, for the time being gave up on him.

When she left, Giroux reached for the scrapbook drawer, changed his mind, slammed it shut. At the desk he put his head in his hands and wept.

Arms resting comfortably, Jaiyavara sat in a straight back chair. Her hair was freshly washed and brushed by Alexis. In her clean white robe she looked bland, virginal; she was content.

The cell, Giroux noticed was not clouded with smoke.

"Where are your cigarettes?" he asked, agitated.

"I threw them away. I've quit."

Some of the discoloration had slid from the left side of his face to his neck. His left eye was still a swollen slit. Gloom swooped down from his black shoulders. How ugly he is, she thought, and the attempted condescension in his swollen face, ludicrous. As he glowered before her Jaiyavara put both bandaged hands protectively to her slightly swollen belly.

"I will not tolerate it!" he erupted. "I will not allow you to corrupt everyone. I will not allow you to parade your repulsive and flagrant vulgarity before the entire. . . ."

". . . collection of pseudo-saints?"

"You are to be confined. You are not to leave this cell, do you understand?"

Lifting her chin, she said nothing.

Stalking up and down, he spoke with quiet fury. "Like mother, like daughter. Another bastard. And when your little bastard is born it is to be confined with you."

Refusing, for the sake of the child to fight with him, she waited, by her silence letting it reverberate, letting him hear his own vileness. As he came to a standstill she said calmly, "I will never again be alone, Giroux. You wanted a great symbol. Remember? A female symbol, a mother symbol. How utterly male, that the real thing is just too damned much for you."

Fixedly, his good eye glittered. He looked, she thought, suddenly very old, a defeated fanatic.

Hearing the door close, hearing the key turn in the lock, she lowered her head, cradled her belly. "Don't worry, don't worry, I'll take care of you. He can't hurt us now. We will sing in our chains like the sea. . . ."

Soft . . . slow . . . opening herald. Measured. In darkness her eyes moved upward. Sunrise gradually would frame itself in that small high window. From nowhere. Everywhere. Music. She could make music. A full orchestration. Hear it as she created it. Salvini was right. Other ways.

Before the first hint of light the melody opened, reached. Beautiful! She had only to lie there and listen. As real it was as the infinite romantic yearning . . . never ending . . . never realized . . . never fulfilled, yet never lost . . . never conquered.

Now the music reaching, lyrical, passionate, with growing intensity; she rose from the bed, in the cage of cell paced. Rushing now, exorbitant music. Louder. Seething. Exalting. She whirled, ran into the wall. Head to wall, eyes closed, she could not stop the music; it dragged her on and on in a roaring undertow.

Then it slowed, released her a little, gave her a breathing space.

Once more it swelled, expanded. It was all that existed.

Now resigned . . . coming down, coming down again, and she turned and looked to the high window . . . as the music ended . . . the obscure light was born.

Mid morning. A yearly commemoration ceremony of the monastery's founding. In white robes monks gathered on the patio, waiting for a signal from Giroux to begin the chanting procession into the Zendo.

Jaiyavara, in her place, sat waiting for the music.

When it came her eyelids widened, her body went taunt. Elbows at a jutting angle, her exposed fingertips curved downward like talons. When it came it made her fingertips spread, stretch, hold rigid in hysteria. Her body began to move and sway. Glorious, glorious music! Swooping! Rushing! Louder! Louder! She could fly, she could soar! Triumph of music! In a clinging nightgown she leapt from the chair, danced and laughed.

Crashing into the table, with a swoop of her bandaged arm she sent everything on it to the floor. That sobered her a moment, but the music took her again, flung her about the room. She rushed back to the table, tried to move it with her fingertips, grimaced in pain. Placing rigid arms beneath it she wiggled and pulled it to the side of the bed. Struggling to lift it with straight forearms her teeth gritted, in manic determination, panting, groaning, she worked the table finally to the top of the bed. Wet with perspiration she climbed on the bed, pushed the table with her body against the wall. Back to the wall, panting, eyes glazed, she rested a moment while relentless music roared in her head. Holding precariously she got one knee on the table, then the other, against the wall, balancing by her shoulder she got her feet beneath her, steadied the table on the hard mattress with her feet wide apart, braced she stood, clinging to the wall. She could see through the window, she could see it all, all there below in their hooded white robes, their faces hidden, marching slowly, herded toward the Zendo. Torrents of music! Her wild laughter shrilled out like a cracked bell. Her will was sublime, she was both delirious and supremely sane. In a crazy screech that strained and tore and scraped she was singing through the window.

The monks below were stopped in their tracks. Looking up to her window, under the unmistakable anguish of her unholy screeches, for a few moments they tried to ignore her, tried to proceed. The two lines broke up. Monks scattered in every direction.

Swiftly Giroux moved from the Zendo porch to the back steps, striving for decorum, he refused to run to the tower. Once inside, he raced up the stairs, unlocked, flung open the door. Against the wall in the transparent nightgown, on top of the table, Jaiyavara singing. Giroux leaped on the bed, lifted her from the table, dragged her to the floor. Loud, loud, still she was singing. He slapped her hard.

"What's the matter with you?" Her bewilderment was genuine. "What are you doing? Why did you hit me?"

"You're driving everyone away! You're driving everyone crazy! Do you want to destroy everything!"

"Oh," she said, and her eyes cleared somewhat. "Am I? Destroying? Yes, I want to. And I will. I will."

He grabbed her by the throat, pulled her face close to his. "I'll see you dead first! I'll see you in hell!"

That evening a small group of monks met in Doyle's cell to talk of leaving.

"I don't understand anything now. . . ."

"Ruben hanging himself. That was a very bad omen."

"Why is he keeping her locked in up there? That's not what this place is supposed to be about."

"Everything has gone to hell here. But I'm afraid it's worse out there."

"If we leave, are you with us, Doyle?"

"I don't know. I don't know."

"He won't let us leave. . . ."

"Jethro and Anthony and Bethune left."

"If we leave," said Karen, ". . . should we take her with us?"

"We can't take her with us," Doyle said. "She's pregnant."

"Pregnant . . . and mad. . . ." said Sebastian.

That evening Alexis found Jaiyavara sitting in the chair, head bowed, used up, in a stupor of compliance.

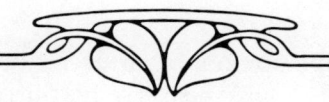

Chapter Twenty

Where was the resolution? The blow Jaiyavara dealt Giroux had left a stigmatism, the left eyelid lowered, eyesight in the left eye permanently impaired; he could not decide if the constant ache in his face was due to the blow or to more teeth going bad. But that was the least of his worries. He could not, despite the threat, keep her locked up forever. What was he to do with her now?

He had no one to turn to, no one to confide in. He was blocked, frustrated, stagnant. Bethune, once an avid listener, had helped him sort his thoughts. (And where by now were the banished malcontents, and how did they fare?) Not one thinker left in the entire miserable lot. Peripherally, he noticed, and despised himself for noticing, Karen no longer tagged after him like a lovesick calf. The deepest cut of all, Alexis' challenge, defection, in misguided defense of Jaiyavara, simply because she was incapable of grasping the significance of the situation. Admiration motivated him, inspired him; yet now he saw in every eye suspicious mistrust. He, provider and protector, he, with the best intentions in the world, was now being regarded as some sort of villain!

Just as he was beginning to believe that Jaiyavara was about to make a vital transition through her own visions, she had in fact, become an acute embarrassment, a stone about his neck, weighing him down.

Is this, she said, the only idea of your life?

But if he were to give up on it, abandon it, what could possibly replace it? What would be his meaning, his purpose in life? Perhaps the slow, torturous evolution of civilization was after all, nothing but a ghastly mistake. Things kept getting worse and worse, a process of progressive deterioration. Perhaps the entire human race was being drawn ever more swiftly and inevitably to a horrible conclusion.

Never had he felt so discouraged, so morbid, so helpless.

And yet . . . if Jaiyavara ever grasped the need, backed him up, stood beside him as intended, that psychic marriage might yet bring guidance to those lost, famished souls; those who thirsted and hungered for more than mere survival.

In the middle of the night Jaiyavara woke. No sounds. No music. The tower cell was pitch black. She was nauseated. Her eyes burned. Her heart raced. The earth seemed to have fallen away. In the vise of an incomprehensible fear, she could hardly breathe.

Within her body, a strange, subtle movement. Smooth and sensual, a continuous movement, a rolling, bulging. Rising on her elbows, she looked down upon her body. Her belly was transparent. Within her body, slowly writhing, a golden serpent.

In the cell below, Alexis jerked awake. It took her a few moments to identify it as human—that piercing scream. Leaping from the bed she raced up the stairs.

In the lamp-lit outer hallway Giroux was unlocking the door. Alexis rushed in ahead of him to Jaiyavara gasping, threw both arms around her.

"Help me! Help me! Get it out of me! Get it out of me! A serpent in my body!"

"Oh, no, no, no, my darling! It's only a dream!"

Holding the lamp aloof Giroux came forward.

He saw Jaiyavara thrashing on the bed. "Help me! I begged you! I begged you to kill me!"

"Quickly," Giroux said. "Get John. I'll hold her." It took all his strength to hold her as she flung her head back and forth, tried to fling her writhing body against the stone wall.

Half way down the stairs Alexis met John on the way up. "I heard her," he panted. "Everyone heard. The whole place is awake." They rushed up the stairs into the cell. While Giroux restrained Jaiyavara, John Bain administered the injection. "Don't let go of her yet," he warned. "She fights it. It'll take a few minutes, but I gave her enough to knock out a horse."

Unable to hide her emotion, Alexis turned her back on them all. Still Jaiyavara fought Giroux, incoherently moaning. He did not talk to her or try to soothe her. When she became a little quieter Giroux said to John, "It's all right. I think she'll be all right now."

"I doubt it," John Bain answered. "I'm not trained to cope with this sort of thing."

"It's all right, John. Alexis and I will stay with her. Leave us alone now, please."

But the usually mild, deferential John Bain was not to be so easily dismissed. He was very angry. "I don't know what you've done to her," he said, "or why. But I hold you responsible. And I warned you at the beginning. I explained to you in detail all the physiological signs. I will never forgive you for this Giroux. Never."

As John left Alexis took a deep breath, regained control, went back to the bed. Pushing in between Giroux and Jaiyavara, she took Jaiyavara in her arms. "Be still now. I'm here. I'm with you. It was only a dream."

Wary, Giroux relinquished her, pulled up a chair close to the bed.

"No, I saw it . . . I saw it," she repeated, her face buried in Alexis' arms. "I was awake. Not a dream. I feel it still. Put your hands there. Can't you feel it? It's a serpent. I'm going to deliver a serpent and I'm going to die." She held to Alexis.

Alexis looked up to Giroux. "It's a false pregnancy. It's all in her head."

"But she's enlarged."

"False, I tell you, from the beginning. Her body believes. . . ."

"But why?"

"Her hands are useless. Her body creates. . . ."

As it dawned upon Giroux that Alexis was right, in slow amazement the knot of despair within him was loosened, released.

Stroking her hair, in a rocking motion Alexis held Jaiyavara. Lifting her head Jaiyavara pulled back a little, said drunkenly, ". . . doesn't matter. Don't understand . . . but I'm all right . . . now I am, Alexis."

"Are you sure?"

". . . accept it. Yes. It doesn't matter. I'm all right now."

Alexis released her, avoiding Giroux, walked around the foot of the bed, sat down on the other side.

"Doesn't matter," Jaiyavara repeated. Her eyelids drooped, her voice slurred. "I want to die. That's all I want." With effort she focused on Giroux. "I never belonged here. You captured me like a fish in a net. You promise. You give me an oath that when I die. . . ."

"Don't be absurd. You had a bad dream. You're not going to die."

"I am. You know I am. I want to and I will. You give me an oath. Now."

Half humoring her, half believing, he went along with it. "What oath?"

"That when I die . . . you will take my body to the sea. All I ask. Little enough to ask in return for. . . ." Her eyes closed.

Giroux leaned forward in the chair. "In return for what?"

Her body spread, euphorically sank down. ". . . the myth."

Caught up in the stupendous fantasy, at last they were in communication. Tentatively, Giroux put his hand to her bandaged arm. "I agree. Whatever oath you desire."

She did not answer.

"Don't sleep yet. Jaiyavara, hear me. What oath?"

She smiled. Her eyes opened. Drunk with the narcotic her eyes were deep and dark and prophetic. "Say it. For the dancing mother . . . the eighth daughter. Say it, Giroux."

His pulse quickened, his mind raced. "The dancing mother," he repeated. "The eighth daughter."

". . . golden serpent," she whispered.

"Golden serpent."

"I promise to take Jaiyavara to the sea. Say it," she said.

"I promise."

"No. Say it exactly . . . word for word."

"I promise," he repeated, "to take Jaiyavara to the sea."

Her head turned. "Alexis?"

"I'm right here, my darling, right here."

". . . my witness. Make him keep his word."

"I will," Alexis said.

". . . don't trust him, ever. Make him, Alexis. Make him keep his word."

"I will. I promise you I will. Go to sleep now," Alexis pleaded. "I'll be with you. Don't be afraid."

". . . not afraid." She licked her dry lips. "Accept it all." Once more she turned to Giroux. "I carry her. She's the one you've waited for. When it happens you'll understand. Her father is Varrick. You thought he was dead, didn't you? He is dead, but he fought through to me. A serpent now . . . but that's only . . . I accept it . . . when she's born . . . a beautiful daughter. As my mother told me. And she will be . . . she will be. . . ." She sighed. Her eyes closed.

Listening intently, Giroux wanted to ask more but Alexis stopped him with her fierce eyes. In the high narrow cell, silence. Giroux sat motionless watching Jaiyavara. Dark hair clung to her moist forehead. She was breathing evenly, deeply. At last he withdrew his hand from her bandaged arm. Sleeping, she turned on her side, curved one knee over the other.

"Well," Alexis said with terrible scorn, "are you satisfied?"

Giroux sank down in his chair. His eyes never left Jaiyavara. "How fragile . . . how fragile . . . the dancing mind."

Looking up, Giroux saw that the path he walked led straight to the bench of the large and very fat monk. Veering off, he avoided it, turned toward the path beside the stream, lost in thought. She had given him clues. She had given him symbols. They were working in him. And as if fearful that seeing her in a completely different state might break the spell, with little concern for Jaiyavara's emotional or physical welfare, he left her entirely to John and Alexis.

Dancing mother. Eighth daughter. Golden serpent. Why serpent? Why golden? Her way of admitting to herself that it was all a fiction? Well, if so, no more than ordinary life. He could not figure it out, he was a philosopher, not a psychiatrist. And what did the intricate why's and wherefore's matter as long as the dross was burned away. Serpent? And she accepted it. And how quickly, before his eyes, she transformed something dreadful, loathsome, into something beautiful, something to wait for, hope for.

Unaware, he came upon them, young monks at the pool. The few there sat on the banks, spiritless, dejected. They looked up at him as an intruder. No one spoke. No one was splashing, playing in the water, no one was swimming. As he turned away, continued his walk, he realized how they were different now, and remorselessly shrugged. They were all fully clothed.

"If you persist in this," Alexis warned, "you're going to lose everyone, everything. They have always thought of her as eccentric, but they all care for her."

At the window of his study Giroux stood with his back to Alexis. "Which is," he replied without turning, "as it should be."

"She's in grave danger. Her blood pressure is extremely high."

"That's up to John. . . ."

"John can't do everything! Get Simeon on the radio. Get help for her. She needs better care than we can give her here. I keep trying to talk to her but it does no good. She keeps saying she will die!"

At last Giroux turned to face Alexis. "Then, no doubt, she will."

"Talk to her!" Alexis begged. "Tell her she's free to leave, to try to work again. That's all she's ever wanted."

"No."

"All the years I've trusted you, helped you, do you owe me nothing?"

"I owe you nothing."

"She keeps saying she will die!"

"Then, no doubt, she will," Giroux said matter of factly. "She is very stubborn. Pride, wrath, envy, avarice, sloth, lust, gluttony . . . the seven deadly sins, I have at one time or another been guilty of every one. But there is an eighth sin, Alexis. The death wish. I have never been guilty of that."

"Oh." Her mouth spread to an ugly sneer. "Oh . . . you . . . you sanctimonious son-of-a-bitch. How dare you! Of what use to you is her dead body?"

Giroux picked up a pen on the desk, tapped it thoughtfully. "You *owe* me, Alexis. Something is unfolding here. Something important. I *allow* you to participate in an extraordinary event. The Grail appears to those who are spiritually eligible. She will yield the pearl. I will have the victory. I will bestow the symbol."

"Her dead body! You have tortured her to insanity! If she dies you are responsible!"

"But this," he explained, "is the result. It's not madness," Giroux insisted. "She knows exactly what she's doing. Well . . . something knows."

Twisting her hands, Alexis was utterly distraught. Angry tears burst from her eyes. "May God have mercy! I see it now! You're as crazy as she is! You've always been crazy! I should have helped her escape long ago! God have mercy, deliver me from insane mystics! The insane asylums are full of messages!"

In calm certitude Giroux regarded her. "Why, yes . . . Alexis. I thought you knew that. I thought *everyone* knew that."

Day after day . . . Jaiyavara's stillness.

And the weather was peculiar. Oppressive morning heat squeezed the life out, left the monks lethargic, despondent. Every afternoon or evening a high wind rose, the trees moaned and lashed, dead pine needles scattered, a storm was anticipated. At the edges of the valley thunder growled like a marauding panther, but the storm passed them by, the release never came.

Jaiyavara's stillness . . . Giroux gave it wide berth, as if to look upon her now would turn him to a pillar of salt. Only bare necessities were managed. His neglect of the monks left them uncentered, cast adrift. Rituals were slowly forsaken, finally abandoned. Only the old man of the Zendo lit candles for whoever might wander in to meditate; sounded the gongs, the drums, the clacking sticks, kept the timeless vigil.

Lounging like actors off-stage waiting for a cue, the monks played poker or bridge, cast horoscopes, consulted the I Ching, the Tarot, the predictions of Nostradamus. From the cellar library someone dug out an ancient manuscript on alchemy. Several monks asked to see Jaiyavara. Giroux refused. Little by little the bizarre tale of what was happening in the tower cell was pieced together, there were various versions, as with each person it was added to, distorted.

The young pine trees were dying. No one knew why. Rusty pine needles covered the paths and walkways, were swept from the patio, clogged the stream. Only the pine trees, only the young. Monks began gathering at night in private cells, to drink wine, to talk; they drank to excess, there were arguments, fights, defiant spurts of hilarity. But on occasion in the evenings, when the storm which circled had once more passed them by, a few monks would gather beneath Jaiyavara's high small window to sing old, old songs, remembered from childhood, songs from a simpler, more innocent time, which Giroux in his study did not hear or have to tolerate. Jaiyavara listened to their lifted, sweet, slightly drunken voices and knew what they were saying to her in the only way they could.

She listened also to the swallows, the starlings. In some shaft of the wall they had made a nest. All through the hot, long days she listened to the contented little twitterings and chirpings of the baby birds. Each dawn the parents left to hunt for food to bring to them. Each dawn the powerful beating of their wings, the upward swoosh of flight thrilled her.

And so it continued . . . Jaiyavara's stillness; it gathered, accumulated, radiated from the tower cell until it seemed to batter the stones of the high surrounding walls. There was much talk among the monks of leaving . . . yet no one left. Under the tension and stress of some morbid expectation still hanging, unresolved, there was an all pervasive pallidness, joylessness, the sense of life half-lived, the sense of being stranded in some anteroom of existence.

In the back of every mind it was seeping in, the harsh realization that there are no saved, no chosen, no spared; that there is no place to hide. Her stillness seemed destined to drive them into the world beyond the gates, into risks and terrors so long ignored, so long avoided . . . but not yet . . . not yet. Jaiyavara's stillness lay seige to the fortress of each separate ego, each separate defense, and held each suspended in her helpless, bandaged hands.

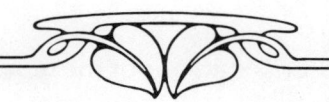

Chapter Twenty-One

That sultry morning Giroux rode out alone, through the gates, up the narrow, twisted, ascending mountain path. The air was clearer, cooler when he reached the mountain top. At a plodding, steady pace he crossed the wide grassy plateau and came in full view of the open sea.

Far below, he looked down to the cove, water so clear and brilliant in sunlight it made his eyes burn. There the sands formed a half-circling bar so that the cove was separated, stood out like an enormous turquoise ring. For a long while he sat still on the good horse gazing out to sea. Faintly he seemed to hear a far off humming. Dolphins? Mermaids? The fabled Sirens? Listening, his face was strained, taunt with a bereavement he could not name. Or was it the sea singing to itself, celebrating to itself its own opaque mysteries?

Turning back he let the solemn horse take his time plodding homeward, planting his huge hooves firmly on the steep downward trail. The gentle swinging motion of the horse helped him shake off recent nightmares of his mother, his father. By the time Giroux returned, stabled the horse and headed toward the tower he felt bone-weary, formless.

Alexis rushed out to him. "Come quickly. She thinks she's in labor."

Directly below Jaiyavara's window monks were gathered, anxiously looking up to the window, listening. As Giroux approached he too heard the grunting moans.

"Where have you been?" said one of the monks. "Why is it you can leave and we can't?"

"Do I have to watch you every moment? I needed some time to myself."

"What have you done to her now?" another accused.

"As you can see . . ." he spread his arms, "I'm doing nothing." None of them wore the habitual black robes. They were to him now un-individual, unrecognizable. He could remember none of their names. My entire life, he thought, devoted to them?

"We've all been psychically seduced," one of the women said. "We're leaving."

"You need the outcome of this as much as I do."

In every face he saw raw aversion, hostility, as sounds from the high window goaded their anger. "We're leaving. You can't stop us."

Giroux's tongue flicked to the space of missing tooth. His mouth went dry, his throat was parched. He tried to make his voice authoritative, commanding. "We have all been through the fire. We could all become heroes. This is no time to leave. This is the beginning."

"Bullshit!" Leon cackled, wagging his head, as he danced a mincing little cat dance.

"Fraud!" Karen shouted, and hurled a stone. It glanced off his shoulder.

"Liar! Liar!" Another stone was hurled.

"These women," said phlegmatic Doyle, advancing a little, "are getting very unhappy."

Giroux found his voice. "I have taught you!" he thundered. "Protected and provided for you! I have prepared you for a great deal more than mere happiness. I have loved you like a father." But as he moved toward them, arms outstretched, the sounds from above were hard and tearing; the monks backed off, turning away.

"For yourself," one said, looking over his shoulder. "We've been nothing but your stooges."

"Leave, then! Leave!" he shouted. "You want everything easy, handed up to you on a silver platter! Cowards! Ingrates! You are all hideously petty! Take your stupid misconceptions elsewhere!" He turned, stalked back toward the entrance, Alexis close behind.

Glancing down to the bench of the large and very fat monk he saw that the bench was empty, stopped abruptly. His face drained, his eyes were desolate. "Where is he, Alexis?"

"I don't know. He disappeared sometime this morning."

"He wears . . . the mask of God."

"What are you talking about?"

Giroux shook his head—it was unexplainable—he went in as she followed, resolutely climbed the stairs.

Amid limp trampled sheets which hung awry off the bed, Jaiyavara on her knees on the bed, moaning, moving, turning. Between the open folds of a man's oversize shirt which clung damply to her body her naked abdomen bulged out, shining, a pale mirror of flesh, a dome. The steamy fecund odor in the close cell was almost sickening. Her face and body were streaked with sweat, her hair was tangled, her eyes glassy. She looked like a trapped she-wolf.

"It's hot as hell in here," Giroux said, and propped the door open wide with a chair.

Jaiyavara moved in mindless circles on her knees.

Did his own mother, he wondered, bring him to life in such travail? Around and around, he thought, watching her . . . and down the cosmic drain?

"No idea . . ." she panted, "that it would hurt so."

"No need to drag this out now," Alexis scolded, made her lie back and wiped her face with a damp cloth. "We must do this quickly now and get it over with."

"We?" Jaiyavara repeated through clenched teeth. "Where did you go, Alexis?"

"To get Giroux."

"What for? What can he do?"

"Never mind that."

"Where's John?"

"John can't be here. John has a migraine. Never mind that. I've attended many deliveries. No need to drag this out, it's entirely up to you."

Fascinated by their conspiracy—Alexis behaving as if they were on the verge of something real—Giroux stood on the sidelines. But it occurred to him that he had perhaps underestimated Alexis. It occurred to him that she was a true midwife, that without her Jaiyavara might not bring it to pass.

"You've had pain before," Alexis was saying. "Use it. Work with it. Work through it. How far apart are the pains now?"

"Not apart . . . just one enormous everything. . . ."

Why, Giroux wondered, must they suffer so? Old, old, he thought, the re-enactment. In reality, it had happened on the planet billions of times, and yet for every female, it was new, it was the creation of the world. Why must her body play out this fantastic charade? He had to keep reminding himself that nothing could come of it, one way or another, but her release. She did not whine or complain. Would she remain to the very last moment this courageous? Could one die of a fantasy? Or . . . if she thought that a birth was actual, might she not say . . . Well, that's done now. Let's get on with it, and yet with all the creative work she had achieved why was he certain that this birthing, this work of her body was a rare crowning, her greatest accomplishment?

As if answering his thoughts she threw him a ravaged look of triumph. ". . . wait and see . . . wait and see. . . ." Enlarged veins of her throat and face stood out like chords, looked ready to burst. He could see every throb, every heartbeat. Even as she spoke another contraction hit, her face contorted, her mouth curled back in a growling snarl.

"Push down, push down!" Alexis urged.

". . . no hands . . . no hands."

Alexis grabbed her elbows, braced her. "Push with your elbows. Hard! Push hard!"

Her head moved forward, down, legs spread Jaiyavara arched her back, straining, pushing, her elbows braced by Alexis' strong hands.

Alexis glanced at Giroux. "Quick. Help us. Get on the other side. Hurry."

He found himself doing as he was told, participating.

"Hold her shoulder. Hold her elbow."

But by the time he took a bracing stance in a shuddering wave the pain passed through her and she collapsed back on the bed. Once more Alexis wiped her face. Jaiyavara sniffed, said to Giroux, "Pretty useless, aren't you?"

"I'll do better next time."

"See that you do. It's your last chance."

Alexis put both hands to Jaiyavara's abdomen. "It's very close now. The next one we'll both hold you, brace you, when it comes for God's sake push with all your strength."

". . . with all that I have. Water."

Giroux poured the water, lifted her, held it to her lips. Time. Beginning and end. Full circle. When first she woke she had asked for water. "Do you remember?" he said.

Their eyes met. "Yes. I remember. The dream I told you."

"I'll never forget it," he promised. "We should never have become enemies."

Remembering that dream she withdrew, turned inward; preparing to enter one more fathomless, final, as if to herself she said, ". . . if I had not fought him . . . how different it all might have been. . . ."

Jaiyavara turned to Alexis. "The terrible things I said to you. Forgive me. I didn't mean them. Please forgive me. I love you."

"No need to forgive. I love you."

"I'm not worthy, Alexis. You should be her mother."

"I'll be her godmother."

"God . . . Mother . . ." she repeated. "Yes, that's what we yearn for. But she won't need care. She's a new creature. She'll be born with wings . . . just as birds evolved from serpents. She'll fly to the sea. Oh, God . . . it's coming. Hold me, Alexis. Hold me."

They grabbed her elbows and shoulders. Mouth open, her body went rigid. That low inhuman moaning howl . . . he thought if it didn't end he would go insane. And then the sound ended, yet somehow continued, reverberated. Throwing her head, still she fought the pain, labored with it, pushing, straining, and her last strength was stupendous. Her abdomen bunched, quivered, and gradually eased down. It made his spine tingle. From her entire body there was an animal sound of release, satisfaction.

Through the high small window sunlight slanted. Blinded by that light Jaiyavara's face slowly softened to rapture. That madness . . . Giroux thought. It must be like looking at God.

". . . so beautiful . . . she's so beautiful. I knew she would be. It's finished."

To look more deeply into her eyes, wanting some small fragment of that ecstasy, Giroux leaned between her and the light. Something . . . some unknowable force was peering at him through her dark dark eyes, something mischievous, twinkling, radiant.

"Finished," she whispered. "Put me in water. Put me in water." Head back, she stretched, sank down, her eyes closed. Her bandaged arms spread out as if she were floating. She became very still.

The moments passed. She did not move. Giroux whispered to Alexis, "Do something. Get John. Make him help her."

"It's too late. There's nothing anyone can do."

"Are you sure?"

Alexis' voice was flat. "It's too late, I tell you. She's beyond us. . . ."

"Is she dead?"

"Not quite. Not yet."

"What is it, a stroke?"

Alexis lifted each eyelid. There was no response. "Probably. Coma. Her suffering is over. I'm glad it's over." In her sorrow, with movements deep and fluid Alexis pulled the edge of the pillow from beneath Jaiyavara's head, gently straightened her legs, pulled the sheet over the lower half of her body. In vague distraction she straightened articles on the table beside the bed, then slumped into a chair.

"What did she see, Alexis?"

No answer. Giroux thought that perhaps Alexis was going into shock. Before he could repeat the question, without looking at him Alexis spoke. "She saw what she wanted to see. People near death do that. She saw an infant daughter that no one can ever imprison . . . hovering in air . . . poised for flight."

How long Alexis sat mutely beside her he did not know. Holding to the railing at the foot of the bed he could not think, he could not feel, he could not weep.

Jaiyavara's stillness. Now it was final. It was just a matter of waiting for the breath to leave her body. Her face was composed. Perfect. Finished. So like a photograph. More perfect, more beautiful, he thought than any of the photographs in his keeping. Finally he realized that without a word to him Alexis had left.

"Is it always too late?" he asked, speaking to a point in the wall just above her head. "We should have been great allies, bound by a common cause. Perhaps it's not too late, after all. What am I saying? I don't know . . . I don't know. I keep thinking of my mother. She died horribly. It took a long time. Why I keep thinking of her now I don't understand. Inch by inch, she dragged it out for over a year. My father and I were chained to her all that time. . . ."

His eyes moved upward to the stone wall beside her bed. "There should have been a better window in here. I didn't realize how close and hot this room could be in summer." He took a deep breath. "She didn't want much . . . my mother . . . only the impossible. She wanted to be elegant . . . and she was vulgar. She wanted to be brilliant . . . and she was trite. She wanted to be tall and dark and slender, like you, Jaiyavara . . . and she was short and fat and dumpy . . . and her eyes were yellow. Yellow. Yes, yellow . . . believe me." Sadly, he smiled. "Have you ever seen anyone with yellow eyes? Topaz, she called them . . . of course. And her hair. Oh, her hair . . ." he lifted his eyes heavenward, shook his head. "Her hair was a disaster. What could have been a mild mousey brown . . . that horrible rusty orange . . . from bleaching. Well," he shrugged, "what does it matter now?"

Head down, both hands on the railing he became lost in the past. "My father was a surgeon," he explained. "Highly respected. Devoted to me. We did everything together . . . long talks, long trips. He taught me everything. She was excluded, you see. Why he stayed with her I'll never understand . . . a frumpy fat drunkard, growing old. An embarrassment. Of course there were other women. She knew that. Well, what did she expect from him? Why am I telling you this? I don't know. When I was very small I think I loved her. I seem to remember that she was playful once, a certain zest, but always selfish. At one time I must have felt some compassion for her. But he weaned me of that. Without ever saying it, in so many words he made me understand that to love someone stupid and weak is a terrible weakness. Maybe Ruben . . . maybe I tried to refute that. Maybe the entire cast of my life has been an attempt to refute that. But by the time I was grown I had no love for her, none, only disgust, contempt. Is this a confession? Here lately . . . such disturbing dreams. I've been dreaming that we murdered her. Isn't that strange? After all this time?"

He longed to weep. A few tears . . . no matter how weak, how futile, how hypocritical. But none would come.

Looking up then he saw them, monks huddled just outside the open door. Like naughty children they had ever so quietly crept up the stairs. Wide-eyed, they were, curious and frightened. His first impulse was to order them to leave. Time alone now he needed . . . infinite time alone with Jaiyavara.

Yet he could tell by their demeanor that they would not leave. Others sneaking up the stairs pressed from behind, close to the stone walls they edged through the doors, edged into the cell with the stealth of shadows. Giroux walked to the outer hallway. No one spoke. They made way for him. And there they were, standing, sitting, leaning, aligned all up and down the stairs. At the foot of the stairs Karen looked up at him, her anger had passed, yet he had no idea what she was thinking. She looked at him so strangely.

Stepping through them—they were sitting on the floor, leaving space around Jaiyavara's bed—Giroux returned to his chair, a little to the right at the foot of the bed.

Afternoon passed into evening. Nothing sounded from the Zendo. No gongs. No drums. No clacking sticks. They were all, it seemed, determined to wait it out. Someone now and then, in the hall or on the stairs, coughed discretely.

Someone lit the lamps.

When Alexis returned, someone guided her to her chair. On the opposite side of the bed from Giroux, she sat down very close to Jaiyavara. Alexis had been with none of her sons at their death. In attending Jaiyavara, a process of grief was becoming resolved for her, some part of her bitter pain at last being laid to rest.

All through the night the monks stayed near. No one left.

And all through the night at long intervals, from different points, ever nearer, they heard the wolf howl. It seemed to be circling very close outside the wall.

At dawn the old man of the Zendo made his way through monks curled and bunched together like sleeping puppies on the stairs. He wore a white robe. He carried his large whacking stick. As he passed through the monks they woke. Feeble, but untottering, he made his way into the cell and came to stand at the foot of Jaiyavara's bed, looking down upon her sternly.

As if on signal every monk dozing or sleeping awoke, sat up straight, came to attention. And there he stood, like a querulous little white angel of death.

The old man of the Zendo had never been known to waste time or energy.

Quietly some of the monks rose to their knees, others silently stood. All watched intently. For perhaps ten or fifteen minutes the old man of the Zendo stood before Jaiyavara perfectly motionless, but ready, alert.

The birds began to twitter and chirp. There was a soft swoosh and rush of beating wings as the starlings left the nest. The whacking stick in both hands, the old man of the Zendo raised both arms straight and high above his head to signify her release. Deeply then, he bowed to her, and reverently placed the whacking stick on the bed at her feet.

As he left, he was smiling.

Chapter Twenty-Two

Sullen sky. A cold wet overcast day. Pieces of the broken gates standing ajar clanked in the moaning wind. Bundled in her heavy coat Alexis tried to head off a small brown and white spotted cow escaping through a hole in the crumbling wall. Alexis had rapidly aged, she was bent and shrunken, she looked like a peasant. Her hair, wild in the wind, had grown out white, was streaked with dark. "Get back! Get back! Who do you think is going to milk you out there, you misbegotten bitch!"

But the cow tossed her head, showed the whites of her eyes and galloped out of reach, then turned, planted her feet, lowered her head and looked at Alexis sedately. To keep other cows from escaping Alexis dragged a log to the hole, propped it as a barrier. Breathless then, she just sat down on the cold ground. Giving vent to her anger she hit the earth with a stick, three hard whacks. "What's the sense of it?" she growled. "Might as well beat a dead horse." Whack! She hit it again. In sheer frustration she wept a little, but it was over quickly and she wiped her nose on the sleeve of her coat.

High on the road above the broken gates a strange object soundlessly appeared. It made her gasp. She squinted and gaped. A metalic silver-pink, it seemed to change color, shimmer to pale lavendar before her eyes. What on earth? An automobile? The door opened. A man got out. Alexis got to her feet, stumbling ran forward waving her arms. "Help! Help! I'm here, I'm here. Help!"

Closer, somewhat fearful, she stopped to get a better look. "Simeon! My God, it's Simeon!" She ran forward, threw herself upon him, cried and laughed as they embraced.

He held her at arms length. "Your hair. I didn't recognize you with hair. How are you, Alexis."

"Terrible! Terrible! Can't you see! Everything's terrible!"

He too had changed. He looked older, thinner, not quite so tough. His face was splotched as with a youthful acne of swollen red bumps.

"I've tried to reach Giroux on the radio. No one answers. Where is everyone?"

"They've left. They've all left. How did you get here? Is the road repaired?"

"The road, yes. A lot of repairs. What happened to the wall?"

"We had a small quake. Three, in fact. Scared me to death, the first one. Oh, you look so tired. Come, I'll fix you something to eat. Tell me everything."

Arm in arm they walked down the path, kept hugging as they walked. "A lot of changes," said Simeon. "People regrouping in odd configurations. Former enemies . . . as after a war, now the best of friends. Picking up the pieces. The space program, would you believe, will soon be started again. So," he said cheerfully, "we can send our viruses to other worlds like good missionaries."

"I prayed you'd come. What else? Do we have a president?"

"He's called that. Hugh Powers, a dictator, but benevolent. He's getting things done."

"But what about Thandon?"

"I couldn't find him. He's out there somewhere, hiding out. Or dead. I don't know." As they walked Simeon took in the disrepair, neglect. "Everything looks different. Where's Giroux? I'm anxious to talk with him."

"No, you're not."

"What do you mean?"

Alexis shook her head. "You'll see, you'll see. He's not the same at all, Simeon. You won't recognize him."

"What's the matter with him?"

"Useless without an audience. Totally incompetent. We'll soon starve."

"That bad?" Simeon frowned.

"Worse. You'll see. I hope you can help him."

"Where's Jaiyavara?"

"Dead. He killed her."

"What?" Simeon halted. "How? What happened? He loved her."

"Loved her, killed her." Alexis threw out her arms. "What's the difference? One and the same thing with him. She died of a contagious vision. His. Oh, don't look at me like that, Simeon. I'm not crazy. But what's the advantage, when everyone else is? Tell me that."

"Slow down, slow down," he said. "I don't understand."

"Oh, you will," she asserted, "when you see him. The truth is not in him! He promised to take her body to the sea, a solemn oath she got from him before she died, and she called me as witness, because she knew him. Oh, she knew him. He lied! Her things, relics he calls them. And she's still a prisoner. He sits with her body day and night. He hardly eats. I don't know when he sleeps. And he talks to her and he talks to her, all the time."

Deeply concerned, incredulous, Simeon asked, "Where is he now?"

"In the Zendo, as usual. With her."

"I want to see him."

"Oh, eat first. Rest a little. There's plenty of time."

"No. I want to see him now." Surely she exaggerated. Alexis seemed, he thought, a little crazed herself. Her voice was brittle, and she kept trying to scratch at her shoulders and arms through her heavy coat.

Climbing the wooden steps to the Zendo in agitation she stumbled, he took her arm as they circled around the slated porch to the entrance. Finger to her lips, she warned him to silence. Simeon peered into the dark interior, lit with only four candles. All the high windows were closed. It looked nothing like the starkly elegant, inspiring place he remembered. It now resembled a medieval chapel. Giroux sat on a heavy wooden bench like a pew, his back to them. He was mumbling. It took some time for Simeon's eyes to adjust. There was something on the meditation shelf which Giroux devoutly faced. It was, he realized, a glass coffin filled with green liquid. A floating cloud of dark hair within the coffin.

A body.

Simeon withdrew, leaned against the outer wall in horror. "Merciful God. In the coffin . . . is it. . . ?"

"Yes, I told you. It's Jaiyavara."

"Merciful God."

"No mercy," Alexis whispered. "Anywhere." She pulled him back to the porch corner so that Giroux would not overhear. "You see? Didn't I tell you?"

"How long . . . ?"

"Six months . . . maybe eight. With everyone gone I lose track of time. I used to keep up with it. You see how he is? He won't help me do anything. He just sits there with her."

He took her arm, guided her to the back steps. "Let's sit down . . . we need to talk. I can't take this in yet." Simeon lit a cigar. They got settled. "Why has her body not decomposed?"

"It's an embalming fluid he was saving for himself. I never knew he had it. The coffin, it was for him. All the years I worked, helped him, you see how he kept secrets from me?"

Simeon rubbed his forehead. "Macabre."

"Yes."

"It's demented."

"Yes!"

"But why? What happened? Merciful God!"

"They were fighting all the time. He didn't want her to paint. Oh, if only you knew how she fought him."

"My God, I'm the one who brought her here!"

"No, listen, don't blame yourself. You couldn't know. None of us knew."

"I asked him once," Simeon ruminated, "if he loved her, and he said something I thought very odd. He said, if only it were that simple. What was it, Alexis? What did he want from her?"

"It's hard to explain . . . I never understood exactly. But she did. It was something like . . . listen, he wanted her for something like a statue, you know, like the Virgin Mary in the Catholic church. To help him start some sort of new religion. And she wouldn't budge. And he wouldn't quit. Deadly enemies. Until the very last, that is . . . and then . . . then it was as if all that was on the surface. As if at the very last there was a deeper, unspoken dialogue between them. Between their souls. Do you understand? Because, you see, at last . . . she complied. She gave him what he wanted. All her fantasies and visions, she gave him. I can't explain it, but it was almost at the very last as if they were lovers. I'm old, Simeon. I loved her. It took so much out of me, all that fighting. You have to help me. You may not believe this either, but it's true, I tell you, true. The sea knows what he promised her. Ever since she died the sea has been raging at that mountain, trying to get through, trying to take her. . . ."

"Oh, Alexis . . . come, now . . . that's. . . ."

"No, it's true, it's true, I tell you! You have to help me!"

"Help you what?"

Alexis gestured extravagantly. "If my word means nothing, I might as well be dead! Coffin and all, we must take her to the sea. That's what I promised. I'll have no peace until it's done. Yes, listen, we must! And, setting her free . . . maybe that will bring Giroux to his senses."

In wordless amazement, Simeon stared.

Alexis stared right back at him, slowly nodded her head up and down, looking into his eyes with bleak, desperate conviction. "I can drug him while we take her. Otherwise, he's going to sit there talking to her until he rots. Yes, Simeon. Yes. We must."

"God help him," Simeon groaned. "All right . . . all right . . . I'll help you."

And so . . . Alexis led Giroux's dark red, thick-necked horse, which pulled the wooden make-shift wagon. On the wagon, the coffin. Simeon walked at the rear to make sure it did not slide off, to push if the wheels got stuck. Within the sealed coffin Jaiyavara's dark hair stirred, floating with every motion as the green liquid sloshed. They struggled slowly up the mountain path. Alexis staggered with exertion, and had to rest now and then, yet she was strangely exhilarated, goaded beyond her normal strength and endurance. They both felt it, sensed it; it was almost as if they could hear it . . . as if the entire world was made of nothing but music—deep, powerful, music, urging them onward.

Twice when they stopped Simeon pleaded with Alexis to go back, to let him do it alone, but she refused.

The wind was against them until they neared the crest. Suddenly, it shifted, blasting at their backs. They could hear the roaring sea.

As they gained the crest Simeon yelled for Alexis to stop and rest, but she shook her head and would not stop until they came to the place where Giroux and Jaiyavara had lunch beneath the tree, drank wine, and talked. Alexis paused there. Jaiyavara had told her of that conversation. Then on they went, to the very edge of the cliff facing the open sea. Easing it down, Simeon slid the coffin on boards from the wagon to the ground.

With folded arms, Alexis looked down to the cove. Yes, the water was deep enough there to float the coffin out to sea. Yes. This was the place. With a screwdriver Simeon pried open the lid, tilted the coffin, let some of the liquid flow out so that it would not be so heavy. On dry earth the embalming liquid seeped in quickly between the stones, staining the brown, green. "Are you ready?" Simeon asked.

Alexis looked long at the coffin. She had an urge to kneel beside it, to try to look once more upon Jaiyavara, but she denied that urge. That thing in the coffin . . . so now like a green fish . . . that obscene thing . . . that was not Jaiyavara.

The task was almost beyond Alexis, yet she found the strength, helped Simeon lift the coffin at the edge of the cliff. They swung it back once and hurled it over the edge. Green and gold, it streaked a gleaming arc in air, shattered as it hit the water into a million sparkling pieces. The gold lock depicting Adam and Eve, the Forbidden Fruit, and the Golden Serpent sank quickly.

Over the sea the sun broke through. The wind became quiet. At the edge of the cliff Alexis sank to her knees, sobbing.

No one to talk to. Least of all him. I need to talk to someone about so many things. Someone . . . about how I ran into Anthony in a bar one night and he said the world has gone crazy, and it's not just the aftermath of the Plague. I've been disoriented, he said, ever since I left the monastery. Giroux is a saint, he said, compared to some of the people I've run into. He kept saying the world has gone crazy, and I said I hadn't noticed. How do you mean? And Anthony said there's this all pervasive mechanical and automatic greed. I don't own a telephone, he said, because every time it rang there was a recording trying to sell me something. And there are all these people like the old-fashioned positive thinkers—Act enthusiastic and you'll be enthusiastic!—all these people with answers and remedies that are utterly simplistic and selfish.

I keep remembering a word you taught me. Ambivalence. How you explained what it meant. In a way I guess that's how I feel about you. Anthony asked about you and I told him you were dead, and we both got very drunk that night and he took me back to his loft. We just fell across the bed and slept, we didn't make love. The next morning we made love but it was messy and fumbling, not very good, not like it used to be, and right after Anthony vomited, and I said to him . . . what has she done to you? He didn't answer. I need to talk to someone. . . . Later he showed me some of the stuff he was working on, sketches and canvases . . . I couldn't tell if they were good or not, but he seemed to want to be working on them all the time. All the time! Damn it was boring for me. He said that Jethro was becoming very militant, always stirring up something, in trouble, going to jail, making speeches. He said he didn't know about Jethro, he could go either way, become a fugitive and outlaw or run for Congress, not much difference he said, and laughed, and Bethune he said was working in one of those places for derelicts and prostitutes and drug addicts, and that Bethune was looking good and gaining weight and had gotten contact lenses. Jesus, I said. I said I can't imagine Bethune without his foggish glasses. So I stayed with Anthony three weeks or so, and I thought wouldn't it be wierd if after all this time we got something serious going, as I had been bumming around since I left the monastery, sleeping here and there, wherever I landed. I couldn't get settled. Men were good to me, you know that. Anthony kept asking about you, Jaiyavara. I told him everything I knew, how your hands got crushed, how you . . . excuse me, got so crazy and how Giroux kept you locked up and how you thought you were pregnant, but weren't, all of it I told him. And he was never satisfied, still he kept talking about you, asking me more and more questions, and he said . . . if this helps at all . . . that he really regretted leaving you at the monastery. So, see, I knew it would never work out with us, and I was ready to leave then, and he was ready for me to leave, and he gave me some money, although he didn't have much, and we parted as friends. He said if ever I needed anything to let him know. I appreciate him more now than I used to. He's a sweet man, Jaiyavara. And you know . . . he said to me, what about you, Karen? What are you going to do now? I'm going to become an actress, I said. You've got the looks for it, he said. But I lied. I knew it would be too hard, that I wouldn't have the guts for it. And I think he knew I lied but gallantly acted like he believed me.

And then I met this Harvey at another bar, he lived in a cheap hotel and drove a taxi, and he was a writer of sorts, you would have really liked him, sensitive and quiet and easy to be with, really one of the most fascinating men I've ever known, and I think I stayed with him at least a month and would have stayed longer, maybe forever, except well . . . early one morning his wife comes home to that cheap hotel dragging with her these three little woebegotten kids. He never told me he was married. So much for that.

So it was getting to be the same old story over and over again, and yes, men were good to me, except that last bastard who beat me up because he was so jealous, but except for him, I won't even mention his name, every man I've known has treated me better than Giroux. And I know what a bastard he is too, in his own way. But it isn't as if I actually decided. There was just a sort of fate to it, really. I know it was fate because I didn't really intend it, because I was with these three guys one night, and one of them was this cowboy named Elbert, and we were all drinking and decided just like that we were going to Texas, or maybe even further, all the way to the South, just to see what that was like for a while. And I thought wouldn't it be funny, we might even go as far as Mississippi, and I might even see the place where you grew up, or who knows . . . even meet this Lou Iris you told me about . . . no big deal, just out of curiosity, and then Elbert's car broke down and we had to split up, hitchhiked, and so I was in the back seat of this car, an elderly couple, he sold life insurance and tried to sell me some while he was driving, they wanted to see the scenery, but I sort of woke up in the back seat and, my God, realized where I was, that we were very close, and I sat up straight and said let me out here, I know where I am now. They were going so close I had only a mile or so to walk. But walking I thought . . . what if it's deserted, what if there's no one there at all? But there was. You see how it was just my fate?

What a shock. When I saw Giroux. Poor Giroux. Not the way I used to love him, a different way. But my heart ached for him. My God, my God, I said to him. What has she done to you? Just like Anthony, he didn't answer either. But who does he have now but me and Alexis? And Alexis is getting very old.

I once told Harvey a lot of this . . . all through the night we talked, before his wife came home and spoiled everything . . . all through one night about you and Giroux. How you danced, and how you got drunk, how you advised me to seduce Giroux. Even how some of us thought that you thought you were going to . . . excuse me, give birth to a serpent . . . of all things. Harvey was fascinated. He said he'd like to come here some day, you know, he said . . . just soak up atmosphere. He might do that some day, who knows. But I'm not holding my breath. I never saw you in that glass casket. It's hard to believe. But Alexis told me and she has never lied to me. Wow. I'm sorry I missed that. By just a few days I missed it. I can't even imagine it. Wow.

I never understood you. I could never figure you out. I said to Harvey that night, the only person who could explain Jaiyavara to me would be Jaiyavara herself, and it's too late for that. She can't say anything now. Harvey said, maybe she can, through the work she left. But I can't find any of the work, Jaiyavara. I said to Harvey, from the moment she got there Giroux was not the same. She had a terrible effect on Giroux . . . and yes, I said . . . that's hard for me to forgive. That night we were talking all night . . . I used that word. Ambivalence. And Harvey, when I said that word, he understood right away. Harvey, he liked that word a lot.

On the dirt road above the broken gates that bright morning four young men with backpacks and a female child of twelve appeared. "This is the place," one of them said. "It looks deserted," said another, yet they made their way down the path through the gates to begin their search.

Behind Giroux's back in the darkened Zendo, as the door opened, raw sunlight streaked in. Giroux slowly turned, squinting in the glare. He was very thin, unshaven, his black robe wrinkled and dirty.

"We beg your pardon," said one of the young men, as they approached. "Are you in charge here?"

Blinking stupidly in the blinding light, Giroux tried to get his bearings.

"We don't mean to intrude," said another, "but we've come a long way. Could you tell us something about this place?"

"Alexis . . ." Giroux mumbled. "Where's Alexis?"

"Who?"

"If you're hungry," Giroux managed, "Alexis will feed you."

"My name is Wendall," said the young man. "And this is Adrian. And this is George. And this is Michael. And this," he said, placing his hands on the girl child's shoulders, "is our adopted little sister, Vanassa. We heard stories from some monks who once lived here. . . . We're from Sacramento."

"What stories?" Giroux asked.

"A woman named Jaiyavara."

"A dancer . . ." said George.

"A painter . . ." said Adrian.

"We'd like, if possible," Michael said, "to see her work. Do you know her? Can you tell us where to find her?"

Giroux could not speak.

"Is she," Wendall asked, "by any chance, still here?"

Waiting, impatiently they shifted weight from one foot to the other. Michael and George unstrapped their heavy backpacks, eased them to the floor. "Do you understand what we're saying?" Michael said louder. "We've come a long way. We're very tired. We're looking for Jaiyavara."

Taking the initiative, the female child went to Giroux, offered him her hand.

Grasping her small hand, Giroux unsteadily rose to his feet.

"I know it seems strange," Wendall said, "but the stories we heard. . . ."

"This child," Michael said of the girl, "is extremely talented. She paints. We want her to have instruction from Jaiyavara."

"The stories we heard," Wendall repeated, "we're very anxious to find Jaiyavara."

Giroux's face was slowly transformed. "Not strange at all," he replied at last. "There is much to tell."

"Back on his feet," Alexis said to Karen as she glanced through the kitchen window at Giroux, the young men, the child, on the patio. "New faces. It's been good for him."

Karen came to stand beside her. "Basking in the limelight. He has to have it to live."

❦

"... and Jaiyavara said," Giroux expounded, "... yes, it was on this very spot. 'I'm capable of anything.' No, wait. 'I'm capable of becoming anything.' That's how she said it. Her words precisely. And don't you see, she meant by that, so are you. Yes. You also. So are you."

Greedily, they listened. Mesmerized.

But the girl child was restless and pouting. "I want to see the paintings. Show us the paintings."

"We'll find them, we'll find them," Giroux assured her. "They're here somewhere. Jaiyavara, I have to admit, was very secretive about her work."

"Why?" asked the child. "Why was she secretive?"

"Come," Giroux suggested, "let's walk up to the chapel. You really haven't seen the chapel yet."

Through the kitchen window Karen appraised the four young men. And found them wanting. Like so many of the former monks, she thought them too feminine, too malleable. She watched as Giroux led them up the path to the chapel, as he now called it. Old fool, she thought. He'll need me some day . . . if only to sit by his death bed.

"You see . . ." said Giroux, breathing heavily, slowly leading the way—he had to stop after the climb to get his breath—"... there was . . . a force in her beyond the normal. A thrust of higher evolution. A leap of the spirit. That's why the stories were repeated, why you heard them. Everyone who knew her was aware of it. A great platonic love," he said, opening wide the doors to the chapel, "between Anthony and Jaiyavara. He'll return one day. They all will."

Following his example they removed their shoes before entering.

"Paintings will hang here one day. Paintings of the stories she told, the dreams, paintings depicting the way she once danced."

Surveying the high bare walls, which to her cried aloud for adornment, the female child said, "If you will tell me the dreams, I can paint them."

"Of course I'll tell you. And I'll show you the photographs. That's what I'm here for. In a sense, I've been expecting you. How long, you'll never know."

"Was Jaiyavara," Wendall asked, "pure of heart? Did she abstain from meat? Did she abstain from sex?"

Stumped momentarily, unprepared, Giroux quickly improvised, yet even as he spoke an image flashed before him, Jaiyavara puffing on a cigarette like a paratrooper. "We must begin with the truth," he piously. "That's most essential. No meat was ever served here. How crass, how gross it is to satisfy a desire for meat at the expense of the entire life of a living creature. But . . . she was a passionate woman, and in the crude vernacular, although this is confidential, and I don't want it repeated, she was a great lay. How do I know? She told me herself. I hope this does not shock you."

Blandly Adrian asked, "Were you her lover?"

"In spirit only. Which is, after all, all that matters. I'm sure she meant when she was much younger. I'm sure she had, by the time I knew her, transcended sex. And you see, my son, that sort of question does not pertain. The body is, after all, only a garment. We must wear it lightly, lightly. On these very walls Anthony, or some artist, will depict a dream she revealed to me as if in a trance, a dream she confided to me when I first rescued her."

"You deserve," said Michael reverently, "a special place in our hearts for that rescue."

"Well, yes, thank you, I do," Giroux smiled. "I have never been unduly fettered by fake modesty."

"How did you know?" George mused. "How did you know her . . . as who and what she was?"

"Oh, I knew the first moment I saw her . . . years before she ever came here. When I first saw her the time was not right. All things vital move slowly to completion. There is, so to speak, no shortage of time. And you, as the first pilgrims, also deserve a place of honor among those who will follow, those who will come later. An inexorable destiny led you here. This is your home now. All that I have is yours. I've been waiting to share with you so much, so much." Giroux laid his hand on the girl child's head. "How beautiful your eyes are. Dark, like hers. You look . . . do you realize . . . a great deal like her."

Slow delight filled the child's eyes. But in a twinkling she changed, lifted her chin. "I don't look like anyone. I only look like myself."

"We need, Giroux said, "to open this place up, air it out." With a long pole he went to the windows. Window by window, as they were opened the chapel was lifted from gloom. Light spread to the musty corners spun with cobwebs.

"But what does it mean?" Wendall asked as they followed him. "I don't understand why Jaiyavara was at first afraid . . . or why she gave birth to a serpent."

"No, no, a serpent at conception, not at birth. Listen carefully," he said, turning to face them, "this is important."

But the female child was very inquisitive, and weary of Giroux's sermonizing slipped away unnoticed to explore on her own.

"It was her way of seeing the truth, the pure symbol. The Serpent said, 'Every Dream Can Be Willed Into Existence By Those Strong Enough To Believe In it.' Now . . ." Giroux held out his arms to them. "Can you remember that?"

Yes. Solemnly they agreed. They could remember.

"Mind," he continued, tapping his forehead, "on an atomic level . . . where all miracles, all wonders are possible. For instance, Christ rose from the dead on the third day. Do you believe that?"

Yes, they said. They certainly did. In a world battered by disease and raging destruction, there was nothing they believed in so much as miracles.

"The Serpent is wisdom. Even in that old, out-dated myth of the garden of Eden, there was a serpent, remember? That myth is no longer luminous, it no longer draws our projections, it was for a different time. Through Jaiyavara we have been given a new meaning. For Jaiyavara it was visible. It would not have been visible, actual, for an ordinary person. She carried that wisdom in her body to completion. But it was an actual birth in the sense of a new creation, an opening, a breakthrough. The Serpent changed at the moment of birth to a new creature, symbolizing a new beginning, a glorious infant daughter with wings. She'll fly to the sea, Jaiyavara said. She is Vijana, a higher plane of consciousness."

Looking into their earnest seeking faces he saw that they needed it, that they accepted it. Giroux gathered them close, like a father instructing them.

At the entrance of the chapel Alexis lurked, listening apprehensively. Her hands trembled. Her head wobbled.

"Jaiyavara once said to me," Giroux continued, gaining strength with every spoken word, "that had it not been for the love of his dead wife, Varrick would never have become a great warrior, defending persecuted creatures. Had it not been for my love for Varrick, she said, I would never have danced, never have painted. Don't you see how this linking chain of love goes forward from the past into the future. . . ."

"I see. . . ." Wendall said. "And goes forward through you and your love for Jaiyavara."

Ferociously Alexis whispered to herself. "Never through you, Giroux. Never! Never! As I live to tell it!"

"What did Jaiyavara teach of Satori?" Michael asked.

"Only the truth," Giroux assured him. "Only that it comes and goes." As he turned, herded them toward the chapel entrance, Alexis darted behind a screen. As the last young man, Adrian, the youngest, tarried, Alexis leaned out, beckoning to him. "Psbt! Psbt! Here. Come here, come here."

The others left. Dutifully, he gave her his attention.

She stuck her face close to his, leering with anger. "Satori, is it! Ha! Don't listen to him! It's all lies! Satori! She never had it! She never wanted it!"

But the delicate young man, regarding Alexis as dottering, senile, politely excused himself to follow blindly after Giroux.

They returned to the patio to find the female child amusing herself, marching up and down like a little soldier, brandishing a large flat stick, slashing and whacking at the air with it. Her feet were bare, she wore loose pirate pants, her waist tightly cinched with a bright pink sash. Her long thin arms were bare, her small budding breasts visible with every movement under a short open vest. With karate gestures she was advancing, retreating, lifting her leg high, leaping, whirling, threatening an imaginary adversary.

"What? Where did you get that?" Giroux demanded.

She pointed to the tower. "Up there. One of those dirty old rooms. I found it on the bed."

"Give it to me," he said severely. "That's not to play with. That's a relic."

"No. I found it. It's mine."

"Give it to me, I said!"

Just then Karen came out of the kitchen and the female child ran to her with the whacking stick, hid stubbornly behind her long skirts. "Oh, what difference does it make?" Karen said to Giroux. "If it pleases her, Jaiyavara would want her to have it. She's only a child. Leave her alone."

Giroux turned back to the four young men who attentively watched this domestic interplay. "Women!" he said, and threw up his hands.

Less than a week later ceremoniously on foot Giroux led the four young men and the female child up the mountain path, a long trek, led them across the plateau to the edge of the cliff, facing the sea. George, Michael, Wendall, and Adrian wore traditional black robes. The girl child wore a green toga laced at the waist with a golden cord. For warmth Jaiyavara's rust fringed shawl was draped about her small shoulders. Giroux had showered her with gifts, her every whim was indulged. Already this orphaned child was rather spoiled, beginning to lord it over her adopted older brothers. Her dark hair was crowned with Jaiyavara's golden ornaments, and she was beginning, under Giroux's influence, to speak of Jaiyavara as her spiritual mother.

Giroux still teaching, indoctrinating. He did not have to shout against a wind. If necessary, breathless as he was, he would have shouted. Had a strong wind hurled his words back into his face they would have seen his mouth resolutely moving. But nature complied. All was bright; sunlit, quiet and calm. A perfect day.

"This," said Giroux, "is where her body entered the sea." He spoke, due to another missing tooth, with a slight lisp. "Simeon and Alexis had to do it. I had not the courage to part with her." His voice choked with emotion. One tear slid from the corner of his good eye. "But . . ." he swallowed, "all is now as it should be. Down there," he pointed. "Look. The beautiful cove. I envision it all, as it will be some day. There, you see? We will build a temple. The temple will be anchored, floating on water. Anthony, or some great artist will create her image. Art in the service of truth. Yes. Can't you see it? Jaiyavara dancing on water . . . one leg lifted . . . she will be naked and as pure as dawn . . . her arms lifted as she dances . . . releasing into the air as she dances the infant daughter with wings."

A long silence.

"Yes . . . yes. . . ." Adrian whispered.

"And you . . ." Giroux said to the female child, his hand tenderly poised above her head, "a great future awaits you. You will grow to be a beautiful woman, tall and wise and brave, and you will become a high priestess. And when I am gone you will teach others all that I now teach you. And you will comprehend . . . all these mysteries."

"We'll help you," said Michael.

"We'll build the temple," said George.

And so they stood at the very edge of the cliff, inspired by the sea, glowing with inner hopes and aspirations.

At the very edge of the cliff, outlined by limitless sky and endless sea, these human figures were very small.

Here stark mountains march down to the sea. High in the air above sea and mountains, the birds congregate.

In the sea the dolphins congregate. Playfully, they dive and swoop, circle and frolic.

Breaking away, one dolphin turns toward the land, slicing through warm undulating currents alone, flinging itself toward the cove, attracted by a curious dark speck almost hidden among huge rocks and boulders at the base of the mountain.

The large and very fat monk sits on a large dark slab of rock facing the sea, doing nothing but dreaming.

Dreaming pleases him immensely.

So. Giroux makes myths. But then . . . Alexis, perhaps Anthony, Karen, will speak also, and perhaps someone will listen to their side of the story. The seeds of dissension are sown in every beginning.

The large and very fat monk shrugs and smiles. *But then, on the other hand . . . I must admit . . . I rather like it. The image. A woman dancing on water.*

The dolphin swims very near, as close as possible to the large and very fat monk. A suspended moment . . . everything stops.

Waves . . . sea spraying foam against jagged boulders . . . overhead birds in flight . . . folds of the monk's robe fluttering in wind

. . . for the dolphin in that moment, everything stops, all is motionless. As if all the world were a painting . . . a rich living thickness and tapestry of colors laid on in lush heavy brush strokes.

Pulled into the compassionate eyes of the large and very fat monk, in that moment the pigments of the monk's eyes become for the dolphin boundless space, the infinite universe; within that space all the whirling seething gasses and fires and stars and explosions . . . the dancing density of creation.

Then the dolphin breaks from the spell and returns to the sea. And the sea, as ever, is singing.